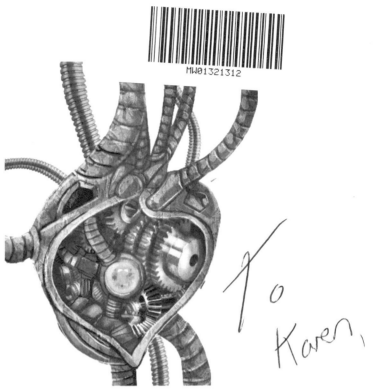

THE LAST MAGUS
A Clockwork Heart

Mark Piggott

Copyright © 2021 Mark Piggott

Cover Art by Anna-Lena Spies

Title Page Art by Dennis Saputra

Interior Map Art by Dewi Hargreaves

All rights reserved.

ISBN: 978-1-6671-1169-8

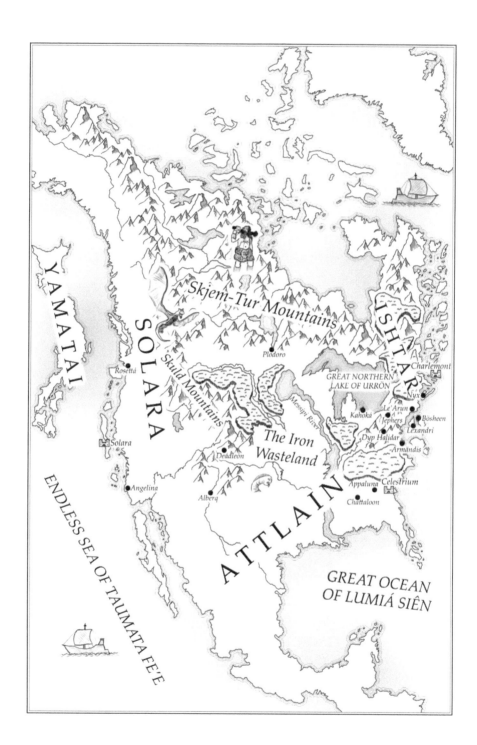

To the writers, the dreamers, the storytellers, and those who believe in all things make-believe…

TABLE OF CONTENTS

	Acknowledgments	I
	Prologue	1
1	A Clockwork Heart	6
2	The Magus of Attlain	23
3	The Black Wolf Guild	41
4	Passing the Torch	50
5	The Magus vs. The Guildmaster	62
6	The Forest of Ponshu	78
7	The Basilon Magic Academy	96
8	The Entrance Exam	105
9	A Fateful Encounter	116
10	The History of the Magus	133
11	To Restart a Clockwork Heart	151
12	A Basilon Tradition at the Red Door	167
13	Kidnapping a Princess	183
14	A Romance and an Ambush	201
15	The Paladin of Le'Arun	219
	Epilogue	231

ACKNOWLEDGMENTS

I would like to acknowledge my family, one and all, who supported me on every step of my journey as a writer. It has not always been fun, at least for them, but through it all, they have helped me achieve my goal of being a published author. Thank you, from the bottom of my heart!
I love you all!

MARK PIGGOTT

PROLOGUE
A STRANGER IN A STRANGE LAND

Gideon's Journal – Attlain is a strange world of magic and miracles. It has cities built on the technological might of modern marvels called "Magius Engines" powered by magic, lighting the darkness by electric lamps, connecting the towns in all directions by a network of Magius-powered trains and iron-hulled ships. Many different people inhabit this world, both humans and demi-humans of various races—alfs, dwarves, catsei, and many others. That's just the basics of what I learned about Attlain from the books I've read. Beyond that, my memories of who I am and where I came from are meager. I remember the ocean, sailing on a warship, but nothing about family or friends. I'm as much of a mystery as this brilliant world.

The only possession that provides me clues to my previous experience is a book that I can't even read. Its pages are waterlogged an illegible. I have no idea what it is, but I can't let it go. Everything about my past is blank, yet this place seems familiar to me. My memories began at the crossroads outside Armändis on the edge of the forest of Imeströs, where I died, and then I was saved.

At first, there was darkness. Not the kind that you'd find at the bottom of a well or on a moonless night. It was just a blank emptiness. All he could sense was a crushing nothingness and pain. His head throbbed with a persistent dull ache that never seemed to stop. He tried as hard as he could to open his eyes, but they wouldn't open. He could hear someone talking, but the voice sounded like an echo from way off in the distance. At the same time, he felt someone kicking his feet.

This continued—the jolting kicks, the demanding voice, the dull headache—and still he couldn't open his eyes or shake off the darkness of disorientation. Minutes or more passed. More kicking and more shouting, and then something hit his face, something cold and liquid. Instantly his eyes popped open.

He blinked several times, trying to clear his blurry vision. Slowly his surroundings came into focus. He looked around. He was lying on the ground, a dirt road, surrounded by several men and women. They were dressed in various armor and carried an assortment of weaponry. Over their armor, they wore uniforms that resembled long blue coats. It was an emblem that signified them as part of some organization—a black howling wolf's head with red eyes—but he didn't recognize it. They were gathered together at what appeared to be a crossroads, where four roads merged at one point at the edge of an immense forest.

The forest looked ancient, with gnarled roots, stretching branches, and towering trees. A thick canopy of leaves blocked the sky but allowed little rays of light to pierce the veil. The forest stretched on for miles to the east and the west, with a dark pathway heading south into the woods; to the north it opened to rolling hills and meadows.

He could see a sign at the intersection with arrows pointing down the different roads. He could barely make out the name "Armändis" on one of the indicators, and "Le'Arun" and "Bösheen" on the others.

One man was standing over him with a leather canteen, pouring water on his face and kicking his feet now and then. He was bulky for his size, quite muscular and completely bald, devoid of any hair over his entire body. He was chewing on a toothpick, moving it around his mouth as he spoke. "Come on, wake up!" he said. "We ain't got all day!"

He started to cough as the water went down his throat. He rolled over and lifted himself on his hands, trying to sit up. He looked down over his body. He wore such simple clothes: a tunic and pants that were tattered, but no shoes or sandals. They hung off his body, baggy and oversized. He ran his fingers through his long black hair, rubbed his rough beard, feeling every inch of his face to maybe help him come to his senses.

"What's your name, stranger?" the man asked him. "Come on, now, answer me? What's your name?"

He shook his head again, trying to regain his senses, but he drew a blank. He had no memory of who he was, where he was, or how he got there. "I . . . I don't know. . . ."

"Come on, mate, you've got to know your name!" the man argued with him. "What is it now?"

He shook his head, placing his hands on his temples as he clenched his teeth, trying to force himself to remember. "I don't know . . . I can't remember . . . I must have hit my head!" he screamed.

The man looked down and picked up a leather-bound book with red trim sitting on the ground next to the stranger. He flipped through it.

"Looks like some kind of holy book, can't read it though. The words are washed out," he said as he continued to flip through it. Then on the inside cover, he found an inscription. "Is your name, Gideon?"

"Gideon?" the stranger stammered as he tried to think. "My name is Gideon."

"Gideon, huh? Is that your family name? Come on, what's your full name?" he demanded. Gideon grabbed his head as he tried to focus past the pain to answer the question.

"I can't remember, okay . . . I just can't remember!" Gideon screamed.

"Come on, Po, quit messing around!" one of the other men shouted. "We haven't killed anything all day. He isn't a goblin or an orc, but he shouldn't be here either. Let's get on with it!"

"Back off, Heller, you can't kill an unarmed man for no reason," a woman argued. "Where's the sport in that?"

"Wait, if that's a holy book, maybe he's a cleric," another one chimed in, "We can't kill a cleric."

"What? Who says we can't kill a cleric? You're ridiculous, Benji!"

"Where . . . where am I, and who are you?" Gideon slowly got to his feet.

The bald man shifted the toothpick in his mouth again. He was getting angrier with each passing moment. "My name is Po Kildevil, and we are from the Black Wolf Guild of Armändis. We hunt down the goblins, orcs, and other creatures that inhabit these woods. Unfortunately, there's been no activity today, and we're bored out of our minds."

Po tossed Gideon's book to Heller, and then pulled Heller's sword from its sheath. "So, I tell you what, Gideon," Po said, throwing the sword down at Gideon's feet. "I'll give you a fighting chance to save yourself. Go on, pick it up."

Gideon looked around at the men surrounding him as they cheered on for the upcoming fight. He knew he had no chance of running off, and there were too many to fight one-on-one, but Gideon realized that he was dead the moment he picked up that sword.

"No," he said, trembling with fear. "I have no reason to fight you, and you have no reason to kill me. Give me back my book, and I'll be on my way."

"Sorry, but it doesn't work that way," Po said. "I don't need a reason to kill you. You fight, or you die. It's your choice."

Gideon stood there and sighed. He contemplated every possibility in his aching head, but it seemed as if he had no choice in the matter.

Heller stepped up and said, "Let's go, pal, we ain't got all day." He shoved Gideon toward Po. Gideon spun around, as if on reflex, and slammed his open palm against Heller to push him away, but instead of physical force, a wave of energy poured out of Gideon, throwing Heller across the road and into a tree trunk. Gideon stared at his hand, not understanding what he did or how he did it. The others rushed to help Heller, who was lying on the ground, face down and not moving.

"He's out cold," one of the guild members said. Po was furious now as he drew his sword.

"So, you're a rogue magic caster, huh?" he gritted. "Well, that makes this a whole lot easier!" He charged at Gideon, thrusting his sword as he lunged. Instinctively, Gideon dodged, leapt, and rolled across the ground, grabbing the sword left there for him. Gideon spun around to face Po as the guildsman swung at him. Gideon parried the attack and then pushed Po back and took a swipe.

His slash caused Po to jump back to avoid the blade. "You're pretty capable with a sword after all," he surmised. "You're full of surprises, aren't you?"

Gideon said nothing. He gripped the sword with both hands, his palms sweating, waiting for the guildsman's next attack. Po swung hard, bashing relentlessly at Gideon. Try as he might, Gideon couldn't block every assault. His arms and chest were cut sporadically—some deep, some superficial. He was weak and the blade started to quiver in his hand after every hit. Po gained an advantage and overwhelmed Gideon and knocked the sword from his hand. Po then thrust his blade at Gideon's chest, stabbing him right through the heart.

"Not good enough!" Po joked as he forced his blade deeper.

All Gideon could do was stand there impaled with Po's sword. He grabbed onto the blade and tried to pull it out. The sharp edge sliced into his palms but Gideon kept pulling, unsuccessfully, blood gushing out with each beat of his heart. Gideon began to spit blood and slowly lose consciousness. Po gripped the sword and kicked Gideon in the stomach. Gideon came off the sword, stumbled backwards, and fell hard to the ground. Blood poured out of the gaping wound in his heart. He clenched his chest, hoping to stem to the tide, but it seemed too late.

"Nice one, Po!" one of the men cheered.

"Yeah, he's as good as dead!" another said as he helped Heller to his feet. "Come on, let's head over to Marion's Tavern to celebrate!"

"What about him?" the woman asked. "You can't just leave him here!"

"Why not?" Po said. "Some goblins or orcs will come along and have him for dinner. There will be nothing left of him for anyone to find, except maybe this." Po causally tossed the mystery book onto the ground next to Gideon and ordered his men to leave the area.

With his remaining strength, Gideon reached out and grabbed it. He held it close. Although he couldn't remember what connection he had to this book, deep down, Gideon knew it was important to him. His breathing became labored and he slowly faded out of consciousness.

Is this where I'm going to die? he wondered. *I don't even know where I am, or even who I am, and I'm going to die. Why God? Why me?*

Minutes seemed like hours as time passed slowly. Gideon closed his eyes as the darkness turned into a bright light. He felt a peace about him as he headed into the light.

"Come on, lad, don't die on me!" he heard a voice cry out to him. It was an older voice, pleading with him to stay alive. As much as he longed for the serenity offered by the light, he knew it wasn't his time.

1 A CLOCKWORK HEART

Gideon's Journal – I can't say dying was all it lived up to be. I mean, everyone talks about your life flashing before your eyes, but I didn't experience any of that. Maybe it's because I have no memories from before I woke up at the crossroads outside Armändis. I can remember scents and tastes—the salt air of the ocean, fresh apple pie, thick black smoke, and savory grilled meat. My past is uncertain, and so is my future, but perhaps this is a start to a new life for me. Either way, I can certainly say I didn't like dying and never want to do it again, but I don't think I'll have a choice in the matter when the time comes. I think that's going to be my new goal in life—to live forever!

Gideon felt terrible. His whole body hurt, though his chest ached the worst. He reached down and ran his fingers across his chest and found bandages stained with blood. He tried to look around the room, but it was too painful to move. He looked out the open window next to him and saw it was night, so he knew he had been unconscious for some time. He tried to sit up, but was too weak to move.

"Best not try to move, lad; you might rip open those stitches," a voice said. "Sorry, but my sewing's seen better days."

Gideon turned his head to see an older man sitting next to him. He was fairly messy in his appearance, ragged and unkempt. His clothes were bloodstained, most likely from whatever the stranger did to save Gideon. Though he was hefty at the waist, Gideon could see the muscles underneath all that bulk. He was probably some kind of a fighter at one time in his life. His mass was the likely result of years of misuse and abuse.

He had long black hair and a beard mixed with deep streaks of gray. His face was careworn. Looking at him, you could see the years in his eyes, as if each battle, every death, was etched on it. He took long swigs from the wine jug sitting next to him, something he seemed pretty comfortable doing. He appeared like a man who used drinking as a form of stress relief and recreation rather than sustenance.

"Where am I? And who . . . who are you?" Gideon stuttered as he tried to clear his mind, ease the pain in his body.

"My name is Henri Botàn. You're in my house with a hole in your chest where your heart used to be," he answered. "Your heart," Botàn continued, pointing across the room to where bloody instruments, knives, and bandages spread across the table. Amongst all the carnage was a human heart, sliced right in half. "Well, damaged as it was, I had to use an alternative."

"An alternative? What alternative?" Gideon asked. "How am I still alive?"

Botàn got up and pulled his chair over to Gideon's bed. "This is going to be a bit startling, so brace yourself, okay?" Gideon nodded and looked down at his chest. He expected Botàn to unwrap his bandages, but he did something completely unexpected.

He held out his hand across Gideon's chest. *"Revelá!"* chanted Botàn as a runic magic circle appeared beneath his open palm. The bandage faded, then the skin, muscle, and bone, revealing the miracle underneath. Where his heart once sat in his chest, there was a mass of clicking gears, springs, and mechanisms—a mechanical heart, beating a steady rhythm as harmonious as a heartbeat. Like the magic that exposed his chest, it also glowed with magical energy all its own.

"What is it? A mechanized heart?" Gideon asked, confused and concerned as his motorized heart droned to a faster beat. The uncertainty of his condition caused fear to race through him.

"I like to think of it as a clockwork heart," Botàn explained. "It was created by an associate of mine. A watchmaker by trade, but he liked to venture into new possibilities. I . . . uh . . . never found a need for it until I found you down by the crossroads.

"Inside it, there's a thunderstone. It uses mana to replenish the magic, and your body seems to have an abundance of mana to spare," he continued. Mana was the energy source that magic casters tapped into to cast their spells. "You must be a brilliant magic caster."

"I don't know if I am. I never studied magic . . . At least, I don't think I have. I can't remember anything before I woke up on that crossroads."

This revelation stunned Botàn. He pulled his hand back and canceled his reveal spell before returning to his wine. "You don't remember anything about your life? You've got to be, what, twenty-three, twenty-four years old? You're not a young man. You must have done something with your life."

THE LAST MAGUS: A CLOCKWORK HEART

Gideon pushed himself to see if he could remember anything. The only image that came to mind was the ocean, rolling waves out on the open sea. "I remember the ocean, deep blue water," Gideon said. "I think maybe I was a sailor."

"A sailor, well, that narrows it down," Botàn remarked. "You probably came from Bösheen. It's the biggest port in Attlain. Plenty of ships there."

"Bösheen? Is it a nice place?" Gideon asked, trying to use anything to regain his memories.

Botàn laughed. "It's a shithole! That place, as a wise, old man once said, is 'a wretched hive of scum and villainy.' I would have left, too, if I were you."

His answer was no help. Gideon lay there, contemplating everything that had happened to him since he regained consciousness at the crossroads. "How did you find me?" he asked.

"I was foraging for mushrooms when I came across your body, and it was lucky that I did. If I had gotten there any later, you would have been a dead man. I used a magical life support cocoon to suspend your body's functions until I could get you back here. It's a miracle that you're still alive at all."

"Are you a magic user, a healer?" he asked Botàn, causing the old man to break out in laughter.

"A healer? Me? No, I'm afraid not. I dabbled in magic in my youth, so I know a few spells. Now I'm just a humble blacksmith."

Now it was Gideon's turn to be stunned and worried. "A blacksmith? Then how did you know how to replace my heart with this thing?" he asked.

"Oh, that was easy. I just had to cut out your damaged heart and put that contraption in its place. It did the rest itself," Botàn joked as he took another drink. "I was surprised it worked."

"What? You never did this before? You could've killed me!"

Botàn took offense to Gideon's tone, sneering at him. "You were already dead and dying, you ungrateful son-of-a-bitch! I took a chance and saved your life. A simple thank you would suffice!"

Gideon lay there and reconsidered his attitude. "You're right . . . I'm sorry, and I'm grateful for what you did to save my life. Thank you, sir."

His apology caught Botàn off guard. It was rare for someone to have such honesty and humility at a time like this. "Well, I'm just glad it worked, lad. What's your name, anyway?"

"They told me my name is Gideon, since it was inscribed inside a book I was carrying—my book, where's my book?" Gideon shouted. Botàn got up and walked across the room to the table. He picked up the book and gave it to Gideon.

"You were clutching it over your heart when I found you. I figured it was important to you," he explained. "That might have been what kept you alive. I can't read the language inside, but the inscription inside the cover says 'M.

Gideon.'"

"M. Gideon? They must have missed the M." Gideon closed his eyes and tried to remember. What is it? Michael, Morris, Marceau, Mark? No, not Mark. Marcus maybe? That seemed familiar. Yes, it was coming back to him now. "I think my name is Marcus Gideon."

Botàn poured a cup of wine for Gideon and handed it to him. "It's always nice to know your name, eh Marcus?" He tapped his goblet against Gideon's for a toast. "Drink that slowly; you're still recovering from surgery."

Gideon sipped the wine, savoring its delicate, sweet flavor while Botàn gulped it down. "By the way, you said they told you your name was Gideon. Who are they?"

"These men, they said they were with the Black Wolf Guild of Armändis," Gideon said as he took another sip. "They're the ones that tried to kill me."

"Did you happen to get their names?"

Gideon thought back to the crossroads. He was trying so hard to learn his name; he wasn't sure who was there. "There was someone named Heller, Benji, I think I heard one say, and Po . . . Po Kildevil."

That last name caused Botàn to spit out his wine, nearly choking on it. He coughed until his throat was clear, then he took a big swig to calm his nerves.

"Po Kildevil, are you sure about that?" he demanded.

"Yeah, he's the one that did this to me," Gideon said, pointing at his chest. "He tossed a sword on the ground and told me to defend myself or die. I lost. . . ."

Gideon saw the anger seethe inside Botàn as his blood began to boil. "That bastard," he cursed. "These guild adventurers—as they like to call themselves—keep the woods free from the odd creatures that pop up now and then and threaten the town: goblins, ogres, orcs and the sort; but when those cowards get bored, they kill wayward travelers for sport."

"Then, why don't you tell the local magistrate and have them arrested?"

"Don't you think I have? They won't do a damn thing because of Herrod," Botàn cursed again as he took another drink.

"Herrod?"

"Maximillian Herrod, Guildmaster of the Black Wolf Guild of Armändis," he explained. "He runs this town with an iron fist. Most of those serving in the guild are good people, but a select few follow his lead. Sure, he keeps the monsters out there at bay, but it leaves Armändis like a prison. His guild does what they want, to who they want, and when they want, without question."

"So, people like me usually end up dead," Gideon interjected. "And no one asks why?"

Botàn raised his cup toasting Gideon's correct answer before he gulped down the rest and then poured himself some more wine. "Do not worry yourself over this, Marcus. Unfortunately, this is the way things are here in

Armändis."

"And you're okay with that? You don't seem to be the type just to let things go on like this."

Botàn drank some more before he answered. "Maybe at one time, but the longer things go on, the more we become set in our ways. It's hard for an old man like me to fight back when there is no hope for victory."

"But if you don't fight back, there will never be any hope for anyone."

Botàn considered everything this young man said before finishing his wine. When he tried to refill his cup, his wine jug was empty. "Well, if we're going to start getting into philosophical discussions, I'm going to need more wine." He got up to get another jug.

"If you don't mind, can we save that for later? I'm exhausted."

"Of course, you need your rest," Botàn said. "I'll let you sleep. I'll change your bandages and get you something to eat in the morning. Good night, Gideon." He started to leave and Gideon stopped him.

"Master Botàn, thank you again for saving my life."

The old blacksmith just smiled and nodded his head as he left the room. Gideon lay there and looked out at the stars. He remembered a line from an old poem he heard somewhere before: *Stars are memories, forever shining in the sky.* He had no memory of these stars nor the twin crescent moons that hung in the night sky. All he knew was he had to heal up and get stronger to get revenge on those who tried to kill him. The Black Wolf Guild will not harm another innocent life, I swear, Gideon thought as he drifted off to sleep. Armändis may not know justice, but he would show them.

Gideon's Journal – Master Botàn gave me this journal to write down my thoughts. He said it might help me stir my memories of my past. To be honest, I'm not worried about my previous life. I'm more concerned about my future.

The first time I met Maximillian Herrod, I was in no condition to fight him or the rest of the Black Wolf Guild of Armändis. They could have killed me right on the spot, again, but they didn't. I think that's their weakness. They're arrogant. They believe that they can do whatever they want and get away with it. It's like a spoiled child never told "no" growing up. Someone needs to start being the adult in the room and enact some discipline on these children for once in their miserable lives. I just hope that when that happens, I'm there to see it.

As the sun started to peep through the window, Gideon slowly woke up. He felt relatively well-rested from all the sleep he'd been getting, but he was still sore all over. As he shook the slumber out of his head, he heard another distinct sound: hoofbeats in the distance, growing louder and louder as they came closer.

Botàn suddenly appeared in the window, panicked. "Stay inside and keep quiet," he ordered Gideon. "Whatever you do, don't make a sound or come outside. Do you hear me?" Gideon didn't say a word as Botàn closed the wooden shutters and latched them shut.

Gideon sat up as best as he could, being careful not to rip any of the stitches in his chest. He peeked through the crack in the shutters to see what had Botàn scared. The blacksmith stood outside, next to what appeared to be his blacksmith shop and barn across from the house. The shutters opened wide, exposing the work area as smoke billowed from the forge.

Suddenly, a group of horsemen rode up to the barn. They all wore the same uniform, one Gideon recognized immediately. They were with the Black Wolf Guild of Armändis. Their horses were burdened down with the weight of various weapons, from swords and axes to daggers and spears. As they gathered around Botàn, Gideon immediately recognized Po Kildevil sitting astride one of the horses. His bald head was easy to spot amongst the men there. He even recognized a few of them from the crossroads when they attacked him, but one man stood out amongst them.

The man's appearance was different from the others. He was clean, his hair and beard neatly trimmed, his armor shined, and his uniform was pristine. He wore no gauntlets, but on his right hand he wore a large, ornate ring. It was a black onyx ring shaped like a wolf's head with rubies for eyes. On his back, the man carried a large curved sword. The blade looked too heavy to wield, so Gideon was unsure whether it was real or just for show.

"What can I do for you, Herrod?" Botàn asked. Gideon knew that name from his conversation last night. Here was the guildmaster of the Black Wolf Guild and the man who held everyone in an iron grip. He grimaced with each move he made, trying to sit up and get a better view. He wanted to make sure he heard every word they said.

"It's been a rough week of hunting for the guild," Herrod said. "We need our weapons sharpened and fixed by next week." With a nod of his head, the men began to unload the weapons.

"Come on, Herrod, you have to give me more than a week to get this done," Botàn complained. "This is too much for one man to do alone."

"Well then, maybe it's time for you to hire on some assistants," Herrod butted in.

"You know I can't afford to do that with the scraps you pay me."

"I pay you what the guild sets as fair pricing for services rendered, nothing more," Herrod interjected. "I'm sure you can find someone to lend you a hand."

"He has someone!" came a voice from the house. Botàn was stunned that Gideon didn't listen to him, but not as shocked as Po and the other guild members were, seeing him alive. Herrod, on the other hand, looked at him with intense curiosity. It took every ounce of strength Gideon had to walk out there. He leaned against the door, bracing himself as he walked out.

"And just who are you, stranger?"

"My name is Marcus Gideon. Master Botàn was kind enough to heal my wounds after he found me out at the crossroads," Gideon said.

Herrod glared over at Po, who was seething in anger. "The crossroads, you say? What happened to you out there?"

Gideon thought about it for a minute. He could nail these guys right in front of their boss, but all that would do is get him and maybe Botàn killed. It might be better to embarrass them instead.

"I don't remember much about what happened," he started to say. "I was knocked unconscious and stabbed in the chest. I think they were bandits, but they were just cowards to me. I mean, attacking someone near death. That's something only a coward would do, am I right?"

Po was shaking violently, gritting his teeth at the insults Gideon was aiming toward him. He had one hand on his sword and looked about ready to lash out and cut him down.

"Is there a problem, Po?" Herrod asked his deputy. Po was stunned, not knowing how to answer.

"No, sir, it's just . . ." he paused, trying to come up with an answer.

"Just what? You were out at the crossroads the other day. Did you happen to see the bandits that attacked him?" Herrod asked him directly. Gideon watched as Po struggled to answer, as if one wrong answer could get him killed.

"No . . . no, I didn't."

"Alright, now sit there and be quiet," Herrod ordered, embarrassing his subordinate, and then turned his attention to Gideon. "What are you doing in Armändis?"

"Passing through on my way to Le'Arun."

"Oh? And what do you plan on doing there?" Herrod inquired. Gideon realized he was hammering him with questions to try and get him to slip up, so he had to be careful.

"I was going to check out a magical school there, see if it's possible to enroll."

"Magic school? Aren't you a little old for school?" Herrod laughed. "What have you been doing all your life?"

"I was a sailor out of Bösheen. It was a hard life, so I decided it was time for something new." Gideon lied, basing his answer on what little memories he could recall. It made sense to try and throw Herrod off track with a fib. As frustrating as it was for him, Gideon doubted the guildmaster would send someone all the way to Bösheen to check out his story.

"Bösheen, huh? That's a nice place. Who'd want to leave there?" Herrod joked.

Gideon chuckled himself. "I guess you've never been to Bösheen," he remarked. "It's a pile of shit on top of a shithole. I couldn't wait to get out of there."

Herrod just sat there, stone-faced, until he broke out laughing. "Ha, you got me there, boy! That place is a real shithole. I'm surprised it took you that long to leave," he chuckled loudly as the others joined in. "How long will you be staying in Armändis."

"I owe Master Botàn a debt for saving my life," Gideon replied. "I'll be staying with him until that debt's paid, that is, if that's alright with you?"

Gideon knew it was a risk to ask for permission, but Herrod looked like he was never one to shy away from danger. To him, it helped alleviate the boredom. "It makes no matter to me. The debt is yours to pay. It's nice to find someone who has a sense of honor and duty," he added as a jab at Po. "Botàn, I'll expect those weapons by next week."

Herrod turned and rode off, with the rest of his men right behind him. As soon as they rode far enough away from Botàn's home, Po rode up next to Herrod to question his decision.

"Sir, why are you letting him live? He's the one we—" Before Po could say another word, Herrod backhanded him across the face. Po was stunned as he rubbed the sting from his cheek.

"His life is your mistake, Po. You should have made sure he was dead," Herrod explained. "I let him live so that your failure will stare you in the face every time you see him. Maybe next time, you'll do it right."

"Then let me go back there, and this time I'll get it right!"

Herrod backhanded him again, this time harder. "I told you he will stay alive for now. Botàn could use the help, so that benefits us. You don't touch him until he leaves Armändis for Le'Arun. Then you can do what you want. Do I make myself clear?"

Po knew better than to cross Herrod, so he just nodded his head. "Yes, sir, perfectly."

Botàn helped Gideon back to bed, cursing at him with every step. "Are you out of your goddamn mind? Are you trying to get us both killed?"

"I took a chance and it paid off, give me a break." Gideon moaned as he laid back down. "Besides, if I didn't do that, they would have killed me the moment I tried to leave Armändis."

"They might still do that anyway," Botàn replied. Although what Gideon said made sense, the whole situation still made him angry. "And I never agreed to take you on. I don't need any help, especially from a half-dead slacker like you."

"Oh, like hell, you don't. You're the one who said you couldn't finish the job without some help. The way I see it, you need me, just as much as I need you."

Botàn stood there, frustrated and angry, but this was one of those moments when he knew arguing would be useless. "Alright, fine, but you listen to me," he said, "you have to do everything I say, exactly as I tell you, no arguments. One word of back talk out of you, and you're on the road, on your own."

Gideon smiled. He was grateful that the old blacksmith listened to him. "Okay, you've got a deal. When do we start?"

"Tomorrow!" Botàn yelled. "Today, you need to rest so that you'll have enough strength to survive a proper magic healing later tonight. That should fix you up enough to start work tomorrow."

"Sounds good, Master Botàn," he replied as he laid back and closed his eyes.

"Just Botàn, or Henri if you must. I'm not your master."

Gideon was already fast asleep. Botàn smiled as he left him to rest. There was something about this young man that Botàn liked. *Maybe he is the one that was foretold to me,* Botàn thought, *the one I have been waiting for.*

Gideon's Journal – I don't know what kind of magic caster Botàn is, but he's a damn good one. His healing spell did the trick. By the following morning, I was back on my feet. The pain was practically gone as if they never killed me (I keep reading that, and I still can't believe it sometimes). He is a miracle worker. The one thing Botàn does know how to do is be a slave driver. The man is relentless! He expects me to get it right the first time, even though I've never done blacksmithing before. Still, it's a worthwhile trade. The heat of the forge reminds me of the fire in a steamship boiler, another lost memory fighting its way to the surface. The good news is that being his apprentice has helped me get stronger. He's even showed me some sword fighting techniques, so I know I'll be better prepared if I ever cross swords with Po Kildevil again.

The other thing Master Botàn does know how to do is drink. I swear he goes through at least three jugs of wine a week. Still, the more he drinks, the better his stories are. He's told me about many of his adventures across Attlain. He's fought dragons, vampires, goblins, giants, orcs, and every type of monster out there. He's fought alongside paladins like Sir Duarté Dartagni, beautiful mages (his words) like Lady Jacqueline Celestra, and even a renegade goblin named Bok. They seem to be quite a collection of characters.

Still, every time I've asked Master Botàn about teaching me some magic, he's reluctant. He tells me I have "great potential" to be a magic caster, but he won't teach me a single thing. He's hiding something, but I just can't put my finger on what it is. It's like that armored pauldron he wears all the time. He told me he wears it because of a bad shoulder, but I know he's lying. He swings a hammer better than anyone I've ever seen. And besides that, there's something strange about it. The runes on it glow every time he gets too close to the forge. I swear it's true. Botàn is like a puzzle with one too many pieces, but those questions will have to wait for another time.

Armändis was like any other small town in Attlain. It was a cobbling of stone and wooden homes, rich and poor parts of town, with a little something for everyone. The town was surrounded by a wall, tall enough to keep the monsters out but low enough for people to enjoy the beauty of the forest around them. The city was a modern miracle, lit brightly by electric lights using crystal filaments that sparked when burned. All courtesy of a dwarvish innovation, magic-powered steam turbines called Magius Engines. These miracle machines used a slew of magical engineering and science to produce enough energy for everyone to have these valuable modern conveniences, from light at night to heat in the winter.

Also, massive steam locomotives powered by Magius Engines provided speedy transportation between the major cities, keeping travel time between towns to a minimum; and allowing the people to avoid the long, weary roads that were the hunting grounds of bandits and monsters. It also allowed the shops to carry all kinds of goods brought in from Le'Arun, the capital city of Celestrium, Solara's desert city, and even the distant island of Yamatai. However, even with all those luxuries, there was an air of despair in Armändis. The guild heavily taxed the people—prices controlled and regulated for goods, services, security, and even the power for lights—to pay for the apparent center of the town, the Black Wolf Guild headquarters.

They built it like a fortress. There were armed parapets with mounted multi-shot ballistae that could fire down onto the streets. Only the guild members were allowed inside, so very few of the townspeople have ever seen this impressive structure's interior. They lived in the lap of luxury, with the best food, spirits, and furnishings. They had enough stores to hold out for months inside the monstrous keep. That's how Guildmaster Herrod wanted it. It not only allowed him to control the guild members, but it also kept the locals at bay.

What surprised Gideon the most was how the people of Armändis treated Master Botàn. He was a popular man with the people, even if he wasn't one with the guild. Botàn could charm barmaid and merchant alike, talking his way to discount prices on liquor or for an extra loaf of bread. In return, he did favors for them at every turn, whether he repaired tools, tossed a few coins out to help, or gave out some herbs or meat caught in the forest when someone was in need. He was a friend to all, and they appreciated him for it. In turn, Gideon also became a recipient of their generosity and well wishes.

There were a few decent taverns in Armändis, away from the control of the guild along the perimeter, but Marion's Tavern was the best. Members of the Black Wolf Guild frequented it often, so they had a lot more income when it came to good drinks, good food, and pretty waitresses. Marion's also carried the best wine in the region, importing jugs of hundred-year-old Merwàn from Oliviérs' Winery in Deádleon, making it a favorite of Botàn's. He usually came into Armändis once a month to pick up supplies from the general store, but he also made a special stop at Marion's to get at least ten jugs of wine. That's double what he would typically purchase, especially since Gideon decided to stay with him.

Six months passed since Gideon arrived in Armändis. For all the work he did for Botàn, he found himself doing most of the heavy lifting for the blacksmith, but to be honest, he didn't have a problem with that. As far as he was concerned, he owed him a debt he could never repay. Gideon was a lot like Jupiter, Botàn's one and only horse. Jupiter was an old gelding, strong enough to pull the cart to-and-from town, but he took his own sweet time doing it. Botàn frequently cursed at Jupiter for being a slowpoke, just like he did Gideon from time to time, so they were both kindred spirits.

The problem today for Gideon was not Jupiter nor his sluggish demeanor, but rather the crowd of guild members sitting outside Marion's. Their cavorting and drunken behavior only accentuated the steady stream of insults they threw at Gideon. Herrod may have stopped them from killing him, but that didn't mean they couldn't antagonize him.

The group seated out front were made up of the same hooligans that attacked Gideon at the crossroads, with one exception. Dominic Evergreen sat there enjoying his ale, not joining in the vicious insults hurled at the apprentice blacksmith. He was older than most of the other guild members; the gray hair in his beard and on his temples was evident. He did his job, earned his pay, and wanted nothing more. He propped his feet up, drank his ale, and ignored the petty antics of the ruffians. Po Kildevil, however, was not as quiet. As Gideon loaded the jugs into Botàn's cart, Po decided to try and torment him a little.

"Look at this one," he joked. "He's a slave to that old blacksmith. It's a wonder that the old man gets anything done for the guild."

"It's called doing a hard day's work, Kildevil," Gideon snapped right back at him. "You could learn a thing or two about that."

"What do you know? We just spent half the day clearing out the forest!"

"Yeah? Did you happen to clear out a nest of bugbears?" Gideon asked. "Botàn and I found some tracks near the north ridge yesterday morning. Did you happen to hunt them down?"

"Bugbears? We didn't find any tracks. You must have been mistaken, but that's to be expected by a hapless apprentice," Po retorted. The other guild members laughed at Gideon's expense, except for Dominic.

Before Gideon could say or do anything, he received a smack on the back of his head, courtesy of Botàn. "What are you doing? You're supposed to be loading the cart."

"Sorry, Master Botàn. I was just informing the guild of our discovery in the forest yesterday, nothing more."

Botàn glared over at the guild before nodding his head. Gideon knew that Po was just trying to goad him into a fight. That was the last thing Botàn would have wanted. "And stop calling me master. How many times do I have to tell you that?"

"Sorry, it's a force of habit. My parents must have taught me to respect my elders," Gideon joked with him. Even though he didn't remember his parents, he liked to act like he did. It reminded him that he wasn't born out of thin air.

Botàn smiled and chuckled a little bit before they were interrupted.

"Botàn! I found the last two jugs of the '48 Charblan." shouted tavern owner Fenwick Shamshaw as he walked up the cellar steps with another case of wine. His long gray hair showed his age, but he kept himself reasonably fit. His muscular body bulged from under his tight-fitting clothes. He needed to be fit to keep all the troublemakers out of his tavern. "These are the last ones I'll have for quite a while. Are you sure you want them?"

"Are you daft? Of course, I want them!" Botàn shouted. "Finish loading these up, Marcus, while I help Fenwick with those jugs, and stay out of trouble." He poked Gideon in the chest with that last order as he went with Fenwick down to the cellar.

While Gideon loaded the last of the jugs, the waitress came out carrying another round for the guild. Ester was a beautiful young woman with long blonde hair and quite a buxom figure. Once she laid out the drinks, she handed Gideon a small cup of wine from her tray.

"Here you go. I thought you might be thirsty," she said politely. Gideon gladly took the cup of sweet wine.

"Thanks, Ester, I appreciate it." he gulped it down greedily to satiate his thirst. For some reason, this angered Po.

"What the hell are you doing, giving him a free drink?" Po asked.

"Because he doesn't have the tab that you do!" Ester snapped back as she started to load the empty pints onto her tray. Gideon chuckled at Ester's slam on Po, but Po didn't like the joke.

"My tab isn't that bad! How do you know what my tab is?" he shouted back. This time, the rest of the guild laughed at him.

"Everyone knows about your tab, Po," Dominic interjected. "It's legendary." Everyone started laughing again, but louder. It angered Po even more.

He grabbed Ester by the arm, causing her to fling all the cups off her tray, and shook her violently. "What are you telling people, wench! How dare you insult my character!"

"What character?" Ester shot back at him. When Po reared back to hit her, Gideon grabbed him by the wrist. The look on Po's face showed how surprised he was at how strong Gideon had gotten in such a short amount of time.

"Let her go," he ordered.

Po struggled against his grip. "You've gotten stronger, haven't you, pup?"

Gideon smirked but continued to hold him tight. "Strong enough to take on a sad sack like you."

Po flew into a rage as he released Ester and swung at Gideon with his right hand. Gideon blocked his punch easily and pushed him away before stepping back himself. Po didn't like being brushed aside like that and turned to the other guild members to assist him.

"Well, why are you sitting there? Get him," Po ordered.

"No, you don't," Dominic said, interrupting before anyone could step up. "Herrod said the boy's off limits as long as he's working for Botàn. I wouldn't recommend disobeying Herrod, would you?" The others took Dominic's words to heart and stayed right where they were. Po gritted his teeth at Dominic's defiance, but Gideon was confused.

Why would Herrod give them such an order? he wondered. He was brought out of his stupor as Po drew his sword and started moving toward Gideon.

"Well now, this seems familiar," Gideon remarked as he stepped backward. "You always pick fights with an unarmed man?"

"I don't care if you're armed or unarmed. This time, I'll make sure you stay dead."

"Gideon!" came a voice as a sword flew toward him. Botàn flung it from the cellar door. It was a broad sword, more than three feet long, with a basket hilt shaped like a lion's head. For such a large sword, it felt light in his hand. Gideon caught the blade just as Po swung his sword down on him.

Gideon blocked his strike with ease, holding him back before pushing him back. Seeing that it was Po, he didn't want to be the aggressor. Better not anger Herrod unknowingly. He tried to stay on the defensive, for now, only striking back if necessary. With this sword in hand, it was easy to block Po's wild strikes at him. He barely felt a thing. The blade was so sturdy that it absorbed the impact of each blow. While the fight rattled Po's hands, Gideon stood firm. It was a new sensation for Gideon, compared to their first fight.

Finally, he had enough of Po's bashing attacks. Gideon swung hard after blocking another strike, hoping to knock the sword out of his hands. Instead, Po's blade snapped in half from the strike. The tip flew, nearly missing one of the other guild members before embedding into the wall of the tavern. Po fell backward as he dropped his broken sword. Gideon stood over him, holding his sword square at his throat.

"Alright, Gideon, that's enough!" came a voice from the street. Stepping over toward him was Tyrion LoFan, Magistrate of Armändis. The older gentleman had been the magistrate for more than twenty years, and it showed. His long hair and beard flowed with a smattering of salt and pepper color. His face, scarred from years of fighting in the Attlain military, sported an eye patch where he lost his right eye. He wore a simple leather and ring mail armor with a long sword hanging around his waist, though he rarely drew it. There was not a lot of lawlessness in a town where the guild ruled.

"Lower your sword and step back," he ordered. Gideon knew that Tyrion was a good man, but he couldn't perform his duties properly due to the guild. Gideon lowered his sword and stepped back, as ordered, as Botàn came to his side.

Po got to his feet, smiling as if he'd won the fight. "Well, what are you waiting for, magistrate? Arrest him?" he cooed.

"Arrest him? For what? For defending himself? I watched the whole thing from over there, Po Kildevil. You attacked an unarmed man who was defending poor Ester from a beating by you! If it hadn't been for Botàn throwing him a weapon, I'd be arresting you for murder."

Po grew angry at Tyrion's refusal to act and got right in his face. "I don't care what you think you saw. He attacked a guild member without reason. Do your job and arrest him!"

"No, you don't! I'll be damned if I let you arrest Gideon just because he kicked your sorry ass!" Botàn screamed at Po. "It's about time you idiots learn that we're not expendable to the likes of you." The rest of the people gathered around and supported Botàn and Gideon. For the first time, people stood up to the Black Wolf Guild and their bullying tactics.

"Well now, what's going on here!" shouted Herrod as he walked up to the tavern. The commotion suddenly got quiet as the Guildmaster of Armändis approached them. Walking next to him was Cyrus Pipster, scribe and personal aide to Herrod. He was a squirrely man, thin and lean, with tiny glasses that rested just on the bridge of his nose. He was young, barely shaving, with long hair pulled back into a ponytail. With a quill pen in hand, he carried a wooden board with an inkwell built into it, layered with mounds of paper.

Tyrion walked over to Herrod while Po kept away. He knew he was probably in trouble with the guildmaster, but Tyrion was confident he could rely on the other guild members to back him up.

"Po was having a disagreement with young Ester over there and raised his hand to her," Tyrion explained. "Gideon stopped him from hitting her, and Po retaliated by drawing his sword. Once Gideon was given a blade, the two fought with Gideon snapping Po's blade with his own." Tyrion pointed out the piece of the sword still sticking in the wall of the tavern.

"Is that how it went down?" Herrod asked the other Black Wolf Guild members standing there.

"No, it wasn't," Po interjected. "That son of a bitch—"

"I wasn't talking to you," Herrod interrupted. Po immediately shut his mouth and just stood there. "I asked you lot," he said, pointing to the guild members. "Is that how it happened?"

They remained quiet until Dominic spoke up. "Yeah, that's how it happened. Exactly as Tyrion said."

Po's anger grew as Dominic sided against him, but he should have known better. Dominic was never one to oppose Herrod.

"Well, there you are. It seems Gideon was defending a young lady's honor. You should know better, Po," Herrod said, reprimanding his subordinate. "However," he continued to say as he turned toward Gideon and Botàn. "Since you broke his sword, it would only be fair if you replaced it with a new one. Wouldn't you agree?"

Botàn and Gideon knew Herrod pushed them into a corner. If they refused to make Po a new sword, Herrod could change his mind and have Gideon jailed, or worse. "No, that won't be a problem, Herrod. We'll make him a new sword," Botàn replied.

Herrod smiled a wicked grin. He was the consummate politician, playing both sides to get his way. "Excellent." He glowered. "Now, the rest of you have work to do. Get back to the guild!" They gulped down their drinks as quickly as possible before they ran off to the headquarters. Po scowled at Botàn and Gideon before he followed behind them.

Gideon kept a close eye on Po as he left, and once he was gone, Gideon went to hand the sword back to Botàn, but the weapon vanished from his hand. He looked around, thinking he dropped it. The blade was nowhere. He was about to apologize to Botàn when he noticed something strange. One of the runes on Botàn's pauldron softly glowed before it faded away. The rune looked like a lion's head.

Ester snuck up on Gideon and kissed him deeply while he was distracted, wrapping her arms around his head. When she finally released him, she leaned up and whispered in his ear. "Thank you for saving me. If you come back to the tavern tonight, I'll give you a proper thank you."

As she walked away, Gideon licked his lips, tasting her kiss. He smiled. He was going to have to come back and take her up on her offer.

Herrod slowly walked back toward the guild with Cyrus close in tow. He did his best not to show any emotion for what he saw in Po's duel with Gideon. "Was that one of them, Cyrus?" he asked his assistant.

Cyrus flipped through his papers, checking through each page thoroughly until he found the correct sheet. "It's not on the list, but it is an unusual weapon," he replied. "I can send a message to see if it is one of the artifacts, but it could take time to get a proper response. You know how adventurers can be."

"I don't care how long it takes. I won't ruin this by delivering the wrong merchandise. Just get it done," Herrod ordered. As Cyrus took off ahead of him, Po caught up to Herrod, flustered.

"Herrod, that punk got lucky, that's all. Let me take care of him and—" But before he could say another word, Herrod drew a dagger and slashed Po across the cheek. He grabbed Po by the scruff of his tunic and shoved him into the wall, holding the blade at his throat. Everyone around them ignored what was going on, knowing better than to interfere in guild business.

"That's twice now, Po, twice that you failed to kill a man who is nothing but a whelp, and yet he easily bested you," he gruffed. "How do you think that makes the guild look, makes me look, being my deputy and all?"

Herrod could see that Po was genuinely scared. He would kill Po without hesitation if necessary. "Now, if you let that man get the best of you one more time, I'll kill you myself. Is that clear?" Herrod stepped back and sheathed his dagger.

"But, Herrod, every breath he takes is an insult to me. Why can't I—" he stopped talking when Herrod reached for his sword. He did not draw it, not even an inch from its hilt. He just stood there with his hand on it. That was enough to frighten Po to death.

"Are you challenging my orders, Po?" Herrod asked.

"N-n-no, Herrod. I would never."

"Good, then we have an understanding." Herrod removed his hand from his hilt, much to the relief of Po. "Now, go get another sword and head back into the forest. There's a group of bugbears spotted by the north ridge. Take some men and deal with them."

Po nodded his head and rushed away as fast as he could to get away from Herrod's wrath. Herrod watched him run away and reveled in the power he held over the guild, but then his glee turned sour as he looked back at Botàn and Gideon. Those two continued to give him headaches, threatening his way of life here in Armändis, but maybe, just maybe, they will be the source of his most incredible windfall ever, and that made him very happy.

The ride back to Botàn's little stone house was quiet. Although Gideon had plenty of questions, especially about that sword Botàn tossed to him in his fight with Po, they remained silent. Once they arrived at the house, Botàn jumped down immediately and started to unload the cart. Gideon got down slowly and moved around to help.

"So, how much longer are you going to ignore me, or are you just letting your anger build until you can't hold it in anymore and explode? If you keep doing that, you'll give yourself a heart attack."

Botàn's face contorted and twitched so many times Gideon thought he was having a heart attack. Finally, he let it all out. "You idiot! What the hell were you thinking? Challenging the Black Wolf Guild all by yourself? If you want to get yourself killed, then you can leave now!"

"So, all that talk about the people of Armändis no longer being expendable was all for what? For show? You didn't mean a word of it?" Gideon asked as he attempted to remain calm for the two of them.

"Well, no, of course I meant it! It's just that putting yourself out there for one woman will only get you killed! Those bastards control everything. You should know that by now. The people of Armändis don't stand up for anybody."

"Oh, like you put yourself out there to save me? That kind of self-sacrifice? Is that what you meant?" Gideon blasted back at him as he started yanking things off the cart sporadically. "You know, you seem to be all talk when it comes to standing up to the guild, aren't you?"

"Oh, I suppose I was all talk when I tossed you that sword?"

"Yeah, about that, where exactly did you get it? I mean, you don't have it on you right now, and it disappeared as easily as it appeared, and don't tell me that pauldron is just to support your sore shoulder," Gideon argued before he tapped at the pauldron on Botàn's shoulder. "You have more secrets than anyone I know, and you refuse to clue me in on any of it. I mean, you saved me, let me into your home, become your assistant, tell me stories of adventuring, but nothing more. If you trust me that much, Master Botàn, then trust me a little more."

Botàn heard the pleas of his young apprentice, and his words rang true. He swallowed his pride and headed into the house. "Get the cart unloaded and put Jupiter in the barn," he said quietly.

"Do it yourself," Gideon snapped as he turned to leave.

"Just do what I ask while I make us something to eat," Botàn ordered. "We've got a lot to talk about, and I'm not about to spill my guts to you on an empty stomach. Or sober!"

2 THE MAGUS OF ATTLAIN

*G*ideon's Journal – I don't understand this man. One minute he's yelling at me until he's blue in the face, and the next, he's laying out his life story to me over dinner. Botàn is a lot older than I realized and a lot more experienced as a magic caster and a warrior. He is a puzzle box. No matter what peg you pull out, there's always another secret waiting behind the next peg.

He reminds me of someone, I think, an authority figure I once knew. I can't recall a face or a name, but the anger . . . that's what I remember. Someone in your face, yelling at you for no reason.

He has told me stories of his home in Plodoro. For such an isolated place, he made it seem like a paradise. I can tell how much he misses it, but he could never make the journey there in his current condition. Maybe that's why I'm here, why he took me under his wing. I can sense there's more to it than that. Still, it's good that he trusts me enough to tell me his secrets. I just hope I'm worthy of that trust.

Dinner was as quiet as the ride home from Armändis. They ate a simple meal of roasted pigeons and vegetables. When Botàn finished eating, he poured himself another goblet of wine—his third already that evening. After he gulped down that cup, he finally spoke up.

"Have you ever heard of the Magus, Gideon?" he asked. His apprentice shook his head as Botàn poured some more wine.

"You mean like a magic caster?"

Botàn nodded. "Of sorts." He took a couple swigs of wine and then continued. "The Magus were the protectors of the secrets of magic, but they became so much more."

"I don't understand. What did the Magus protect?" Gideon asked. "Magic is studied all around Attlain. There doesn't seem to be very few secrets to be kept."

"Ah, now that's where you're wrong. There are many secrets to magic, from the ingredients used in a rejuvenation potion to the specific runes needed to summon a demon. The secrets that needed protecting were ones that, if they found their way into the wrong hands, could mean the death of millions of people."

Gideon was intrigued by the conversation and poured Botàn some more wine. "What made the Magus so special?"

Botàn raised his cup to Gideon for his hospitality and took a drink before answering. "Wizards, sorcerers, and mages have power, but they lack the skill to wield the weapons of magic they create. For that, they formed the Magus, skilled magic casters who could fight better than any warrior. They could summon lightning with one hand while swinging a sword with the other. They chose only the strongest initiates with the greatest affinity for magic. They would be the warrior class of magic, guardians at every magical academy, library, and laboratory across Attlain."

"Then why have I never heard of them? Even in your books, there is no mention of the Magus."

"That's because they wiped our names away from history." Botàn cursed as he drank the last of his wine. He went to refill his cup, but Gideon held his hand over it to stop him.

"Slow down," he admonished him. "You start to slur your words after your fifth cup." Botàn frowned but understood his concern. "Why were they written off?"

"Because of this." He pointed to the pauldron on his shoulder. "The Armory of Attlain."

"An armory?" Gideon asked, confused. "But, it's just a piece of armor?"

"Really?" Botàn smiled as he held out his hand and said, *"Come to me, Sirocco, Demon Sword of Wind!"* One of the pauldron's runes glowed and soon a runic circle appeared next to his hand. Slowly, a hilt began to emerge from the center of the ring. Botàn grasped the hilt and drew a sword from within the circle. It was a curved blade, a scimitar, with an ornate gold crossguard embedded with a large green gem at each end of the crossguard and on the pommel.

Gideon was shocked and amazed by the display of magic he had just witnessed. "Is that . . . is that a magic sword?"

"Sirocco, Demon Sword of Wind," Botàn said as he swung the blade, cutting through the air. A gust of wind erupted from where it slashed, blowing over everything in its path. You could hear birds chirp wildly in distress as the wind tossed them through the air.

Botàn released the sword, and it vanished as quickly as it appeared. Gideon got up from his chair and walked over to look more closely at the pauldron. He saw the same rune glow again, indicating that the weapon had somehow returned to it. Botàn took the opportunity to pour himself some more wine while Gideon was distracted.

"How?" Gideon asked as he ran his fingers across the runes. Botàn batted his hand away as he drank some more wine.

"The Magus needed weapons to protect their assigned places of duty, so the mages created them the finest of magical weapons. The weapons were housed in the armories, so the Magus had easy access to them and a variety of choices."

"Okay, that makes sense but I still don't understand something. What happened to the Magus?"

Botàn loudly sighed and took another drink. "What happens to anyone when they obtain too much power? Some of the Magus decided that since they were the strongest magic casters and the strongest warriors, they should be the ones calling the shots. They tried to take control."

"They started a rebellion?" Gideon asked, leaning in to hear more of the story.

"Yes, and the Helios Arcanum crushed the rebellion as quickly as it started," Botàn continued, referencing the magical authority in Attlain. "There was a flaw built into the armories that even the Magus were unaware of. If a Magus should die in battle, the armory was rendered useless to anyone else. Unless a Magus passes control of the armory to someone like an apprentice, it locks the weapons within it. No magic on Attlain can unlock it after a Magus dies.

"Once the remaining Magus were killed or captured, those that declared their loyalty could keep their armories. Most of them became adventurers, while others sequestered themselves into hiding to protect the weapons within their armories. As for the Magus themselves, they were wiped from the pages of history so that no one would know just how powerful they once were, or the weapons they carried," he concluded.

"Which one were you? Adventurer or hermit?" Gideon inquired.

Botàn laughed. "A little bit of both." He took another drink of wine. Gideon was finally beginning to understand why Botàn drank so much. He drank to forgive, and he drank to forget.

"My adventuring days came to an end in the caverns of Golquieth," he continued. "I was tracking down a vampire that had been plaguing the local towns. There were only two of us—me and Duarté Dartagni—who entered those caves. Since he was the better swordsman, I agreed to loan him Durandal from my armory."

"Durandal?" Gideon asked.

"Durandal, Holy Sword of the Archangel Michael," Botàn said as he pointed to an empty space on the armory where a rune once sat. "It was the one weapon that was most effective against the undead."

"What happened?"

Botàn took another drink of his wine as if he was preparing himself to speak the words. "He betrayed me. When we got deep enough into the cavern, we found the vampire's lair. I drew another holy weapon—Orléans, Lance of the Sainted Maiden—for myself. It's just as powerful as Durandal, but Duarté was not as good with pole weapons as swords.

"We were about to engage the creature when Duarté disappeared. I turned around to see him leaving. He used Durandal to split the columns and collapse the ceiling at the cavern entrance. He sealed me inside with the vampire."

"What? Why? I thought he was a paladin and your friend?"

"So did I, Marcus, so did I," Botàn concurred. "I never found out why he did it, at least not from him. Days later, after I defeated the beast and blasted my way out of the cave, I found out that Duarté declared that he had killed the vampire and was blessed by the archangel with the holy sword Durandal. For his actions, he was knighted and declared a Paladin of Attlain."

"What? How could he do that?" Gideon argued. "Didn't they know you had the holy sword in your armory?"

"The Magus kept the weapons of their armory a secret. If too many people knew what weapons you had, the more they were interested in stealing them from you."

"Why didn't you speak up against Duarté and dispute his claim?" Gideon asked.

Botàn paused to drink some more wine. To Gideon, it seemed as if it was a difficult question for him to answer.

The older man continued. "It was too late for that. I didn't have the resolve to stand up to Duarté's lies. My best friend betrayed my trust, turned his back on me, and tried to kill me. I didn't have the stomach for it anymore."

"'Is that why you came to Armändis? To hide away from Duarté?"

"No. I came to Armändis because I fell in love," Botàn said with a smile. "As I crawled out of that cave—dirty, starved, and near death—I was saved by a beautiful young lady, Ophelia, my wife. Armändis was her home, so she brought me here to heal my wounds. We soon fell in love and were married. I apprenticed as a blacksmith under her father, inheriting all this after he died. It was a short time after that I lost Ophelia. She died giving birth to our son, Gabriel."

Gideon could hear the sadness in his voice, something he rarely heard from Botàn. "I still don't understand why you stayed on in Armändis?"

Botàn touched one of the runes on his armory and said, *"Evil Eye."* Immediately a dagger appeared in his hand. It was a Kris, a wavy blade of black steel, about ten inches long, enveloped in smoky darkness—the guard of the dagger curved toward the tip, encircling an all-seeing eye.

"This is Evil Eye, the Dagger of Eternal Darkness," said Botàn. "Besides some other special abilities, the dagger gives the wielder the chance to catch a glimpse into the future."

"Well, that's helpful," Gideon retorted.

"No, not really. Every time you gaze into the future, the enchantment exacts a high cost: one year of your own life."

That revelation surprised Gideon, but it also explained a lot about Botàn. "Is that why you look so old for someone so strong?"

"Yes, exactly. I've used the sight more than I should have. I've been looking for one thing, and I finally found it. You!"

Now Gideon was even more startled. "Me? Why me?"

"The first time I used it was after Ophelia died. I saw myself, still here in Armändis, and I saw the same thing every time for more than twenty years; and the only question I ever asked was where I would find an apprentice. All I ever saw was me, here in Armändis, and then I saw you.

"I saw the attack on you by Po and his men," he added. "I knew I had to save you from death. That's why I had the clockwork heart built. It was the only way to save your life."

"But, couldn't you have just stopped them from stabbing me in the chest?" Gideon quipped.

"No, I'm afraid not. That's another flaw of the dagger's foresight. If you try to change the future, there is a chance you could bring about your own death. One must never chance with fate."

Gideon held his hand over his chest, feeling the steady beat of his clockwork heart. He wondered how much fate played a role in setting him at that crossroads. "You want me to be your apprentice? To become a Magus?"

"Yes, Gideon, because you have the qualities of a true Magus. You're strong of heart, steadfast in your convictions, with the potential to be a great warrior and a great magic caster," Botàn explained. "You are everything that a Magus needs to be. You don't seek power for personal gain. You want it to help people."

"Then why have you been fighting me tooth and nail since I got here," Gideon yelled. "Every time I asked you to teach me more, you turned me away. If you wanted me to be your apprentice so bad, then why did you disregard all my requests?"

"Because I had to be sure," Botàn shouted back at him. "I had to be sure that you were willing to accept the responsibility of becoming a Magus. It's not something to take on lightly. There are weapons in the armory that could level an entire city. You must be able to discern when to use weapons like that and when not to."

Gideon sat back, poured himself another goblet of wine, and chugged it down. He expected to hear something surprising from Botàn but not like this. "How long will it take? Being your apprentice, I mean."

"That depends on you," Botàn answered. "You have an incredible abundance of mana flowing through you, so the power is there, but it's unrefined, raw talent. It's just a matter of seeing if you have the skill to wield magic. It could take a year; it could take two or more. I just don't know yet."

Gideon finished his wine and got up from his chair. "Alright, I'll see you later," he said and started to leave.

"Where the hell are you going?"

"If I'm going to start training as a magic caster tomorrow, this is going to be my last free night for a while. I'm going down to Marion's and take Ester up on her offer of a reward." Gideon smiled as he left the house to head into Armändis.

"Gideon!" Botàn shouted, stopping his apprentice in his tracks. "Don't tell anyone in town about me being a Magus or teaching you magic. No one knows about my past, and I want to keep it that way."

Gideon was surprised to hear that, but it made sense with all that had happened over the past few months. Botàn was hiding in plain sight so that no one would come after him or the armory. "Of course, Master Botàn. I won't tell anyone. Not even during pillow talk with Ester."

Botàn laughed as Gideon left for his night of merriment. He drank some more wine, satisfied that he made the right choice in his new apprentice. Botàn didn't want to pin all this on Gideon, but he had no choice. He needed to pass the torch, and Gideon was his best hope for the future. *The Magus cannot die with me,* he thought to himself.

Gideon's Journal – What a night! Ester is a very loving, lively, and quite flexible young lady. As much as she "thanked" me, I think I made her happy too. It was a night I'll never forget because it's the last one I'll have for a while. The next day, Botàn started training me as a Magus in earnest. We still had our regular blacksmithing work to do for the guild, but I discovered another one of his secrets beyond that.

Beneath the house, there is a cellar. His father-in-law used it for storing food and supplies for the harsh winters in Armändis, but Botàn dedicated it for something else now. He concealed the entrance to the cellar with magic. I never knew it was there until he showed me, and once I got in, I understood why. It is a magical laboratory with books, relics, elixirs, and other magic items. It includes the most valuable artifact of his collection—the "Libru di Magia" or the Book of the Magus. It's a spellbook with specifically designed spells for the Magus, and it's one of the last in existence. The book links to the armory so that, when a Magus dies, his book self-destructs to keep the Magus' secrets.

My brain is going a million miles a minute in twenty different directions. There's so much to do and not enough time in the day to do it all. I thought the search for my past was going to be difficult, but this is at a whole other level. It is going to be a wild ride.

Botàn began his instruction with the basics of magic. Gideon was an apt student, curious and voracious for knowledge. He read every book, every scroll he was given with a thirst for knowledge, unlike anything Botàn had ever seen. The hard part was learning to control the flow of mana.

"Mana is the source of power for a magic caster," he explained. "Sometimes, you release mana unexpectedly, as you did at the crossroads, but by controlling the flow of mana, you control the energy. In short, you can increase or decrease the effect of a spell through that control.

"You can manipulate mana through words used to incite a spell," Botàn continued. "There are two ways to activate a spell—through a long recitation or a single word. Observe."

He held out his hand and focused on a suit of armor propped up on the opposite side of the cellar. *"Lampi!"* he chanted. Runic bands of power encircled his hand as a lightning bolt blasted the armor. The armor rattled loudly as the electrical charge jumped around the empty metal suit. Once the armor settled down, he held up his hand again.

"Thunder dash, and do your dance, sing across the sky anew; ignite the fire within the clouds, lightning strikes my enemy true! Lampi un Stratti!" Botàn's spell slowly built up as he cast his rhythmic chant. As the runic bands of power spun around his hand, the sparks flew until the last word. The lightning bolt blew the armor apart, nearly obliterating it into pieces this time.

"So, depending on how much mana you put into the spell and whether you do a single word or detailed chant will determine how powerful the spell is? The longer the incantation, the more power is built up behind the spell. Right?"

"Yes, exactly. You can also increase the power of a particular spell if you use it in conjunction with an artifact or relic, like a wand or a staff, but you have to be cautious," Botàn added as he poked Gideon in the chest. "Remember, your clockwork heart feeds on your mana to replenish the thunderstone within and keep your heart beating. If you use too much of your mana at one time, you could give yourself a heart attack."

Gideon rubbed his chest, reminded of the pain he felt when Po stabbed him in the heart. "I don't want that to happen. So, how do I control the flow of my mana?"

"We'll start with a simple spell—creating fire. You can practice this in the morning when you light the forge. Just imagine a flame, hot and bright, and then, say the word *Brusgià!*"

"*Brusgià?*" Gideon stuttered, trying to pronounce the word correctly. When he said it, his hand exploded with fire, startling the two of them. The pulsing flame expanded outward like a ball of hot plasma. Gideon noticed that he scorched some of his hair when the fire subsided. Suddenly, they both started laughing out loud.

"Well, I did say you had potential as a magic caster," Botàn joked. "I think you need to be more focused on a target before you repeat it."

"I think you're right," he retorted.

Gideon practiced daily, using the fire spell to ignite the forge daily. There were days when he could easily control the fire, while other days, it was a struggle, leaving him nearly exhausted. It took him time, but he was finally able to learn to control the flow of mana through his body without causing him a lot of discomfort in his heart.

He was like a man obsessed, trying everything and anything he could do with magic. He studied relentlessly, reading everything Botàn had in his collection. He memorized spells and incantations, focusing on the basic elemental, manipulation, and defensive enchantments. Botàn watched his apprentice in awe. He knew his patience had paid off. The faith he put in the foresight bestowed upon him by the Evil Eye was worth the years of waiting.

As they continued the training, Botàn asked even more of Gideon. He began intense weapons training—with sword, spear, ax, hammer, and dagger—to teach Gideon how to handle various weapons before passing the armory onto him. Like everything else he did, Gideon was a fast learner. The strength he built up swinging a hammer as an apprentice blacksmith improved his skill as a warrior.

"You must learn more than the sword," Botàn explained during one of their training sessions. "The weapons in the armory and ones you may add to it yourself will consider you its master. You must be able to wield them, or they will not fight for you or may even turn against you."

"You speak as if they have a mind of their own." Gideon looked down the length of the sword in his hand, pondering that very idea.

"In a way, they do. You see, magical weapons become imbued with the spirit of the person who created them. That *spark* gives them a life of their own. Most will follow the will of its master, but if that master falters—especially in battle—then the magical weapon could reject its wielder."

"So, the weapon controls you, or you control the weapon?"

"A little bit of both," Botàn surmised. "You must become one with the weapon, and it will become one with you. If you try to exude too much control, it will not obey you, but if you let the weapon control you, it could run wild and kill without abandon. That is why the Magus has to be a master of both magic and sword."

"I get it. You must master the weapon to tame the magic inside of it," Gideon said, swinging his blade about to show his mastery. "What's next?"

Botàn chuckled. "You have a long way to go and a lot more to learn, my young apprentice. Be patient."

It became their daily routine: Work in the forge, weapons training, and studying and practicing magic late into the night. Their day usually didn't end until after midnight. At night, Gideon walked outside, feeling the cool breeze on his face as he wiped the sweat from his brow. He looked up at the sky and saw the endless stars reach from horizon to horizon. It always amazed him how beautiful they sparkled in the night, even when the twin moons brightened the night.

He looked over and saw Botàn where he always was at this time of night. Beneath the branches of a dogwood tree, Botàn sat in front of two graves. The simple tombstones had two names on them: Ophelia and Gabriel. Every night, before he turned in, Botàn would come out to say good night to his wife and son.

Gideon could sense the sorrow in him as it built up throughout the day, drinking away his sadness and then coming out at night as he sat by their graves. He felt responsible for continuing to live when they had died, and that burden was overwhelming.

Gideon's Journal – It's been more than a year since I started training with Master Botàn. The regiment has been difficult, but it's rewarding. He even started to show me some of the weapons within the armory. He has more than twenty different magical weapons in there, which, according to Master Botàn, is a lot for a Magus. Over the years, he's met with other former Magus who didn't want to bear their armories anymore. They transferred their weapons to him, adding to his armory.

That's a big part of the responsibility of being a Magus. The weapons in the armory can be helpful as well as quite deadly. There's one that can cause a plague, one that can turn flesh to stone, and another that can summon a swarm of insects. Can you imagine what would happen if these weapons fell into the wrong hands?

It's so much responsibility. I wonder if I'm up to the challenge. Master Botàn has faith in me, so I need to trust his judgment, and hopefully, live up to it. I will master this power and bring honor back to the name of Magus. It is a legacy that Master Botàn has preserved, and it will not end with him.

Hunting was the only way to keep food on the table for the two men, but they rarely had time for it. Botàn had a solution for that. He taught Gideon about setting traps for rabbits, birds, and other small game. They set them along known hunting trails that Botàn had been using for more than twenty years.

Gideon checked the traps while Botàn picked some mushrooms, ramps, and other wild plants. He went to the first trap, where Gideon discovered two rabbits, nice and plump for cooking. "Alright, it looks like we'll be having rabbit stew for dinner tonight," he exclaimed.

"As long as you don't burn it like last time," Botàn retorted. Gideon scowled at him. He knew Master Botàn was just prodding him, and quite sarcastically.

"Hey, that wasn't my fault. I was following your recipe."

"There is nothing wrong with Ophelia's recipe," Botàn shot back. "And two rabbits are not enough to do it justice. There's barely enough meat on them. Now, go check the other traps."

Gideon laughed as he headed off to where they set another trap, but he noticed something wrong when he got there. The animal trap was crushed entirely, including the rabbits that were inside. They were nothing but a bloody pulp of fur and blood, pressed into the ground by an enormous footprint.

"Master Botàn, I think we have a problem here," he shouted. Botàn got on his feet and quickly ran over to see what Gideon meant. Once he saw the massive footprint and bloody mess, he knew what was going on.

"Trolls!"

"Trolls? How can they be out like this in the daylight?" Gideon asked.

"There are parts of the Imestrüs Forest where the canopy blocks out every ray of sunlight," he explained. "But, if they're nearby, that means that they must have somewhere to hide, like a cave or a hollow log."

Gideon looked around, trying to pierce the shadows for any hint that the trolls may be nearby. "Maybe we should pull back to the road," he suggested. "There are too many places to hide around here."

"Agreed. Let's—" But before he could say another word, a giant club swung right at them. The two men jumped aside in the nick of time just before it struck. There was the troll they wanted to avoid. The creature had greenish-gray skin, wearing only a loincloth, carrying a dead tree log as a club. His mouth was large with oversized tusks growing from his jaw, his eyes as small as a quail's egg, with a long ponytail formed from a single tuft of hair on the top of his head.

It roared a low, guttural scream as it swung again, this time smashing a tree in half. Botàn touched the armory and said, *"Come to me, Will O' the Wisp, Bright Bow of the Forest!"* The rune glowed before it faded. A runic circle opened above him, and a wooden bow levitated down from inside. It looked like a twisted tree branch, with tiny leaves growing out of it, carefully shaped into a bow without a bowstring.

Botàn pulled back on the bow; a bowstring shimmered as an arrow formed out of nothing into a brilliant white light. He fired the arrow, shattering the makeshift club into splinters. He fired two more arrows, knocking the troll backward.

"Gideon, finish him off!" he ordered his apprentice.

Gideon knelt, placed his hands on the ground and chanted. *"Earth and stone, heed my call; bend to my will, and split the ground; twist and turn, oh Earthen clay; become my spear, and strike my enemy down! Lancia di Petra!"* The ground beneath them rumbled. The staggered troll lost his footing and fell backward as stone spikes shot up from the ground, running him through his head, body, arms, and legs. The monster twitched and struggled as it bled out from the multiple wounds. Its black-red blood flowed down the spikes until the troll finally died.

The two men looked at each other and smiled, relieved that things worked out okay. It was more than that for Gideon. It was the first time he performed a spell successfully against a living target. Their moment of relief shattered when an ear-piercing scream rattled them. It was another troll, but its clothes and hair differed from the other troll. Botàn knew what it was when he saw it.

"Uh-oh, looks like its mate," Botàn said.

"What? That's a female troll? How can you tell?"

"You mean you don't see that she has boobs?" he snarked back at Gideon. "She also has two ponytails off the top of her head, but that's not the worst problem."

"What problem?" Gideon asked.

"Female trolls are usually magic casters!" he explained when the female troll started shouting in a strange tongue as lightning flew from her fingertips and struck the ground next to the two of them, blasting them back.

Although the blast didn't roast them, they were covered in dirt and bruised from being thrown through the air. Gideon set up a quick shield to protect them, anticipating another attack. *"Scudo!"* he chanted as a runic circle formed in front of him and Botàn, glowing with magical energy. It was a quick-acting spell, not as powerful but effective. He didn't know how long he could hold it without depleting his mana.

The attack he was waiting for never came. The female troll went over to its mate and sobbed over the dead body. Gideon never saw anything like this in a demi-human before. He considered them like animals, sub-human creatures who acted on instinct alone. For the first time, he caught a glimpse of humanity in their souls.

"What do we do?" Gideon asked Botàn as he continued to shield them.

"We need to distract her long enough to get in one good shot," he replied. Gideon weighed their options, but then he saw something out of the corner of his eye. A ray of sunlight piercing through the canopy.

THE LAST MAGUS: A CLOCKWORK HEART

"I've got an idea, but I need you to loan me Freya," he demanded. Gideon's request shocked Botàn. He knew what happened the last time Botàn loaned someone a weapon from the Armory of Attlain. Gideon could see the worried look on his master's face.

"Don't worry, Master Botàn. I'm not going anywhere."

His words comforted Botàn. He trusted in his apprentice this far; he might as well take the next step. *"Come to me, Freya, Fist of the Ice Queen!"* he commanded. A runic magic circle opened, and a handle appeared. Botàn gestured for Gideon to take it. He reached in and pulled out a massive mace. The mace head was a fusion of multiple steel plates covered in a thin layer of frost. An icy mist rose from around it.

"So, what's your plan?" Botàn asked in anticipation.

"Get Sirocco ready," Gideon said. "When I get her in position, blast the canopy just above her with its wind magic. The sunlight should do the rest."

Botàn liked the way his apprentice thought. It was a good plan. "Alright, just be careful out there," he told Gideon. The apprentice smiled, grateful at the trust his master put in him. Botàn summoned the scimitar from the armory, just like before. Gideon moved through the brush carefully, trying to get in behind the grieving troll.

When he finally got into position, he stepped out from behind the brush and screamed at the monster. "Over here! Hey you, ugly!" he shouted. The insults got the troll's attention. She turned toward Gideon and gritted her teeth as slobber dripped out from between them.

"Ugly, am I?" she said, quite clearly for a troll. "I'll show you how ugly I can be!" She screamed as she charged right at Gideon. Her fingernails extended out from her hands, forming razor-sharp claws capable of rendering his flesh with ease.

With all his might, Gideon slammed the mace on the ground. The magical weapon sent out a wave of ice, freezing the earth and everything in its path. The troll was too massive to freeze completely, but the ice captured her legs. She was right where Gideon wanted her.

"Now, Botàn!" he yelled. Botàn stepped forward and swung Sirocco up toward the canopy of the trees, slashing the air multiple times as the wind cut through the branches and leaves. The magical winds blew open the roof, blasting a hole through it and letting in the sunlight. The sun's rays hit the troll straight on. Although it started to melt the ice Gideon summoned, it had a more devastating effect on the troll.

The one weakness of trolls was sunlight. The monster screamed as its flesh began to change to stone. When it was over, the troll stood there, arms and claws extended as it attempted to block out the sun, but to no avail. She was dead, now a statue captured in stone, for all time.

The two men walked up, admiring their achievement. They moved around her, making sure that every inch of the troll was now stone. When they finished examining her, Gideon handed the mace back to Botàn, who stared at him in awe.

"I told you I'd give it back," Gideon said. Botàn returned Sirocco to the armory before taking Freya by the handle.

"That you did, lad, that you did," he said with a grin, satisfied and happy.

"I guess we should report this to the guild," Gideon surmised. "Maybe they'll give us a reward for killing these trolls."

"The bigger reward has got to be around here somewhere," Botàn retorted. "Trolls don't move this freely in the daytime unless their den is nearby. Let's look for it. We may find some treasure on our own."

The two men started exploring the nearby woods, looking for any signs of a troll horde. They soon found it in the hollowed-out trunk of a dead tree. The inside looked like a proper home for a troll. The trolls hollowed it out even more, making room for them to live. There were stools, a small table, a straw bed, even a makeshift stove with the chimney coming out the top of the log for both heat and cooking. It looked like they had been living there for some time.

"Unbelievable," Gideon said as he looked around. "They were trying to make a home here. It's a wonder that the guild never caught them."

"She must have been a good magic caster," Botàn explained. "She probably hid them from sight with illusion magic whenever the guild came around. That chimney pipe goes right through a stump to hide it. They would never have found them unless they broke the spell."

"It's a shame we had to kill them," Gideon added. "It seems all they wanted to do was live their life here in Imestrüs, without anyone to bother them."

"That may be, lad," Botàn said as he continued to ransack the troll's home. "But you never know with this lot. Some demi-humans can be amenable, downright reasonable. Some, however, will turn on you on a whim." Botàn swept away the straw being used for a mattress to reveal a hidden panel on the floor. "Ah! Here it is." He opened it up to reveal a hole with a chest stored inside it. "Give me a hand, Gideon."

The two men leaned down and lifted the heavy chest, scooting it forward as best they could before setting it on the ground. Botàn opened it up to reveal gold and other coins, jewelry of all shapes and sizes with precious gems inlaid in them, some small weapons and even some chain mail armor. Gideon picked it up, but it looked like you'd have to be relatively small to wear it.

"What in the world is this? Armor for a child?" he asked as he held it up. Botàn examined it closely.

"It's mithril, the metal mined by the Dwarves of Ordstran and forged by the Iscandi Alf," he explained. "It looks like a gnome or maybe a halfling could wear it. That should fetch quite a price."

From the woods they heard noises. It sounded like men talking and searching the area, closing in on the trolls' house. Gideon and Botàn instantly recognized those voices as members of the Black Wolf Guild.

"If they find us here, they'll take the treasure for themselves. What do we do?" Gideon whispered.

"We do just like the trolls did and hide in plain sight," Botàn said as he stepped in front of Gideon. He held up his hand and began to cast an illusion spell.

"Whispers in the darkness, silent as the wind, bend the light to my will; Cast your shadow around me, hide me from my enemy, conceal me while I remain still! Muru Invisibili!"

The runic circle enveloping his hand extended outward until it reached the edge of the chest. The air in front of him shimmered as if looking through a pool of water. "Remain perfectly still and silent," Botàn whispered. "Any sudden movement or sound could break the spell.

Gideon nodded his head and stood firm next to Botàn. Within minutes, the sounds grew louder as the guild members walked right by them, peering inside before moving on. The spell was working as it should. Just when they thought they were leaving, two familiar faces walked up to the opening. Po was leading this expedition, and surprisingly, Herrod was with them. Gideon knew that Herrod rarely ventured into the forest with the guild, but perhaps the news of trolls in the woods brought him out to satiate his greed.

"Nothing. They must have just got here. Maybe they were traveling light. It looks like they didn't bring any treasure with them," Po said.

"Maybe, but I doubt it. The bigger question is, who killed those trolls?" Herrod inquired.

"Heller said he found a crushed rabbit trap near the first troll. We know Botàn sets traps out here regularly."

"Botàn is a crummy blacksmith with no balls for fighting, at least not anymore," Herrod snapped. "Not even his witless apprentice could kill one troll, let alone two."

"Should I send some men to check them out, just in case?" Po asked.

"No, leave them alone," Herrod said. "I don't want them getting wind of what I'm planning. We must wait until Gideon leaves for Le'Arun. Then, Botàn will be easy pickings, and his armory will be mine."

"Then let me kill Gideon now!" Po demanded. "The next time he's at Marion's, I'll have Ester lure him upstairs. She's been providing us with good information so far. I know she'll do this for me. He'll be dead before his head hits the pillow."

"You don't get it, do you?" Herrod yelled, smacking Po in the chest. "I want you to kill Gideon after he leaves Armàndis. That way, we can blame Botàn's death on him, and no one will be the wiser. Then, we can retire as rich men once that witch Selene pays us for the armory."

Both Gideon and Botàn were shocked and angered by the overtures laid out by Herrod and Po. Gideon knew they wanted to kill him, but all along, they were after the Armory of Attlain. And Ester, a woman he was close to, was a spy for the guild. It made his blood boil.

Botàn could see Gideon was close to losing control. He slowly reached out with his free hand, knowing he could break the cloaking spell, and placed it on his shoulder. His touch was a welcome presence that brought Gideon back to his senses. He understood what his master wanted and calmed down.

"Any sign of it?" Po shouted to his men.

"No, nothing here! They must have been scavengers. There's no treasure here!" One of the men shouted back. Po looked at Herrod for advice.

"Do you want us to keep searching?" he asked.

"No, let's head back to Armändis, but start asking around to the usual suspects in the taverns and any new ones. Someone knows who killed those trolls, and maybe we'll find their horde too."

Po kicked the trunk in anger as he left, causing the roof to drop down a little. The dust and dirt hit Botàn's illusion, causing it to ripple. The effect was only temporary, but it was enough to cause Herrod to look again down at the trunk. Gideon readied himself for a fight, but Herrod just shook it off as more dust and dirt fell on his head and in his eyes. He spat it out and wiped his face with his sleeve as he left, just as hasty and angry as Po.

Gideon and Botàn waited a few more minutes until the guild's voices faded into the distance. "What do you think? Are they gone?" Gideon whispered.

"Can you do a search spell?" Botàn asked. Gideon nodded his head before kneeling and placing his hand on the ground.

"Creatures of the forest, heed my call, let me see where my enemies are, look out from where I sit, and give me sight to look afar! Sensu Longu!"

Gideon closed his eyes as he "looked" outward from the trunk through the spell he cast. He saw through the eyes of every bird, beast, and insect in the woods. Its effect spread from the tree's trunk, running through the ground, the bushes, and the tree until his spell caught up with the guild as they were leaving the forest, including Herrod and Po. They were long gone.

"They're gone, Master Botàn," he said. "They've already left the forest."

Botàn sighed as he lowered his hand, dispelling the illusion over the trunk. He shook out his arm to relieve the stiffness and pain he felt. "I haven't had to do that in quite a while," he told Gideon. "I forgot how much it hurts to keep your hand raised."

"You should have used your other arm. That's the one you hammer with all the time, so it's a lot stronger," Gideon joked. The two laughed because what they had just overheard was hard to comprehend. "I never suspected that they'd go this far," he said as they both tried to face reality. "I never thought Ester would betray me like that."

"Don't dwell on it, lad," Botàn said. "It will only turn sour in your stomach. Best that we plan how to hit them before they get us. For now, let's get this trunk back to the house and into the cellar."

The two men lifted the heavy trunk and carefully stepped out of the hollowed tree as they started toward home. When they reached the edge of the forest, they were cautious, checking out the area for signs of the guild. They decided to wait until dusk before they left the woods in case anyone was watching. Once they got back to the house, they descended into the cellar, hidden behind magic wards, before going through the chest more thoroughly.

Botàn started pulling out the jewelry, gems, and other precious items, while Gideon opted to look for more unique items, like armor and weapons. Besides the miniature mithril armor, he found some plate armor pieces—not magical but very finely made—as well as a leather longcoat, padded for added protection. Along with a dagger and sword, which probably belonged to the person who owned the leather coat and the armor, he found something unique.

It looked like a flintlock pistol, only broader in scope and size. The barrel flared open wide at the mouth and was heavily reinforced along the barrel as if to contain the force of the blast. "What in the world is this?" Gideon asked as he held up the weapon to Botàn.

"My God, that's a Dwarvish Doomfire!" Botàn took the weapon from Gideon and examined it more closely. "I've never seen one up close before."

"How does it work?" he asked and took back the weapon to examine it himself.

"The dwarves use an alchemical mixture of sulfur, saltpeter, and a mysterious black powder to fire a metal ball out of it. You pull the trigger, the hammer strikes the pad, causing a spark, which ignites the powder. They say it can pierce through even the toughest armor."

"Why don't guilds and adventurers carry them?" Gideon studied the barrel.

"Dwarves are very proprietary when it comes to their inventions," Botàn explained. "It took almost twenty years for the kingdom to negotiate the rights for their Magius Engines, plus another forty to fifty years to build the train tracks, power grid, and other conveniences across Attlain. That little venture nearly bankrupted the kingdom."

Gideon peered down the barrel of the Doomfire. "I think there's something stuck down there," he observed. Botàn grabbed it from his hands.

"Be careful, you idiot," he scolded. "'Do you want to blow your face off?"

"It doesn't look like metal. It's a crystal, I think."

Botàn carefully looked down the barrel of the Doomfire and saw a glint of a red crystalline structure inside. "It can't be." Botàn's eyes widened with disbelief. "Let's take this apart carefully. I think I know what's inside, but I need to be sure."

Over the next hour, the two of them meticulously took the weapon apart, ensuring they cataloged where each screw, pin, and bolt matched up to the piece that held it in place. Finally, they removed the barrel and Botàn was able to see what someone had crammed inside.

"I knew it!" he exclaimed. "It's a dragon's eye!"

"Are you serious?" Gideon said, shocked by the discovery. Botàn took out a magnifying glass to examine the crystal up close. "A jewel made by transmuting a dragon into an element of pure magic through alchemy? I thought they were just a legend?"

"They are very rare indeed," Botàn retorted. "Whoever this warrior was—the one with the armor and sword—he must have shoved the stone down the barrel to keep the trolls from finding it. Can you imagine that female troll with the absolute magic of a dragon's eye? Oh, no—"

He stopped mid-sentence as he discovered something in the stone. "Damn, there's a small crack in it, probably from when he shoved it down the barrel," Botàn said. "It's useless now. If we try to remove it, the eye could shatter. The chain reaction would kill us, and probably half of Armändis." Botàn dropped the barrel on the table, disgusted at losing such a powerful item. Gideon picked up the stone and examined the crack.

"We may not be able to remove it, but it's still a powerful source of magic, right?"

Botàn was curious by his apprentice's question. "Yes, but to use it properly, you have to take it out of there."

"No, I want to leave it in the Doomfire and put it back together," Gideon explained. "You said it was time for me to manufacture myself a wand. Why not use this instead?"

Now Botàn was confused, and Gideon saw that. "Look, we could bind it with some concentric bands along the barrel, and carve the appropriate magical runes in the trigger, hammer, and plate. Then, all I'd have to do is cast the spell and focus the power through the dragon's eye. It would act just like a wand, maybe even better."

"Where did you learn about concentric bands?" Botàn asked.

"It's in one of your books on magic crafting," he said. "We could melt down the mithril armor to make the bands. It would be a weapon that I could use without severely depleting my mana. What do you think?"

Botàn looked at the disassembled Doomfire laid out across his workbench. His ideas were feasible and could benefit them both against Herrod and his machinations. "Doing this would require some additional components and that won't be cheap."

Gideon reached into the chest and picked up a handful of coins. "I don't think we have to worry about that."

"We need to be careful, Marcus. If we start spreading around money like there's no tomorrow, the guild will get suspicious. Herrod will surely know that we were the ones who killed those trolls, and then he may move up his schedule to kill us."

"Then we'll just order from places all around Armändis, not just Marion's," Gideon said.

Botàn considered his apprentice's solution for a moment and decided it was a good plan.

"But, in all seriousness, Master Botàn," Gideon continued, "do you know who this Selene is and why she would want the armory? Someone like that must know that killing you will lock the armory, preventing any weapons from being recovered."

Botàn pondered that point, sighing at the situation. "I don't know any Selene, but if she's a competent sorceress, perhaps she discovered a way to unseal the armories."

"But that's impossible. You said so yourself."

Botàn pulled out the stool from under his workbench and sat down to gather his thoughts before he continued. He knew his next words could scare Gideon away from becoming a Magus. "I have been hearing stories, over the past few years, about someone killing Magus and taking their armories. I even had a few Magus come to me to transfer their weapons to me because they were afraid . . . afraid of dying, being killed, and their magic weapons sealed away forever.

"This woman could be the one killing Magus, taking their armories, and experimenting on them, trying to find a way to unlock the secrets inside," Botàn continued. "It is a good possibility that she finally found a way to do it, but now, it doesn't matter if I'm dead or alive. If she gets my armory, these weapons could change the face of Attlain."

Gideon watched the pain form across Botàn's face. He saw the fear, both for him and for Gideon too. "Well then, I guess we better get started on this, Master Botàn, the sooner the better."

Botàn swelled with pride. The man he chose as his apprentice was courageous, undeterred, and he understood the responsibilities before him. Botàn got up to help him with the task of creating his new weapon, but not before smacking him on the back of the head.

"What did I tell you? Stop calling me Master!"

Gideon just smiled as they got to work.

3 THE BLACK WOLF GUILD

*G*ideon's Journal – *It's not easy keeping a secret, especially in this town. Trying to create a new, magical weapon from scratch was no easy task either. I hated to lie to Fenwick, having to order from his competitors, but I had no choice if we were to keep this from the guild. It worked out exactly as we planned. I bought the necessary components from different merchants across Armändis. Some were genuinely surprised at the requests, but, in the end, they appreciated the business and kept quiet about it. I mean, it's hard to hide the fact that you're buying things like water drawn from a moonlit well, the claws of a werewolf, and hair from the mane of a unicorn. The components and the mithril need to be smelted together before being cast into parts for the new weapon. It won't be easy, and will take a while to complete, but I need this to work. It could turn the tide in the upcoming fight with Herrod and the guild, and with Master Botàn's help, I know we can do it.*

It took a lot of heat to melt down the mithril armor. Botàn had to amplify the fire in the forge with magic to get the mithril to the right temperature. The next step was pouring the molten metal into molds to form the four metal bands. Gideon etched the bands with magic runes, just as it instructed in the magic crafting book. Botàn and Gideon bent them around the barrel in place of the reinforced plating. These bands would act as amplifiers for the magic. They also recast the hammer, trigger, and striking plate in mithril with carved runes. Lastly, they had to carefully pour some of the mithril down the barrel to encase the dragon's eye in the precious metal. Not enough to seal it, but rather to complete the "circuit" between the caster and the dragon's eye through the mithril, powering the weapon. It took them more than a month, but they finally finished it.

Gideon added his little flare to the weapon, carving the wooden handle and body to resemble a dragon. Instead of keeping the name Doomfire, he renamed it Dragoon. According to the instructions in the book, he needed a power word to activate the weapon. He chose Dragoon and etched the new name in magical runes on the last concentric ring. With the weapon complete there was only one thing left to do. Test it.

Master and apprentice went outside. It was near dusk, so no one in town would notice whatever they did. The two went down the hill toward the forest, where an old stump protruded from the ground. Botàn cut that tree down years ago, but its roots grew down deep. He could never get the stump out of the earth. It made a perfect target.

"Alright then, give it a go. Let's see if we're as clever as dwarves," Botàn said.

Gideon planted his feet firmly on the ground. He raised the Dragoon and aimed toward the stump, cocking back the trigger before he cast his spell.

He began chanting. *"Brusgià, Focu di Dragone, Dragoon!"* Runic circles built up around the barrel burning orange like the fire within the spell, one over each concentric band, as his mana flowed into the dragon's eye in the barrel. As the power poured into the weapon, something extraordinary happened. A dragon made of magical fire swirled around his arm and down the barrel of the Dragoon. When he pulled the trigger, completing the spell, all hell broke loose. The weapon exploded, sending a fireball toward the stump. The impact was devastating. The stump burst into a fire pillar that shot upwards into the sky. The blast knocked the two men back across the ground. When the ringing stopped in their ears, they sat up to see that the explosion destroyed the stump.

"Wow!" Gideon exclaimed. "Well, it worked!"

"Yeah, a little too well," Botàn added. "You might need to cut back on one part of the incantation to decrease the power to a more manageable level."

"Yeah, I'll have to experiment with it a little bit to get it right where I want it," Gideon said. "Still, that was a good test."

"Yes, but it may have attracted some attention from town. We'll need to come up with an excuse before anyone starts asking questions."

"Well, you told me to get rid of that stump, so I tried blowing it up and burning it out," he concocted. "It worked a little too well, causing that massive explosion."

Botàn nodded his head. It was a good idea. With the Dragoon, Gideon added a powerful element to his arsenal. He would need it for the battle ahead. There wasn't much time left, and Botàn knew it.

Gideon grunted as he lifted the bags of flour and potatoes onto the cart. Usually Botàn would help him with the supply run, but they decided to venture out into town separately from now on. Knowing the guild's plans for them, one target was better than two. They would deny the guild any opportunity to put one, or both, down at the same time. He knew they wouldn't target Gideon while in town, so Botàn would sequester himself away in the cellar while Gideon was out.

Ester followed Gideon like a lost puppy, fawning over him, trying to get him to come back to the tavern later. She cooed and wrapped her arms around his. "You haven't been to the tavern in over a month." She batted her eyes and pouted her lips, trying to look as provocative as she could. "I need you."

Gideon felt himself throw up a little in his mouth. He knew that Ester was just trying to get him down to the tavern for more information for the guild, or worse, set him up. "Sorry Ester, but we've got a lot of work to do at the shop. Why do you think Master Botàn isn't here helping me?"

"Yes, but you're not working at night, are you?" She ran her fingers across his lips, pulling on them enticingly. Gideon knew he couldn't turn her down completely, otherwise, it might raise suspicions when she reported back to the guild. Before he could say anything, he heard someone calling his name.

Gideon looked up the street and saw a little boy running toward him. It was Collin Wildman. The ten-year-old boy's eyes were red from crying.

He was the son of Janus and Merrie Wildman. They were both in the Black Wolf Guild and Botàn and Gideon's friends. Some people within the guild cared about Armändis, and the Wildman's were some of them.

Gideon rushed over to the crying child, knelt, and wrapped his arms around the little boy to comfort him. "Collin, what's wrong?"

"They're beating my father," he cried. "They tied him up and are whipping him out in front of the guild."

"What? Who's whipping him?"

"Guildmaster Herrod is beating my father, all because he kept a couple of gold pieces for himself," Collin explained. "We needed the money to pay for some medicine for my mother."

Ester walked up beside Gideon and the boy and interjected. "It's the rule of the guild. If you steal from the guild, you get twenty lashes in front of everyone."

Gideon's blood boiled as anger riled up inside of him. They were beating a man for trying to provide medicine for his wife. "Come on, Collin, let's go!" Gideon grabbed the boy by the hand and raced down the street, hurrying to reach the guild before it was too late.

When they reached the guild headquarters, Gideon was shocked at what he saw. They gathered everyone from the guild on the stairs and across the stone porch in front of the guild. At the top of the steps, Herrod sat on an oversized chair, like a king on his throne. He sat there, munching on a ripe, juicy apple, looking down at the activities below him. Collin's father, Janus, was stretched out between two posts, his shirt ripped off his back. His skin was bloody, ripped from the whipping he'd already received. His head and face were bruised and swollen, bloodied by the beating he acquired before his punishment began. He hung there, nearly lifeless, as Heller, the guild master-at-arms, carried out the task of whipping him with a cat o' nine tails.

The rest of the town looked on, shocked at the pain and agony inflicted. Collin's mother, Merrie, was being comforted by Magistrate LoFan, who could do nothing about this. It was the guild's business, so he had no authority in stopping this atrocity from happening.

"Ten!" Po Kildevil counted out the punishment, standing next to Herrod. As the master-at-arms reared back for his next swing, Gideon stepped in front of Janus. The whip snapped toward him, but Gideon was able to catch it in his hand. The barbs cut into his palm, but he ignored the pain and held fast onto the whip.

"What the hell do you think you're doing, boy? Let go of the whip! It's guild business and none of yours!" Po shouted, angry at Gideon's interference. Herrod sat there and said nothing.

"Since when is it the guild's job to beat an innocent man? If he's done something wrong, it's up to the magistrate to determine his guilt and punishment, not you, Herrod!"

Now Herrod stood up, held up a hand instructing Po to be quiet, and addressed Gideon. "He stole from the guild, and as such, the magistrate has left his punishment to my discretion. Isn't that right, LoFan?"

Tyrion could do nothing but nod his head, agreeing to Herrod's every word. He was powerless against the master of the Black Wolf Guild.

"Now, get out of the way, Gideon, before I have you removed by force!" Herrod motioned for two of his men to move toward Gideon.

"If you continue beating him, he'll die! That's not punishment. It's murder!" Gideon shouted.

"If he dies, it only means he was weak and shouldn't be in the guild," Herrod said as he sat back down. Gideon stood his ground as the two men moved in to remove him. He had to think fast or they would kill Janus.

"Then, I'll take his remaining lashes!" Gideon exclaimed. Everyone was shocked and amazed by his proclamation, including Herrod.

"You'll what?"

"Cut Janus down, and I'll take the other lashes for him. Will that be satisfactory for you, Guildmaster?"

Herrod liked this idea. He didn't want to kill Gideon, but he needed to teach him a lesson for all his impertinence. Besides, it'll send a message to everyone in the town not to oppose him or the guild.

"Alright, if you're willing to take his punishment, then so be it! Cut him down!" Herrod ordered. Instead of removing Gideon, the two guild members cut down Janus and helped him to the ground. Collin and Merrie rushed over to help, but Merrie was more concerned about Gideon.

"Gideon, I can't ask you to do this!" she pleaded.

"Don't worry about me, Merrie. Take care of Janus and Collin, okay?" Gideon said as he removed his shirt. They went to tie his hands in the ropes, but Gideon pulled his hand away.

"You don't need to tie me up," he said. "I'm not going anywhere." Gideon leaned against one of the posts as he braced himself for the lashes. Once Heller was in position, Herrod gestured for him to continue.

"Hang on!" Po said as he walked down and took the whip from him. "I got this!" He sneered as he walked up behind Gideon and whispered in his ear, "I'm going to enjoy this."

Gideon tightened up his muscles in preparation for the lashes. Po reared back and swung the whip, hitting him squarely on the back. "Eleven!" Herrod shouted as he took over counting out the lashes.

The next four were just as brutal, digging deep into Gideon's back. He gritted his teeth and dug his fingers deep into the post.

"What's the matter, Gideon? Regretting your decision to take his punishment?" Po laughed.

Gideon looked at Po and smiled. "Are you kidding? My grandmother whipped me harder than this."

The small crowd of townspeople and guildsmen laughed at Gideon's joke. Po looked bad in front of everyone now and that angered him even more. The guildsman lashed out, striking Gideon several times. The cat o' nine tails ripped into his back, but Gideon held on, standing his ground against the onslaught from Po.

"That's enough!" Herrod shouted.

Po finally stopped, breathing heavily from all that activity. The crowd was silent.

"He took the remaining lashes. Let him go." Herrod rose from his chair to go back inside, happy with his little demonstration, but then something caught his eye. The townspeople were rushing to Gideon's aid, helping him. Herrod, thinking this would be a display of his power, saw that it had the opposite effect. The people were rallying to Gideon in appreciation for what he did, not in fear of the guild.

Herrod's mood soured as he stormed back into the guild. Tyrion and the others helped Gideon over to the steps of the magistrate's office across from the guild, where Janus was being healed. The guild employed clerics—magic-based healers imbued with divine power to perform miracles. The newest member of the guild, Cerise Junquets, tried her best to heal Janus's wounds.

She was a catsei, a race of demi-humans with cat-like features. Although she looked human, she had large, cat-like ears poking out the top of her head and a long, fuzzy tail. She was a beautiful, young girl, fresh out of the Paragon Temple, looking for adventure in the outer wilds of Attlain. Her long black hair matched her tail and ears, which were soft, silky, and tipped in white. She held her hands over Janus's back, chanting a prayer as her divine energy healed his wounds.

Merrie held her husband's head in her lap while Cerise finished her healing ritual. "That should stop the bleeding, but he's going to need plenty of rest," she advised Merrie. "Take him home, and I'll come by tomorrow to check up on him."

"No, you won't," Po said as he stepped over to them. "Janus is no longer part of the guild. Herrod kicked him out. If you want to heal him anymore, he's going to have to pay for it, just like everyone else. The same goes for Gideon. You don't touch him unless he pays, Cerise."

Angry at his orders, Cerise stood up and got in Po's face. "I am Cleric of the Great Goddess Bast! I will not turn away from someone in desperate need of healing."

"You will as long as you're with us," Po snapped back at her. "A healing costs one gold piece."

"One gold piece? Are you insane? That's three times the cost in other cities!" Cerise shouted.

"This ain't other cities, this is Armändis, and the price for a cleric's healing is one gold piece. On top of that, Janus owes us two gold pieces for what he stole from the guild."

Gideon gritted his teeth as he tried to get to his feet. Tyrion helped him up as he reached into his pocket and pulled out four gold coins. He grabbed Po by the hand and slapped the coins into his palm. "That takes care of Janus's debt and pays for my healing today and another for Janus tomorrow. Is that alright with you?"

In excruciating pain, Gideon stood there defiant against Po and the guild. Po looked down at the gold, wondering where this lowlife apprentice could get gold coins. He clenched them in his hand before he spat on the ground in front of Gideon and walked away in a huff.

After Po disappeared into the guild's headquarters, Gideon nearly collapsed on the ground as his legs finally gave way. Tyrion held him up before sitting him back down on the steps. "You're a damn fool, Gideon. A brave one, but a damn fool," he scolded. Cerise placed her hands over Gideon's back and began the healing process.

"You sound just like Botàn," Gideon chuckled, trying not to wince from the pain.

Tyrion said, "Well, I'm standing in for him right now. You can't take on the guild on your own like that. You're going to get yourself killed."

"If I didn't take Janus's place, he'd be dead by now. We can't have Collin growing up without a father, now can we?" He reached out and patted the little boy on his head, rubbing it slightly.

Tyrion agreed with Gideon's logic, just not his method. Merrie, however, was a little more appreciative. She walked over and grabbed his face with both hands lovingly and kissed him.

"Thank you, Gideon," she said as tears rolled down her face. "I don't think we could ever repay you for what you did today."

Gideon was happy to hear her say it. Collin hugged him tight around the neck, which made his wounds sting, but he didn't mind it at all.

"Thank you for saving my dad," the little boy said. All Gideon could do was smile. It was why he stepped in for Janus.

Janus was loaded onto a stretcher and carried back to his home, with Merrie and Collin following close behind. As they walked off, Dominic Evergreen stepped up to Gideon.

"Don't tell me, are you going to yell at me too?" Gideon asked, too tired and in pain to argue.

"No, I'm not," Dominic said. "I just wanted to say thank you."

Gideon was surprised to hear that. "Really? That's not the usual guild line, Dom."

"Yeah, well, some of us aren't like that lot," Dominic replied, nodding his head back toward Po. "I've been a guildsman for more than forty years. I stand with my brothers and sisters in the guild, just like you did for Janus today, and for that, I wanted to say thank you."

Dominic held out his hand. Gideon was impressed to hear that, especially from Dominic. He offered his own hand and the men shook. He had heard that Dom was one of the few guild leaders with morals, and they were right. "Dom, you know that Herrod is wrong. He's corrupt, evil, and unjust. Why don't you stand up to him?"

Dom mused over it before answering. "There can only be one guildmaster, and right now, that's Maximillian Herrod. Just watch your back, Gideon. You and Botàn too. I don't know what he has planned, but it ain't good." Dom left and walked back to the guild.

Once Cerise finished the healing process, she said, "He's right, Gideon. Something is going on, but Herrod and his minions are being hush-hush about it. Be careful, okay. I haven't done a resurrection yet, so don't get yourself killed. I don't want you to be my first."

"I doubt I could afford one at the guild's prices," he retorted as he looked around for his shirt.

Cerise found it and handed Gideon his shirt as he carefully worked to put it back on, still feeling a twinge of pain, even after her healing. "Thanks, Cerise. I appreciate your delicate, healing touch."

"You're going to be a little tender back there for a couple of days," she said.

"I'd put some wormwood paste on that tonight to help reduce the swelling. I'm sure Botàn knows how to mix that up, so make sure you take care of it."

"Yeah, I will as soon as I get my ass chewed out by him for what I did today."

Cerise stepped up on her tiptoes and kissed Gideon on the cheek. "To tell you the truth, I'm with Dom on this one. Thank you!"

Cerise headed back to the guild, leaving Gideon with Tyrion. "Let me help you back to Marion's, Gideon," Tyrion offered. "You'll need some help unloading the cart once you get back to Botàn's house."

"Thanks, Tyrion. You too, huh?"

"Well, call it a guilt complex," he explained. "I can't stop Herrod from doing what he wants to do, so it's the least I can do to make up for it." The older magistrate carefully helped Gideon up, wrapping his arm low so as not to touch his wounds. The two men slowly made their way down the street.

"Yeah, can you please explain that one to me?" Gideon asked. "Why doesn't anyone stand up to him?"

Tyrion took a deep breath, putting his thoughts together before trying to explain things. He explained that Herrod was not only an excellent swordsman, he also carried a cursed weapon. A demon sword that burned with a black hellflame. The sword could not only kill you physically, but it could destroy your soul too. With that sword, no one dared challenge Herrod.

When they reached Marion's Tavern, Gideon paid Fenwick while Tyrion finished loading the cart for him. The tavern owner even helped Gideon up on the wagon. There was a genuine look of concern on Ester's face too. It had amazed Gideon how one act of kindness could change everyone's attitude in Armändis.

Maybe it's just what they needed to bring the people together against Herrod, Gideon thought.

It was a slow, bumpy ride back to Botàn's. Tyrion did his best to take it easy on Gideon, which made the ride last a lot longer than usual, even at Jupiter's sluggish pace. Once there, Botàn waited patiently outside, confused and concerned at seeing Tyrion on the cart with Gideon. Tyrion jumped down first to explain everything that happened, while Gideon sauntered inside and lay down in his bed to rest.

The two of them unloaded the cart and put Jupiter in the barn before Tyrion walked back to Armändis. Botàn finally checked on Gideon.

Gideon lay face down in bed, waiting for the scolding he would get about being reckless, but, instead, Botàn said nothing, not a single word. He just pulled up a chair and sat next to Gideon. "Pull up your shirt and let me see your wounds," he said calmly and politely.

Gideon raised a little bit, grimacing as he pulled his tunic up and over his head. Botàn carefully examined his back, ensuring the wounds were closed and healing. He knew the cleric's healing would stop the bleeding and heal his injuries, but there was still a chance for infection and other complications. He looked over him quietly. Gideon didn't know what was more disconcerting—all this silence or waiting for him to yell.

"Aren't you going to say something?" Gideon asked.

"And what would you like me to say?"

"Oh, I don't know. Usually, by now, you'd be telling me I was a careless idiot who was trying to get myself killed, et cetera, et cetera."

Botàn smiled and continued his examination. "Nope, no yelling, no scolding, not a single word. You did good, Gideon. You did good. Just rest up, okay. I don't want you ripping open those wounds. We'll put some wormwood paste on your back later tonight."

Gideon was amazed as Botàn walked away. He couldn't believe it. His master finally understood him and his reasoning. After two years, they finally connected the dots.

4 PASSING THE TORCH

Gideon's Journal – *The pain from the beating took a few days to subside. The wormwood paste did the trick. The swelling went down, and my skin healed up nicely. On the other hand, the scars will be with me for the rest of my life. It'll make a nice story to tell down the road, especially to a certain young lady with whom I was trying to entice into my bed. I know it's probably not the most ethical thing to do, using an injury like that, but you need to be creative sometimes.*

That beating did stir some more memories to the forefront. I remembered a time at school—a religious school I think—when I was a boy. I was passing a note and I got caught. The teacher beat me across my hands with a ruler. I couldn't write neatly for a week. Pain is a memory we never forget.

Botàn and I are getting along better than ever. We seemed to hit our stride—with the trolls' defeat, making the Dragoon, and being whipped by the guild— and have reached a better place, like master and apprentice. We're even talking about leaving Armändis and heading to Le'Arun together. One of his former adventurer friends, Lady Jacqueline Celestra, is now an instructor at the Basilon Magical Academy. She could be a big help in finishing my training as a magic caster.

This is something we need to do together. The last thing I will do is leave Master Botàn here by himself.

The forge was a place of peace for Gideon. The hammer's rhythmic drumbeat against the hot steel kept his mind clear for other things. The heat from the fire caused him to sweat out his frustrations. Forging a new blade from raw iron gave him the satisfaction of his work through the whole process. To him, the time in the forge was like a day of meditation.

While Gideon hammered out the weapons to the beat of his hammer, Botàn ground down and sharpened the edges of his stone wheel. He powered the spinning stone with his feet, pumping relentlessly to keep it moving at high speed to form a sharp edge. He would douse the stone with water, now and then, to keep the stone smooth.

It was their routine, six days a week, from sunrise to sunset. The guild was notorious for ruining blades, chipping and bending them from their constant abuse. There were quite a few guild members who didn't know how to use a sword, ax, or spear. The guild liked to employ a tactic of throwing bodies at the monsters. They used the inexperienced warriors to distract the creatures while the more experienced struck them down. This tactic led to broken weapons and dead and injured warriors. It was a demonstrable stratagem, but the cost was very high.

A child's voice called out to the two men, who both stopped working and looked up to see little Collin Wildman running toward them. It had only been a few days since the public beating his father received, so it was strange to see the little boy out here by himself.

"What's the matter, boy?" Botàn shouted. When Collin got to the forge, he stopped but was so out of breath, he couldn't speak. Gideon took a ladle of water from the barrel and handed it to Collin. The little boy gulped it down greedily.

"It's alright," Gideon assured him. "What's happened? Is it your father?"

"His wounds are infected," the boy said, his head nodding in rapid succession. "My mother sent me out to get some wormwood to help him, but they're all sold out. They said the guild bought out every leaf to replenish the inventory in their stores."

"That's bullshit!" Gideon said. "They knew that Janus, or I, might need it, so they bought it out to make us suffer. Damn that Herrod!"

"And let me guess, the guild won't sell you any either," Botàn surmised. Collin shook his head.

"Please, you gotta help me!" Collin pleaded. "My father's in so much pain. He's getting worse and worse."

"We don't have any wormwood, Collin. Botàn used the last of what he had on me," Gideon said.

"Not to worry," Botàn said. He wiped the sweat from his brow and the dirt from his hands. "I know where some wormwood grows inside the Imestrüs Forest. We'll have an ample supply for your father in no time. Come on, Gideon!"

Collin begged them to let him come along, but Botàn was reluctant. Gideon, however, sided with the little boy. He didn't like the idea of leaving him there by himself, in case the guild might show up. In the end, Botàn couldn't argue with them and gave in.

"Alright, but you will do as I say, no backtalk. Otherwise, you can stay here. Understand?"

Collin nodded his head and smiled as Botàn went inside the house to get ready. Gideon leaned down and whispered to Collin. "Don't worry. He said the same thing to me when I first got here."

The little boy was happy to hear that. Gideon patted him on the head one more time before joining Botàn in the house. The three of them soon left together and headed for the Imestrüs Forest. Botàn led them to a small clearing, away from the usual monster-hunting sites. It took nearly thirty minutes to reach his "secret spot," and they began searching for the elusive wormwood plant.

"Look around the base of the trees that are well lit," Botàn said. "Wormwood likes plenty of sunlight and not a lot of water. That's why you have to look in places like this for it."

Gideon kept Collin close to him as they searched for the plant. Finally, they came across some near the base of a giant oak tree.

"I found some here too. Remember to cut it at the base, don't pull up the roots. That way, they can grow back and supply us with more," Botàn replied as he got down and pulled out a knife to cut the plants he found. Gideon did the same, carefully cutting the leaves off and handing them to Collin. They had quite a haul.

"This should make your dad feel a lot better," Gideon said. Collin smiled and nodded. Gideon was about to cut the last plant when he noticed something next to the oak tree's roots. It was a track, but one he'd never seen before. It looked like the footprint chickens make, but several times bigger, and then it hit him.

"Cockatrice! I found a cockatrice track!" But before he could say another word, the creature emerged from behind the tree. It stood nearly fourteen feet tall on two legs. The monster had a dragon's body but a rooster's head and feet. Its dragon-like wings were too small to carry its immense weight, so the monster was bound to the ground, just like its bird-like cousins. The cockatrice screeched, its bellow an ungodly howl that frightened all three of them.

"Get Collin away from there!" Botàn ordered. "And don't look into its eyes! It'll petrify you if you look in its eyes!" Gideon grabbed Collin by the waist and lifted him, running away as fast as possible. Botàn held out his hand to summon a weapon. *"Come to me, Thornrose!"* A long wooden handle appeared from inside a runic circle. Botàn grabbed the shaft and pulled out a spiked flail. The chain, more than three feet long, had razor-sharp barbs on each link. Long spikes varied in shape, size, and length on the heavy ball at the end of the flail.

Botàn swung the flail around before directing it at the cockatrice. The chain magically extended outward more than thirty feet before it wrapped around the neck of the cockatrice—the spiked ball embedded in the side of its rooster-shaped head, causing the creature to screech once more. Botàn was doing his best to hold it steady while Gideon moved Collin to safety, but he wasn't the viral young man he once was. He struggled against the strength of this giant creature.

Gideon set Collin down inside the trunk of a dead tree and ordered him to stay. The little boy looked scared out of his mind. Gideon took a dirty handkerchief out of his pocket and wrapped it carefully around Collin's head to shield his eyes. "Don't take this off until I tell you to, okay?"

Collin nodded his head as Gideon drew his Dragoon, preparing to join the fight. He saw that Collin was shaking in fear. The apprentice reached down and laid his hand reassuringly on Collin's shoulder. "Don't worry, Collin, you've got a couple of secret magic casters with you!" he said slyly. He smiled a slight grin from underneath the blindfold, reassured by his friend.

Gideon ran back toward Botàn and the cockatrice. He saw his master struggling against the pull of the monster. Botàn screamed for help.

Gideon aimed his Dragoon and chanted: *"Congelatu! Onda di Gelo! Ghiacciu! Dragoon!"* The magic built up within the Dragoon. The runic circles of frosty white spun around the barrel. An icy dragon formed like before. Gideon pulled the trigger causing a wintry blast to explode from the barrel. It struck the ground beneath the monster, allowing the ice to spread as it engulfed the cockatrice exponentially. The monster bellowed out one last time, a purple mist spewing from its mouth that headed right for Botàn. Gideon knew that the cockatrice could petrify you with its stare and its breath from his research.

He shouted a warning to his master, but it was too late. The petrifying mist caught Botàn on the right hand. He screamed as his fingers turned to stone, spreading slowly up his hand and into his forearm. He dropped Thornrose, causing the magical weapon to disappear and return to the armory. The frost wave finally enveloped the monster, freezing it solid. Once he saw the ice contained the creature, Gideon ran over to aid his master.

"Master Botàn! Are you alright?" he pleaded.

"Stop screaming at me!" Botàn replied. "Put a damn tourniquet around my arm to keep it from spreading any further!"

Gideon understood what he wanted, but he had already used his only handkerchief. He shouted for Collin to bring him the item. The little boy removed the blindfold and ran over to the two of them. Gideon took the cloth and wrapped it around Botàn's right arm, just above his elbow. He tightened it down hard, which caused Botàn to wince. Only then, Gideon heard the ice cracking behind him. Any moment now the cockatrice would break free.

"Collin, help Botàn out of the forest," he told the little boy. "I'll follow right behind as soon as I've dealt with this monster."

"Don't be daft, Gideon," Botàn interrupted. "The boy doesn't have the strength to help an old man like me. We'll stay here while you finish it off, but to do that, you'll need this." He unbuckled the belt holding his armory in place and removed the pauldron, handing it to Gideon.

Gideon was shocked that Botàn would give him the Armory of Attlain. "Master, I . . . I can't. I'm not ready."

"You've been ready, Gideon. I've just been too stubborn to let go," he replied with a reassuring tone.

Gideon was reluctant at first, but he knew this is what he agreed to when Botàn started training him. He reached out and touched the armory with Botàn. They had rehearsed this moment but never completed the ceremony. This time, it was for real.

"I, Henri Louis Botàn, Master of the Armory of Attlain, with this sacred trust, bestow ownership to Marcus Gideon. I deem him worthy of the title of Magus and relinquish the armory into his care. I rescind any claim that I have to Armory of Attlain or the weapons entrusted therein."

Gideon tried to ignore the sound of ice cracking as the cockatrice continued to struggle to break free from the spell; he cleared his mind and took a deep breath. "I, Marcus Gideon, now accept the title of Magus and responsibility as the Master of the Armory of Attlain," he responded. "I do this of my own free will, becoming the master of the weapons entrusted therein. I swear to pass on this armory to a worthy apprentice so that the Magus will live on forever."

The magic passed from Botàn to Gideon, making the ceremony complete.

"Now, go kill that thing," Botàn said, trying to fight through the pain of the petrification.

With a sly grin, Gideon holstered his Dragoon and buckled the pauldron on his shoulder. At that moment, the cockatrice broke free from its icy prison and Gideon went into action.

"Dragonfly! Come to me!" he commanded as a runic circle opened, and a chakram flew out and into his hand. The steel circle was rimmed in gold teeth, pointing inward on the curved blade. Between each tooth was a rune shaped like an insect.

He threw the chakram at the cockatrice. The spinning blade buzzed around the monster like a fly, nipping and cutting at it with every pass. While it kept the beast busy, Gideon made his next move. *"Now, Frostfire!"* he commanded as he held out his hand. A hilt emerged from another runic circle. He grabbed it, pulling out a broad sword, as Dragonfly faded and returned to the armory. Frostfire was an executions blade, with a curved tip instead of a point, that burned with an icy blue flame. It was the Sword of Fire and Ice.

Gideon raced toward it before dropping down and sliding across the ground. He skimmed under the cockatrice with the blade held high, slicing into it from front to back. The blade's magic burned the wound while its icy touch kept the injury from healing. The damage caused the cockatrice to fall to the ground. As Gideon moved behind the monster, he dismissed Frostfire and drew one more weapon from the armory.

"Gorgon, Hammer of the God Killer, to me!" he ordered. A long wooden handle emerged from a runic circle. He pulled out a giant hammer. The visage of Medusa held the two hammerheads together as the snakes from her hair reached out from the center. It looked unwieldy, but it was relatively easy for him to swing.

With the cockatrice on the ground, Gideon ran up its tail, across its back, before he leaped into the air. He screamed as he swung at the creature's head. It snapped its neck, but then, the effect of the hammer did more than just that. The cockatrice got a taste of its own medicine. Gorgon's unique ability began to turn the creature into stone. Within minutes, there was nothing but a stone statue lying there.

Gideon breathed out as he released Gorgon, returning it to the armory. He had one thing left to do. Gideon drew his Dragoon and aimed it at the petrified cockatrice. *"Meteore! Focu di Dragone! Brusgià! Dragoon!"* he chanted as the magical energy built up again. Once he pulled the trigger, a dragon of burning white flame roared and flew at the petrified monster. The explosion from the impact shattered it into dust.

Gideon holstered his weapon before he took a deep breath. The entire fight took a lot out of him. He could feel the strain in his clockwork heart, just a little twinge of pain, but he put it aside as he rushed back to where he had left his ailing master and Collin. "How are you feeling? Are you able to move?" he asked, the concern reeked through his voice.

"Well, I don't think I'll be playing the violin again," Botàn joked as he held up his petrified hand. It got a laugh from both Gideon and Collin. "I think the tourniquet has stopped the spread of the curse, but without proper healing, it'll continue to turn my body to stone."

Gideon thought for a moment before he reached into his pocket for a couple of coins. "Listen to me, Collin. I want you to gather up all the wormwood you can. When we get to the edge of the forest, run home and give that to your mother; then, go to the guild and ask for the cleric Cerise."

He placed two gold coins in the palm of the little boy's hand. "Bring her to Master Botàn's right away. The money should pay for her services. Do you understand?"

Collin nodded his head before he started gathering up all the wormwood they collected before the cockatrice attacked. "And Collin," Gideon added, stopping the boy in his tracks, "you can't tell anyone about what you saw here today. No one in the guild can know that we can use magic. Okay? Can you keep it a secret?" Collin just nodded his head again as he went back to collecting the wormwood.

Gideon helped Botàn up to his feet, but the former Magus was more worried about Collin than himself. "You shouldn't involve the boy like this, Gideon. I don't want him to get hurt!"

"Neither do I, Master Botàn, but I can't run into Armändis and leave you alone like this, defenseless," Gideon answered.

"Defenseless? I've got a hand of stone that'll put you in your place," Botàn threatened him with his petrified fist. "And dammit, stop calling me master! You are the Magus now. I'm not your master."

"You will always be my master, Master Botàn, and you'll never convince me otherwise," Gideon said with a smile. Botàn chuckled as he patted him on the chest. Gideon moved as quickly as possible to get Botàn home. As soon as they reached the edge of the forest, Collin did what they told him and took off as fast as he could for Armändis.

Collin rushed into the guild headquarters, although he wasn't supposed to. It was usually off-limits to everyone in town, but most guild members knew Collin. The little boy practically grew up in the guild—his father was one of the guild's best fighters, and his mother was a cook in the kitchen—so no one usually paid him any mind when he would wander in.

Just inside the guild's main doors was a large lobby area, filled with various plush, comfortable chairs and lounges for the guild members to relax in. There was an assignment board delineating teams and patrol areas and a large desk for Cyrus Pipster. The squirrely man sat there—day after day—with his staff, filling out paperwork, cataloging treasure found, and paying out a bounty to its members. There was no artwork of any kind in the hall, except for Herrod's giant self-portrait of him standing in uniform next to a black wolf. The painting looked like he was staring at you, no matter where you stood in the guild. It was a reminder that the guildmaster was always watching you.

Though others tried to stop and say hello to Collin, asking about how his father was doing, he didn't have time. He was looking for the cleric.

The first person that was finally able to stop him was Dominic Evergreen. "Hold on a minute, Collin," Dominic said as he stopped the boy from going any further. "You can't be in here anymore. You know that?"

"I'm sorry, Mister Dominic, but I'm looking for Miss Cerise. It's not for my dad. It's for Master Botàn."

"Botàn? What happened to him?" Dominic asked.

"Hey, runt!" someone shouted before Collin could answer. Po stormed across the room toward the little boy. "I told you not to come in here anymore. We don't have any wormwood for your deadbeat dad. Now get out of here!"

"I'm not here for wormwood or my dad," Collin said defiantly. "Gideon and Master Botàn helped me find some in the forest, but Master Botàn got hurt by a cockatrice. His right hand has turned to stone. I'm supposed to find Miss Cerise and take her to him." Collin held up Gideon's coins to show that he could pay for her services.

Everyone in the room was shocked to hear about Botàn's injury and the cockatrice. Po, though, wickedly grinned at the news and said, "Those idiots don't know when to stay out of the woods, now do they?"

"Maybe they wouldn't have to if you did your job right and kept the forest clear of monsters," Collin shot back at him. His father told him never to talk back to the guild members, but he didn't like Po. The rest of the guild laughed at Collin's verbal smackdown, which pissed off the deputy guildmaster. He walked over and raised his hand, about to slap the boy when Cerise grabbed it and stopped him. The catsei were surprisingly strong for their build, and she held back the big man with ease.

"If you lay a finger on that boy, I'll cast a diseased curse on you that'll give you every venereal disease in the known world. No woman will touch you for years," she said with a fierce conviction. Po was scared by her threat and backed away.

She took the coins from Collin and slapped them into Po's hands. "Let's go, Collin," she said, taking him by the hand and walking out with her little charge.

"Po!" Herrod shouted from behind, motioning for him to come over to him. Herrod slowly walked next to Cyrus. He glared at the guild members standing around the desk, waiting for payment. All it took was a look to make them move away from him as quickly as they could. Po walked over as Cyrus held out his hand, waiting for him to turn over the payment. Po felt slighted and insulted that the bookkeeper would consider him a thief, but he didn't say anything about it. He just tossed the coins down on the table before Herrod could speak.

"The jug is ready, in my office," Herrod said. "Take it down to Marion's and tell Ester to take it out to them as soon as Cerise gets back to town. Once she returns, Cyrus, you'll go out and wait for them to succumb to the poison's effect."

"Me? Why me?" Cyrus asked, wondering why they dragged him into it.

"Because if anyone sees Po out there, they'll get suspicious. You won't raise any alarms because no one thinks that a scared, little man like you could be a threat," Herrod snapped back. Po laughed at the little clerk's expense. "When all is said and done, you go in and take the armory off his dead body and bring it to me, got it?"

He nodded his head, knowing it was better not to argue with Herrod, but something caught his eye. "Excuse me, Guildmaster, but where's your guild ring?" Cyrus asked.

Herrod looked at his hand, noticing that his pride and joy, the symbol of his leadership, was missing. "Huh? I must've left it in my room."

Gideon's Journal – Cerise arrived just in time. Her healing powers stopped the petrification from spreading any farther. It'll be a while before his arm returns to normal, but at least he was spared the worst. Cerise promised to stop by every couple of days to check on his progress. She also said not to worry about the guild payment, as she'll be doing it in her free time. Collin passed on a message from his parents, thanking us not only for the wormwood but for protecting him from the cockatrice.

I don't understand why everyone feels the need to thank me for helping them. It's a part of human nature to help your fellow man, isn't it? At least for those of us who act human, unlike Herrod and his motley crew. I can't stand by anymore and let innocent people get used and abused by him anymore. Now that I'm the bearer of the Armory of Attlain, a Magus, things will change in Armändis. I'm taking the fight to him!

Gideon looked through the wine inventory and searched for the jug that Botàn requested. Although he kept a large stock in storage, Botàn liked a particular vintage when he was sick or injured. Unfortunately, it seemed that Botàn drank through his favorites. Gideon grabbed what he could and carried it out to his injured master.

Botàn was laid up, in bed, waiting patiently for something to drink. He laid there, wrapped in a simple robe so as not to constrict him. He finally breathed a sigh of relief when he saw Gideon walking in with his wine. "It's about bloody time!" he shouted at his former apprentice. "Did you find the '52 Arménz?"

"No, you drank the last one last week. All I found was the '55!" Gideon said as he handed him the jug.

"Ah, that's piss water," Botàn complained. Gideon pulled it back to return it to storage.

"Well, if you don't want it," he said as he pulled it back. Botàn snatched it from his hand before he could take it away.

"Don't be daft!" he exclaimed. "It's piss water, but it still numbs the pain." He took a big swig of the wine right from the jug before noticing the goblet Gideon was holding out for him. He stopped drinking from the pitcher, wiping his mouth with his hand before taking the goblet from him.

"Measure out your drinks," Gideon told him. "Otherwise, you'll spoil your dinner."

"What dinner?" Botàn asked.

"I'm heading down to the meadow to flush out some quail for us," Gideon said. "I should only be gone for an hour. Try not to get too drunk in that time."

"Yeah, fat chance of that," Botàn said.

Just then, a knock rattled the front door. The two men looked at each other, startled and concerned. Gideon walked over to answer the door but hesitated when Botàn called out his name. When the older man pointed to his shoulder, Gideon understood what he was saying. He wanted him to hide the armory. Using one of Botàn's dirty shirts, he laid it across his shoulder, concealing the armory. He proceeded to open the door, amazed to see Ester standing there, holding a jug of wine in her hands.

"Ester? What are you doing here?" he asked.

She hesitated for a moment before speaking. "Well, Fenwick heard about what happened to Botàn, and he sent me out here with this," she said, handing the jug of wine to Gideon. He took the wine and looked at it carefully.

"Wow, a '48 Charblan! Where did he find this? I thought he couldn't get anymore?" Gideon said. Ester hesitated again, looking around as if she was trying to find the answer. Her behavior was suspicious, but then Gideon knew that she was a little flighty at times.

"Well, he said he found one through a competitor of his," she explained. "Fenwick bought it because he knew he could charge Botàn whatever he wanted for it, and Botàn would pay."

"Yeah, that sounds like Fenwick, always looking for a way to make a few extra coins," Gideon said. "So, how much do I owe you for this?"

"Oh, Fenwick said you could settle up next time you're in town," Ester lied. "He just thought it might help Botàn feel better."

"Well, tell him I said thank you. I'll be by tomorrow to settle things. Goodnight, Ester."

Ester just smiled as Gideon closed the door. As she headed back to Armändis, her smile went away, and she began to cry a little bit. She knew it was the last time she'd see Gideon alive.

Gideon brought the jug into Botàn, knowing how happy this would make him. "Well, it seems you have a friend down at Marion's," he said. "Look what Fenwick sent out for you." He handed Botàn the jug and, when he saw it, he couldn't believe his eyes.

"A '48! But he said there were no more." Botàn popped the cork and smelled the delicate bouquet before he savored a sip of the wine. "Oh yeah, that's the good stuff. You can drink that piss water when you get back. This one is all mine!"

Gideon shook his head and smiled. Botàn would never change, and he was happy with that. Without saying another word Gideon left. He was hoping to catch some quail for dinner, but more than likely, Botàn would drink himself to sleep.

For the next half hour, Botàn lay in bed and savored each sip of the wine. It was delicate to the palate yet full of flavor, and he loved it. He must have drunk half the jug when a strange feeling came over him. The numbing effects of alcohol never fazed him, but this feeling was different. His body started to go rigid. Every joint ached; a stabbing pain shot through them even if he tried to move just a little. He took another drink to calm his nerves, but then he noticed something in his goblet. At the bottom of the cup were tiny bits of white, not sediment but rather slivers of a delicate white petal. He recognized it almost immediately as a white chrysalis. Though beautiful, these flower petals could create a deadly poison when ground up and allowed to ferment. Inside a full-bodied wine like the '48 Charblan, the poison would spread without affecting the wine's taste.

Botàn threw the jug across the room, shattering it against the wall. Just that effort caused him immense pain throughout his body. He collapsed back on the bed as his whole body began to tense up. He could barely move. His mind raced with a hundred different things, but more importantly, he hoped Gideon would get back soon. He had something to tell him before he died, something vital.

The door opened, causing Botàn to breathe a sigh of relief, but it wasn't who he expected. In walked Cyrus Pipster. The skinny, little man had a grin like a cat that ate the canary—wicked and evil. Immediately, Botàn knew who poisoned the wine and why. He was thankful that Gideon didn't drink any of it.

"My, my, how the mighty have fallen! Herrod knew that your love of wine would be your downfall and look at you now!" Cyrus bantered. "Now, let me relieve you of your armory, and I'll be on my way before Gideon gets back!"

Cyrus pulled back his robe, but there was no armory. He started to panic as he almost ripped the robe off to find the armory. Botàn winced and cringed in pain every time he thrashed him around. "Where is it?" Cyrus screamed. "Where is it, you crazy old man?"

Botàn just chuckled, as best as he could, knowing that they had outwitted Herrod and his goons. His laughter made Cyrus angry, and he slapped the old man repeatedly about the head. "Stop laughing at me," he shouted. "Where is your armory? I've seen you carry it with you every day since I arrived in Armändis. I know it's here somewhere. Where is it?"

Botàn laughed again. "It's out of your reach, boy!" he muttered as best as he could. "You'll never have it, never!"

Cyrus panicked. He knew that if he went back to the guild without the armory, Herrod would kill him. He started searching, looking in every drawer, on every shelf, and in every chest he could find; he ransacked the place, but came up empty-handed. It caused him to panic even more.

"No! No! Where is it? Where is the armory?" he screamed again.

"Right here!" Gideon said from behind him. As soon as Cyrus turned around, Gideon hit him in the side of his head with his Dragoon, stunning

Cyrus. Gideon then grabbed him by his collar and belt and flung him as hard as he could. Cyrus slammed into the wall with such force that he crumpled on the ground, unconscious.

Gideon rushed over to his ailing master, seeing that he was in so much agony. "Master Botàn, are you alright? What did he do to you?"

Botàn struggled to speak, but he was beginning to succumb to the poison. "The wine," he rasped. "They poisoned the wine with chrysalis petals. I can barely move."

"There's got to be a cure. Tell me and I'll get it!"

"N-no cure," he stuttered, forcing each breath he took. "I don't have a lot of time, so listen carefully." Gideon just nodded his head, wanting to obey his master's last wish. "Down in the cellar, that small chest on my workbench, there are four envelopes. Follow the instructions to the letter, Gideon, please."

Holding tightly onto Botàn's hand, Gideon nodded and said he would do whatever his Master asked. Tears rolled down his cheeks as he tried to hold back the emotions.

"Protect the Armory of Attlain," he continued as he patted the pauldron strapped across Gideon's shoulder. "It is your most solemn duty now. You are the last Magus."

"I wouldn't be if it weren't for you, Master Botàn," Gideon replied. "You saved my life, gave me purpose. I wouldn't even be here if it wasn't for you."

Botàn smiled. "No, my boy, you saved me," he said, his voice wavering. "If not for you, I would be dead, and the armory would be in Herrod's possession. Now, I can join my wife, Ophelia, and my son, Gabriel, in paradise, knowing that the legacy of the Magus is in good hands."

He took his other hand and reached up to touch Gideon's face. He wiped the tears from his eyes and patted him on the cheek. "You know, I look at you, and I imagine what my Gabriel would have been like had he had the chance to grow up. You've been like a son to me, Marcus, and I am very proud of you. Stay strong. . . fight hard. . . and live."

With his last words, Botàn slowly faded away. His hand fell away as he stared off into heaven. Gideon saw a slight smile on his face. He imagined Botàn being greeted by his wife and son as he crossed over to the other side. The Magus of Attlain was finally at peace. Gideon cried for a few minutes, grieving the loss of his master, but then he heard a groaning sound behind him. Cyrus began to stir, and the grief inside Gideon turned to rage.

As Cyrus's eyes fluttered open, Gideon kicked him in the head in one swift motion and knocked him out again. It would be a while before he would wake up.

5 THE MAGUS VS. THE GUILDMASTER

G*ideon's Journal – I buried Botàn next to his wife and son underneath the dogwood tree. I didn't even have to read his instructions to know to do that. Botàn sat there every evening, saying goodnight to his family. Now, he will be with them forever. To be honest, I was initially hesitant to open Master Botàn's instructions, but I knew it had to be done. In the end, it turned out there was nothing to be afraid of. I packed up the cellar, making sure to seal away all the magical books and artifacts behind magical wards in the trunks. You can't have that stuff in the hands of some amateur. Who knows what they'd do? Next, I have three letters to deliver for him. That will take some time to accomplish, but at least two of them are on my way to Le'Arun.*

I kept a couple of books out for myself, including my holy book. I haven't been able to interpret any of the book as of yet, but then again, the language of the Saints is only taught to clerics. Still, it's comforting to have it with me. In addition to the armor pieces and padded coat we found in the troll horde, I packed a few other things from Botàn's adventuring days. He has this magic item called a coin purse. It's like a bottomless pit inside a tiny pouch. I put the entire contents of the money, gems, and jewelry we found in the troll's trunk inside. I reach in, say what I want, and it'll appear in my hand. It's like carrying a safety deposit box around with me.

I packed a couple of saddlebags for my journey across Attlain. I want to travel light, but I have something else to deal with first. Master Botàn specifically told me not to go after Herrod. He must have known that the guildmaster would be the death of him. I know I promised to follow his instructions to the letter, but I just can't do it.

If I leave without dealing with Herrod and Po, they'll just come after me; or worse, they'll take it out on the people of Armändis. Plus, I need to know more about this witch, Selene. I'm sorry, Master Botàn, but I must disobey you this one time. Herrod's reign of terror has to end, here and now. I must do this, for you and for Armändis.

Gideon finished cleaning up the room that Cyrus had ransacked, and that he had subsequently trashed by tossing the guildsman around. He had already been working half the night, but he didn't want to leave Botàn's house a mess. As he picked up the shattered pieces of the wine jug, he noticed something shiny beneath the broken pieces. A ring. Gideon had seen this guild ring many times before and knew it belonged to Herrod. Tiny bits of the chrysalis petals were caught in the setting. It was the proof he needed against Herrod for Botàn's murder, but it wasn't enough. Gideon wanted to know more about the mysterious Selene and why she was after the armory. He had an idea on where to get that information.

He walked over to the forge with a purpose. The storm doors were closed, but not for bad weather. Instead, he wanted to keep any prying eyes from seeing what he was about to do. Inside the forge, Gideon had Cyrus strung up against the wall. He stripped him down to his undergarments. His arms and legs were stretched out, held apart with tight ropes. He gagged his mouth so he couldn't call out, not that anyone could hear him out here. Cyrus was quivering with fear, awaiting his pending interrogation.

Gideon closed the storm door behind him and walked over to Cyrus. He ripped the gag from his mouth as the guild bookkeeper gasped for air. "You're dead," he shouted. "Herrod's going to rip you apart, but if you let me go and give me the armory, I'll give you a head start. You can leave Armändis, start somewhere else. Just untie me and give me the armory."

Gideon stared at Cyrus with rage in his eyes as the guildsman swallowed hard. He would not be deterred from his quest for the truth and Cyrus was a wellspring of information.

"If you don't release me soon, they're going to come out looking for me," he said, trying a different tactic. "You'll have forty-plus guild members surrounding this entire place soon. Then what'll you do?"

"No one's coming for you," Gideon said. "You see, I cast a shadow spy spell to see what was going on in town. Po is getting his rocks off with Ester at Marion's Tavern, along with twenty assorted other guild members. Herrod is asleep in his bed, with two whores at his side.

"No one, except those two, know you're here. Herrod probably thinks you're bumbling your way through everything, being thorough like you always are, and will turn up tomorrow morning with the armory. We'll be alone here all night, giving me plenty of time to get everything I need out of you."

Cyrus laughed. "I won't tell you shit!"

"We'll see." Gideon smiled slyly, held out his hand, and chanted, *"Come to me, Freya, Fist of the Ice Queen!"* An ice-laden mace appeared in his hand. Cyrus's eyes widened with shock and fear.

"Every time you lie to me or refuse to tell me what I want to know, I'm going to hit you with Freya. The first hit will freeze it solid, and the second will shatter it into a million pieces.

Cyrus's mind was going in so many different directions, unsure of what he should do or say, or even if he should believe that Gideon would hurt him.

"Tell me the full name of this woman Selene who is after the armory, and where can I find her?" Gideon asked.

Cyrus didn't say a word.

"Nothing, huh? You don't think I'll use this?" Gideon held up the mace, pointed it close to Cyrus's face.

"You won't if you know what's good for—"

Before Cyrus could finish, Gideon slammed the mace into his left knee. Cyrus screamed in agony as Freya's icy effect froze his knee solid.

Gideon grabbed him by the face and squeezed. "Rest assured, little man, I will take you apart, bit by bit, until you tell me what I want to know."

Cyrus spat on Gideon's face. Not the smartest thing to do as Gideon reared back and hit his left knee again. The ice shattered, destroying his leg from the knee down this time. Cyrus screamed in agony as Gideon took a step back.

"I know you receive all the contracts coming in and out of the guild," he explained. "You know who sent the request for the armory and where it originated. So, I'll ask you again, who sent the contract and from where?"

"Piss off!" Cyrus said, ever defiant.

"Wrong answer!" Gideon shouted as he slammed Freya into his right knee. Not only did the impact shatter his kneecap, but the icy touch also froze everything down to the marrow, and this wasn't a numbing cold. It was a painful, stabbing chill. Cyrus screamed again, lashing out as he struggled against his bonds. The problem was, he thrashed about with his frozen leg, causing it to shatter all on its own.

"Well, that saves me from having to do it myself," Gideon chuckled. "How about now, Cyrus? You want to tell me who sent the request out?"

Cyrus said nothing as he was overwhelmed with pain. Gideon walked back up to him and readied to hit his left elbow, but he suddenly paused before he struck. "You're right-handed, aren't you?" He switched sides to attack the right elbow, raised the mace and readied it for another strike.

Cyrus frantically shook his head, squirming to be free of the bonds. "Alright! Alright! I'll tell you! Her name is Selene Dartagni from Le'Arun!"

Gideon stopped in mid-swing. He heard that last name before but associated it with someone else. He placed Freya under Cyrus's chin. The mist emanating from the mace started pricking at his chin, like tiny icicles stabbing him repeatedly. Gideon said, "Say that name again!"

"Selene Dartagni from Le'Arun!" Cyrus repeated, breathless from the pain he was suffering.

Gideon stepped back and dismissed Freya as he tried to comprehend what Cyrus just told him. "Selene Dartagni? By any chance, is she related to Sir Duarté Dartagni, the Paladin of Le'Arun?"

Cyrus nodded his head. "His wife."

Gideon was shocked and dismayed. The man who tried to kill Botàn once before was at it again, and this time he succeeded. Gideon couldn't let this go unpunished, not this time. He picked up a dagger from a pile of weapons nearby and cut Cyrus down. He fell to the dirt floor, lying on the ground as he recovered from his frozen wounds. Unfortunately for him, his frozen extremities kept him from bleeding to death.

Gideon left Cyrus lying on the floor of the forge while he went out to retrieve his horse. He found it in the gulley behind the house, tied to a fallen tree. Once he had the horse secured outside the forge, Gideon brought out a stool and set it next to the horse. He then picked up Cyrus and sat him down in the chair. Gideon did all this without saying a word to the injured guildsman, which scared him even more.

"What are you doing? Are you letting me go?" Cyrus asked.

"Yes, I am," Gideon said as he tied the reigns around one of Cyrus's hands.

"You're not going to kill me?"

"No, Cyrus, I'm not . . . ," but before Gideon could say another word, he smacked the horse on the backside, causing the beast to take off toward the forest, dragging Cyrus along with him. "The orcs in Imestrüs will do that for me!" he shouted as they disappeared into the darkness. Cyrus's screams filled the forest as every rock and stick cut him open, putting the smell of blood into the air. Within minutes, orcs were shouting in unison as they reveled in the meat provided to them. Both the horse and Cyrus cried out as they were dismembered and eaten alive by the orc raiding party. Soon there was nothing but silence in the dark.

Gideon spent the rest of the early morning hours packing up the house and getting ready to head into town. Botàn left him a hooded tunic. The white cloth was embroidered in red around the hood and collar in ancient runes. The runes spelled the motto of the Magus: Protect the Secrets, Defend the Magic, Secure the Future for the Magus! On top of it, he wore a black leather vest that had once belonged to Botàn—embroidered with magical runes and protection spells. Over that, he wore the padded leather long coat with the armored vambraces and the armory attached to it. He laid a simple cloak over his shoulder to hide the armory from prying eyes. Once he strapped his Dragoon on his hip, he was ready to go.

Gideon had been up all night, but he was far from tired. One of the lessons

Master Botàn taught him was that adventurers had to work through long days and nights, sometimes on less than three to four hours of sleep. He showed him how to mix an herbal concoction—with a bit of wine, of course—that would keep you alert and ready.

He stopped over at Botàn's grave and laid a flower over it, saying a little prayer for his friend and master before he headed into Armändis. As he made his way into town, most people recognized him but were confused by what he was wearing and where he was going. He didn't speak to anyone, even those who greeted to him, which caused even more stares and bewildered looks. Gideon made a beeline for Marion's Tavern. Although the establishment had been open late, it always opened early in the morning to rouse those out of the girls' beds and off to work.

Gideon walked into Marion's. He looked around for Po, but he was nowhere around. He noticed a few guildsmen hanging around, many were surprised to see him dressed like that. From behind the bar, Gideon spotted Fenwick cleaning up after the late-night frivolities. He greeted Gideon and said, "What are you doing here? Are you going somewhere?"

"I am," Gideon said as he walked over to the bar. "I'm finally heading to Le'Arun. I just wanted to settle up some things with you before I go."

"Settle up what?"

"Well, Ester brought me the '48 Charblan you sent up for Botàn, so I came down to settle our account. I know how much that must have cost you."

"A '48 Charblan?" Fenwick said, surprised. "I haven't been able to find any of the '48 in months. And you say Ester brought it out to you and said it was from me?"

"Yes, she said you heard about Botàn's injuries from the cockatrice, and you were kind enough to send up the '48 Charblan to cheer him up." Just then, Gideon saw Ester walking down the stairs, buttoning her dress. When she saw Gideon looking at her, she stopped, a surprised look on her face, and quickly turned to go back upstairs, but before she could get away, Fenwick called out her name and waved her over to the bar.

"What's this about you taking a '48 Charblan up to Botàn? I didn't give you any wine to take out to him."

Ester smiled and, with a sultry and demure voice, said, "No? I could have sworn you gave it to me. It must have been someone else who was concerned about Botàn's injury."

"Who gave it to you?" Gideon demanded.

"I-I don't remember," Ester said as she backed away.

"Lionheart!" Gideon whispered as the broadsword appeared in his hand. He placed it under Ester's chin in one swift stroke, right at her throat, while gripping her arm so she couldn't move away. Other guild members in the tavern went for their weapons, but all Gideon had to do was stare at them, and

they quickly backed down.

"I'm going to ask you again—Who gave you the wine?" He pressed the broadsword a little more firmly against her chin, not enough to break skin, but enough to show he meant business.

"Gideon, are you mad? What are you doing? What would Botàn say if he would see you doing this?" Fenwick interceded.

"Botàn is dead!" he shouted, stunning everyone in the room. "He died from drinking wine poisoned with chrysalis petals, from the wine jug she brought me. She helped them kill Botàn."

Ester looked around the room for help, but no one would help her. They all glared at her with the same hate and contempt that Gideon had for her.

"I'll ask you again, who gave you the wine jug?" He bore down against her, this time the blade cutting slightly into her skin. Her face flooded with panic and fear but Gideon had no sympathy.

Loud lumbering footsteps and a man's deep boisterous laugh came down the steps then. Gideon glanced over and saw it was Po.

"Goddamn, woman, you are a wonder between the sheets," Po said as he tucked in his tunic. When he reached the bottom of the stairs, he looked up and saw Gideon standing there with a sword to Ester's throat. He fumbled for his sword, trying to hold his pants up while he drew it, giving Gideon time to draw his Dragoon.

"Spider! Sita! Dragoon!" he chanted as a spider-like creature crawled around his weapon. When he pulled the trigger, a spiderweb shot out and pinned him to the wall. With his arms restrained, his pants fell around his ankles. Gideon moved quickly by releasing Ester and placing the blade to Po's throat. Po looked at him with disdain and helplessness.

"Surprised to see me? Or are you more surprised to see this?" Gideon pulled back the cloak to reveal the armory on his shoulder.

"I don't know what you're talking about, but if you don't get this sword off my throat, you will be sorry." Po motioned for the other guildsmen to move in.

Keeping his blade on Po's throat, Gideon swung around and pointed the Dragoon at the men around the room. "Before any of you lift a finger to help this man, I want you to think about something!" Gideon shouted. "Ask yourself, when was the last time Maximillian Herrod or Po Kildevil lifted a finger to help any of you? Then ask yourself, when was the last time Henri Botàn offered to help you?"

Gideon watched as the men stood there and considered everything he said, comparing the overbearing machinations of Herrod and Po next to the kindness and gratitude they got from Botàn. "Do you want to help the men that murdered Henri Botàn?" Gideon added. That cinched it for most of them as they sheathed their weapons and sat back down.

Infuriated, Po swore under his breath as he glared at everyone in the room.

Now that everyone else in the tavern had settled down, Gideon returned his attention to Po and pointed his Dragoon at him. "Cyrus already gave me the rundown on where the contract to steal the armory came from, but what I want you to do is to tell everyone here what you and Herrod did to facilitate it."

"Like hell I will," Po said in defiance. "I ain't telling you shit!"

"You know, Cyrus said the same thing. Then I started freezing body parts and shattering them into a million pieces," Gideon snapped. "He lost both legs at the knees before he confessed, but I know you're a lot tougher than that. So, I prefer something a little more drastic."

"What did you do to Cyrus? Where is he?" Po yelled. Gideon lowered his weapon and pointed it directly at Po's exposed groin. The big man grew quiet.

"Now, my Dragoon has a four-step spell . . . four words before I pull the trigger. In other words, to dumb it down for a simple mind like yours, that gives you to the count of five to start talking before I freeze those two olives and a carrot stick you call your manhood. The blast will freeze them solid as an icicle in winter. At this range, no regeneration would ever be able to heal it."

Po's eyes doubled in size as sweat beaded off his forehead. Everyone watched and waited as Gideon pulled back the hammer and began his spell, pausing between each word to emphasize each step as a form of intimidation.

"Congelatu!" . . . Po struggled against the web to no avail as a frost dragon swirled around the Dragoon.

"Onda di Gelo!" . . . Po looked desperately around the tavern, but no one stepped in to help. Only Ester looked concerned.

"Ghiacciu!" . . . Everyone knew if he talked, Herrod would kill him. Which was better, death or a frozen crotch?

"Dragoon!" . . . Po closed his eyes, waiting for the final blow, but he couldn't take it anymore.

"Alright! Stop! Just stop! I'll tell you everything! Just don't do it!"

Gideon stepped back, dismissing Lionheart, but he kept magic in effect within his Dragoon. The runic circles swirled around each concentric band, held in place, ready to fire with the pull of the trigger in case Gideon didn't like his answers.

"After Herrod saw the contract, he remembered the pauldron that Botàn always wore," Po said. "It fit the description in the contract, but it wasn't enough to kill Botàn until the fight you and I had. It took a while, but Herrod finally confirmed it was an armory. He was just waiting for the right time to kill Botàn, steal it, and blame you."

Gideon was shocked at this revelation. He wondered if it was his fault, then, that Botàn was targeted and killed for the armory. "Keep going!" he ordered. "Where did Herrod get the chrysalis petals?"

"Are you kidding?" Po answered with a chuckle. "He keeps a potted plant in his office just in case he needs to eliminate someone. He's gotten very good at developing the poison just right."

Everyone in the room went silent at his confession. "Insufferable bastard!" Fenwick said stoically and softly. "We're nothing but sheep to you, aren't we? It doesn't matter if we live or die, as long as you and Herrod make a profit."

"You're one to talk," Po shot back at him. "All you care about is how much money you can make!"

"I don't poison my customers when they can't pay up, now do I, you son-of-a-bitch!" Fenwick screamed. Gideon held up his hand to silence him.

"How much?" Gideon asked. "How much was Botàn's life worth to you and Herrod?"

Po hesitated but finally said, "Five thousand gold." There was a collective gasp as the revelation of the absurd amount sent shockwaves throughout the tavern.

"What? You said it was a thousand gold!" Ester shouted. "You promised me a cut if I delivered that wine to them! You promised me, Po!"

Everyone in the room turned their attention to Ester. For years, the girl most had known turned out to be someone else entirely. "I guess you do have a price, don't you, Ester?" Gideon shot back at her, seeing how his words angered her, but then she looked around the room. They were all staring at her, angry and upset that she helped kill a man they all called a friend.

"You can pack up and get the hell out of my tavern, ungrateful wench!" Fenwick yelled at her. "And I never want to see you around here, ever again! Do you hear me?"

Ester, visibly shaken, began to cry. She ran toward the stairs, pushing past Gideon until he grabbed her by the arm and pulled her in close to his face. "I'm not going to kill you for what you did to Botàn, so consider this mercy. But know this—If I ever see you again, my face will be the last thing you will ever see in this world. Leave Attlain, travel to Ishtar, Solara or Yamatai, because you don't want to be working some dive in Celestrium and have me walk in. Do you understand?"

Ester nodded her head in rapid succession. Once Gideon let her go, she pushed her way past Po and ran up to her room to pack. Gideon then turned his attention to Po; his mood still soured from the greed that caused them to kill Master Botàn. He snapped his fingers, causing the web to dissipate, freeing Po, who quickly pulled up his pants, tucked in his tunic, and tightened his belt.

"So, what now?" Po asked. "Are you hoping the magistrate will arrest me? Ha! Fat chance of that!" He laughed.

"Oh, I know, Po! I know!" Gideon lunged forward and stuck the barrel of his Dragoon over Po's heart. He pulled the trigger, causing the Dragoon to explode with a freezing blast at point-blank range. The burst had nowhere to go but deep inside Po, freezing his heart, his lungs, his entire chest cavity in a block of ice.

Still standing, Po lost the ability to speak. His bodily functions began to stop. He couldn't breathe; he couldn't swallow; his heart stopped. Gideon leaned into his face, staring him right in the eyes, and whispered, "You stabbed me in the heart. I froze yours. Consider us even!"

Gideon walked away and holstered his Dragoon as Po slumped to the floor, dead.

Gideon tossed a coin down on the bar for a drink. Fenwick knew what he wanted. He reached below the counter and pulled out a bottle of a hundred-year-old Calderian Whiskey, pouring a glass for himself and Gideon. The two men picked up the glasses and clinked them together.

"To Botàn!" Fenwick said.

"To Botàn!" Gideon saluted back as they both drank down the sweet, vibrant liquid. Gideon put his glass down while Fenwick poured another round for them.

"Fenwick, I have a couple of favors to ask," Gideon said as he picked up the glass and drank down his second one.

"Anything, Gideon, what do you need?"

"I buried Botàn next to his wife and child under the dogwood tree," he said as he reached into his coin purse and pulled out about twenty silver coins and laid them on the bar. "Will you make sure he gets a nice headstone?"

Fenwick scooped up the coins. "Yeah, of course, I will. I'll take care of it myself. What else?"

"Is it alright if I leave my saddlebags here for a little bit?" he asked. "I've got one more thing to take care of." Gideon turned to leave the tavern but Fenwick stopped him.

"Where are you going?" the tavern owner asked.

Gideon paused as he opened the door to leave and then announced to everyone, "To kill Herrod." Without another word, he left the bar. Shortly after, everyone in the tavern took off after him. It was a fight they had all been waiting to see.

Herrod walked down the stairs in the guild lobby. He expected to see Cyrus sitting at his desk, with Po standing next to him, ready to give him the armory he took off the dead body of Henri Botàn. With Gideon and Botàn both dead, he would collect his reward and retire somewhere far away from this place, but first he needed the armory. Unfortunately, neither of them was there, while the rest of the guild were mulling around with nothing to do. Without Cyrus or Po, no one knew their assignments that day.

"Any of you seen Po or Cyrus yet this morning?" Herrod asked.

"I saw Po go upstairs with Ester at Marion's last night," Dominic replied. "He might still be down there."

"Well, then send someone down to get him, you idiot," Herrod cursed. "Do I have to do everything myself?" Dominic grabbed one of the men and shoved him out the door after Po. Herrod continued. "What about Cyrus? Where's he at?"

"He never returned from that errand you sent him on yesterday," Dominic said. "No one's seen him since."

That worried Herrod. If the poison did its work, Cyrus should have returned by now, unless something unforeseen happened. Just then, the door to the guild burst open as the man who was supposed to get Po ran back in, looking scared out of his wits, his face flushed with fear.

"What the hell's a matter with you? What are you doing back here?" Herrod screamed.

Out of breath, and in between huffs, the man said, "Master Herrod, it's Gideon!" he yelled. "He's . . . he's wearing some sort of mage's outfit, walking toward the guild. People say he killed Cyrus and Po, and now . . . now he's coming here . . . for you!"

Herrod was both outraged and upset. His plans had gone to hell. Now he had to deal with Gideon. "Alright, you lot, listen up!" he shouted. "Man the ballistae and get ready to fight! Gideon killed two of our own, and now he's coming here for us! We need to kill him before he gets here!"

"Why's he after us?" Dominic asked. "If he did kill Cyrus and Po, why? What did they do to him?"

Herrod walked over to Dominic and got right in his face. "You don't need to ask questions; you do as your told. Now, get the men to their posts!"

Before Dominic could comply, the windows in front exploded in a massive fireball, shattering glass and wood into the air. Everyone ducked for cover as more explosions happened all over the building. Timber and stone crumbled around them.

"He took out the ballistae!" one guild member shouted from above. As people helped each other up and took care of the wounded, a voice cried out from outside the guild.

"Herrod! Get your fat ass out here!"

It was Gideon. He was challenging the guildmaster. Herrod stood there and scowled. The man he considered a stupid little punk was a lot more proficient in magic than he led anyone to believe. If Po weren't already dead, Herrod would have killed him for his utter incompetence.

"You in the guild, listen up! This is between Herrod and me!" Gideon shouted. "Stay out of my way, and you won't get hurt! I don't have a beef with any of you, only with Herrod! Leave your men out of this and face me, you cowardly bastard!"

The anger in Herrod grew when Gideon called him a coward. He wasn't a coward; he just knew how to manipulate others to do his dirty work for him. "Get out there and finish him off!" Herrod ordered the guild members, but they were hesitant to take on Gideon. Herrod looked around and saw he was losing control, thanks to this whelp.

"You heard me!" he said as he grabbed one man by his tunic. "Get out there and kill him!"

"Don't any of you move!" Dominic said as he stepped up to Herrod. "Gideon said he wasn't after anyone in the guild. His beef is with you. It's your fight, not ours."

Herrod was tired of Dominic's insubordination, so he grabbed him by the tunic with one hand and put his other hand on his sword hilt. "You want to challenge me, Dom?"

"I'm not the one you have to worry about, guildmaster. I wouldn't draw that just yet!" Dominic said, his voice stern and steady before they heard Gideon again.

"Herrod! How long are you going to make me wait! I promise you that I will bring that building down around your head, and you damn well know I can do it! Quit playing around and face me like a man!"

Herrod said nothing to Gideon's rants and kept staring at Dominic, but then the floor dropped out from beneath him as Gideon said something that got everyone's attention.

"You killed Henri Botàn, you bastard, and you're going to pay for what you did!" Gideon shouted.

Those words caught everyone off guard as their fear of Gideon turned to anger at Herrod. The guildmaster looked around the room and saw every eye on him, but not in support or fear. They were angry, pissed off. He killed someone who the guild respected, but they didn't know why.

Herrod saw that the only way he would regain control of the situation was to kill Gideon. He pushed Dominic away, glaring at all the men and women around him. "Get this place cleaned up," he ordered and headed for the door, but no one listened to him. They all gathered around the door and windows to watch what would happen next.

Herrod stepped out onto the landing at the top of the guild's steps. He looked down and saw Gideon standing at the bottom of the stairs. Besides the new clothes he wore, Herrod noticed the armory now slung on his shoulder and a Dwarfish Doomfire in his hand. With all this activity encircling the front of the guild headquarters, the crowd had grown large around him. It was as if everyone in town had gathered around, including Magistrate LoFan. Even Fenwick closed his tavern door to be here, something he hadn't done since he opened the place.

Herrod knew he had to be cautious and sly about this. He couldn't tell what

Cyrus or Po told him, so he thought it best to play dumb. "You're gonna pay for all these damages, I hope you know," Herrod said, snapping at Gideon while wagging his finger.

"The only one paying for anything today is you, Herrod," Gideon replied. "For the murder of Henri Botàn."

"Really? Says who? You?" Herrod taunted.

"Cyrus and Po already confessed to their part in his murder—Ester too—and everyone knows those two don't take a piss without orders from you." Everyone gathered around laughed at that joke, mainly because they knew it was true.

"Look, I don't know what those idiots told you—"

"Oh, cut the crap, Herrod!" Gideon shouted over him. "You killed Botàn for this." He pointed at the armory. "Human life never gets in the way of your greed."

"Really? Got any proof of that? I mean, you killed the two men you say confessed to this. Did anyone hear those confessions besides you?"

"I heard it!" Fenwick spoke up as he stepped forward. "Po admitted to everything, including poisoning the wine! Why don't we look in your office for a chrysalis plant, huh? The one Po said you keep just in case someone needs to be taken care of."

The crowd started getting agitated and angry as people talked about the mysterious deaths over the past few years. Many of them were people who opposed Herrod at one time or another. Now, Herrod began to worry, but he remained steadfast in his demeanor.

"So, besides a dead man's confession, one that was probably coerced by you, you don't have any other proof of my involvement in Botàn's death, do you?" he sneered. Gideon holstered his Dragoon and reached into his coat pocket. He pulled out Herrod's guild ring and showed it to the crowd. You could hear a collective gasp from the people gathered.

"The next time you kill someone, you better check where you leave your jewelry. It was at the bottom of the wine jug you poisoned," Gideon said as he tossed the ring back to Herrod. He looked at his guild ring and was about to lick it to get it to slide on his finger when Gideon spoke up. "I wouldn't do that if I were you," he exclaimed. "It still has chrysalis petals embedded in the settings."

Herrod stopped himself and looked at the ring. Strips of the delicate white flower were there, caught in the prongs that held the red gems in the eyes of the wolf's head. Without licking it then, he shoved it on his finger.

"Alright, I killed Botàn. What are you going to do about it? What are any of you going to do about it?" he shouted out to the crowd. The people were silent as their fear of the guildmaster returned to them. "Just as I thought. Now, I'll let you in on something. That is an Armory of Attlain," he shouted as he pointed at Gideon's shoulder. "Botàn has been deceiving us for years. He was a Magus, the cursed magic casters who rebelled against the crown. He was hiding away so that none of us knew who or what he was. Now that armory's worth ten thousand gold! Anyone who kills Gideon and brings that armory to me will get a cut of the bounty, that I promise."

The crowd started talking amongst themselves. The people couldn't believe the reward offered for that and wondered if it was worth the risk, but their discussion was interrupted by Gideon's laughter. "What's so funny?" Herrod blasted him.

"You are, Herrod!" Gideon tossed right back at him. "First off, do you think anyone here believes that you would share any part of the reward? Do you?" The audience agreed with Gideon. They all knew that Herrod didn't share any money with anyone. "On top of that," he continued, "Po said it was five thousand gold, so either you're lying now, or you lied to him. No one trusts you, Herrod. Never has, never will!

"You think Botàn was hiding? You're damn right he was. He was hiding from people like you," Gideon added, pointing his finger at Herrod. "Greedy bastards who wanted the secrets of the armory for themselves or the profit. He was abiding by the Laws of the Magus, to protect the secrets of the magic within the armories. More importantly, he was defending the people of Armändis from you!

"You used every advantage you have as guildmaster to gut the people of this town," he continued, turning to address the people around them. "Did you know that he charges you three times what other guilds charge for services and pays the guild members only half of what he should?"

As Gideon continued his barrage, all Herrod could do was stand there and take it from him.

"And what did Botàn do? He helped wherever he could. He fixed farming implements for free, repaired damaged weapons for guild members who knew you would charge them for it. Henri Botàn gave back to this community. All you did was tear it down, all to line your pockets with our money."

Herrod stood there, fuming. He looked around the crowd and saw what he saw the other day—people were standing together, not in fear of him but rather against him. "Like I said, what are you lot going to do about it?" he snarled at them as he tried to regain some foothold over them. "You can't live without me, and you know it. Now, if you'll excuse me, I've got a guild to run." He turned to head back into the guild, but not before Gideon lashed out.

"Freya!" he commanded, summoning the ice-laden mace into his hand. Botàn had shown him how he could call a weapon with a single word, especially those he used the most. He took Freya and slammed it into the ground, sending a wave of ice up the steps and underneath Herrod's feet. He slipped on the ice and fell backward down the stairs, landing right in front of

Gideon. The crowd laughed at Herrod's fall, angering him even more as he got to his feet. He looked up at Gideon and saw the whelp had no look of fear in his eyes. He was ready to fight, prepared to die. It was the first time in ages that Herrod saw that kind of determination in a man facing death.

"We're not done," Gideon said. "So why don't you draw that pig-sticker of yours and let's finish this, man-to-man."

Herrod got to his feet and smiled as he placed one hand on the hilt of the sword. "Are you sure you want me to do that, boy?" he asked. "Do you know what happens when I draw this sword?"

"I do, so quit stalling and pull it out already," Gideon said as he dismissed Freya, sending it back into the armory. Herrod chuckled under his breath as he pulled out his sword and held it in front of him with two hands. It was a long sword with a slight curve to the blade held up by a two-handed hilt. A fluid black flame flickered all along the edge. The air smelled of sulfur as the sword burned.

"This is Brimstone, Demon Sword of the Black Flame," Herrod stated. "Unfortunately, it's a cursed sword. You see, whenever I draw it, I have to kill someone with it; otherwise, it'll kill me, and I don't intend on dying."

"It's never what you intend, Herrod. It's what's inevitable," Gideon said as he held out his hand. *"Come to me, Fafnir, Spear of the Dragonslayer!"* A runic circle appeared above his hand as a spear shaft slowly descended from it. Gideon grabbed it and pulled out the spear, holding it in front of him. It was quite an ordinary-looking spear. A simple wooden shaft with a double-edged tip that was more than a foot long. At the base, points curved up, down, and outward from the cap.

It was Herrod's turn to laugh at Gideon. "Of all the weapons in that thing, that's what you pull out? You think that toothpick is a match for Brimstone?"

"You of all people should know, Herrod—as I'm sure you've heard from many of the women you slept with—it's not the size that matters," Gideon said. Everyone laughed at Herrod, especially the women who slept with him and now whispered and laughed as they told people about his "shortcomings" down there. It did what Gideon wanted to do. It made Herrod lash out. He raised the sword over his head and charged at him. That was the opening Gideon wanted.

"Seger!" Gideon shouted, and, in an instant, the spear shaft grew, shooting out at Herrod. The spearhead doubled in size as it sliced right through Herrod's head. It cut him through his mouth and out the back of his head. Gideon didn't even move from where he was standing. He just held the spear in place, and the magic within the weapon did the rest. The crowd was shocked about how quickly he killed Herrod and how disgusting of a death it was.

Herrod's body twitched and shuttered as he dropped the sword, impaling it into the ground. Once the body collapsed, his head slid off the spearhead and fell to the ground. That's when the magic of Brimstone kicked in. The black flame increased until it enveloped Herrod's body completely. The flame burned as it touched his body, burning through clothes, skin, muscles, and bones, until there was nothing left of Herrod except for his guild ring.

Gideon dismissed Fafnir, causing the spear to disappear back into the armory. He went over and picked up Brimstone, holding it in his hands. "Brimstone, Demon Sword of the Black Flame, I claim you as your master for the Armory of Attlain. As a Magus, I swear to wield you with the honor you deserve. Accept me as your master! Become one with the Armory!"

Brimstone glowed brighter as Gideon struggled against the sword, fighting with it to prove himself worthy. Finally, once it accepted Gideon as the master of the sword, Brimstone faded away and a new rune appeared on the armory.

The crowd breathed a sigh of relief. The man, and the weapon he used to terrorize the people of Armändis, was gone. The people cheered and congratulated Gideon, knowing that he helped free them from under his control. Once people made their rounds, Gideon walked over to where Herrod once stood and picked up the guild ring that still laid on the ground. He looked up to see Dominic standing at the top of the steps.

"Dom!" he shouted to get his attention before tossing him the ring. Dominic caught it, staring at it closely. "There's an opening for Guildmaster of the Black Wolf Guild."

"You think I'm the right man for the job?" he asked with a sly grin. Gideon nodded his head as Dom slid the ring on his finger and turned back to address the guild members. "What are you all standing around for? We've got work to do! Half of you start cleaning up this mess while the rest of you get yourselves armed and ready to head out! We've still got a town to protect! Let's go!"

Gideon knew Dominic was going to do great things for the guild. Both Fenwick and LoFan came up to speak to him, but Gideon stopped them when Janus Wildman and his family approached. "Give me a moment, will you please?" he asked them as he walked up and shook his hand, hugged Merrie, and patted Collin on the head before asking him to run down to Marion's and retrieve his saddlebags. Collin nodded his head—getting his parents' permission before he ran down the street.

"How are you feeling, Janus?" Gideon asked.

"Much better, thanks to you and Botàn. I'm sorry that you had to take those lashes for me, Gideon. I wish there were something I could do."

"There is . . . if I remember correctly, you once told me you worked in your father's blacksmith shop. This town is going to need a new blacksmith, especially for all the work Dominic is going to have for you." Gideon reached into his coat pocket and pulled out a sealed envelope. "This is the deed to Botàn's house, the forge, and the land it's on. It's yours on two conditions: One, there are trunks in the cellar that are off-limits. I've magically sealed them, and I'll send for them once I get settled elsewhere. For now, just leave them alone, and make sure Collin doesn't try to get into them."

This revelation concerned the two parents, but they agreed to it. "And two," Gideon continued, "The dogwood tree where Botàn and his family are laid to rest. Please take care of it and their graves for me."

The two agreed, without hesitation, as Gideon handed them the deed. "And take good care of Jupiter," he added. "He's an old horse, but he'll get the job done." Janus and Merrie agreed before they hugged each other, happy that they now have a home and a purpose in Armändis. When Collin returned with Gideon's saddlebags, they told him the good news as the family headed off to gather their things to move into their new home.

"That is a good thing you did, Gideon," Fenwick congratulated him.

"Yeah, well, they deserve a little happiness and a good place to raise Collin."

"So, where will you go now?" Tyrion asked.

"Le'Arun," he replied. "I need to finish my training as a magic caster. Botàn was good friends with one of the instructors at the Basilon Magical Academy."

"Well, if you're going to Le'Arun, then take this with you," Tyrion interjected as he handed a coin to Gideon. He took the coin and stared at it curiously. It had the seal of Attlain—a castle rising from the sea with two cross swords beneath and angel wings above—on one side. On the other side was a different type of seal, like a family crest. It was a shield with a hawk in flight behind a spear pointing downward.

"What is it?" Gideon asked.

"Call it a get out of jail free card, of sorts," he explained. "I know the magistrate in Le'Arun quite well. I also know your penchant for causing trouble, so this should help you out of it at least once while you're there."

All three men laughed at the joke. Gideon shook their hands, said his final farewells as he departed Armändis for the last time. He walked out the city gates, never turning back as he started for Ponshu Forest. His destiny laid ahead of him, not behind.

6 THE FOREST OF PONSHU

Gideon's Journal – Leaving Armändis was not as difficult as I thought it would be. I just kept walking, never looking back . . . At least not until I got to the top of the first hill. I stopped there for a moment and looked back at the place I called home these past two years. It looked much smaller from a distance, but still, I just wanted to look one more time. I doubt I'll ever go back there ever again.

What concerns me now is Ponshu Forest. Botàn asked me to find someone named Bok, a goblin who "doesn't act like a goblin," whatever that means. He somehow befriended this Bok and owed him a debt or something like that. He even told me to bring him a book, of all things, to give to him. A goblin who reads—that's a new one. Still, I'm not sure where to find him. All his instructions say is to head toward Ponshu and, once I reach the split in the road, walk into the woods. Wonderful!

The woods outside Ponshu were dense on the outer edges but cleared out the farther you traveled into the forest's interior. There, the forest was magical. Clear pools of luminescent waters flowed out from under and behind rocks. Plants of a wide variety and nature—from giant man-eaters to blooming buds that glow in the moonlight—can be found there. From faeries to hippogriffs and phantom cats to centaurs, every magical creature found a home in Ponshu. It was a refuge, of sorts, from the wilds and wicked creatures in Imestrüs Forest to the south and the dark and desolate Crowsfeld Woods in the west.

With every step into the forest of Ponshu, Gideon was amazed at the sights and sounds of these woods. It was nothing like Imestrüs. This forest was alive with life. He could feel the mana flowing through the trees, the plants, and the creatures. These woods were inviting, as if it wanted you to be a part of its life cycle, unlike Imestrüs, trying to kill you at every turn.

He saw the sun had started to go down, which concerned him. He had hoped to find this Bok before nightfall, but he had no luck so far. The deeper he walked in, the more confused he got at his surroundings. There were no distinct trails, no pathways, not even ones for hunters or trappers. It was as if no one ever came in here with ill intent.

He heard the cry of an eagle above him, but louder and more resonant. He looked up and saw something he'd never seen before. Floating down from the sky flew a griffon—a creature with a lion's body, eagle's head, and wings. Once it landed, it stood nearly ten feet tall, with a wingspan of more than forty feet, from tip to tip. It cried out again, warning Gideon away as if it wanted him to leave the forest.

Gideon was in awe of this beautiful creature. He could not turn away from it. He held out his hand and slowly walked toward it, hoping to put the griffon at ease. The beast cried out and clawed at the ground as it continued to try and intimidate Gideon, but the Magus kept his footing and continued to inch forward. He was inches away when the creature finally started to calm down as if it sensed no danger from Gideon. However, he did sense danger coming toward him.

Out of nowhere, a leather and steel braided whip wrapped around Gideon's extended arm, stopping him from touching the griffon. Gideon was suddenly pulled through the air and flipped onto the ground. The impact knocked the wind out of him, but he had to be ready for an oncoming attack. His Dragoon became dislodged as he was flung through the air, so that was out of the question. He needed something light and fast, and he knew just what weapon to summon.

"Legionnaire!" he shouted, calling a new weapon from the Armory of Attlain to his free hand. It was a saber with a basket of woven metal rods shaped in the design of a fleur-de-lis over the hilt. As his attacker moved over him with the whip held tight in one hand and a broad sword in the other, Gideon brought up his sword to block him.

Standing over him was a large goblin, over seven feet tall and quite muscular. His skin was a dark purple with an almost lizard-like texture. He was bald with several metal piercings in his ears and across the bridge of his nose. He had two large tusk-like teeth protruding from his lower jaw. He wore a crossed bandolier with various throwing knives and a multicolored kilt with chainmail underneath held up by a heavy leather belt. He wore a pendant around his neck with what appeared to be goblin tusks of various shapes and sizes attached to it.

The goblin kept a tight grip on the whip in one hand, keeping Gideon off balance. His sword was a curved, leaf-shaped blade with hooks underneath and on top of the sword. Hanging from the hilt of the sword was even more disturbing—a shrunken head so disfigured Gideon couldn't tell what race it originally was.

Although Gideon kept his sword pressed against the goblin's blade, it was only temporary. The goblin had the upper hand. "What are you doing here?" he demanded, his voice low and gruff.

Gideon paused for a moment before answering. "Are you Bok?" he asked, which startled the goblin.

"Who wants to know?"

"My name is Marcus Gideon. I was Henri Botàn's apprentice. He sent me to find you and deliver a message," Gideon answered.

"Was?" the goblin replied. "The old man is dead?" Gideon nodded his head. The goblin sighed before he lowered his weapon. "Yeah, I'm Bok," he said as he snapped the whip, releasing Gideon from its grip. Once Bok hung the whip back on his belt and sheathed his sword across his back, Gideon dismissed his saber and got back on his feet.

"When did he die?" Bok asked.

"A few days ago, in Armändis," Gideon explained. "You were the first one on his list for me to seek out."

Gideon waited as Bok stood there, thinking. His mind was trying to wrap around everything he just heard. While he was thinking, the griffon came up behind him, cooing like a bird as it cuddled next to him, rubbing its head on his arm. Bok reached under and patted the griffon on the head, scratching it lightly.

"It's a beautiful creature," Gideon said. "What is its name?"

"Her name is Sarusasha." Bok corrected him. "Follow me; you're just in time for dinner." The goblin turned and walked away, the griffon walking right beside him. Gideon realized he had no choice but to stay with him for now.

After a short stroll into the Ponshu Forest, they reached a clearing. There was a small wooden hut with a thatch roof. A makeshift rack sat next to it, where skinned meat hung out to dry. A roaring fire burned with a bubbling pot of stew and a couple of sturdy logs for seating.

"Have a seat," Bok said as he pulled his sword off his shoulder and set it down next to the front door of the hut. He stepped inside while Gideon sat down on one of the log seats. Sarusasha started sniffing around the pot until Bok came back out, carrying a couple of bowls, cups, and a jug. He smacked her away before she could get her beak into the pot.

"Get away from there! That's not your dinner!" The griffon squealed a few times as if she asked for something to eat. Bok grabbed one of the rabbits hanging on the rack and tossed it over to her. Sarusasha caught it in mid-air and started eating it. "You gotta learn to hunt for yourself, like your brother," Bok said as he sat down next to Gideon.

He took the lid off the pot and scooped out some stew into a bowl before handing it to Gideon. Gideon accepted the food with a thank you and smelled the stew, expecting something gross considering a goblin cooked it, but instead, it was oddly familiar. Once he tasted it, he realized what it was. "Botàn's rabbit stew! How did you learn to cook it?"

"It's the only good thing that old man knew how to cook," Bok explained as he spooned himself a bowlful. "I had to watch him do it, over and over again, before I got it right."

Gideon was getting more and more impressed with this goblin. "You're not like other goblin's I've run into, are you? I mean, the goblins in Imestrüs were these nasty little buggers, but not you."

Bok became a little agitated with him. "You mean I'm not some mindless beast scrounging for its next meal, killing anything in sight? That what you mean?"

"Well, yes," Gideon answered. "Why is that?"

"Goblin's have a class system. Our breeding is so out of whack that we have to stick to a strict system so that we don't fuck our way into genocide," Bok explained. Gideon almost spat out his food when he heard Bok speak that way. It was so strange to listen to a goblin talk like that. "The smallest of goblins are called kobolds, they mostly work in remote, dark places like mines, but they're also good at stealth, hiding in shadows. Then, there are hobgoblins. They're a crafty bunch, mischievous and sneaky, and intelligent too. Hobgoblins are the magic casters of our race.

"Knockers are your basic grunts," he continued. "They're strong, fearless, and all-around tough. Most of that type go on raiding parties, war parties, and the like. Then there's me. I'm an umber. We are at the top of the class when it comes to goblins. Smart, strong, and bigger than all others. We are set above as leaders among the goblin race."

"Then, what are you doing, out here, on your own?" Gideon asked.

Bok sat there and ate some more of his stew. "That's a story you're not ready for yet, boy," he answered quietly. Gideon could see it was not an issue to push with him, not yet, at least.

"Let's just say I'm not welcome with the goblin clans right now and leave it at that. Now, you said you had a message for me?"

Gideon put down his bowl and reached for his saddlebags. He searched through it until he found the book Botàn asked him to deliver. He handed it to Bok, who quickly set down his bowl to take the book. "Ah, a new one!" Bok said with glee. He looked at the title and quietly mouthed the words. "Hah, it's the one he promised me!"

"You like to read?" Gideon asked.

"Of course, I do!" Bok snapped back. "How else am I going to learn about the world?"

Gideon started to feel guilty. He kept treating Bok as any other goblin, but he was quite a unique fellow. "Oh, this is for you too," Gideon said as he reached into his coat pocket and pulled out one of the envelopes with Bok's name on it.

"You read it to me, boy," Bok said as he waved Gideon off. "I could never read that scribble of his."

Maybe Gideon's estimation of Bok wasn't exactly right, but he still had some tendencies associated with goblins. He broke the wax seal on the letter and read it aloud.

Bok,

Well, my old friend, the time is finally here. If you're reading this, or instead my apprentice is reading it to you, then I'm dead. Don't worry about avenging my death, as I'm sure my apprentice disobeyed me and took care of it himself. In any case, I have one final favor to ask of you, Bok, and maybe I'll finally be able to even the score.

My apprentice is a capable fighter, but he's rough around the edges. He needs some fine-tuning that I know you can fix. Teach him as much as you can, but you don't have a lot of time. He needs to be in Le'Arun by the end of summer. Do what you can, old friend. I know I'm asking a lot of you, but don't worry, this is the last time.

If you can, teach him to fight Dartagni. Since he's going to Le'Arun, I know he'll probably run into the bastard. I want you to prepare him for the fight ahead. Do your best, my friend. I have faith in you.

I can never forgive myself for not being there for you. You lost more than anyone should have too. I hope you finish your quest and find peace someday, as I have now. No one deserves it more than you, Bok.

Henri

Gideon didn't know what was more surprising: Botàn's under-appreciation of his fighting skills or the fact that he knew more about his impending death than he led on. He looked over at Bok and saw another side to this strange goblin. Bok was solemn, not even looking at the book Botàn left for him. He just picked at his dinner as if he was holding back any emotion he might have felt.

Bok set down his bowl, picked up the jug, poured the dark liquid into the cups, and handed one to Gideon. "To Botàn," Bok said, holding up his beverage. Gideon clinked his cup against Bok's and both men drank to Botàn. The liquid instantly burned its way down Gideon's throat, making him sputter and cough.

"What the hell is that?" he said as he coughed some more. It was not the sweet wine that he was expecting.

"Hexson Gin, the best drink goblins make," Bok said with a smile. Gideon assumed he was smiling, even with his tusks, but it was hard to tell. "Too much for you, boy?"

Gideon took another swig and then said, "I've drunk worse at the taverns in Armändis." He coughed again, making Bok chuckle some more. Another swig finished off Gideon's cup, but it did not satisfy his thirst or his curiosity.

"How do you know Botàn?" he asked.

Bok sat there in silence before answering. As well-spoken as he was, it seemed as if he needed time to gather his thoughts before he spoke. "I used to live on the southern side of Imestrüs," he started to explain. "I was out hunting with my daughter, Alna, when we ran into a giant wild boar. The beast knocked over a tree on top of me, pinning me to the ground. It was about to attack Alna when Botàn stepped in. He saved her and freed me from under the tree. No human ever did that for me before."

The story sounded just like Botàn. Gideon said, "Botàn never turned his back on someone in need, whether it be human or demi-human."

"Yeah, he even gave Alna a dagger to protect herself should it ever happen again in the future," Bok said. "Though my wife, Griet, gave me an earful when I got home that night."

"Where are your wife and daughter now?" Gideon asked, but even before he finished that sentence, he could see a change in Bok's demeanor. He became sad, quiet, and reserved. The goblin took one more drink of his Hexson Gin and then stood up.

"You can sleep out here by the fire," he said. "Get some rest. We start training early in the morning."

Bok headed back to the hut, leaving Gideon there without another word. Something about his wife and daughter must have caused all this pain, but Gideon knew better than to press an issue like that too soon.

That night, Gideon slept better than he had in a long time. Maybe it was the magic of the forest that soothed him as he slept, but it was the most relaxed he'd been in quite a while. It's a good thing he got such a good night's sleep because he was awakened early in the morning by the thud of a sword dropping next to his head and Bok commanding him to get up.

"Let's go, boy," he said in his calm, gruff voice. "Let's see what you're capable of."

Gideon sat up before grabbing the sword. "Whatever happened to breakfast before training?" he grumbled.

"The only thing you get to eat this morning is my steel!" Bok growled as he swung at Gideon. He jumped back as his sword struck the ground. Gideon quickly shook the cobwebs from his rattled mind and held the sword up in front of him, ready for the next strike. He wondered if being on the defensive would be best to gauge Bok's abilities, but the goblin made him pay for that.

Bok's strikes were powerful. It took all Gideon had to hold them off. Gideon fought back, matching his blows, but just barely. This asshole is getting on my nerves, Gideon thought as he finally decided to go on the offensive. He started to attack, changing up his moves from the previous maneuvers. Gideon targeted Bok's arms and legs instead of vital organs and the head and neck. When that didn't work, he did something outside the box. He kicked Bok right in the groin.

He remembered the goblin had chain mail under his kilt, so he measured his kick to reach just beyond and hit him where it hurts. At least maybe it would if he was human, but Bok didn't seem to care what Gideon did. It didn't affect him at all.

"Weak!" Bok shouted as he retaliated with a kick of his own, right to Gideon's gut. The impact hurled him across the clearing, knocking the wind out of him. "What is it with you humans and always going for the balls? That trick doesn't work on goblins! Don't you know that?" He rushed over to kick him again, but this time, Gideon was ready for him. He grabbed Bok by the foot and flipped him backward.

"How about that trick? Does that work for you?" Gideon said, getting to his feet, ready for his next strike. He waited for Bok to get up and attack again, but the goblin just lay there and laughed.

"Damn boy, you got some spunk. I'll give you that," he groaned. "Not much skill, but plenty of spunk, and all that'll do is get you killed."

Bok got to his feet and walked back toward the fire to get it going again. "Go clean yourself up, and then we'll talk. There's a spring that way," he said, pointing away from the camp. "Just, don't look at anything in the water. You'll lose more than your life."

Gideon didn't know what to make of his goblin drill instructor. He was a lot like Botàn. Rough, demanding, and overbearing. He'd worry more about it later. At the moment, he needed to wash the dirt and sweat off him. He jabbed the sword into the ground before heading toward the spring.

The spring was a small water pool, bathed in magical light as faeries danced above it. The water poured out from a large rock as a steady waterfall blanketed it. There were strange plants Gideon had never seen before, blossoming around the water's edge. The thick greenery surrounded the pool as colorful flowers poked through, filling the air with sweet scents. It was a beautiful sight to behold.

He walked up to the waterfall and held his hand under it. It was cool to the touch and refreshing to taste as he gulped it down. He pulled off his tunic and tossed it aside before he dunked his head under the water to invigorate himself.

He splashed some more water on his body as he tried to wake up. After Gideon washed his face one more time, he spotted something in the water. He rubbed his eyes to clear his vision, and then he saw it.

From underneath the water, he saw a pair of eyes staring back at him. He rubbed his eyes, trying to clear his vision, wondering if he imagined it all. He looked again and realized he didn't imagine it. There was a pair of eyes looking right at him. The eyes were bigger than average, dark with no visible pupil. He ignored Bok's warning as he couldn't resist what he saw. Her head slowly rose out of the water, and it became clear to Gideon what it was.

Behind those eyes was a beautiful face with light green skin and dark, full lips. Her hair was like a dark green seaweed, flowing across her shoulders and down her back. She was completely naked, her breasts firm and supple, but he couldn't see anything below her waist. It was as if she was a part of the water itself.

"My, aren't you a handsome man. I haven't seen a human for a very long time," she said, her voice sweet and intoxicating as she reached out to touch Gideon. He grabbed her hand and stopped her, but something strange overcame him as soon as he touched her skin. He felt drawn to her, a longing for her.

"What . . . who . . . who are you?" Gideon stammered as he tried to fight against her control.

"My name is Lyllia. I'm a naiad, a water nymph," she said seductively. "What's your name?"

"Gideon . . . Marcus Gideon. . . ."

"My, my, Gideon. You are a delight to see," she cooed. "I bet you taste even better!" She reached up and kissed him deeply, her tongue swirling in his mouth. He couldn't resist her kiss, which drew him in even more, as if her saliva was infused with an aphrodisiac.

"No fair, Lyllia," said another naiad emerging from the water. "Don't keep him all to yourself." This one was just as beautiful as the first, but her hair was a reddish seaweed instead. "Let me have a taste," she said as she grabbed Gideon and kissed him too. She wrapped her arms around his head and pulled him close. Her tongue went deep into his mouth as if she were trying to swallow his lips.

"Stop it, Auren!" Lyllia complained. "I saw him first!"

"Oh no, you don't, Lyllia!" argued another naiad coming up from beneath the water. This one had a light brown seaweed for hair. "He's the first human man we've seen in months. You're not keeping him all to yourself!"

The third naiad pushed Auren out of the way as she took Gideon by the face, licked him on his lips, and bit his earlobes before kissing him.

"Come one, Doru, not you too!" Lyllia grumbled as she pushed her aside to kiss Gideon again.

"Let's just pull him in here with us. That way, we all get a turn with him!" Auren said, and she grabbed one of his arms while Doru grabbed the other. The three naiads started to drag Gideon into the water with them. He was already underwater when he realized that he was drowning. He couldn't breathe, and yet he couldn't resist them. They passed him around, from one to the other. Each one's kiss was just as irresistible as the next. He was gasping for air, but he couldn't stop himself. He kept on kissing them, touching them all over on their lips and breasts. He was insatiable.

As the lack of oxygen overcame him, Gideon started to blackout. The naiads tried to have their way with him as much as possible, but before they could do any more, a hand reached in and pulled Gideon from the water. Bok tossed him on the ground, face down, pushing on his back to pump the water out of him. Gideon coughed the rest of the water out of him as he gasped for air.

"Don't you listen? I told you not to look at anything in the water," he screamed at Gideon before turning his attention on the three naiads. "And you three! What did I tell you about luring humans into the water? Unless you want to go back to that muck in Crowsfeld, I suggest you leave Gideon alone. Got it?"

"We're sorry, Bok. We just wanted to have a little fun," Auren said. "He's so tasty!"

"Drowning is not fun for a human!" he continued to scold them. "Now beat it!"

"Come back anytime you want to play, Gideon!" Lyllia shouted as the naiads giggled before they dove beneath the water and disappeared.

As Gideon got to his feet, he laughed and coughed out more water. Stammering, he said, "Damn, Bok, you could have warned me there were naiads in the spring."

"If I told you they were there, how would you learn to avoid them?" Bok snapped back at him. "There are too many things in this world that can get you killed, including beautiful ones like them. I swear, you humans think with your cock, and not your brains."

Gideon couldn't argue with him as he picked up his clothes. "I can't argue with you there," he conceded. "But still, what a way to go."

Both of them got a laugh as they made their way back to camp. They sat down and ate some leftover rabbit stew. Every time Gideon ate it, it reminded him of Botàn. It was weird to him how much someone like Bok enjoyed it so much. He's seen goblins eat animal parts raw, so watching one enjoy a cooked meal was unique.

"I can tell Botàn's been training you," Bok said. "You've got the basics down but no refinement. The old man was the same way. He could fight, but he relied too much on those magical weapons. You need to be better than the weapon you wield."

"Is that why he sent me to find you?" Gideon asked. "You seem to have a lot of experience fighting humans."

"Yeah, I've run into your lot too many times. I even survived a fight against the Paladin of Le'Arun."

"Dartagni?" Gideon exclaimed. He wanted to know more about that knight, especially with his sordid past with Master Botàn. "What kind of fighter is he?"

"He's a brawler, not refined, a lot like Botàn," Bok explained. "But he's got his wits about him. He knows how to adapt to a fight. You'll have to learn how to counter his adaptability, be one step ahead of him if you want to beat him.

"On top of that, you're strong, but not strong enough, boy," he continued, explaining his evaluation of their earlier fight. "It takes more than arm strength to wield a weapon. You need every muscle in your body."

"What do you mean?" Gideon asked, confused as he questioned his fighting style.

"Have you ever fought goblins before? Not just regular knockers, I mean kobolds and hobgoblins too?"

"A few times, yeah. Botàn and I came across a few raiding parties when we were hunting or foraging in Imestrüs," Gideon recalled. "They were tough little bastards."

"Yeah, well, that's because all goblins go through a regiment we call *Nært Crid*. It means strength from within," Bok explained. "We do it every day, from kobolds to umbers, to make us equal in strength and power. A kobold who does the Nært Crid has just as much strength, for its size, as an umber."

"So, this Nært Crid is some kind of exercise?"

"Come on, I'll show you, and once you master it, we'll start working on your weapon skills," Bok said as he put his bowl down and got up. "But we don't have a lot of time, so pay attention."

Gideon was surprised to hear this goblin was willing to share secrets of its race to make him a better Magus. How could he refuse? "Okay, let's get started!"

Gideon's Journal – Bok was right; the Nært Crid was unexpected and powerful. It's not what I anticipated. After doing it a few times, I can understand why goblins could be so resilient. It's a series of movements with the sword, slow and repetitive with muscles tensed, stepping through each swing, watching your breathing, etc. It takes a lot of concentration and strength to perform, from your gut to your chest and arms and legs. I did it the first two times, and it wore me out immediately. It took half the day to recover.

THE LAST MAGUS: A CLOCKWORK HEART

Once you get the hang of it, it's amazingly refreshing.

When he started to teach me fighting techniques, I can see why Botàn sent me to him. He knows his stuff. He's fought everything and everyone, so he has a lot of skill in all weapons. He has shown me more in the past few weeks than I learned in the past two years. It's not that Botàn lacked in skill. He focused more on magic with me. Maybe he did rely more on the magic in the weapons than himself. It must be why he pushed me so hard to be better.

Bok is such a strange person. When he's not training me, he's either teaching me about the creatures of the forest or telling me stories about his adventures with Botàn. I must admit his stories are much better than Botàn's. He knows Lady Jacqueline, too, although he calls her "Lady Jay" instead. It's impressive for a goblin. Bok has connections all over Attlain. He even knows a goblin mercenary squad from Ishtar. The one thing Bok hasn't told me about is his family. He's not very talkative about them either, something he has in common with Master Botàn. They both have secrets and like it that way. I hope to get him to trust me a little more and talk to me about it. I like this crusty, old goblin.

It had been a few weeks since Gideon started training with Bok, and his days had become relatively routine, even more so than when he was working as an apprentice blacksmith. The morning started with the Nært Crid, followed by breakfast, then weapons training. In the afternoon, Bok patrolled Ponshu Forest, making sure the creatures under his watchful eye were alright. Before dinner, the second round of Nært Crid before food, drink, and plenty of stories.

Gideon washed himself up in the spring before dinner. He splashed water on himself, washing the day's sweat from his body. Gideon felt stronger in these past weeks. He wasn't sure at first about training with Bok, but since it all started, he was stronger, faster, and more proficient with the sword. He had grown so much in a short period, but he still had a long way to go.

As he washed himself off, he spotted a hand reaching up for him from beneath the water out of the corner of his eye. "Stop it, Auren!" Gideon scolded. "You know better than to try that again."

The naiad Auren surfaced from the water as she pulled her hand back. "Aww, come on, Gideon. I just want a kiss," she cooed seductively.

"Yes, and a kiss will lead to you pulling me into the water and drowning," he shot back at her. "Sorry, Auren, but I need to breathe air, not water."

"Oh, Gideon, you're no fun!" Lyllia said as she surfaced next to Auren with Doru. "You're hanging around with Bok too much."

"Well, it is the reason I'm here. Besides, do you think I like wearing this every time I come down here?" Gideon said as he held up a pouch he wore around his neck. It wreaked of skunk cabbage, a smelly plant usually found around ponds and waterways. It's the one thing that can keep a naiad at bay, and it worked. The three of them backed away from Gideon as they swatted away at the foul smell.

"No fair!" Doru shouted. "Why did Bok have to give you that?"

"Look, I would love to spend more time with you three, but I can't without dying. So, unless you know a spell that would allow me to breathe underwater, I have to wear this." Gideon looked at the naiads and could see the sadness in their eyes. All they wanted was a little love and some male companionship. They couldn't help it that they lived under the water. "I tell you what," he continued, "I'm going to be leaving soon for Le'Arun to attend the Basilon Magical Academy. If I can find a spell there that would allow me to breathe underwater, I'll come back and visit you. I promise."

The naiad's eyes grew wide, and their smiles brightened at the promise of Gideon returning to be with them; but before they could say anything, a few faeries flew overhead. Their lights flickered off and on as if they were speaking to the naiads. Gideon knew something was wrong.

"What is it?" he asked.

"Goblins, goblins in Ponshu Forest!" Auren cried. "And they've got Bok!"

Gideon knew he had to act fast. He grabbed his tunic and the armory and put them on as quickly as he could. "Can you ask them to lead me to them?"

The naiads complied, speaking to the faeries in a high-pitched gibberish that he couldn't begin to understand. The faeries flew off with Gideon in pursuit right behind them. He drew his Dragoon and started chanting a spell. He knew if other goblins were here, Bok was in trouble.

Bok struggled against the two goblins holding him fast against the tree. A third goblin had a metal cord wrapped around his neck, pinning his head against the tree while choking him out. The three knockers were joined by two more, along with a hobgoblin magic caster and an umber goblin. Although they looked practically the same—pointed ears, no hair, upward tusks from the lower jaw with metal piercings all over—they each had slightly different clothes, armor, and weapons. The knockers looked like regular goblins—green scales with leather and metal armor. The hobgoblin had torn robes and a crooked staff with a gem suspended in an opening at the top. It also had a pale-yellow coloring to its scales.

The umber was like Bok, but he wore an ornate red cape decorated with human bones and skulls around the collar. He also carried a staff, but this one was different. It had metal spikes and rings all along with the shaft, in addition to several shrunken heads hanging from the top. This umber was Mækto, one of the five chiefs of the Goblin Nation.

"My, my Bok. How the mighty have fallen!" Mækto crowed.

"Tell these grunts to let me go, and I'll show you how a fallen goblin kicks your ass!" Bok growled as the cord tightened around his neck.

"Oh no, I need you right there!" he boasted as one of the grunts handed him Bok's sword. "I want to add your head to my staff, and that's the perfect position for execution." He looked at the head hanging off the end of Bok's sword. "Ah, poor Toroq! We will miss him."

"You're gonna be joining him soon, dangling there from the end of my sword!" Bok threatened, defiant to the end.

"Sorry to disappoint you, Bok, but no one is coming to save you. You'll die like your pitiful wife and daughter did, begging for their lives!"

Mækto's words angered Bok as he struggled even harder against his captors. "Shut your filthy mouth!" he screamed. "Don't you dare talk about them like you give a shit!" His struggles caused his captors to lash out and pummeled him about the head and body. They hit Bok repeatedly until his left eye swelled shut, and his lip bled out. Bloody, bruised, and beaten, Bok hung lifeless from his captor's arms as they bashed the fight out of him.

"You know the law, Bok. Their life became forfeit once you left that filthy human alive," Mækto said. "If you would have done your duty, they would still be alive. Their deaths are on you, not us."

Bok roared back at the goblin chief, but his cries were to no avail. He was helpless in their hands. Mækto handed his staff to the hobgoblin wizard as the chief stepped forward and wrapped both his hands around the hilt of Bok's sword. He raised it upright to Bok's throat, getting his aim just right before he swung. "Your little quest for revenge is over!" He reared back to strike but stopped when he heard a scream. He turned to see the hobgoblin engulfed in flames. A burning white dragon was swirling around as the magic caster turned to ash.

All the other goblins finally saw who did it. Gideon was standing there, and his Dragoon pointed right at them. He knew he had to take out the magic caster first. Now, he could turn his attention to the rest of them.

"I suggest you let Bok go right now, that is, if you want to leave this forest alive," Gideon said.

The goblins all broke out laughing at him as they drew their weapons, all except for the one holding Bok by the throat. He held on to keep him from joining in against the others. "You think you can get all of us with that Doomfire, boy? It takes dwarves forever to reload those things."

"This?" he asked, holding out his weapon. "This is a Dragoon, not a Doomfire, and unlike the dwarf weapon, it works off magic, but I'm not going to fight you with this." He holstered his weapon before he held out his hand. *"Come to me, Gæl Bölg, the Goblin Destroyer!"*

That name made all the goblins shake with fear as a runic circle appeared above Gideon's hand. A handle descended downward as he grabbed it, pulling out a massive weapon. It was a two-handed ax that resembled a giant meat cleaver, nearly two feet in length and several inches wide. It was held to the ax by the skull of an enormous goblin. Rumored to be the skull of the first goblin king killed by the first King of Attlain, they forged it into the weapon to infuse the magic.

The goblin's fear increased when they saw the actual weapon in his hand. Most of them considered it only a legend, a story made up to scare goblin children; but it wasn't. It was real, and they were looking right at it. Even Mækto was terrified at the sight of the Goblin Destroyer.

"No, that's not possible! How do you have Gæl Bölg?" His voice quivered with fear.

Gideon held the ax out in front of him in both hands, smiled. "Why don't you come here and find out, *Feur Muc!*" He cursed at him in goblin, one of the many swear words that Bok had taught him over the past few weeks. It did its job as Mækto was angered and insulted.

"What are you waiting for, idiots? Get him!" he commanded but the others froze on the spot from fear.

"Allow me!" Gideon said as he jumped forward and attacked them. He sliced through the first one from his collar bone down to his groin, cutting right through what little armor it had, like a knife through butter. That was the magic of the Gæl Bölg; nothing could stop it from killing goblins. Gideon spun around and decapitated the second one with ease before slamming the ax handle into Mækto's gut and up into his chin, knocking him down and stunning him.

He then turned his attention to the three holding Bok hostage, but he didn't need to worry about them. Bok grabbed the two in front of him by their heads and smashed them together, crushing their skulls. Gideon moved around the tree and attacked the last goblin. In one stroke, he decapitated it, embedding its ax into the tree as its body slumped to the ground.

Bok coughed violently, trying to catch his breath. In the meantime, Gideon turned his attention to the goblin chief, whom he had intentionally left for last. Mækto, still on the ground from being stunned earlier, started to recover. As he rolled onto his hands and knees, Gideon kicked him in the gut, sending him flying into a tree. He landed on his back, spitting out blood as he held out his hands, pleading for his life.

"Why are you interfering, human? You are meddling in goblin affairs! What does the life of this renegade mean to you?"

Gideon stopped and stared at the goblin. He couldn't believe how much of a coward this umber was. "Because he's my friend, that's why," Gideon answered.

"Friend?! Friend?! You lie! Goblins don't have friends, especially human scum!"

Angered by this, Gideon stepped up and threatened him. Mækto pleaded and begged for his life.

"Oh, don't worry. I'm not going to kill you." Gideon tossed the ax to Bok then, who caught it with ease and walked right up to Mækto, putting even more fear into the goblin chief.

"Bok, I was only following the law!" he pleaded, but Bok heard none of it. He took off his head in one swing of the ax. He stood there and stared at Mækto's dead body before spitting on it. His blood and spittle splattered over the corpse, giving him absolute satisfaction.

"Are you okay?" Gideon asked of his injured friend.

"Yeah, I'll be alright," he grunted, the pain so evident in his voice, and yet he fought through it. He held up the ax and looked at it closely. "I didn't know Botàn had this in his armory."

"The first rule of the Magus—Don't tell people what you have in your armory. The more they know, the more they may want what you have," Gideon said.

Bok tossed the ax back and Gideon returned it to the armory, the weapon disappearing in a twinkling of magical light.

"And you left yourself wide open with that second swing," Bok scolded him. "If this idiot had any skill as a warrior, he could have cut you down before you hit him in the gut." Bok motioned toward the goblin chief's corpse before he went over and picked up his head. He groaned as his injuries got the best of him. Bok almost went down to one knee. Gideon grabbed his free arm as he helped the goblin to his feet.

"Come on, you old fool. I'll do what I can to heal you once we get back to camp," Gideon said. Bok would have usually shrugged off such help, but his pride was a little beaten too. He held on as the two of them walked back toward Bok's hut.

"What about their bodies? Do I need to dispose of them later?"

"Nah, the forest will take care of it for us. The bodies will be gone by the morning, souring in some poor animal's belly." Gideon couldn't help but gag at the thought of that, but as he looked back at the bodies, some smaller animals were already chewing on them. "In a place like this, nothing goes to waste," he mused.

As night fell over Ponshu Forest, Bok quietly sat by the fire where a pot boiled slowly over the open flame. Gideon healed the goblin's wounds as best as possible and bandaged his ribs and swollen eye until he could try another healing in the morning. Over the fire, a few quails roasted on a spit as Gideon slowly turned them.

"How's your project coming?" Gideon asked, just to try and start a conversation. Bok lifted the lid to the pot and pulled on a string dangling off the side. At the end of the line was the goblin chief's head, shrunken to about half the original size.

"Still got a few hours to go," Bok replied as he lowered it back into the boiling liquid before putting the lid back on.

"Where in the world did you learn to shrink heads?"

"My mother taught me," Bok explained. "It's a family secret, passed down for generations. . . ." His voice trailed off and he became solemn.

"I heard what the goblin chief said about your family. I'm very sorry."

"It's my fault, like he said," Bok said, quiet and emotionless. "My actions got them killed. After we got back to the village, Alna told some of her friends about meeting Botàn, even showed them the dagger he gave her. Once the word spread through the village, the Council of Chiefs brought me in for discipline. Normally, they would have killed me, but they decided to punish me instead. So, they executed Alna and Griet and made me watch, all because I let Botàn live."

"That's ridiculous. What were you supposed to do? Kill Botàn after he saved you and your daughter?"

"It's goblin law," Bok explained. "You come across a human. You kill them before they can kill you. It doesn't matter if it's today or tomorrow; you kill any humans."

"That's bullshit, and now you're the one making excuses for them!" Gideon argued. "You respected the man that saved you and your daughter, that's all. Don't justify their reasons for killing your family. Why are you hunting down the chiefs then and hanging their heads on your sword? Is that for you or them?"

Bok said nothing. Gideon wanted to get through to him but couldn't reach Bok in his current state of mind. They sat there, in silence, for several minutes until Gideon realized what might shift his perception.

"Gæl Bölg!" he said, summoning the ax.

This move caught Bok off guard as he jumped to his feet. Gideon stood up slowly and handed Gæl Bölg to Bok.

"What are you doing?" he asked.

"I'm giving Gæl Bölg to you," Gideon explained as he held out the weapon to Bok. "As a Magus of Attlain, I relinquish my rights as master of this ax and remove it from the Armory of Attlain. I do this freely and without any reservations." As he said those words, the rune faded from the armory.

Bok looked confused as he reached out and took the ax from Gideon. "Why would you do this for me?"

"This will make your revenge even sweeter, and maybe—just maybe—it'll scare those bastards enough to stay away from you, at least while you're in Ponshu. Besides, I trust you," Gideon said as he sat back down and returned to turning the spit. "You can return it to me once you get all of your trophies."

Bok looked at Gideon, as if trying to understand this strange human who confused him as much as Botàn had. "I don't like being indebted to anyone," Bok said as he sat back down.

"You're not. I'm paying you back," Gideon explained. "I mean, you've been training me for the past few weeks. It's the least I can do to pay you back, right?" He smiled at Bok, and for the first time, Gideon saw that crotchety old goblin smile right back at him. He wondered if maybe, just maybe, he found a friend in Bok. It was something he sorely needed now that Botàn was dead.

As the sun broke over the next day, Bok and Gideon walked out of Ponshu Forest. Sarusasha followed close behind Bok, nudging him as they walked as if she was looking to get something to eat from him. Gideon dressed for travel, his saddlebags slung over his shoulder. Bok showed off his new hardware, with Gæl Bölg slung across his back with two shrunken heads dangling from the ax handle.

"Sarusasha can take you as far as Jephers," Bok said, patting the griffon on the side of the head. "Just make sure you land on the outskirts of town. You can then take one of those steel snakes into Le'Arun."

Gideon laughed at the thought of riding inside a steel snake as Bok described it. "It's called a train, Bok. A mechanical engine that pulls cars along a track, and it's faster than walking."

"You'll never catch me riding in one of those. In any case, just let Sarusasha go once you get there. She'll come home to Ponshu, quick as she can."

Gideon listened to Bok and knew he wasn't kidding. He raised this griffon, and its twin brother, since they were hatchlings. They were the only family Bok had. He took his saddlebags and laid them across the griffon's shoulders and then jumped on its back. "I won't let anything happen to her," Gideon said as he patted her on the side.

"By the way, the naiads wanted me to give you a parting gift," Bok said as he reached into his pouch. "I think it's their way of making sure you keep your promise." He pulled out a small crystal orb, only a few inches in diameter. In the light, the crystal glowed with fire all its own as tiny lights danced around inside. "It's a fairy orb. If you're ever in need of help, you can summon three fairies through this."

Gideon stared at the orb, appreciative of the gift but questioning what value it had in a fight. "What can three faeries do?" he asked. Bok just laughed at him.

"Damn boy, you don't know much about anything, do you?"

Gideon studied the orb and figured it might come in handy someday. He put the ball away and reached out to shake Bok's hand.

"I can't thank you enough, my friend, for everything," Gideon said. Bok gruffed as he reached out and took his hand.

"No, thank you, Gideon, for making me see the purpose of my life from here on out. I know now what to do. It's not just killing the chiefs. I have to make the goblins see that we can live with humans, not just kill them for the sake of killing them."

"It sounds like a plan to me," Gideon replied. "And you'll come to Le'Arun six months from now? By next spring?"

"I'll be there, don't you worry. You just get your magic training done," he said as he patted Sarusasha on the behind, sending the griffon flying into the air. "And don't forget to say hi to Lady Jay for me!" he added as the two of them soared high into the sky. Gideon offered a wave as they flew off.

Bok watched until they finally disappeared.

"Well, Botàn, you picked yourself a helluva apprentice," he said to himself. "I just hope he's ready for what's to come."

7 THE BASILON MAGICAL ACADEMY

G*ideon's Journal – I can honestly say I love to fly. Riding on the back of Sarusasha was incredible and relatively easy too. She knew just where to go. And wouldn't you know it, right on cue, as soon as I got down off her, she headed straight back toward Ponshu. She was a homebody.*

Jephers is a small town, even smaller than Armändis. A quick, simple stop for the train, which allowed people to stretch their legs, get a bite to eat, and enjoy the beautiful countryside while the engine was refilled with water. Plus, it made it easier for the southbound train to get by as most of the tracks traversing Attlain were on a single rail line. This required precise scheduling and easy transition points in the major cities. Luckily, I caught it right at the transition between the two and made the northbound train to Le'Arun. It'll take another week to get there, and unfortunately, the other passengers bought out all the sleeping spaces. So, for me, it's sitting up, night and day, while riding into Le'Arun. Luckily, I know a few deep meditation spells that'll allow me to sleep soundly but keep me alert enough should danger arise. They say the trains are relatively safe, but you never know.

The one thing I plan to do during the journey is study some more. Some of Botàn's books that I brought focus on a couple of things: The Laws of Attlain, regarding the Magus; his spellbook on runic summoning, in case I need to know some advanced magic techniques; and the guidelines for being accepted to the Basilon Magical Academy. It also allowed me time to study my holy book and try to stir some more memories. There's a phrase that's repeated throughout the book—"Patris, et Filiis, et Spiritus Sanctis"—and it seems so familiar to me. I don't know where, but the words "Father, Son, and the Holy Spirit" come to mind when I read those words. I don't know for sure, but I think I was related to a priest or a cleric. I don't see myself as a holy man, so maybe this book belonged to a relative. It might be something passed down through my family and ended up with me. Just another mystery to include in my search for the past.

I'm doing all this preparation for Basilon, but the fact is I don't know if they'll oppose having a Magus attend the school. I need to understand how to respond to any of their objections. I know that Lady Jacqueline's there, but I don't know what kind of pull she has at the school. The truth is, I don't know a lot about her, period, except through the stories Botàn and Bok told me.

I don't think Master Botàn would put me on this path if the goal were unobtainable. He knew what he was doing when he saved me. He set all this in motion. I don't know if it's all from his use of Evil Eye to see into the future, but it had to give him some insight. He prepared for every contingency. He had to know.

As the train pulled into the station at Le'Arun, Gideon got his first glimpse at the second-largest city in Attlain, next to the capital of Celestrium. Shaped like a triangle and bounded by three rivers in a valley, mountains rose along either side of Le'Arun. Massive stone bridges stretched across the rivers, connecting the entire city. The city center was where all commercial activity took place, the stores, taverns, and inns were all scattered about the cityscape. Whether by rail or by water, goods regularly traveled in and out of Le'Arun.

The people of Le'Arun were like no other. They were warm, cheerful, and full of life, and yet, at the same time, conniving and scheming to make some coin. The merchants would sell you their mother if they could make a decent profit. They talked up their wares, night and day, and there was always someone willing to buy it. The taverns and inns were some of the best in Attlain. They kept the adventurers occupied after traversing the surrounding areas.

Hordes of magical creatures surrounded Le'Arun. Only the high peaks and rivers kept the monsters away, and the adventurers regularly patrolled the outer area, just like they did in Armändis, to keep the goblins, orcs, and others at bay. After weeks of slogging about the wilderness, they longed to come back to a warm bed, cold brew, good food, and inviting companionship, all of which were readily available at an inn or tavern in Le'Arun.

While the center of Le'Arun was a hornet's nest, the city's slopes were a quiet retreat. Away from the hustle and bustle of the city, people lived along the valley's sloping sides that encased the town below. They lived in the serene heights above the city, where the simple homelife kept the business separate. Children played in the streets while men and women took care of their homes. Whether they were wealthy or poor, it didn't matter. They all lived together in Le'Arun.

Sitting at the top of the highest point above the city of Le'Arun was the

Basilon Magical Academy. The school resembled an ancient castle, with towering spires and high walls. It was well fortified for a school, but it wasn't just an institution of higher learning. It was also a storehouse of magical knowledge, and it protected those secrets with all due diligence.

As Gideon left the train, he was mesmerized by the city that blossomed around him. He'd never seen anything quite like it before in his lifetime. While Gideon marveled at the cityscape around him, people pushed by as they went about their business. He began to feel out of place and in the way.

Gideon spied an open-air wine bar just off the station, serving refreshments to weary travelers as they boarded and disembarked the trains. A few people were sitting around the makeshift bar that consisted of a wooden cart with a canopy surrounded by short stools. One of the drinkers caught Gideon's eye. It was a young man wearing what appeared to be a student wizard's robe. The question was, what was a student from Basilon doing down here?

Gideon sauntered up to the bar and ordered a wine. The bartender quickly poured him a goblet and set it down in front of him. "Five coppers, if you please!" he said politely. Gideon reached into his pouch and laid the coins down on the bar. He picked up his goblet and quickly chugged down the sweet wine.

"That's pretty tasty after two weeks of stale wine on the train, my compliments," Gideon said to the owner.

"We aim to please," he said with a nod of his head. "Would you care for another?"

"Yes, please," Gideon said as he put his goblet down and laid another five copper coins on the bar. "Could you tell me how to get to the Basilon Magical Academy from here?"

"Oh, are you a new instructor for the school?" the bartender asked, piquing the curiosity of the young man in the wizard's robe.

"No, not hardly," Gideon said as he took another drink of wine. He knew he shouldn't say too much as they may misconstrue the presence of a Magus at the academy. "I'm a messenger. I have to speak to one of the instructors at the school."

"Well then, Guilfoy can take you there," the bartender said, pointing over to the young wizard. He was dressed in a purple wizard's robe, draped across his thin frame by a simple shirt and tie, vest, and pants. His disheveled black hair flopped around his head, his face framed by a pair of thick rimmed glasses. He looked to be in his late teens.

"Oh, well, yes . . . I'd be happy too," Guilfoy announced as he took another swig of his wine. "Guilfoy Guilderhof, at your service, sir." He held out his hand to Gideon, who took it with a curious stare.

"Gideon, Marcus Gideon," he introduced himself. "Tell me, why is a student down by the train station, in the middle of the day, drinking what appears to be his fifth goblet of wine?"

Guilfoy looked at Gideon quite curiously. "I thought you said you weren't an instructor?"

"I'm not. It's just a question out of sheer curiosity," Gideon replied. "My former master would start his day drinking around this time. I would hate to see a promising young wizard follow suit."

"Oh, well, no need to worry. Believe it or not, this is all part of my training," Guilfoy said with a smile as he chugged down some more wine. "You see, my specialty is shadow magic, and to better control the dark powers within me, I need to feed my dark desires, and the best way to do that is through the massive consumption of alcohol."

Gideon laughed at the outrageous explanation Guilfoy gave him. "That has to be the most bullshit excuse to drink that I've ever heard!"

"It works!" Guilfoy snapped back. "Besides that, Montag here makes the best wine in Le'Arun. He's only in town once a week, so I take my lunch away from the academy when he's here." Guilfoy raised his goblet to Montag, who smiled and nodded his head.

"You still have to pay your tab, Guilfoy," Montag said. "You're up to three gold."

The young wizard finished his drink as Gideon noticed the student thinking of a way to get out of paying his tab. He'd seen it before at Marion's Tavern. So, before he could answer, Gideon laid three gold coins on the bar. "I'll take care of your tab if you take me to Basilon. Deal?" Guilfoy reached for the gold, but Montag swept them up before he could.

"He'd be happy to take you there, that is, if he wants to get another drink from me ever again," Montag said. He then snatched the goblet out of Guilfoy's hand, giving him no other choice.

Guilfoy guided Gideon through the winding streets of Le'Arun. The roads were winding and quite crowded, making it difficult to navigate. Gideon knew it would take him some time to learn the city's unique layout. They crossed one of the bridges connecting the city's center to the mountainside. Once there, they followed the sloping roads upward toward the Basilon Magical Academy.

Guilfoy didn't seem talkative like he was at the bar. Gideon wondered if his tongue only loosened up with a drink, like Botàn's. "So, tell me a little about the academy, Guilfoy. What's it like there?"

"Oh, it's probably the most boring place in the world," Guilfoy said. "I'm going on my third year, and with luck, this will be my last. I mean, all we do is study spells and magical history, but no practical application."

"It is a school, isn't it? You have to crawl before you learn to walk, right?" Gideon asked. "Besides, I heard that the academy has a reputation for its magical dueling, correct?"

"Yeah, but you can only use tier-two spells, nothing too dangerous. I mean, it's not like real magical combat."

Gideon chuckled under his breath at the student, minding not to insult him. "No, it's not."

"You're a magic caster, right? Are you a professional adventurer?"

"No, not yet, at least. My master died recently, so I'm fulfilling his final wishes before I move on to other things."

"So, are you planning to stay in Le'Arun for a while?"

"Well, that depends on how things go. I have to talk to Lady Jacqueline first," Gideon replied.

"Lady Jacqueline Celestra? What a coincidence, she's one of my teachers!" Guilfoy exclaimed.

"Oh, can you give me an introduction? It would make things a lot easier for me."

"I would, but you can't get into Basilon without first seeing the administrator, Master Dieter von Straithmore," he explained with a sly grin. "He's a bit of a prick, always got his nose in everyone else's business."

They continued their walk through Le'Arun as Gideon listened to Guilfoy recounting all the gossip from within the walls of Basilon, from the magical and noble pedigrees—or lack thereof—of his fellow students to the secret passages within the school. These passages were used for everything from getting to class on time to secret rendezvous between students.

Throughout their walk, Gideon could sense the "fun-loving" façade that Guilfoy used to hide some real pain. He had been separated from his family for the entirety of his time at Basilon, part of a "family tradition" as Guilfoy explained. Still, Gideon sympathized with the young student and understood why he turned to the bottle. He wondered if this was something most magic casters did.

Once they arrived on the school grounds, Guilfoy pointed and said, "If you go through that gate there, the sentry will escort you to the administrator's office." He then drew a dagger from inside his robe. It was a Kris—a wavy, curved blade—that glowed with dark, magical energy. He stabbed it into a shadow on the wall next to them.

"Aren't you coming in?" Gideon queried curiously.

"Oh no, at least not through the front door," Guilfoy stated. "You see, it's against the rules to leave the academy during the day, so if I walk through the front gate, it'll be a demerit for me. That's why I use this— *Porta!*" Guilfoy stepped into the shadow and disappeared.

Gideon marveled at the shadow magic and made a mental note to learn that spell. There was no telling when it would come in handy.

Just as Guilfoy said, the sentry was more than willing to escort Gideon to the administrator's office. Once inside the school grounds, Gideon got his first look at Basilon. The castle looked ancient but well maintained. An enormous staff of workers took care of everything from groundskeeping to security to everyday household needs. The students themselves walked about the grounds, going from class to class. They wore robes of red, blue, and purple, indicating what year they were enrolled in, from first to third. They were from various races—both human and demi-human—including catsei, alfs, gnomes, and dwarves. Alfs had pointed ears, pale skin, and white hair. Gnomes and dwarves were shorter than the average human—gnomes averaged about three feet tall while dwarves topped out at four feet tall; both looked quite similar in appearance. They carried their schoolwork and various staffs, wands, and other devices, with a passion for the craft. Many hoped to be an adventurer or part of a magical guild someday. They all looked at Gideon with quiet curiosity.

Once inside, the sentry led Gideon straight to the administrator's office where it was a beehive of activity. The administrative staff scurried about helping students, paying vendors, and dealing with the myriad of issues that came with running a magical school. Gideon patiently waited until someone was available to assist him.

"Can I help you, sir?" a young scribe finally asked him. He reminded Gideon of Cyrus Pipster—a skinny, little man using layers of clothing to bulk himself up.

"Yes, I need to speak with Lady Jacqueline Celestra," Gideon responded.

"Lady Jacqueline, yes, of course . . . give me a moment and I'll send a messenger to see if she's available." he started to say as he waved over one of the messenger boys.

"One moment, Gerard," came a voice from behind. Gideon knew in an instant that this must be Master Dieter von Straithmore. His robes denoted his position—regal red and black with gold adornments. He walked with an ornamental black obsidian staff encrusted with precious gems and capped with a golden orb floating inside a ring. His head was devoid of any hair, facial or otherwise. Instead, he had gold discs embedded in his skin, from the middle of the forehead across the back.

"What is your business with Lady Jacqueline Celestra?" Dieter asked, his voice he said, his voice stern and straightforward.

"I'm here to deliver a personal message to her from my master."

"I see," Dieter said. "And who did you say your master is?"

"I didn't," Gideon snapped back, not giving him an ounce of information. "As I said, it's a personal message for Lady Jacqueline."

"Well, our instructors are quite busy during the school day. Perhaps you could give me the message, and I'll see to it that she gets it."

"I'm afraid I can't do that. My instructions were to give Lady Jacqueline the message and no one else. I don't mind waiting until she's available."

Gideon could tell his refusal to pass along the message perturbed Dieter, but the administrator didn't try to press Gideon on the issue. All he did was instruct him to wait in the hall and he'd let Gideon know if and when she became available.

Gideon bowed politely and went out into the hall. More than three hours passed while Gideon sat on a stone bench and waited patiently. He knew that the administrator was trying to force his hand, but he calmly sat reading one of his books to pass the time.

At some point, Guilfoy showed up. "What are you still doing here?"

"I'm still waiting," he answered as he turned the page of his book. "You were right, the administrator is a prick."

"Guilfoy!" shouted the administrator from his office door. "Do you know this man?"

"Uh . . . no . . . I was just asking him if he needed anything. You know, being a good student and all."

"Well, get to your next class and leave him alone. I'm handling his request."

Guilfoy didn't say another word, but he gave Gideon a sly grin and a wink before he left. He wasn't sure what that meant, but Gideon knew that he would try and help. Another half hour passed and the sun started to dip in the sky before Dieter came out to speak to Gideon one more time.

"I'm afraid the academy is about to close. Are you sure you won't reconsider giving me the message for Lady Jacqueline? Otherwise, you'll have to come back tomorrow."

"And even then, you can't guarantee I'll see her. Is that how it is, Administrator von Straithmore?" Gideon stood up, agitated by the continued delay.

"I'm not sure I like your tone, young man," Dieter said. "Do you know who I am?"

"Yes, as a matter of fact, I do," Gideon interjected. "You are a bureaucrat who thinks he has to know everyone's business to do his job, but I'm not going to give you what you want. The question is, are you going to continue to interfere with a personal messenger, or are you going to let me speak to Lady Jacqueline?"

"Fortunately, that's not for him to decide," said a female voice from down the hall. Both men turned to see Lady Jacqueline Celestra walking toward them. Gideon never met her before, but he quickly recognized her from the many stories Master Botàn told him about her. Her long blonde hair was neatly tied up on top of her head in an intricate design with a simple tiara holding it in place. It framed her beautiful face, ageless in appearance for someone rumored to be over one hundred years old. She wore a flowing green dress that rustled as it moved around her. As she walked, the golden staff she carried jingled from the many golden rings dangling from it.

She averted her eyes, not looking at either man. Dieter was shaking and seemed nervous. He stumbled and stuttered as he tried to make his case.

"Lady Jacqueline, I was just trying to verify this gentleman's story, but he refused to—"

Interrupting, Lady Jacqueline said, "Administrator von Straithmore, in the future, if a personal messenger arrives for me at this school, you will send one of your underlings to find me immediately. My affairs are no concern of yours. Is that clear?"

Dieter acquiesced, and, with a wave of her hand, backed away toward his office. Lady Jacqueline then turned her attention to Gideon.

"Now then, I apologize for the delay. I am Lady Jacqueline Celestra."

Gideon bowed politely to her before speaking. "Milady, my name is Marcus Gideon. I apprenticed under Master Henri Botàn."

Jacqueline's face lit up upon hearing his name. "Henri? Oh my, well, how is he. . . ." Her voice trailed off, and Gideon knew it was his fault. He was never one to hide his emotions. "What's happened to Henri?"

Gideon reached inside his coat and pulled out an envelope and a pendant hanging on a gold chain. It was a gold locket with an emerald embedded on the outside. "I'm very sorry, milady, but Master Botàn is dead. He asked me to bring this to you."

She took the locket from him and looked at it lovingly. "He held onto it after all these years," she said softly. She looked down at the envelope with her name on it and recognized Botàn's handwriting. "Would you mind?" she asked as she handed Gideon her staff. He took it from her as she took the envelope from his hand. She broke the wax seal and began to read the letter. She took her time reading it, laughing then crying, as she went through the pages. Gideon watched her expressions change, like walking back through time, reliving all the beautiful memories Jacqueline shared with Henri Botàn.

When she finished the last page, she carefully folded up the letter and placed it and the locket in her pocket. She went over to Gideon and took her staff from him and then reached out and touched his face. To his surprise, she leaned in and kissed him on the cheek.

"Thank you, Marcus, for bringing this to me. Your dedication shows me why Henri picked you as his apprentice."

"I'm just glad to see that his stories were true for once," Gideon replied. "You are as beautiful as he described."

Lady Jacqueline laughed imagining what stories Botàn told him. "Ha! I see you learned flattery from your master as well," she remarked. "In any case, thank you for taking the time to come see me."

"I would have been here sooner, but Master Botàn had me stop and see Bok in Ponshu Forest before coming to Le'Arun."

"Ah, Bok. How is that grumpy old goblin?"

"He's fine, sends his regards," Gideon said. "He taught me a few things I needed to know before coming here." Jacqueline understood what he meant as she reached under his cloak and rubbed her hand across the armory. To her, it was like caressing a long, lost lover.

"Yes, I bet he did," she whispered, not even looking up at Gideon. Looking at the armory took her elsewhere, to another time, another place. When she came back to her senses, she pulled his cloak down to hide the armory again.

"Now, Henri said there is something I need to do for you," she started to say. "Administrator von Straithmore . . ." Even though she barely spoke his name, Dieter jumped out from the doorway to the administration offices almost immediately, as if he had been there listening in.

"Yes, Lady Jacqueline, what can I do for you?"

"Please have Preceptor de Maestre and Prefect Simralin meet me in the sixth-floor arena immediately."

"Y-yes, milady. May I ask why? . . . In case the instructors inquire about it?"

"For an entrance exam," she replied without hesitation. "Gideon, follow me, please." Lady Jacqueline took off immediately down the hall, with Gideon following close behind.

Her swift departure left Dieter speechless, but the old administrator knew he had better do as she asked and as quickly as possible. He would be there, though, to see just who and what this Marcus Gideon was.

8 THE ENTRANCE EXAM

Gideon quickened his pace to keep up with Lady Jacqueline, but he was a little concerned about her urgency in getting him admission to the academy.

"Milady, are you sure it's necessary to do this right now?" he asked. "I don't want to cause any problems with the administrator, or the other teachers, on my behalf."

"Oh, believe me, if I give that man a chance, he'll find some way to keep you out of Basilon," she said. "We need to do this now. Besides, I have faith that you will find a way to stand out and make your presence known. You are working on completing the task which Henri started to do a long time ago, and you'll need all the necessary tools to do it.

"Just remember this," she said as she paused and turned back to Gideon. "You must be more than a Magus. The armory is not enough to get you admitted to the school." She patted at the pauldron under his cloak. "I know Henri taught you more than just how to use it. You need to be a magic caster, first and foremost, to get into this academy. Show them those skills, and you'll be fine."

Gideon appreciated the confidence she had in him. The two continued onto the arena, which was more of a theater than a stadium. The gradient seating surrounded the lower floor in a semi-circle, rising higher along the walls. The upper seating was box seating, where instructors and staff could casually observe the classes. The ceiling was domed, painted with stars, constellations, Zodiac signs, and other magical runes.

Currently, a class was under instruction in the art of magical dueling. It was the closest thing to combat these future adventurers experienced while at the school. Each student stood within a ten-foot circle etched on the floor, spaced fifty feet apart. They had to stay within the ring while dueling, using whatever magic was at their disposal to shield, dodge, and attack their opponent. The first to concede, be knocked out, or cause their opponent to step out of their circle won.

The class was primarily second-year students in blue robes, with some third-year students waiting in the stands for their turn. Their instructor was quite an unusual sight to see. Lady Angelica Lumos was a dwarf magic caster. She stood under four feet tall, except for her beehive hairstyle that added another foot to her height. Under her dark green instructor's robe, she wore something unusual for a magic caster, a coat of mithril chainmail that hung to the floor. Dwarves were known to be ready for a fight, also evident by her magical staff. Most would consider it a spear since it did have a mithril pike at the top. Many students felt the jab if they got out of line or didn't listen to her instructions.

Recognized as a stern but fair instructor, Lady Angelica had an unapproachable demeanor. She was remarkably gifted at teaching the students proper combat techniques with military-like precision. She kept the students in line, ensuring they followed the correct procedures in their duels. They knew better than to step out of line or disobey her.

Everyone noticed when Lady Jacqueline entered the room, mostly because she was with someone they had ever seen before. Angelica seemed a bit perturbed that her class was interrupted. "Is there something I can help you with, Lady Jacqueline?"

"I apologize in advance, Angelica, but I need the use of the arena, and you as well, for an entrance exam."

Angelica looked at Gideon, eyeing him up and down as if he were a piece of meat hanging in the butcher shop. "Is this necessary?"

"I wouldn't be asking if it wasn't," Jacqueline said. "Preceptor de Maestre and Prefect Simralin are on their way here to assist."

Her insistency pressed upon Lady Angelica the importance and urgency of the request. "Very well," she said and then turned back to her class. "Second-year students, you can go on to your last class. We'll pick this up tomorrow." The disgruntled students went to leave while Lady Jacqueline turned her attention to the third-year students in the stands.

"Ladies and gentlemen, you can take your last period for free study. I will give you some additional dueling time later this week. I would suggest that you study up on runic summoning circles before the test next week. There are still quite a few of you that are not drawing the runes properly."

There were grumbles and complaints as the students left the arena disappointed. They all looked at Gideon with a curious stare, but one caught his eye. She was a beautiful young woman with flowing red hair, deep green eyes, and full red lips. She was enchanting to see.

He came to his senses when Guilfoy walked over with a sly grin across his face. "It's nice to see that you finally got to meet up with Lady Jacqueline," he crowed. Gideon knew, right then and there, that the young wizard had something to do with her coming to see him.

"I had a feeling you had something to do with that. Thanks, Guilfoy, I owe you," he said as the two exchanged a fist bump, one on top of the other.

"You can buy the first round when Montag comes to town again."

"You're on," Gideon assured, which caught Lady Jacqueline's attention.

"Marcus, how do you know Mister Guilderhof?" she inquired. "You didn't happen to run into him at a certain wine merchant down by the train station?"

Gideon didn't want to get Guilfoy in trouble, but he also didn't want to lie to Lady Jacqueline. He was conflicted by the problem. "Well, I was at a bar down by the station when I ran into—"

Guilfoy interrupted. "I went down to the station during my lunch to pick up a package from my parents."

"He was kind enough to bring me to the academy," Gideon added. "We had a nice conversation on our way up here and just hit it off, as they say."

Jacqueline looked at the two suspiciously but must have decided that wasn't the time or place to discuss things. "Alright then, thank you Guilderhof, you may go."

Guilfoy bowed politely before leaving as fast as he could. In his haste, he almost collided with Preceptor Xavier de Maestre, the head instructor at the Basilon Magical Academy. Prefect Nigel Simralin, one of the senior instructors, followed close behind with Administrator von Straithmore. Guilfoy bowed once again as he hurried out of the room.

Preceptor Xavier de Maestre was human, walking tall and dignified, with long, flowing black hair held back by a simple silver headband. He was a handsome man who looked relatively young for his age, with deep blue eyes that pierced through to the soul. Xavier wore regal robes of deep purple, magenta, and black with intricate silver embroidery. He carried no staff but rather a wand of red oak with a yellow sapphire that was tucked neatly in his sash.

Prefect Nigel Simralin was an alf, with stark white skin and eyes that signified his race. His long white hair was pulled back into a topknot ponytail that stuck out from the top of his head and flowed down his back. It allowed his pointy ears to stick out nearly four inches from the side of his head. He wore a simple white robe with neat blue and gold trimmings that enhanced his monochromatic appearance. He walked with a white birch staff embedded with a quartz crystal rod jutting out from the top.

They waited until the students were all gone before Lady Jacqueline spoke up. "I apologize for pulling you away from your classes, especially so late in the day, but this is an unusual circumstance. I would like to introduce you to Marcus Gideon. Marcus apprenticed with a very dear friend of mine, Henri

Botàn, for the past two years."

"Henri Botàn, I'm afraid I am unfamiliar with that wizard's name," Dieter interrupted, getting the ire of Lady Jacqueline.

"And there is a reason for that if I may continue," she snapped back at the administrator. "Unfortunately, Henri passed away recently, and it was his dying wish that Marcus finishes his education here at Basilon. I would like to add Marcus to the current third-year class so that he may complete his training."

The request confused the other instructors. It was unprecedented in the school's history, and they were all unsure if this was something within their power to do.

"This is highly unusual, Lady Jacqueline, besides the fact that he appears to be almost ten years older than most of our students," Preceptor de Maestre said, his voice steady and stern. "May I ask why you started your training so late in life, Gideon?"

"Well, I spent my formative years as a sailor out of Bösheen. When I had enough of that, I decided to pursue something else and set out for Le'Arun. One my way here, I met Master Botàn, and he saw the potential in me and took me under his wing as his apprentice."

"That may be understandable circumstances, but we have never allowed someone to join a class midstream. Besides the fact that the other students may show some resentment toward someone jumping into their midst, right out of the blue," Prefect Simralin added, his voice light and airy, like the wind.

"I must agree with Prefect Simralin. What makes him different that he should deserve such preferred consideration?" Xavier interjected.

"Because Marcus Gideon is a Magus," Jacqueline stated. They were all taken aback, shocked to hear that this young man trained as one of the forbidden orders of warrior mages.

"That's impossible," Dieter countered. "To be a Magus, he would have to have an armory."

Jacqueline looked at Gideon and simply nodded her head. Marcus pulled back his cloak to expose the Armor of Attlain, buckled to his shoulder. The sight of such a powerful magical artifact left them all stunned.

"Oh, my word," Lady Angelica exclaimed. "Kneel down here, boy, and let me take a look at it." Gideon followed her instructions and knelt. Angelica examined the armory closely, looking at every aspect of the pauldron. "What a beauty! Forged by my ancestors at Hjerte Ibrann, the first great forge of the dwarves. I never thought I would see one in my lifetime. Oh, this is a rare sight indeed."

As she examined the armory, she noticed something peculiar about it. "You must have more than twenty weapons in here, Gideon," she observed. "How did your master come about so many magical weapons?"

Gideon was hesitant to answer, but he knew they must already know the truth. "Over the years, other Magus sought out my master, to transfer their weapons to him so that they could leave their life as a Magus behind."

"But why would they do that?" Nigel asked.

"Because they were being hunted and killed!" Gideon shouted as he quickly rose to his feet. He was angry at their ignorance of this fact. "Someone found a way to remove the weapons from the armory without the consent of the Magus. They were killed off, one by one, for the weapons within their armories. Including Master Botàn."

Gideon's revelation shocked everyone, including Lady Jacqueline. He recounted the events around Guildmaster Herrod and his scheme to kill Botàn, frame Gideon, and then sell the armory to the party that contracted the guild. He did, however, leave out Selene Dartagni's name.

"And what happened to this guildmaster?" Xavier inquired.

"I challenged him to a duel and cut off his head," Gideon said plainly. Everyone was quite impressed with this young man, except for Dieter, who was rather disgusted by it.

"That is why my friend is unknown to most of you," Jacqueline added. "Henri decided to give up adventuring himself, but he kept his armory just in case. It seems that his going into hiding was all for naught."

"I cannot believe that someone found a way to remove the weapons from an armory," Angelica surmised. "It should not be possible."

"A further question is how they discovered the names of these Magus," Nigel added. "Those records were kept confidential after the purge, in case anyone else sought out revenge against them."

"That is a question we'll need to explore later. I will inform the Helios Arcanum of the situation, and they can decide what to do. Gideon, can you please give us a demonstration of the armory?" Xavier asked. Gideon was happy to oblige as he took a few steps back and held out his hand.

"Come to me, Ouroboros, dragon spear of infinite illusion!" he commanded as a runic circle appeared above him. A shaft descended out of it and he grabbed the pole and pulled out the spear. It was nearly eight feet long, a spearhead with two curved crescent blades below the point, extending out from the edge. The spearhead was attached to the wooden shaft by an ornamental metal dragon wrapped around the post.

Gideon held it out in front of him, ready to strike, and the assembled group understood why it was called the dragon spear of infinite illusion. As he held the spear, as if to attack, a dragon appeared out of thin air, flying around the pole arm and extended out, flying from the tip of the spear. The illusion confused enemies as to where the spear point was at any given time.

While most of the group was in awe of the Magus weapon, the administrator spoke up. "I wonder if it's acceptable to allow this novice to wield such a powerful magical item."

The administrator's question caught everyone off guard, but before anyone could say anything, Gideon piped in. "Fortunately, Administrator, that's not something that you or anyone in this room can do anything about."

"I beg your pardon! How dare you? Do you have any idea who you are speaking to?"

"Yes, I do, and none of you are the king," Gideon asserted. "According to the Magus Law of Honor and Loyalty, once a Magus declared their loyalty to the crown and proved said loyalty, the king granted said Magus the ability to select their apprentice to pass on their armory. Only the king can remove an armory from a Magus."

"And how do we know your master had earned such a distinct honor?" Dieter snapped back with a snarky attitude.

"Because I was there when he earned that distinction from the king," Lady Jacqueline interrupted. "Unless you doubt my word, Administrator?"

Dieter was flabbergasted and began to stutter. "N-no, milady, I would never doubt you." The administrator stepped back and withdrew his objection.

"Besides your training as a Magus, what other magical instruction did your master teach you?" Nigel asked to continue the conversation and get past the room's uncomfortable air.

"Well, he taught me the basic spells, both attack and defensive magic, but he focused mostly on elemental magic," Gideon answered. "Master Botàn was of the mind that a Magus needed to know a variety of elemental spells, to be able to adapt to whatever the situation required. I can read and write seven of the thirteen magical languages used in magic casting, I know some runic spells, dabbled a little in alchemy, and I've done magical crafting."

"Magical crafting? So, you've created your wand then?" Xavier asked.

"Not exactly," Gideon replied as he drew his Dragoon. Once again, the instructors were astonished at the surprises this young Magus demonstrated.

"That's a Dwarvish Doomfire!" Angelica proclaimed.

"Yes, milady, well, it was. I found it in a troll horde in the Imestrüs Forest, but it was in bad shape. The previous owner pushed a dragon's eye down the barrel. It's jammed in there so tight that removing it would destroy it. So, I added concentric bands around the barrel and recast the hammer, trigger, and striking plate in mithril—with the proper runes engraved—to make it a working weapon that allows me to focus my magic like a wand. I call it a Dragoon."

Gideon handed the Dragoon to Preceptor de Maestre. He examined the weapon before passing it around to the others. "This is quite a unique configuration, Gideon. I would like to have our magical crafting workshop examine it a little more closely if you don't mind?" Nigel stated.

"No, not at all. Although I don't know if it would work with other magical power stones, the dragon's eye seemed to be the right fit for it."

"I don't know what bothers me more," Lady Angelica said as she examined the Dragoon. "That you found it in a troll horde or that you may have improved on its original design."

Gideon chuckled a little at her observation. "I assure you, Lady Angelica, that I didn't improve on anything. I adapted it to help me focus my magic power properly."

"What do you mean?" Lady Jacqueline interjected.

"Master Botàn said I have an abundance of mana, but for some reason, I can't utilize it properly," Gideon explained. "It fluctuates erratically, and I don't know why. I was hoping that you would be able to help me along those lines."

"Indeed, that is an interesting conundrum," Xavier said. "Can you give us a demonstration of what you're capable of with it?"

"Of course, what would you like me to shoot at?" Gideon asked as he took the Dragoon back.

Nigel walked over to the far dueling circle and tapped his staff three times on the ground. *"Arise and live, a creature of rock and sand; breathe life into your being, set truth into your soul; come forth and serve my bidding, my golem of stone! Petra Giallu!"* The sand swirled beneath his feet. He stepped back and they all watched as the rock and sand formed together. First, a human-shaped head formed, then shoulders, arms, and hands as the monster lifted itself out of the ground. Soon, it stood on its own, more than fifteen feet tall. A massive stone golem.

Gideon looked carefully at the monster, calculating what he needed to do to bring it down. He stepped into the other dueling circle as the instructors and the administrator stepped back to see what the young initiate could do.

Gideon raised his Dragoon and cocked the hammer. *"Ventu! Tronu! Lampi! Dragoon!"* The runic circles formed around the concentric bands, one by one with each word spoken, building up the power as the dragon form swirled around his arm and Dragoon. With the hammer's strike on the plate, the spell fired at the golem with a thunderous boom. It was a ball of wind, thunder, and lightning that incrementally grew as it hurtled toward its target. It struck the golem with a massive explosion that shattered the creature. Stones and sand were sent scattering across the arena. Nothing was left except for its feet, which slowly dissolved back into the floor.

The gathered magic casters were astonished at the power they just witnessed. "That was no ordinary lightning spell," Dieter surmised. "What did you do?"

"The Dragoon allows me to combine one-word spells to make a whole new spell. I call that one Thunderball as it combines wind and lightning."

"I think I've seen enough," Xavier remarked. "You are a prodigy, Marcus

Gideon, but unrefined. I think you would do well under our instruction. I concur with Lady Jacqueline's request to admit you to our current third-year class."

Lady Angelica and Nigel offered their support as well. Gideon bowed politely to the assembled instructors and said his thanks.

"I will take Gideon to get settled into the dormitory," Lady Jacqueline interjected. "Administrator, if you will, please have someone bring the necessary books and supplies to Gideon so he will be ready to start class tomorrow."

"Of course, Lady Jacqueline, however, there is the matter of tuition and room and board. We are not a charity establishment, after all, and for one year, it equals out to fifty gold pieces." The administrator smiled like a tax collector waltzing into a poor village. Gideon, however, was unfazed.

Before Lady Jacqueline could say anything, Gideon walked up to the administrator as he reached into the magical coin purse that Botàn gave him. He grabbed Dieter by the hand and slapped five platinum coins in it. Since one platinum coin equaled ten gold, it totaled out to fifty gold pieces.

"This should be sufficient, but if there's any other costs, administrator, please don't hesitate to let me know," Gideon said with a sarcastic grin.

Dieter clenched the coins in his fist with fury as he spun around and left the arena in a huff. Once the administrator was out of sight, all the instructors had a good laugh.

The group exchanged some pleasantries before they all departed. Lady Jacqueline took Gideon to the dormitories to get him settled. The dormitories were in a separate building from the classrooms, had two separate wings with a central common area, and were divided by boys and girls, with an area on each floor for an entire one-year class. The common areas housed baths, a cafeteria, and rooms for study, games, and relaxation.

"I'm going to introduce you to Madam Kokishi. She runs the dormitories," Jacqueline said. "She'll get you settled into a room and go over the rules of the dormitories with you. I suggest you listen to her intently as she doesn't like to repeat things to new students."

"Of course, Lady Jacqueline. Will I be required to wear a robe like the other students?"

Gideon's question caught her curiosity. "Is that a problem?" she asked.

"Well, Prefect Simralin mentioned that the students might not like having someone thrust into their class," he explained. "These students have gone through two years together, earning their robes along the way. I haven't done that with them, so I wouldn't want to add to any already lingering problems."

Jacqueline nodded her head in concurrence. His logic was quite sound. "Alright then, you can wear the Magus robe that Henri left you. That will suffice for your time here."

"Thank you, milady."

"I also want to caution you against forming any relationships with the female students here," Jacqueline warned him. "You are quite older than them, and most of the young ladies here are inexperienced in the areas of romance. Most of them are—"

"You need not say anymore, Lady Jacqueline," Gideon interrupted. "I am not in the habit of, pardon me, deflowering young women to satiate my desires. If I have any needs to fulfill, I'm sure there are plenty of taverns in Le'Arun that are more than capable."

"Well, that's fine. I don't want to give the administrator any reason to expel you." Jacqueline explained that Administrator von Straithmore cultivated relationships with many of the wealthy and noble families. His influence extended beyond Basilon, so any negative interactions between Gideon and the student body could provide him with the necessary ammunition to expel him.

She led him to a large double door with two smaller doors built into it. Students walked in and out of the large doors while female gnomes went in and out of the smaller doors. Day and night, they carried sheets and blankets, laundry bundles, and other amenities throughout the dormitories. They were an efficient workforce that enjoyed their work.

Once inside, the two walked up to the head of the housekeeping staff, Madam Rosalia Kokishi. For such a diminutive person, she commanded a lot of authority. Her voice echoed above everyone else's as she dictated orders to both students and staff. They were going on, carrying laundry, passing out toiletries, and answering students' complaints. It was a virtual beehive of activity around the clock, keeping the students happy and their quarters well maintained.

Rosalia's stark white hair was tucked neatly under the gnomes' traditional pointed hat. Her face was careworn but quite stern, yet there was sincerity behind her eyes. She held onto her clipboard with a tight grip in one hand and a pencil in the other. Her notes were meticulously kept and consistently accurate. She immediately noticed Lady Jacqueline enter the room, and since instructors don't usually venture into the dormitories, it caught her curiosity.

"Lady Jacqueline, what brings you to my little corner of hell? Showing around a new instructor?"

"A new student, actually," she answered. "This is Marcus Gideon; he will be joining the current third-year class. I wanted to make sure we got him settled into a room tonight."

Rosalia looked through her list of current room assignments to find a room suitable for him. All the while, Gideon felt like the little woman was sizing him up, wondering what made him worthy of being a student at Basilon. After some skillful negotiation by Lady Jacqueline, Gideon was granted a private room—no roommate—to aid in securing the armory.

"Very well, follow me, Marcus Gideon, and I'll get you your prerequisites," Madam Kokishi said as she headed toward the supply room.

"Gideon, I'll leave you with Madam Kokishi, but I would like to talk to you some more about Henri and the school as well, perhaps over dinner tonight. I'll send someone to bring you to my quarters at around eight o'clock."

"Alright, Lady Jacqueline, I look forward to it."

"Gideon!" Madam Kokishi shouted, bringing him back to his senses. Gideon didn't waste any time and caught up with her, remembering Lady Jacqueline's warning about her temperament. He followed her into one of the back rooms, lined with shelves filled with everything necessary for each room: sheets, pillows, pillowcases, blankets, towels, and the like. The shelves reached up high, seemingly inaccessible to the diminutive gnomes, except for a rolling set of ladders that rolled around them like bookcases in a library.

Rosalia climbed up one ladder and started handing items to him as she explained things. "We change your bed linens twice a week, but you must make your bed every day and keep the room clean. I don't pick up after people, especially those who keep their rooms a mess."

"I understand, Madam Kokishi," Gideon answered immediately. He tried to keep a handle on the stack of linens, blankets, and other items she slowly piled upon him.

"We do the student's laundry twice a week. You put your laundry in this bag and leave it on your bed on your designated days. You will have clean laundry returned to you by the end of the school day."

She moved over to another stack of shelves and passed him toiletries, towels, robe, and sandals. "There are communal baths on each floor. The girls use the baths from six o'clock to six thirty in the evening, and the boys from six thirty to seven o'clock. Beyond that, they are open for anyone to use at any time. Just make sure you put the appropriate sign up at the door. You don't want to walk in on someone or have someone walk in on you."

"Do I have time to take one now?" Gideon asked. "I've been traveling for more than two weeks with very little chance to do anything more than wash up."

Madam Kokishi looked at her watch that hung neatly around her neck. "It's still early. You have about half an hour until the classes are completed for the day. There should be time, especially if you're going to have dinner with Lady Jacqueline. Now, follow me," she said as she wiggled her finger for Gideon to follow her.

As she led him up three flights of stairs toward his room, they chatted about Botàn. It turned out that Rosalia remembered Gideon's former master from his school days. "Henri Botàn was an exceptional magic caster, a bit slovenly though, and an occasional drunkard," she said.

Gideon laughed at how perfectly she described Master Botàn. "I guess you did know him."

"I am sorry to hear he died, but for a Magus, it was inevitable," she said. Gideon was shocked to hear her use the word "Magus" so casually.

"How did you know he was a Magus?" Gideon inquired. Rosalia just laughed at his insinuation.

"Of all the Magus that came through this school, Henri Botàn was the best of them," she answered. "Did you know that he led the fight against those who rebelled against the kingdom? That's what earned him the distinction of being the first Magus to retain his armory after the purge."

Gideon was surprised by that information. "He never told me that," he replied.

"Did I mention that he was quite the secretive lot," she said with a sly grin as they finally reached the door to his room. She pulled out a ring of keys from her apron pocket. After a quick search, she took one key off the ring and used it to open the door. The two stepped inside and Gideon surveyed his new home for the next few months.

It was a quaint little room with sparse furnishings: A simple bed, small desk, oversized wardrobe, wash table with a mirror, and a plush chair. There was only one small window. Madam Kokishi pulled back the curtain and opened it to air out the room. Gideon placed his supplies on the bed with his saddlebags.

"This is your only key," Rosalia said as she handed it to him. "If you lose it, it'll cost you ten silver coins to replace the lock and give you a new key, so my advice is don't lose it."

Gideon took the key from her and bowed politely. "Thank you, Madam Kokishi. I appreciate all your help this evening."

"If Henri Botàn picked you to be his apprentice, there must be something special about you, Marcus Gideon. What is it?" Madam Kokishi looked at him intensely, as if trying to see right into his mind.

Gideon smiled. This little woman was quite wise and full of insight. He liked her a lot. "Perhaps that's what I'm here to find out."

"Leave those clothes on your bed and I'll have them laundered while you take your bath. That way, you have something clean to wear for dinner tonight."

Gideon bowed politely again, appreciative of her help. Once she left the room and closed the door, Gideon looked out the window and gazed at the sun setting over Le'Arun. "I made it, Master Botàn," he said to himself. "Now, I just need to find Dartagni."

9 A FATEFUL ENCOUNTER

Gideon's Journal – I was off to a rocky start at Basilon—between the run-in with an overbearing administrator, an intense entrance exam, a beautiful ally, and a diminutive drill sergeant—but it has all led to this. I'm here. It was what Master Botàn wanted, and I'm finally here. Now comes the hard part of living up to all their expectations.

I must admit that I was pretty drained after my little entrance test in the arena. I haven't used magic a lot during my journey to Le'Arun. My mana is not recovering as fast as before. The more I use magic, the more drained I feel, and the longer it takes me to recover. It's even affecting my clockwork heart. My chest hurts when I use too much magic. It's like a signal for me not to overdo it.

Right now, though, I need to get ready for my dinner with Lady Jacqueline. I'm sure she has many questions for me, probably as many as I do for her. I'm hoping she knows something about this heart of mine, maybe something Master Botàn told her. She seemed very happy to get a letter from him in any case. Were they long-lost lovers? He talked about her all the time, as a friend but never like that. Madam Kokishi was right. Botàn was very secretive.

Gideon leaned against the wall as he relished the steamy, hot water that enveloped him. He savored his first bath in weeks and intended to enjoy every minute he could. The baths in Basilon were quite impressive. The mountains supplied a natural hot spring that fed into the academy. The baths provided a relaxing atmosphere to relieve both the students' and the teachers' daily stress. Gideon hadn't been able to relax like this for weeks—between his time with Bok in Ponshu Forest and the long train ride to Le'Arun—just being able to wash clean was a blessing in disguise.

He rubbed the scruffy hair on his face. His beard had gotten longer and thicker over the past few weeks. Perhaps he should clean up a little more, given his place here. Gideon dunked his whole body under the water one last time. He knew he needed to leave soon before the female student's bath time began. He remembered Madam Kokishi's instructions and placed the appropriate signage at the door, so he should be alright.

However, his concern may have been well-founded as he surfaced out of the bath. As his eyes adjusted to the steamy mist that filled the room, something caught his attention—something he had seen earlier in the day. Her flowing red hair, piercing green eyes, and voluptuous red lips framed the beauty in her face. The curve of her hips and the fullness of her breasts were accentuated by her porcelain skin. He was astounded by the woman standing before him.

She, on the other hand, was not so captivated. She cried out as she ducked behind the short wall that separated the wash area from the bathing area. "What are you doing here?" she shouted.

Gideon wanted to be diplomatic in a situation like this, especially after Lady Jacqueline warned him about potential fraternization issues, but he knew he wasn't in the wrong here. She walked in on him, not vice versa. "I could ask the same of you," Gideon said, ever so plainly. "I did put the sign on the door saying 'occupied,' didn't I?"

"Well, yes, but, it's our bath time, not the boys," she said, quite flabbergasted.

"Well, you see, that was your first mistake. I'm not a boy." Gideon's snappy remark got her ire. "Secondly, I was permitted by Madam Kokishi to use the bath before the ladies' bath time at six o'clock. Judging by the sun outside, it's almost six, but not quite."

"Well, some of us got out early and," she started to say before she realized she was still naked, talking to a naked man. "Would you please turn around?"

"I'm sorry?"

"I would like to put my robe on, so would you please turn around?" She insisted. Gideon did as he was asked and turned around, looking away from the young lady. Quickly, she rushed out to grab her robe and slip it on, but when she picked it up, a key dropped out and clanged on the floor.

"That's my robe," Gideon said when he heard the sound.

"What? Are you peaking?" she snapped as she quickly covered herself with her hands.

"I'm not peaking. I put my key on top of my robe when I came in here." He snickered at the partial lie he told her. Yes, he did put his key on his robe, but no, he was peaking. He saw her reflection on the surface of the water. He just couldn't help but admire her beauty.

Once she got her robe on, the young lady collected her thoughts to give

Gideon a piece of her mind. As the mist cleared, something caught her eye. She saw his back and the deep scars that spread across it—scars from his beating at the hands of the guild in Armändis. She'd never seen someone so severely injured yet still able to function normally.

"What are you doing here, anyway? This bath is for third-year students."

"Do you mind if I turn around? I don't like talking to someone with my back to them?" Gideon asked.

"Y-yes, yes, you can."

Gideon turned around to see her covered from head to toe in her bathrobe but still just as lovely. He explained the events of the day, from traveling to Le'Arun and being admitted to the academy to Madam Kokishi giving him permission to use the baths. Gideon asked to be allowed to leave so the third-year girls could then use the baths.

"Well, alright then," she said in a huff, crossing her arms and standing defiantly. Gideon, on the other hand, was waiting impatiently.

"Would you mind stepping outside? I would rather not cause either of us further embarrassment if I step out of the water." As Gideon stepped forward and his body began to rise out of the water, the young lady turned beet red in her embarrassment and rushed out of the bath. Gideon laughed to himself as he stepped out of the large tub. "I think I'm going to like it here!" he teased.

Wren hurried out of the bath and quickly closed the door behind her, leaning against the wall. Her breathing was heavy, and her heart was beating as fast as a racehorse. She couldn't believe that she let this stranger get under her skin like that, and yet, she found it quite exhilarating. *Who is this man, and why does he vex me so?* she pondered.

A voice called out her name, breaking her concentration. Leading a group of girls toward the bath was two of Wren's closest friends. Trini Alofo was a diminutive, dark-skinned beauty. Her wavy black hair was tied up on top of her head, framing her beautiful face. Although she looked tiny, she was rather muscular with an attitude that made her larger than life. Behind her was Fiona Greenleaf, an alf who stood tall above her friend. She looked like the other alfs—long white hair with white skin and eyes like an albino—but her voluptuous figure made her stand out amongst her classmates. Her quiet demeanor was the opposite of Trini, making them an unusual pair of friends.

"Why did you run ahead of us? Trying to get some extra bath time all to yourself?" Trini asserted.

"Yeah, I was, but . . . there's someone in the bath right now."

"What? It's our bath time! Who the hell is in there?" Trini shouted.

"Calm down, Trini, I'm sure there's a reasonable explanation," Fiona interjected.

"He's a new student. Madam Kokishi said he could take a bath before us, but I . . ." Wren stuttered, unsure of how to explain her encounter with Gideon.

"Wait a minute; you walked in on him?" Trini asked. "Did you see him naked? Did he see you?"

Wren didn't answer right away as the embarrassment of the situation got the better of her. "Well, it was my fault really for ignoring the sign."

"Oh, I'm sure you left the poor little boy in a state of shock," Trini joked. "He probably never saw a real woman before."

"Look, Trini, he's not some little boy. He's—"

At that moment, the bath door opened, and Gideon stepped out. Instead of regularly wearing the robe, he tied the sleeves around his waist, covering his waist and legs and exposing his muscular upper body. Gideon draped the towel across his head and shoulders as he dried his hair. As he stepped out, all the girls stared at him in awe. They were used to other students the same age as them, not someone like Gideon. His broad chest and shoulders, muscular arms, and dashing good looks stood out amongst the other male students at Basilon.

He bowed politely to all the girls. "My apologies for taking away from your bath time, ladies. It's all yours." Gideon walked by them and headed back to his room. The girls gazed at him as he walked by.

"Oh, please tell me he's joining our class!" Trini gasped as she lustfully eyed Gideon from head to toe.

"He certainly is impressive," Fiona said. "He looks more like a warrior than a magic caster."

"Who cares? I just want to know if he's available or not," Trini replied as she noticed something different about him. "Wow, look at those scars on his back. I wonder how he got those?"

"Good evening, ladies!" came a voice from behind them, breaking their fixated stares at Gideon. It was Lady Jacqueline. They were so busy looking at Gideon that they didn't notice her approach them.

"Good evening, Lady Jacqueline," they all said in unison.

"Is there something wrong with the bath?" she asked. "You're wasting time standing out here, gawking."

"Sorry, Lady Jacqueline. We were just waiting for someone to finish," Wren said as she changed the sign on the bath for the girls. Once she did that, they started to head inside.

"Wren, would you please stop by my room later, before you go to dinner. I have a small favor to ask of you."

"Of course, Lady Jacqueline. I would be happy to," Wren said with a polite curtsey. With that, Lady Jacqueline turned and left them.

"And yes, Trini, he will be joining your class," she said as she left, leaving a smile on Trini's face as she pumped her fist in the air. Before joining the others, Wren turned one last time to look at Gideon slowly strolling down the hall. She looked at this strange man with curiosity.

Who are you, Marcus Gideon? she wondered.

Gideon gazed in the mirror. He shaved his beard to a goatee—clean and well-kept—to look more the part as a Magus, in both power and appearance. Gideon knew the school would give him the control he needed. It was just a cosmetic change. He didn't want to look like a scruffy, apprentice blacksmith anymore. Mind you, there was nothing wrong with being a blacksmith. He rather enjoyed the power to forge steel to make a formidable weapon. Now, he just wanted to focus on one thing and one thing only. Being a Magus.

Madam Kokishi and her staff did a great job laundering his clothes in such a short amount of time. Gideon usually did things for himself, but he rather liked having someone else take care of him for a change. It was something he could get used to quite quickly.

He dressed in his regular clothes, except for his armored leather jacket. He didn't think he needed to wear that here. His hooded tunic and vest were enough, with the armory strapped across his shoulder. He wondered if he should wear his cloak to conceal it but decided against it. It was a school, and word would spread quickly—if it already hadn't—that a Magus was attending Basilon. Inside the school, there was no need to hide who he was.

As he finished getting dressed, his mind wandered back to the bath. He couldn't get that redhead out of his mind. There was just something about her beyond her beauty and charm. Maybe it was just his lustful self, seeing someone as beautiful as that naked, but he didn't think so. It was something from memory, locked away inside his head, trying to emerge and break out. It nagged him, and he hated that feeling, the feeling of knowing something and yet, not knowing it.

A knock rapped against his door. He finished buckling the armory before he opened the door. To his surprise, it was Wren. She was dressed in a blue dress with a red corset and white blouse under her purple student magician's robe. Her brilliant smile, framed by her flowing red hair, made Gideon's night.

"Well, this is certainly a surprise," Gideon said.

"Lady Jacqueline asked me to show you to her quarters for dinner. It's the least I could do," she replied.

"Well, thank you for that, Miss . . ."

"Wren, you can call me Wren," she said with a smile. "By the way, you clean up rather nicely."

"Thank you very much," Gideon said with a polite bow. "And you can call me Marcus or Gideon if you prefer. If you give me just a moment, I'll be right with you." He stepped back inside his room to grab a couple of last-minute things.

"I would invite you in, but I'm guessing it's against school policy," he shouted from inside the room. Wren just stood there patiently. She was trying to be as polite as possible, wanting to get this over with so she could get to dinner herself, but at the same time, Wren wanted to know more about this new student.

Gideon stepped out and locked his door behind him. "Please, after you," he said as he let her take the lead. The two strolled down the corridor towards the stairs. There was silence at first, so Gideon thought maybe he should break the ice. "You're not still mad at me for earlier, are you?"

"Oh no, Marcus, of course not." Wren answered rather quickly. "It was just as much my fault as it was yours."

"That's true," he joked, "and I appreciate your honesty. I just don't want to get a bad reputation after less than a day at the academy."

"Oh, you don't need to worry about that. Your little walk down the hall was quite enough to give you a glowing reputation, especially amongst the third-year girls." The two laughed at Wren's joke, but she was serious. The girls had all seemingly fallen in love, or at least lust, with the new student.

"So, what brings you to Basilon?" she asked, trying to continue their conversation. "You seem a little too old to be an ordinary student."

"Yeah, I get that a lot. You see, I was studying under my master in Armändis until he died recently," Gideon explained. He could tell that his story hit Wren hard when he told her that, as if she never experienced death before. "Lady Jacqueline was a good friend of my master from their adventuring days. He sent me to Le'Arun to see if she could get me admitted to the school and finish my training."

"So, what's your craftwork?" Wren asked.

"My craftwork?" Gideon had no idea what she was talking about but was rather intrigued to learn more.

"It's your specialty in magic. You see, in the first year at Basilon, we learn the basics of magic. In the second year, we start learning more complex spells, runic magic, and magic crafting. Finally, in the third year, we focus on advanced spells and our craftwork.

"My craftwork is fire magic," Wren continued as she summoned a flame in her hand without even casting a spell. The fire danced around her fingertips until it formed a tiny fire fairy. The small creature floated effortlessly above her hand, dancing in the air.

"That is quite impressive. You didn't even cast a spell to summon it," Gideon commented.

"It's a talent that's always been part of my family lineage, although it skips a generation now and then. I just got the luck of the draw. The only reason I'm here is to learn how to control this power." She waved her hand, and the fire fairy flew off into the air as it slowly burned itself up and disappeared. "So, what's your craftwork?"

"Well, since you put it that way, I guess my craftwork would be Magus."

"Magus? Do you mean to tell me your master was a Magus? Then that means you must have an Armory of Attlain!"

Gideon knocked on his pauldron proudly, making a clang, which got Wren even more excited. She jutted out in front of him to look at it more closely. "Oh my God, it's an actual armory? I've only seen them in books, never up close like this!"

Wren ignored any personal space between them as she ran her fingers delicately across the runes. When she finally realized what she was doing, her face went red with embarrassment as she stepped back. "Oh, I'm so sorry about that," she apologized. "Magical history is a hobby of mine, so when I get a chance to see something like an Armory of Attlain, it's quite special."

"I can appreciate that. In all honesty, I was under the impression the books wiped away the Magus and their history, erased like my master."

"Well, yes, but not to me," Wren explained. "There are those who consider the Magus a wound in the history of magic, but if you look closely, it was only a handful of Magus who rebelled, not all of them. Unfortunately, they all got blamed.

"I think that the people today, outside the magic community, see the Magus as legends, not a threat," she concluded. Her observation piqued Gideon's curiosity.

"Legends? You think that?" he asked.

"Oh, yes, I do. People are in awe of the Magus' power, being both warriors and magic casters. But, for mages, well—"

Gideon spoke up then. "They see the Magus as a continued threat because of the power they wield and keep hidden within the armories. Will I get a lot of that from the other students here?"

"Hard to say," Wren surmised. "We haven't discussed the history of the Magus yet, but I think your presence here will probably change that, hopefully for the better."

The two continued to make their way across the campus to the other side, where the teachers and staff lived separately from the students. Along the way, Wren was more than happy to point out the different buildings and their purposes—from the primary school hall to the laboratories, cafeteria, and sports fields—as well as inform Gideon of the details about their courses and some of the other students in their third-year class. It was quite a lot of information for the short amount of time they were together.

Wren saw that they were nearing Lady Jacqueline's quarters—a row of townhomes at the far end of the campus—and she had one last question she was aching to ask. "Marcus, do you mind if I ask you a personal question?"

"No, of course not. Ask away."

"The scars on your back . . . I noticed them before. How did you get them?"

Gideon saw a look of concern on her face when she asked. At first, he wanted to say something sarcastic about her peeking at him in the bath; but honestly, he appreciated her concern. He explained about the ten lashes and why he had taken them for Janus Wildman.

When he finished, Wren said, "That's incredibly brave."

"Or incredibly stupid," Gideon responded. "In any case, I did what I had to do. Janus has a wife and a little boy. I couldn't let him grow up without his father."

Wren looked at Gideon with admiration and told him how she respected that.

"Now, do you mind if I ask you a question, Wren?" The two continued to walk toward the townhouses, passing students and their curious glances every now and then.

"No, go right ahead."

"Is there a particular reason we're being followed invisibly by two of your friends?" Gideon asked, rather calmly.

"I don't know what you mean?" she said coyly, but her acting skills needed work.

"Dispel!" Gideon waved his hand and summoned a runic circle. He snapped his fingers, and about fifty feet away, a cloak of invisibility dispelled, revealing Trini and Fiona standing behind them. Trini was dressed in a short green skirt and crop top dress, exposing her tone midriff, with a pair of knee-high boots underneath her purple student robe. She had her hair pulled up as before, but this time an ornate scarf of green silk covered in fine jewels and gold held it up. She gripped a narrow wooden staff in her hand. Fiona wore a simple white dress that hugged her curves tightly from head to toe, even underneath her student robe. Her long white hair flowed down the back of her robe, held off her face by a simple mithril tiara. She had a clear crystal wand in her hand. Its magical glow faded once Gideon cast the magic spell on them. The two were embarrassed and surprised that he knew they were there. Trini just waved politely with a smile.

"How did you—" Wren started to ask but Gideon interrupted.

"An invisibility spell is not always enough," he explained. "It masked them visually, but not audibly." He looked back at Trini and Fiona. "Next time, cast a silence spell in conjunction with the invisibility spell!" he shouted. "I heard your footsteps and whispering the whole time you were behind us." Realizing their mistake, the girls decided to step away and wait for Wren.

"How could you hear them? I didn't hear a thing."

"I spent the last two years hunting and foraging in the Imestrüs Forest," he said. "With all the creatures in those woods, you had to develop an ear for every twig snap, rustling grass, or crunching leaves if you wanted to stay alive."

"I'm sorry, it's just that after our meeting in the bath, I didn't know what to expect. I wanted someone with me, just in case, you know," she tried to explain. "But that was before I got to know you on our way here."

"You don't need to explain anything to me, Wren. It's perfectly understandable for a young lady to have an escort," Gideon interrupted. "Besides, if that's what it takes for me to spend time with you, it's well worth it."

Wren turned red. Gideon embarrassed her with his compliment, but he could tell she loved hearing it. Before she could reply, the door to Lady Jacqueline's home opened, and the woman stepped outside. She wistfully smiled when she saw Wren and Gideon standing there. Jacqueline was wearing the same dress as earlier, but with one change. She wore the locket around her neck from Master Botàn that Gideon had returned to her.

Wren curtsied politely to Lady Jacqueline and flashed a smile at Gideon. As she walked away with her friends, Gideon watched closely, admiringly, until Lady Jacqueline cleared her throat and interrupted the moment for him.

"Get those thoughts out of your head, young man, and get in here. Dinner's getting cold," she scolded him. Gideon knew what she was talking about and headed into her house. Jacqueline shook her head before she smacked him on the back of the head, just like Master Botàn used to do. It made Gideon feel right at home.

That was the best meal Gideon had ever eaten: Lamb chops braised in red wine, sautéed vegetables, potatoes au gratin, and crème brûlée for dessert, along with a great '48 Charblan. It seemed Lady Jacqueline had a similar taste in wine as Master Botàn. As Gideon suspected, those two were a lot closer than either of them led on. The strange thing was, Jacqueline never asked him anything further about how he died or about those who killed Botàn.

All through dinner, the two of them swapped stories. Gideon told her about the past two years he spent with Master Botàn. Jacqueline confirmed or denied many of the tales he imparted about their adventures together. After dinner, the two of them sat in front of her fireplace, sipping one-hundred-year-old whiskey and continued their conversation. The two laughed and joked as if they were old friends reuniting for the first time in a year.

"And then, Henri waltzed out of there with the Sultan, arm in arm," Jacqueline explained, trying to contain her laughter. "I guess the Sultan liked more voluptuous women, and who could tell with that disguise."

Gideon never laughed so hard. "I knew there was more to that story," he joked. "He conveniently left that part out when he told it to me."

"Yes, well, Henri didn't like to be embarrassed, so he jutted around the truth whenever it was convenient for him."

The two of them drank a little more before Lady Jacqueline finally dared to ask Gideon the question she'd been patiently waiting to ask him. "Marcus, why are you here in Le'Arun?"

"What do you mean? I'm here to finish my training, just like Master Botàn wanted."

Jacqueline knew he was skirting around the truth, just like Henri. He taught the boy all his nasty habits, she bemused. "I mean, tell me who you're looking for specifically? Perhaps the people who contracted for the armories?"

Gideon nearly spat out his whiskey. Botàn said she was intuitive, like a fortune teller only better. "I've never been good at bluffing," he confessed. "Master Botàn could always beat me at cards. I'd hate to play against you."

"Especially if there's money involved. I'd take everything you have in that magical coin purse of yours," Jacqueline joked. "But seriously, Marcus, who are you looking for?"

Gideon paused for a moment before answering. He knew she would not like his answer. "Selene Dartagni."

Now it was Jacqueline's turn to spit out her drink. "What? Are you sure?"

Gideon nodded. "Her name was on the contract submitted to the guilds. I got that confirmed by all three people from the Black Wolf Guild involved in Master Botàn's murder. It's safe to say she is the sorceress who discovered how to remove magical weapons from the armories."

"That bitch!" Jacqueline exclaimed, catching Gideon off guard. He smiled at the thought of her not being so prim and proper after all.

Jacqueline continued. "I knew Duarté was a desperate fool, but not this desperate. Does he think he can wipe away the Magus and no one would notice? To have all those weapons suddenly reappear in the world. . . . He's mad!"

"From my conversation with Wren, it seems they wiped the Magus from the history of Attlain," Gideon interjected. "No one seemed to miss all the Magus killed for their armories or those who abandoned the ranks of the Magus when they turned their weapons over to Master Botàn.

"My question to you is, where can I find Duarté and Selene Dartagni?" Gideon asked as he leaned forward in his chair. Gideon's stare showed Jacqueline the raw determination in him. Gideon would not stop until he avenged his master. Gideon needed her help, but the question was would she.

"Marcus, you can't go after them, at least not yet. You and I both know how depraved they are, but not to the people of Le'Arun. There are hundreds of adventurers here, working to keep the people safe, and they hold those two in the highest esteem. They have garnered a stellar reputation. If you go after them like this, you'll be fighting not only them but every other adventurer in Le'Arun.

"You need to get stronger first," she continued. "I do not doubt your ability as a Magus, but you told me you have trouble controlling the flow of mana in your body. You need to finish your training and learn to control your magic before you go after them, and even then, you need proof of their involvement."

"Can you help me with that?" Gideon asked. "I know the other teachers mentioned looking at it internally—here at the school and with the Helios Arcanum—but I don't know them, so I don't trust them. I trust you."

"I can help you with that, but it won't be easy. That weasel, Dieter von Straithmore, has his spies all over the school. If he gets wind of this, he'll run interference for sure."

"Why is everyone so afraid of him?" Gideon asked. "He seems like a nobody in a dead-end job."

"And most people would think that, but it's not the case," she said. "He has many powerful friends, including Duarté and Selene Dartagni, and he will do everything in his power to stop any investigation that includes them or anyone connected to it."

"What do you mean? Do you think there are others involved in this?"

"Oh, absolutely," Jacqueline continued. "Duarté is a wealthy man from his years of adventuring but not wealthy enough to pay five thousand gold pieces for every armory they could find. Someone has got to be sponsoring this little venture of his. We need to find them as well; otherwise, they'll hunt you for the rest of your life."

Gideon sat back and took another sip of his whiskey. As much as he hated to admit it, she was right. "Is there anyone you can trust to help us?"

"Here at the school, I trust most of the instructors hired before Administrator von Straithmore got here, but that's only those who were at your entrance exam, so we're limited there. However, I do have someone who I trust implicitly to look into that matter with the Helios Arcanum."

"And who would that be?" Gideon asked.

"My sister, Lady Gwendolyn Celestra. She's the Royal Magician in the Court of King Reghan Glenn Donnelly Sloane Levián III. I'm sure she will be willing to assist in our investigation."

Gideon was shocked to hear that Lady Jacqueline's sister was a Royal Mage. "I never knew you had such far-reaching connections."

"The Celestra family held a position in the royal court since its founding more than five hundred years ago," Jacqueline explained. "Why do you think the capital is named Celestrium?"

"You mean to say your family was one of the founders of Attlain? That's incredible!"

"Well, yes, but we don't talk about it in that sense. Our role has been, and always will be, to serve the royal family of Attlain. Speaking of which, I need to let you in on a little secret about Wren."

"Wren? What about her?" Gideon asked with addled curiosity.

"I see the way you look at her, Gideon," she said. "Be very careful. She is not what she appears to be."

"I'm sorry, Lady Jacqueline, I don't follow you."

"Remember in your admission test when you said there was only one person who could remove the armory from your possession?" Gideon nodded his head as he remembered the conversation. "Well, that one person would be Wren's father."

Gideon considered it for a moment, and then he realized what she meant. "Wren's a princess?"

"Yes, although we do not treat her as such while she's attending the academy. Both she and His Majesty decided it would be best if we treated her like the other students and not as royalty."

Gideon's mind raced, thinking about what she said, and a particular thought worried him. "Is there punishment for seeing a princess naked in the bath?"

Jacqueline laughed and took a sip of her drink. She said, "You don't have to worry about that. Wren told me about it and said it was completely her fault for not paying attention to the door sign. To ensure that no rumors come out of it, I told all the third-year girls to remain quiet on the matter, or they would get detention for the remainder of the school year."

"Detention? Would that stop them from saying anything?"

"I see you don't know about our detention program," Lady Jacqueline said, bemused at his ignorance. She explained that detention meant cleaning rooms, doing laundry, cooking, and serving food to other students. For many of the students from noble and wealthy families, this type of punishment would be considered beneath their status.

Gideon couldn't believe it. The faculty used class warfare as a punishment rather than a privilege. He also couldn't believe that Wren was a princess. He knew he had to reconsider his feelings for her, but he couldn't shake it. She was beautiful, charming, and immensely captivating, and now, she was out of his reach. He passed it from his mind as he had another question to ask her. He reached into his coat and pulled out the holy book he carried for nearly three years.

"Lady Jacqueline, I was wondering if you know someone who could tell me more about this?" he asked as he handed her the book. She put her drink down as she examined the blood-stained cover, nervous about its condition as she glanced up at Gideon. She carefully opened the volume and began thumbing through the pages.

"Where did you get this?"

"I honestly don't know," Gideon said with a laugh. "When I woke up outside Armändis, I was clutching this book. That's how I remembered my name—inscribed inside the cover."

Jacqueline looked inside the cover and saw "M Gideon" inscribed inside. She examined the pages more closely. What words she could make out were written in an ancient language, but most of them were illegible and waterlogged.

"It appears to be a holy book. Our cleric here at the school is fluent in the language of the Saints. With your permission, I'd like to let him examine it." Gideon agreed, happy to have someone try to tell him some more about this mysterious book.

"Now, before you go, there's something I want to see," Jacqueline said as she put the book down and walked over to Gideon. "Marcus, do you mind?"

Gideon was confused. He didn't know what she was asking him. "Milady?"

"It's alright, Marcus. Henri told me about the attack on you in his letter. I want to see how it's working."

Right then and there, Gideon knew what she wanted to see. "Alright, go ahead."

Lady Jacqueline placed her hands over his chest. *"Revelá!"* she chanted as a runic circle of magical energy appeared between her hands. The magic peeled back his clothes, skin, muscles, and bone to reveal his clockwork heart. The heart whirred and clicked as the gears moved like precision clockwork. It beat with a steady drumbeat, keeping Gideon alive as the gears turned, and the clockwork heart kept its rhythm.

"Amazing!" she crowed. "It worked."

"Yeah, kind of shocked me too," Gideon chimed in. "How did you know?"

"Who do you think commissioned the work for Henri?" Jacqueline interjected. "Jacob McMaster is a master clocksmith, and he lives here in Le'Arun. I never understood why Henri needed it until now."

"It saved my life," Gideon said, feeling a sense of gratitude and sadness for his dead master overwhelm him. "I would be dead without it."

"It seems to be working properly, but just to be sure, I'll make an appointment to have Jacob come to see you."

"An appointment? With a clocksmith?" Gideon sounded bemused.

"Jacob is a highly reputable horologist, which makes him a very busy man. He's also quite meticulous with his work, which makes his time rather precious and expensive. It'll take a few weeks to get him here."

"That's alright. It'll give me time to get acquainted with my studies and the other students," Gideon said as he finished his drink and got to his feet. "In the meantime, I do have a small favor to ask."

"Oh, alright. What is it?" Jacqueline asked.

"Do you know a reputable blacksmith in town, or perhaps you have one here at the school?"

"A blacksmith? Whatever for?" she inquired.

"Since I can't use the armory while I'm here, I need a simple sword to do my daily training and exercise."

Jacqueline considered his request. "Wait here one moment," she said as she walked out of the room. When she returned, she was carrying a sword in its scabbard. It appeared to be a long sword with a golden hilt embedded with three jewels—two on either end of the guard and one on the pommel. The handle itself was long enough for one or two hands to wield it. The scabbard was metal with a red silk sash tied around the top.

"This is *Tigru Gattu*, the Tiger's Claw," she said as she handed the sword to Gideon. He took the handle and the scabbard and pulled out the sword halfway to examine the blade. "It belonged to my husband, Sir Leonard Volestra."

"*Le Tigris Regem*. The Tiger King," Gideon said. "I read about his adventures in one of Master Botàn's books. He was one of the greatest knights in all Attlain. His exploits are legendary. Milady, I didn't know you were married to such a famous warrior. Master Botàn never mentioned that you were married at all."

"Yes, well, it was more of a marriage of convenience than anything else," she said with a slightly breathless sigh. "Please don't misunderstand, I loved my husband dearly, but he wasn't my first love," she added as she touched the locket hanging around her neck gently. Gideon knew—from Botàn's stories and hers tonight—that they loved each other, even though they were each committed to someone else.

"Milady, I can't accept this," Gideon said as he put the sword in its scabbard and handed it back to her. "This is too valuable to you and the memory of your husband."

"It's a piece of steel gathering dust in my closet," she said, handing it back to Gideon. "It's not a magic sword, like the ones in the armory, but it's as sharp as it is durable. Consider it my gift to you. It's my way of saying thank you for everything you did for Henri."

Gideon knew better than say no to Lady Jacqueline. He accepted the sword, holding onto it tightly, and bowed to her. "I would be honored to accept this sword, milady. Thank you."

Lady Jacqueline reached up and grabbed his face in her hands. She pulled his head down and kissed him on the forehead. "You have the potential to be a great Magus, Marcus Gideon. Maybe even better than Henri Botàn, and he left it to me to teach you, guide you, and set you on the right path. I won't let him down, and I won't let you down either."

Overwhelmed by her words, Gideon thanked her. He hoped he could live up to her expectations. They said their goodbyes and Gideon headed back to his room. He was genuinely overwhelmed by the events of the day and exhausted.

THE LAST MAGUS: A CLOCKWORK HEART

If Gideon had not been so tired, he might have noticed Administrator Dieter von Straithmore watching him closely from the shadows. He scowled, cursing him under his breath. He despised this young Magus, and deep in his black heart, he vowed to do everything within his power to remove him from Basilon and confiscate the Armory of Attlain.

Mornings at Basilon Magical Academy began well before dawn for most of the staff. With hundreds of students and instructors to contend with, daily chores were an essential part of the morning routine. Preparing breakfast was first and foremost, followed by classroom preparation, cleaning, and laundry.

Before long, the students began to rise and ready themselves for the long day ahead. One by one, they staggered into the cafeteria for breakfast. Spread before them was a feast of eggs, sausage, bacon, fresh fruit, and delectable pastries. No one could leave such a buffet and say they were hungry. There was always plenty to eat, and it was consistently fresh and delicious.

Wren, Trini, and Fiona left the cafeteria and made their way to their first class. Wren had a disappointed look on her face, upset that Gideon was not at breakfast. Trini and Fiona decided to cheer her up with a little bit of fun jabbing.

"I'm sure Gideon just overslept," Trini said. "Maybe Lady Jacqueline tired him out!"

Wren didn't appreciate the joke and elbowed her in the chest. She explained about Lady Jacqueline's friendship with his deceased master, emphasizing that Trini shouldn't allow rumors like to spread.

Trini swallowed her words hard, rethinking what she said. She did not want to get on Lady Jacqueline's bad side. Fiona ignored the conversation as she saw something in the courtyard below them.

"I think he might have had something else to do," she said to her two friends as she motioned for them to look her way. The girls went to the rail and saw something surprising. Gideon was shirtless in the middle of the courtyard, with his tunic, vest, and armory sitting on a nearby bench. He performed an exercise regime with the sword he received from Lady Jacqueline. Gideon made slow and repetitive movements with his muscles tensed, stepping through each swing, concentrating on his breathing.

The girls didn't see the flaws that Gideon did. They watched him in awe of his prowess with a sword as he moved in careful precision and finesse with the blade. "Wow, he's good!" Trini commented. "I've never seen anyone move that graceful with a sword."

"Indeed, if he is a Magus, as you said, Wren, then he must use this regiment to maintain his formidable skills as a warrior," Fiona added. Wren said nothing in response to Fiona. She just stared at Gideon and marveled at this man before her.

He's just a man, an ordinary man, and yet I can't get him out of my mind, she thought. She remembered the apple she had in her pocket. She was saving it for a snack later but decided Gideon could use it instead. She pulled it out and shouted. "Gideon! You missed breakfast!"

Gideon stopped and looked up to see the three girls standing at the rail. Wren tossed the apple toward him. As it tumbled through the air and sailed downward, Gideon spun around in one swift motion and swung his sword up, the sharp blade cutting the apple in half. With his free hand, Gideon easily caught both halves. Separating the two halves then, he took a bite off one and winked and saluted to Wren. She smiled, happy that her gift was well received. Trini's and Fiona's mouths were agape as they stared at their friend.

The girls started to walk away toward the dormitories before heading to their first class. Wren got one last look at Gideon. As he ate the apple, he toweled the sweat off his body. Trini may be right. Gideon seemed to be under her spell, but they failed to see that she was also infatuated with him. However, deep down, she knew it was impossible. Her place as a Princess of Attlain made any romantic encounter with someone like Gideon unlikely, and yet, it was that forbidden love that made it even more enticing to her.

Gideon glanced up at Wren from the courtyard below as she walked away. As a princess, he knew she was off-limits, but he couldn't help himself. The feelings that stirred inside him were utterly new, but it was more than love or even lust. There was something more to this, and he just couldn't shake it.

"Hey Gideon!" someone shouted at him. It was Guilfoy walking down the stairs toward him, happy and optimistic for this early in the morning. "You better get a move on, or you're going to be late for class."

"Yeah, I know, but I never got my schedule or materials from the administrator," Gideon replied. "I don't even know where to go."

"Don't worry, I'll get you there," he crowed. "I'll just keep adding it to your tab."

Gideon laughed, but he knew Guilfoy was quite serious. "By the time I'm finished at Basilon, I'll have to buy out Montag's entire inventory to pay you back."

"Hey, as long as your buying, I don't mind at all," Guilfoy exulted.

Gideon laughed as he got dressed and pulled himself together, but he did have something on his mind. "Guilfoy, what can you tell me about, Wren?"

"What about her?" he queried. "Please don't tell me you've fallen for the 'Inferno Princess?'"

"No, of course not," Gideon lied. "I'm just curious. What is someone like her doing here—wait, Inferno Princess?"

"Well, that's the nickname she's earned since she's been here," Guilfoy explained. "When she gets upset or angry, her fire magic goes out of control and explodes into a fireball. That's why she's here."

"She can't control her power either," Gideon guessed. "Interesting. What about her friends, Trini and Fiona?"

"Well, Trini Alofo is a Solara girl. Her craftwork is wind magic. She's pretty feisty if you know what I mean. It's that western mentality that comes from those nomadic desert tribes. Still, I wouldn't mind getting to know her better, but she's not one for the company outside her circle of friends.

"Fiona Greenleaf is an alf from the southern forest of Appaluna," Guilfoy continued as the two made their way across the campus. "Like most alfs, she's a white mage; you know light and healing magic, that sort of thing. In case you didn't notice, she's got the figure of a woman but the mind of a child. She has no common sense whatsoever. To be honest, she's the opposite of me."

"You mean your shadow magic?" Gideon inquired. "I meant to ask you about that earlier. You seem quite adept with that dagger of yours."

"Oh, this," he said as he pulled out his dagger from inside his robe. The Kris flowed with dark, magical energy. "This is Shadowfax, the Predator of the Dark. It's what I use to project and access my shadow magic. It's a family heirloom, not really what I want, but it'll do for now."

"What do you want?"

"There's this legendary dagger called the Evil Eye," Guilfoy gushed. "It's the ultimate weapon of shadow magic. With that dagger in my hands, I could be the most powerful shadow mage out there."

Gideon swallowed hard as he glanced down at his pauldron. He saw the rune for the Evil Eye, a weapon he carried within the armory, but he decided not to tell Guilfoy about it, for now.

"You know, you still haven't told me about your craftwork . . . Magus!"

He caught Gideon off guard, but he wasn't surprised. In an isolated place like Basilon, rumors spread quickly, especially about a Magus.

"How is that being met by the other students?"

"Well, to be honest, both good and bad. Some students from nobility and other magical families consider the Magus outlaws and rebels. The regular students think of you as something out of legend and mythology."

That's how Wren described it last night. Gideon knew he would have a tough time here, but it was something he would have to deal with sooner or later. Being a Magus was his life now. He would have to teach them the truth.

"And what do you think?" Gideon asked Guilfoy. His friend just flashed a smile as they reached their classroom.

"Me? I think it's cool." He flashed another smile and a thumbs up. "I mean, being around you will either attract pretty girls or trouble, both of which I'm in for."

10 THE HISTORY OF THE MAGUS

Gideon's Journal – Thanks to Guilfoy, I made it to my first class, and I'm happy to have his help. This school is like a maze. I could barely find my way back to the dormitories from Lady Jacqueline's house. Getting around to my different classes will take some time to learn.

It was the first time in weeks that I had been able to do any training with a sword. I am definitely out of practice and weak, but now I have the time to get back to exercise. Plus, seeing Wren was a great way to start my day. I know Lady Jacqueline warned me about her, but I just can't help myself. Seeing her makes me smile, and I want to get to know her better.

She is the next in line for the throne, so my continued existence as a Magus may someday rest on her. It's best for me to form a close relationship with her now, but not too close. I don't want to get on her father's bad side.

Gideon walked into the classroom with Guilfoy, and it was surprising to see things haven't changed at school. Although he didn't remember anything about his life as a child, seeing this did bring back memories of life at school. They divided the desks into three sections with a raised tiered platform in the instruction area. Usually, students separated themselves from their peers—groups of friends who share the same ideas, interests, or cultures. There were less than fifteen students in this class, comprised of humans, demi-humans, alfs, dwarves, and gnomes. Strangely enough, they didn't divide up by their races but mixed into groups based on nobility and status.

Across the room, at the far end, a human male with blond hair and good looks was standing around with a male dwarf and a catsei female. The dwarf was so young that his beard wasn't even grown in yet. Just a rather bushy mustache covered his mouth. The catsei had short black hair with light brown fur with black tips on her ears and tail. She resembled a Siamese cat.

He looked around the room and spotted other groups, including one with a Yamatanese man, wearing the traditional Eastern clothes—a Kimono robe with taught bindings—underneath his purple student robe. He kept his hair tied in a topknot. What set him apart from other students was the bow he carried on his back.

"Good morning, Marcus," Wren said, interrupting his wandering eyes. Her smile was all he needed to break him out of his trance.

"Good morning, Wren. Thanks for breakfast."

"You're welcome, although I doubt you missed it on purpose, did you?" she asked.

"Yeah, I kind of overslept this morning," Gideon explained. "A little too much Jaxouth Whiskey, I think, but I did get a good night's sleep. A little exercise is what I needed to get my mind and body ready for today."

"You have an interesting workout regime. What exactly were you doing?" Wren asked, but before Gideon could answer, Trini got right in his face, placing both of her hands on his chest. Her sudden move caught Gideon by surprise, but especially Wren.

"Trini! What are you doing?" Wren sputtered.

"Hey, I just wanted to see if those muscles he flexed are real," she said as she continued to run her hands over Gideon's chest and arms. much to the shock of Wren and the other female students as they filed into class, although many of them were jealous of Trini, but not as bold. "You are quite a solid specimen, Gideon. I would love to work out with you sometime."

"Wow, Trini, way to breach personal boundaries," Guilfoy said as he pushed her away from Gideon. "It's his first day in class. You want to give the man some room before you wrap yourself around him?"

"You're just jealous, Guilfoy!"

He thought about it for a minute. "Yeah, maybe...."

"So, tell me, Gideon, how do you know Guilfoy?" Trini inquired. "Did you meet him at some bar in Le'Arun?"

Gideon laughed when he suddenly realized the kind of reputation Guilfoy must have at the school. Before he could answer, he heard the familiar clanging of rings against metal as Lady Jacqueline entered the room. She walked diligently, clanging her staff on the stone floor. Under one arm, she carried a set of books.

"Alright, everyone, take your seats," she said as she moved up to the front. When she saw Gideon, her tone had changed from the friendly banter they shared last night. "Gideon, you didn't bring anything with you this morning?"

"I'm sorry, Lady Jacqueline, but no one delivered the materials you requested for me from Administrator von Straithmore's office."

Jacqueline looked quite perturbed. "I see . . ." Jacqueline said before she moved over to the desk and set her stack of books down. She turned to the raven sitting on its perch next to her desk. "Sigmund, please tell Administrator von Straithmore to have all the materials delivered to Marcus Gideon's dormitory room by the end of the day, or I will personally find out why he's ignoring such a simple request."

The raven cawed once before flying out the window. The students muttered amongst themselves, mostly comments about Lady Jacqueline being a "badass" and the administrator's incompetence. As the students went to their assigned seating, Gideon saw Wren motion for him to sit next to her in the front row. *I don't know what it is, but this young woman certainly has a way about her*, he thought as he sat down next to Wren.

It was a little awkward for Gideon as he squirmed in his seat. He was older than all of them, making it somewhat uneasy for him. Lady Jacqueline was about to make him even more uncomfortable. "Class, as you may have noticed, we have a new student. I would like to introduce Marcus Gideon," she said as she motioned toward Gideon to stand. Reluctantly, he did so and gave a polite bow to the class before sitting down.

"Marcus will be joining your class for the remainder of the school year," she continued. "He was apprentice to a master in Armändis until, sadly, he passed away. Gideon is joining us to finish his training as a magic caster. I place the responsibility on all of you to show him the ropes as it were and help him learn the regiment here at Basilon. Any questions?"

The catsei female raised her hand. "Lady Jacqueline, if I may ask, since he's starting with us third-year students, what exactly is his craftwork?"

"Excellent question, Susanna, since that ties into today's lesson in magical history. Gideon is a Magus."

That word created a collective gasp amongst the students. Although some already knew this about Gideon, most of the class was in shock. "That's impossible," a blond-haired student scoffed. "Those traitors were wiped out after the rebellion."

Lady Jacqueline shook her head at her student's ignorance. "That uninformed answer is not something I would expect from a nobility education such as yours, Bartholomew," she quipped. Bartholomew scowled at her, prickling at his lineage. On the other hand, Gideon didn't care for his uppity attitude.

"The Magus were not all traitors, nor were they wiped out," she continued. "The Magus rebellion was brought down by other Magus who disagreed with their order's internal insurrection. Those loyal to both the Crown and the Helios Arcanum informed on the rebels and led the fight to bring them down. These Magus then pledged their loyalty to the king and were given their freedom to become adventurers or chose a different path toward the future. That included the option to choose their successors. This fact is evident by the

Armory of Attlain that Gideon is wearing on his shoulder."

Everyone looked over toward Gideon and saw the pauldron he wore over his tunic. The chatter went back and forth about the Magus' history and how it differed from what they knew, but they were also curious about how Gideon received one.

"I'm sorry, Lady Jacqueline, but that's not what we were taught," Fiona asserted as she held up one of her books. "It's not written that way in the very books you are teaching us from."

"Yes, I know. That's another aspect I wanted to demonstrate here today. It's called revisionist history." Her words shocked the class. It was unusual to hear a teacher talk like this. "You see, many considered the Magus a blight on the history of magic casters throughout Attlain," she continued. "So, what do you do when you have an incident like the Magus rebellion that damages the core beliefs of an organization? You wipe it away. You rewrite history to ensure that something like that never happens again."

"But, isn't that a good thing, milady?" the young dwarf asked. "I mean, if it prevents another uprising, perhaps it is better to erase it."

"That's true, Killian, but then you have to ask yourselves, do the ends justify the means?"

The rest of the class talked amongst themselves as they tried to debate the merits of changing history to better serve the future.

"'Those who cannot remember the past are doomed to repeat it,'" Gideon said out loud. Everyone stopped talking and turned toward him, curious about what this young Magus was saying.

"What?" Bartholomew said.

"It's a saying from a book my master had in his library. 'Those who cannot remember the past are doomed to repeat it.' It means you can't learn from your mistakes by erasing them. All you're doing is dooming future generations by making the same mistakes repeatedly."

Gideon heard the chatter amongst the class, most of them impressed with his answer. None more so than Lady Jacqueline as she expected nothing less from Henri Botàn's apprentice. "That may be, Marcus Gideon," Killian challenged, "but how does a Magus, such as yourself, benefit our magical society when most magic casters view you with disdain and fear?"

Gideon didn't care for his assessment, but he also didn't know how to answer it. "It's because of the Armory of Attlain," Wren stressed as she joined the conversation. "Without the Magus, you would expose many potentially dangerous magical weapons to the world. Within the armory, out of reach of anyone who would harm the people of Attlain, they're protected."

Gideon appreciated the defense Wren presented, as did Lady Jacqueline. "Excellent, Wren, you're correct. Gideon, would you please come up here, so we can demonstrate this fact to the class."

Gideon wasn't sure what she wanted him to do, but he complied with her request and stepped forward. She looked carefully at the runes on his pauldron and pointed to one rune—it was a mask with large eyes and an elongated nose, like a plague doctor.

"This one, Gideon, summon it, please. You have my permission."

Gideon looked at the rune and was shocked that she wanted him to bring out that weapon. "Are you sure, milady?" She nodded her head as she stepped away from him. Gideon breathed a loud sigh, unsure whether he should do as she asked, but then he realized why she asked him to summon that weapon. She wanted to scare them into understanding the purpose of the Magus.

"Come to me, Crimson Sky, Sword of the Red Death!" he shouted. A runic circle appeared in front of him, and the hilt of a sword appeared inside it. Gideon grasped the hilt and pulled out the blade, holding it in both hands in front of him. The sword was a katana—a curved, single-edged blade with a circular guard and a long hilt. The edge was tinted red, a deep crimson red.

The Yamatanese student jumped out of his seat, stunned by the sword's appearance.

"What the hell's wrong with you, Taki? It's just a sword," Bartholomew joked.

"Once again, Bartholomew, your lack of knowledge in magical history is unnerving for someone in your position as class leader," Jacqueline quipped. "Takeshi, would you please tell the class the story of the Crimson Sky?"

His breathing was quite heavy as if gripped in fear of this weapon. "In my country, more than 500 years ago, there was a Samurai named Takeda Yoshitsune," he explained. "He was taking a group of soldiers to a village near the base of Mount Hakkôda. There were reports of smoke, fires, and screams coming from the village. The samurai convinced it was bandits raiding local villages and rushed into the village. When they got to the village, they discovered it burned to the ground, and everyone was dead."

"So, it was the bandits?" Trini interrupted.

"No, the villagers did it themselves. They killed themselves, burned their village down to the last home. An alchemist who lived there accidentally unleashed a plague called the Red Death. It was slowly killing the villagers as it spread. The people were lying there, their bodies bloated with red sores and boils covering them from head to toe.

"Before Yoshitsune could order his men to retreat, they began to succumb to the Red Death. His men fell to the ground, dying from the plague one by one. He soon realized that he was infected and would soon die. Anyone who would come to that village would become infected as well, and soon, all of Yamatai would wilt away to this terrible disease."

"So, what happened?" Susanna wondered as her voice quivered in fear.

"Yoshitsune was also a skilled magic caster in the dark arts. He offered his own life through a ritual suicide called seppuku to cast a spell that drew the plague into his sword. His sacrifice saved my country from falling to the Red Death."

"So, what, this sword has a plague in it? So?" Bartholomew said.

Gideon pointed the sword at Bartholomew, unnerving him. "If you were to prick your finger on this sword, you would become infected with the Red Death and die instantly," Gideon explained. "Your death would then spread the plague, and soon, everyone in Basilon would be infected and die, followed by Le'Arun, then the surrounding villages, then all of Attlain. Dead!"

"So, destroy it or lock it away in the Helios Arcanum," Bartholomew snapped back. "It's gotta be safer there than in his hands."

"You're not thinking, Bart! If you destroy it, you destroy the magic containing the sword's plague. You just killed everyone again," Guilfoy asserted.

"Very good, Guilfoy." Jacqueline marveled at his answer. "Does anyone else see a problem with Bartholomew's assertion?"

"Locking it away at the Helios Arcanum or in a dungeon will leave it susceptible to theft, and once again, Bart, you've killed the world," Trini jeered. All this provocation pointed at him just made Bart even angrier.

"So, what makes it safe in his hands?" Susanna quizzed.

"Specifically, because the armory won't let it fall into the wrong hands, and neither will I," Gideon answered as he dismissed the sword. Crimson Sky faded away from his hand as it returned to the armory.

"Only the Magus can remove weapons kept within the Armory of Attlain," Wren interjected. "If you kill the Magus, the weapons remain locked away in the armory forever." Unfortunately, Gideon knew that wasn't true anymore, as did Lady Jacqueline, but it was a secret they had to keep for now.

"What's to stop some evil wizard or warlord from capturing you and torturing you until you release the weapons from the armory?" Killian asked as he tried to help his friend save face.

"Second rule of the Magus: Under no circumstance do you relinquish weapons under your protection. I would die before I would let these weapons fall into the wrong hands," Gideon avowed.

His answer still didn't sit well with some of the students. "Then what prevents you from using the weapons for your own purposes?" Fiona inquired.

"Third rule of the Magus: You are a servant of the people of Attlain, not a servant of yourself. No Magus would use the weapons within their armory for their benefit."

"And we're supposed to believe the words of an apprentice to a traitor?" Bartholomew spat out, his glib remark causing everyone to gasp in disbelief. Usually, Gideon would lash out violently after a comment like that, but he knew to tap down his temper here.

"With all due respect, Bartholomew, you don't know my master or me, nor would you probably want to. It's safe to say that Magus Henri Botàn did more in his lifetime to keep this world safe than you, or even I, ever will; and you don't even know who he is, and why is that? It's because of attitudes and lies, like yours, that he went into hiding in Armändis. He did it to protect the weapons within this armory, waiting to find an apprentice he could entrust its secrets to. I was fortunate and honored to be chosen by him."

Bartholomew scowled at Gideon. "And I'm supposed to take your word for it that this master of yours was not one of the traitor Magus?"

Lady Jacqueline walked over and stood glaring down at Bartholomew. The young magic caster profusely sweated as he looked up at his instructor. "Henri Botàn was a close and personal friend of mine," she said directly to Bartholomew. "I can personally vouch for his character and his actions as a Magus unless you want to doubt my word."

Bartholomew swallowed hard, not realizing the hole he dug himself with his off-color remarks. "No, Lady Jacqueline," he stuttered. "I would never doubt you."

"Very good," she said as she turned back to her desk. "Thank you, Marcus. You may take your seat." Gideon bowed politely and returned to his seat. Next, Lady Jacqueline instructed the class to take out their *Zosimos History of Alchemy and Magic* textbook and turn to chapter twenty-three.

Wren opened her textbook and moved it over to share with Gideon. As he tried to concentrate on the text, he was distracted by both Wren's beautiful face and the stabbing glare he was getting from Bartholomew. The class leader wasn't happy with how the young Magus stood up to him, and he was showing his obvious displeasure. Gideon didn't want to make enemies here, but nonetheless, it happened.

After a couple of hours of lengthy discussions on the Magus' history, the Laws of Attlain governing the Magus, and some of the more famous weapons wielded by Magus, Gideon was overwhelmed. He considered his lessons with Master Botàn brutal, but Lady Jacqueline completely outdid that mark. It was insightful to learn more about the Magus' history than his own master taught him, but it also left him uneasy. He didn't like being the center of attention, especially on the first day, but he understood why Lady Jacqueline did it. She wanted to ease the students into the idea of having a Magus in their class, especially with their improper education on the matter.

Once the class was over, Gideon was glad that she did. Most of his classmates came over and introduced themselves. The warm welcome made him feel at ease as he got to know them. They were courteous and quite thrilled to make his acquaintance. That became even more apparent when Takeshi stepped forward. He bowed politely to Gideon, who instinctively returned the bow. He read about the many different customs from Yamatai when he studied the other regions of Attlain.

"Gideon-san, on behalf of my people, I want to thank you for bearing the burden of the Crimson Sky," he said as he kept his head bowed.

"Please, you don't need to thank me. It's my duty, and my honor, to do so," Gideon said as he took a closer look at Takeshi's bow. "I've never seen a bow used like a wand or a staff before."

"I was an exceptional archer before my magical abilities emerged, so it only seemed natural for me." Takeshi took off his bow and showed it to him proudly. "It is made from bamboo layered over sakura or what you would call a cherry blossom tree. The wood is from a tree that has thrived on my family's land for more than two thousand years."

Gideon took the bow and felt its weight and apparent strength. He could even sense the magic coursing through it, mainly through the string. "This is beautiful, Takeshi, but what's the bow string made from? It's not hemp or anything I've ever seen before."

"It is made from the hair of a Kitsune the nine-tailed fox," Takeshi explained. "It is a Yokai, a guardian spirit of my family. The Kitsune wove this from his hair to keep me safe on my journey across Attlain to Basilon."

"Most of us students come to Basilon with family heirlooms for our craftwork," Wren interjected. "Usually, it's a wand or staff, or even a dagger and bow in some cases, to focus our magic."

"Do you have a wand, Gideon? Or is your armory your only device?" Fiona inquired. But before Gideon could show them his Dragoon, Bartholomew and his group of friends—Killian and Susanna—sauntered up to him. Bart stepped in between Gideon and Takeshi, ensuring he got right in his face. He just stood there and stared at him, not saying a word as he looked up into Gideon's face.

"Are you just going to stand there and breathe on me, or do you have something to say, class leader?" Gideon jeered.

"Listen, Magus, I don't know who you are or why you're here, but I don't approve of you being in my class," Bartholomew quipped.

"Last time I checked, it's Lady Jacqueline's class, and secondly, I don't need your approval to be here. Unlike you, I'm here to learn magic, not to improve my social status."

"My social status doesn't need improvement, unlike an apparent apprentice of a traitor."

Gideon began to get annoyed by the class leader, but before he could say anything, Wren intervened by shoving Bartholomew back.

"That's enough of that, Bartholomew Ostentatious! You're overbearing and rude for no reason!" Killian and Susanna stepped in front of Bart to protect him. Trini and Guilfoy stepped up between them and Wren, but everyone stopped and looked at Gideon, who was laughing uncontrollably.

"What's so funny?" Bartholomew asked.

"Sorry, it's nothing." Gideon laughed as he rubbed his eyes. "It's just—your name is Bartholomew Ostentatious? Wow, that's quite a mouthful." That got a chuckle out of everyone except for Bartholomew and his friends.

Bartholomew glared at Gideon, angry that someone beneath him made fun of his family name. He took a shillelagh out of his robe—a club of twisted blackthorn with a massive knob on the top. A loud clang of a metal staff on the floor and the clinking of rings brought everyone back to their senses.

"Put that away, Mr. Ostentatious!" Lady Jacqueline scolded him. "Save your adolescent aggression for the dueling circle, not my classroom or any classroom in this academy. Do I make myself clear?"

Bartholomew sighed loudly and slightly trembled as he put his shillelagh back into his robe and left with his two compatriots. "As for the rest of you, get to your next class. Prefect Simralin, like me, does not appreciate tardiness."

Everyone gathered their things together and headed toward the door. Gideon handed Takeshi his bow and paused, wanting to speak to Lady Jacqueline about what happened. But before he took a single step toward her, she spoke up. "You're going to run into this type of opposition here, Gideon," she said without even looking up at him. "You need to find better ways to deal with it than violence or sarcasm."

Gideon understood everything she said. He bowed politely before leaving the room. After all the students left, Jacqueline sat down at her desk and took a deep breath. *For Henri, I have to do this,* she mused. *I can't let Duarté win.*

Gideon's Journal – Who knew going back to school would be so difficult. Master Botàn would be laughing his ass off at me as I go through all this. It's only been a few weeks, and it seems like I've been here for months. The spells are far more complicated than anything Master Botàn taught me. There is so much information to absorb, and I haven't had the two years of instruction here at Basilon like the rest of them. I'm playing catch-up in almost every class. Plus, there's the problem with my clockwork heart. Performing these intricate spells takes a lot more mana out of me, and it's excruciating after just a few attempts. I find myself winded, almost exhausted, and in a considerable amount of pain. I have practically no social life because of the rest I need just to be ready for the next day's class. Lady Jacqueline assures me that the clocksmith is coming to see me, but his time is precious (no pun intended).

The good news is I have plenty of help and support from some of my classmates. Wren, Guilfoy, Trini, and the others are taking Lady Jacqueline's words to heart and are going out of their way to help bring me up to speed. On the other hand, Bartholomew and his allies spend their time making it hard for me to do the work, whether it's taking books from the library or trying to distract me with childish pranks and insults. It's annoying. Add to that, the administrator and his staff are watching my every move. I swear that man is looking for me to make any mistake, so he can expel me or try to take the armory away from me. He is a pain in the ass, but I'll suffer through it. I have to remind myself that I can't just be the weapons in the armory. If I am to succeed as a Magus, I need to master both. Bok gave me the tools to be the warrior; Basilon will give me what I need to be a magic caster.

The one thing I haven't done yet is dueling. Lady Angelica wants me to observe for a few weeks to learn the procedures before I step into the ring. It's understandable as I don't want to hurt these kids. The students think they are refining combat skills that they will use in the future, but they're not. Orcs don't wait between turns for you to set up a shield or let you finish a spell. It's completely impractical, but I don't want to say anything now. I've already got the administrator and some of the students against me. I don't want to start pissing off teachers too.

Inside the arena, the duels were somewhat of a spectacle. Whether in their free time or waiting their turn to face-off, other students watched with enthusiasm at the gladiatorial-style matches that pitted student against student. Some watched for fun, rooting for their favorites, while others watched to learn, trying to find that niche that will make them stronger.

Gideon was among the spectators once again. He watched as Guilfoy dueled with Fiona. It was a very evenly matched contest as shadow magic challenged white magic. The most fascinating part of the match was the diversity in spells. Long-worded spells were used for defense while they attacked with single, short-phrased spells. Students could not use attack spells higher than tier two to avoid severely injuring their opponents. Fiona had a crystalline wall that glowed with a brilliant light in front of her. She held her crystal wand in one hand to attack while maintaining her shield with her free hand. Guilfoy had a colossal shadow beast in front of him, acting as a shield. The creature was like a giant octopus, with dark tentacles reaching out to block her attacks. He used his dagger to fire back at her.

"Ombre Freccia!" he shouted as shadowy arrows fired out rapidly from the tip of his dagger. They pierced the crystal wall, causing multiple cracks throughout her shield.

Gideon saw Fiona hesitate and defend rather than attack. He realized that if she fired back, he might break through her shield on his next attack. *"Star of Tierlîndi, bringer of light, protect me from harm, let your power burn bright! Sciath Réalta!"* She chanted as her shield glowed, and the cracks healed themselves. However, this left her open for another attack by Guilfoy.

"Ombre Strajk!" With that order, his shadow beast attacked Fiona. The dark tentacles, not having to defend, lashed out as they extended toward Fiona.

It repeatedly hit her shield until it exploded, sending Fiona out of the ring. Guilfoy won the duel. He jumped around the circle, celebrating his victory, giving his classmates high fives and fist bumps. Then the two competitors exchanged bows as was part of the courtesies of the duels.

"So, who wants a piece of me?" Guilfoy shouted as he looked around for his next opponent. The winner got to pick their next opponent, and Guilfoy saw who he wanted by the duel-arena rules. "Come on, Gideon, let's finally see what you can do as a caster! What do you say?"

Gideon smiled, even chuckling a little bit. "Are you sure about this, Guilfoy? I wouldn't want to ruin your winning streak!" Everyone "oohed" and "aahed" at the smack talk exchanged. Gideon turned and asked Lady Angelica for permission.

"I think you've had sufficient time to observe and learn the rules of the duel rings," the dwarf instructor said. "If you feel you're up to it, I'll allow it."

Gideon politely bowed before he stepped over to the circle opposite Guilfoy. "Competitors, bow!" Angelica commanded. The two men politely bowed to each other. "Shields up," she ordered.

Guilfoy stabbed his dagger into his own shadow at his feet. *"Come forth, Shadow Beast of the nether world! Protect your master, be my shield and sword! Bona Fiera,"* he shouted. The tentacled beast crawled from out of the shadow and took its place in front of Guilfoy.

Gideon drew his Dragoon in his left hand before extending his right hand in front of him. *"Appear before me, Shield of the Warrior, Aegis Aspida, protect me from my enemies, strengthen my resolve! Magu di Scudu!"* From his hand, a glowing golden shield formed in front of him. It had the face of a Medusa that howled when the protective shield formed, intimidating Guilfoy as well as the others watching.

"Lady Angelica, I've never seen a shield spell like that before. What is it?" Wren asked her teacher.

"That is the Aegis Aspida spell," she explained. "It's a defensive spell specifically designed for the Magus. Only the members of their order know the specifics of this spell. It is a rare privilege to see it used in our duel arena."

"It doesn't look like anything special to me," Bartholomew said, interjecting his sarcasm.

Lady Angelica scoffed away his notion with a jab from her pike. "Then you are not looking at it properly, Bartholomew. That's divine energy in the shield. It makes the Magus practically invincible. However, it takes a lot of mana to maintain the spell, so he must act fast to win the duel before he is unable to fight."

Both students stood at the ready, their shields up, prepared to fight. Lady Angelica held her staff, acknowledging both competitors at the ready, before she smacked her staff on the ground to start the duel.

Guilfoy launched his attack first to test Gideon's shield. *"Ombre Freccia!"* he chanted, summoning a stream of shadowy arrows from the tip of his dagger. Each one of his arrows struck Gideon's shield and glanced off without causing any damage. Guilfoy was shocked to see his spell's ineffectiveness, as was the rest of the students.

"Okay, let's try this. *Ombre Lance!*" He reared back his arm with the dagger until a spear of darkness formed in its place. He threw it at Gideon, but it grazed off his shield just like the shadow arrows. "Oh, come on, Gideon, that's not fair."

"Fights aren't supposed to be fair," Gideon said. "Do you think an orc pack or evil mage is going to fight fair? You have to duel like it's life or death, not some game." Gideon pointed his Dragoon at Guilfoy, then he pointed it upward, over his head. Everyone looked at him like he was crazy.

"Meteore! Cascata Stella! Dragoon!" he shouted as the magic built up in his weapon. Runic circles flowed along with the concentric bands, and the dragon form swirled around it before he pulled the trigger. A burst of white magical energy fired out from the Dragoon. When it hit the arena's ceiling, it floated there as a ball of light.

"That was anticlimactic!" Guilfoy joked, causing some of the other students to start laughing out loud.

"Wait for it," Gideon smirked. Everyone stopped laughing and looked up again at the ball of light. It started to pulse, glowing brighter and brighter, until it exploded, sending shooting stars down on top of Guilfoy. His shadow beast couldn't stop all the magical meteors, blasting Guilfoy out of his ring.

"Match to Gideon!" Lady Angelica shouted, motioning toward him. Gideon dispelled his shield and walked over to Guilfoy. He reached down and offered his hand to help him up.

"You okay?" he asked. Guilfoy took his hand and Gideon pulled him to his feet.

"Yeah, but what the hell was that?"

"Meteor Shower, it's a tier-two spell. I noticed that your shadow beast could reach forward and above but not over or behind you. It was the logical spell to use to get past your defense. If you infuse a little more mana into your shadow beast, you could probably extend his reach to defend you all around."

"Wow, you've been paying close attention to our duels," Guilfoy said.

"Well, you can't look at them as just duels," Gideon said. "You need to treat them like actual magical combat. Otherwise, it's wasted time."

Bartholomew jumped into the conversation then. "And what would you know about actual magical combat?"

"More than you, class leader!" Gideon snapped back. "Tell me, Bartholomew, how much actual fighting have you done?"

Bartholomew scoffed at his assertion. "I'm the undefeated champion of this arena. You should know that."

"I'm not talking about dueling," Gideon said. "I'm talking about actual fighting against orcs, goblins, trolls, and the like."

Bartholomew seemed embarrassed as he tried to come up with an answer. "Well, none, why?"

"Living in Armändis, I had to fight creatures like that daily, just to catch my dinner, and let me tell you this, none of you will survive if you fight out there the way you do in here." He turned his attention to the teacher and added, "No offense, Lady Angelica."

"None taken, I think, but please explain yourself."

Gideon tried to explain things from his perspective as an outsider watching the duels combined with his experiences from Armändis. The students used the same spells repeatedly to wear down an opponent's shield instead of strategizing with various spells to adapt to the duel. He noted, rather bluntly, that if they tried doing that in the real world, they would not survive as magic casters.

None of the students liked the bluntness of Gideon's remark, even Wren. "That's a little harsh, Gideon. We're not novices."

"I'm sorry, Wren, but I'm not going to sugarcoat it for you. Most of you come from sheltered backgrounds. You haven't seen the dangers out in the wild as I have. I've seen many an adventurer in Armändis killed for either their inexperience or ineptitude because they were so full of themselves."

That comment riled everyone up, making them even more perturbed toward the upstart student. "Alright then, let's see if we can prove you wrong," Susanna said as she stepped into the dueling circle to challenge Gideon. Lady Angelica took note and turned to him.

"Gideon, as the winner of the last duel, do you accept Miss Cesseman's challenge?"

Gideon looked at Susanna, and then he looked around the room. Everyone glared at him with a look of discontent and animosity. He hated to make them feel that way, but perhaps, it will save their lives by showing them now instead of later.

He accepted Susanna's challenge and both challengers moved into a circle. Lady Angelica gave them the same commands as before. The two bowed before raising their shields. Susanna pulled out an orb from within her robe. It was made of crystal-clear glass, flawless in its appearance.

"Come forth oh waters of Aquarius, bearer of seas and bringer of life, to protect me with the power of the ocean and prevent my enemies' strife! Acqua di Aquarius!" The orb glowed as it pulled water from different sources—from the ground below and even the moisture in the air around her—until a solid sphere of water surrounded her. It flowed around her in constant motion. Gideon couldn't gauge the ever-changing depth of the water as it moved

around her.

"This is the Water of Aquarius!" Susanna gloated. "Let's see if you can get through my shield, Magus!"

Mesmerized by the motion of the swirling water, he tried searching for any weakness in her defenses. Gideon drew his Dragoon and stood at the ready, but he didn't raise his shield.

"Gideon, shield up!" Lady Angelica commanded.

"It's alright, Lady Angelica. If I can't get through her shield, she deserves to knock me on my ass."

The dwarf nodded her head as she slammed her staff on the ground. "Then competitors, fight!"

The two stood their ground, waiting for the other to make the first move. "I'll give you the first attack, Gideon, but make no mistake, I won't hold back on mine."

"That's good to know," he shot back. "But you should never give your opponent the chance to attack first." He raised his Dragoon and aimed it at Susanna. *"Catina! Dragone! Lampi! Dragoon!"*

Gideon's spell charged in the Dragoon as the runic circles formed and a lighting-charged dragon swirled around it. Once he knew it was ready, Gideon pulled the trigger. A lightning bolt shot out from the Dragoon and sailed across the arena. When it hit her water shield, it didn't even penetrate. Susanna smiled with confidence, thinking she had this duel won, but then she noticed that the lightning bolt didn't dissipate. Instead, it bounced around her shield, jumping about as if the lightning was searching for a way inside. It kept rolling along, like one long chain, until it almost covered her completely. Susanna began to panic and screamed in terror. Her fear paralyzed her from fighting back as she fell to her knees.

"Stop! Stop! I yield! I yield!" she shouted, conceding the match. Gideon snapped his fingers, and the lightning faded away and disappeared. Her shield collapsed, spilling water everywhere. Bartholomew immediately went over to help and comfort her. Once he knew she was alright, he focused his attention on the person he was angry with.

"What the hell was that?" he exploded in anger. "That was not a tier-one or a tier-two spell!"

"Actually, it was," Gideon said as he holstered his Dragoon. "I added the command word 'catina' or chain to a tier-one lightning spell . . . Chain Dragon Lightning. It causes the lightning bolt to jump around to multiple targets until there's nothing left to strike."

"But you were only aiming at her? What other targets were there?" Trini asked.

"You used local water when you cast your spell, am I right, Susanna?" Gideon asked. The catsei just nodded her head, not looking at him. "Water sourced in a big city like Le'Arun is not pure like spring or creek water. It's full of contaminants: Metals, dirt, feces, and the like. My chain lightning was bouncing off those contaminants. Next time cast a purify water spell after you summon your shield. It'll make it stronger against attacks like lightning."

Guilfoy interjected. "You're telling her how to beat you next time just like you did me?"

"We're all here to learn, Guilfoy. If we can't learn from our mistakes, then what good is it. I'm not here to win a dueling competition. I'm here to learn how to be the best magic caster I can be, as I suspect all of you are too."

"You don't know anything about us, traitor!" Bartholomew said, jumping to his feet and getting in Gideon's face. "All you're doing is trying to show us how much better you are than the rest of us. You're nothing but gutter trash, and don't you forget it!"

"That's enough, Mister Ostentatious!" Lady Angelica chastised him. "You might not like his methods, but Gideon has provided all of you with valuable insight that will benefit you after you leave this institution. I suggest you take his advice to heart instead of engaging in unnecessary rhetoric."

Bartholomew listened to his instructor and stepped back before taking out his shillelagh as he stepped into the dueling circle. "Alright, Magus, let's see how you do against the top duelist at this school!"

Gideon felt a twinge in his chest. He wasn't sure if he would last against someone of Bartholomew's caliber and strength, but Gideon also knew that the class would take nothing he said or did here today to heart by walking away. However, Lady Angelica was having none of it.

"You know the rules of the arena, Bartholomew. No more than two duels in one day."

"Begging your pardon, Lady Angelica, but that wasn't even a duel," Bartholomew argued. "Gideon only cast one spell. I'm sure he's got enough mana for one more go around."

Angelica couldn't argue with his logic, but she wasn't going to make that decision. "Gideon, it's up to you, as the winner of the last duel. Do you accept Bartholomew's challenge?"

Gideon looked over at the sly smirk on Bartholomew's face, and then he looked at the other classmates. They all wanted this fight, mainly to see him knocked down a peg after what he did to Susanna. Gideon knew that if he wanted them to understand what he was trying to show them, he had to fight.

"It's alright, Lady Angelica. I accept his challenge." The rest of the class cheered as Gideon moved into the other dueling circle. He drew his Dragoon and prepared to fight.

"Competitors, bow!" Angelica ordered. Gideon bowed, but Bartholomew just stood there. "Bow, Bartholomew, or I will cancel this duel and ban you from the arena for one week!"

He gave in and reluctantly bowed to Gideon.

"Shield's up!"

Gideon summoned the Aegis Aspida as he did before. Bartholomew knelt and tapped his shillelagh on the ground three times. *"Earth and stone, heed my call; bend to my will, and split the ground; twist and turn, oh Earthen clay; become my shield, and protect me now! Terra di Terra!"*

Gideon recognized the spell. He used a variation of it against the trolls. He remembered Guilfoy telling him that Bartholomew used druidic magic, earth, and plant control. Druidic magic was separated into two categories: Attack/Defense and Healing/Purification arts. They both use nature as a source for their power, but it was two different philosophies. He was a warrior in his own right, using the earth itself to attack his enemies.

His spell formed a wall of earth in front of Bartholomew. It molded a semi-circle, sticking to the dueling circle's edges, and was as tall as Bartholomew. Gideon could barely see the top of his head over the shield. Still, he didn't need to see his opponent. He knew where he was.

"Ready?" she asked, as both of them nodded their heads. "Then, fight!" she shouted, slamming her staff on the ground. Gideon wanted to try and end this as quickly as possible, so he decided to go all out from the start.

"Meteore! Focu di Dragone! Brusgià! Dragoon!" He pulled the trigger and a white dragon of blazing dragonfire discharged toward Bartholomew. The beast roared as it impacted the earthen shield. Unfortunately, Bartholomew built up his shield as fast as Gideon's spell broke it down. The explosion did very little to penetrate his shield.

"You'll have to do better than that, old man!" he taunted. *"Petra Jittari!"* he shouted as stones launched from his shield like stone bullets. The rocks impacted Gideon's shield, causing no damage, but he did notice something unusual. The stones crumbled and melted away as if they were mudballs. He realized that the ground over there was still wet from Susanna's water spell, and it gave Gideon an idea of how to beat Bartholomew.

He aimed his Dragoon for a second volley. *"Acqua! Scoppiu! Congelatu! Dragoon!"* The spell caused the magic to build within his weapon. When it was ready, Gideon pulled the trigger and sent a water stream at Bartholomew. The water soaked his earthen shield, seeping deep into the dirt, rock, and stone. Everyone laughed at such a lame attack by Gideon.

"What was that for, Gideon? Trying to give me a bath?" He joined in with his classmate's laughter. However, the laughter stopped when his earthen shield began to freeze from the inside out. Soon, cracks began to form as his stone wall began to crumble and fall apart.

"I guess you never did much gardening," Gideon shot back at him. "At the start of spring, there's always a chance of the ground freezing after a cold rain. All I had to do was let the water get into your shield before freezing it solid.

The rest is nature at work."

As his shield crumbled at his feet, Gideon saw the disbelief build on Bartholomew's face. Even his classmates, once on his side, began to realize what Gideon was trying to show them, and they began to cheer for him. Bartholomew became infuriated as he seethed with rage until, without thinking, he lashed out.

"Gaia, oh Mother Earth, heed my call, lend me your strength, your power, your all . . ." he chanted as he placed the tip of his shillelagh on the ground. Lady Angelica attempted to stop him from using a tier-four spell in a duel.

"Stop right there, Mister Ostentatious! Do not finish that spell!" she shouted, but he ignored her.

"Strike down my enemy with rock and stone! Swallow him up and crush his bones! Pugnu di Stampa!"

The earth split in front of him as a giant earthen hand reached up from the ground. Everyone was shocked as the massive hand clenched into a fist and started bashing against Gideon's shield. It smacked it repeatedly. Try as he might, Gideon could not maintain his protection as his chest began to burn and ache until, finally, his clockwork heart stopped. His shield faded as the giant fist came crashing down on top of Gideon one more time, smashing him into the ground.

Wren and some of the others rushed over to check on Gideon as Bartholomew suddenly realized what he had done. "What the hell, Bart!" Guilfoy chastised as he followed the others.

Lady Angelica shouted, "Bartholomew Ostentatious, that was reckless and inexcusable! You know better than to use a tier-four spell in a duel. You are suspended from this arena for four weeks for that reckless insubordination!"

Wren shouted from across the arena. "Lady Angelica, help!"

Everyone, including Lady Angelica and Bartholomew, rushed over to Gideon. Blood trickled from the corner of his mouth. His chest looked crushed by the weight of Bartholomew's attack. Lady Angelica leaned her head down to check his breathing and feel for a pulse. His breathing was shallow, and she could barely find a heartbeat.

"Someone, go get Canon Cordell, immediately," she ordered. Trini took off toward the infirmary.

Lady Angelica placed one hand gingerly on his chest as she closed her eyes and tried to sense for any traces of life. Since Mana was the life source of a magic caster, all experienced casters could learn to read the flow of mana in the body to determine injuries. It was a prerequisite for instructors at Basilon. Lady Angelica sensed what was wrong with Gideon and said, "He focused all of his mana on his heart, but for some reason, it's almost completely gone. That's what's killing him."

She stood up and placed the spear tip directly over his heart. *"Trasmissioni*

Magicu," she chanted, causing her mana to flow from her body and into Gideon. Gideon was breathing a little more comfortably within moments, but he remained unconscious. Once she stopped transferring her mana, she paused to take a deep breath herself.

"Fiona Greenleaf, can you cast a life support cocoon around Gideon?" Angelica asked her student. Fiona nodded her head. "Then do so and be ready to move him to the infirmary. He's not out of the woods yet."

11 TO RESTART A CLOCKWORK HEART

Gideon's Journal – I don't remember much from the duel. All I saw was this massive fist, and I couldn't move without lowering my shield. If I weren't trying so hard to stay alive, I would've been impressed. After it hit me, I couldn't breathe. I couldn't even feel my heart beating. It was like getting stabbed in the chest all over again.

When Fiona put me in the life support cocoon, it was like my mind was overloaded. I could hear all their voices: Wren, Guilfoy, Trini, just about everyone in the class. Even Bartholomew was telling me to hang on. I never understood how overwhelming that spell is. Yes, it can save your life, but it can also drive you mad. It suspends your body, preventing further injury or death from life-threatening injuries until a cleric could perform proper healing spells. The downside is you feel everything. While saving your life, it opens up every perception you have . . . sight, sound, smell, touch, everything.

It says you are only supposed to keep someone in a life support cocoon for no more than thirty minutes to an hour. I read one incident where a man was in it for more than five hours. Although the body healed, the mind never recovered. He spent the rest of his life sitting in a chair and staring out a window. God, I hope that doesn't happen to me.

"What in God's name were you thinking?" Lady Jacqueline screamed in Bartholomew's face. He just stood there, stoic, taking the senior instructor's verbal rundown. The entire class was standing outside the infirmary, being lectured by Lady Jacqueline, while Canon Cordell tended to Gideon inside. "Using anything higher than a tier-two spell in the arena is absolutely forbidden, driven into students since your first day at Basilon. You should know better than to use 'Gaia's Fist' in a duel!"

"I know, Lady Jacqueline, I'm sorry!" he choked out.

"Sorry? Gideon is lying in there, fighting for his life, and all you can say is you're sorry? And what about the rest of you?" she continued, turning her attention to the rest of the class. "Did you all just stand there and do nothing while he was casting that spell?"

Everyone stood silently, not wanting to answer her in fear of getting a tongue lashing themselves. "It was all happening so fast, we didn't know how to react," Guilfoy admitted. "With Gideon acting as cocky as he was, I guess we all wanted to see him knocked down a bit."

"It's not cockiness, Mr. Guilderhof!" she snapped back at him. "Marcus Gideon meant it when he said he fought for his life, every day in Armändis. Do you know what happened to his master, my friend, Henri Botàn? He was murdered, killed by a local guildmaster for the Armory of Attlain that Gideon now has, and it was Marcus Gideon who hunted down the men responsible and brought them to justice!"

Everyone was shocked to hear that about Gideon. He wasn't kidding when he said he fought his way into Basilon.

"For your sake, I pray that he survives this ordeal because it will mean the difference between standing before the disciplinary committee and the magistrate!" With that, Lady Jacqueline turned in a huff and headed into the infirmary, slamming the door behind her.

Lady Jacqueline was still fuming as she walked through the infirmary. As much as she wanted to continue disciplining her students, she was more concerned about Gideon. She moved briskly through the hospital ward. There were dozens of beds here, but right now, only one patient occupied the room.

Gideon lay in the last bed in the ward. He was covered by a white sheet from the waist down. A catsei nurse held her hands on either side of his head as magical energy flowed between them, keeping him unconscious. Her coloring resembled a calico cat, with blonde hair tied up under a habit. Her ears and tail were blonde with brown, black, and white spots. She wore a nurse's uniform that somewhat resembled a nun's habit with a long, white apron tied in the front.

Next to Gideon, with his hands extended over his chest, was Canon Lucius Cordell. He was the cleric assigned to the school, responsible for the students' care, both physically and mentally. Clerics on this staff comprised the many different faiths worshipped in Attlain. Canon Cordell was an older man, but he still had a full head of brown hair, lightly streaked with gray. His one distinguishing feature was the bulbous nose on his face, broken when he was a child and never healed properly, leaving it misshapen. That life-changing event made him choose the path as a cleric. He didn't want any other child going through life with the deformity he had.

He chanted a soft, melodic prayer, combined with a healing spell, over Gideon's body as he tried to heal his internal injuries. Lady Jacqueline quietly walked up to him, not wanting to disturb him in his work.

"You were a little harsh on your students, Lady Jacqueline," he said with his eyes closed as he continued to focus on his healing magic. "There is a fine line between discipline and abuse."

"They need to understand that their actions have consequences, Lucius," she replied in as stern of a tone as she had with her students. She was genuinely concerned about her students, but Gideon was special to Jacqueline. Lucius never saw her this distraught over a single student before. "How is he?"

He stopped casting his healing spell and took a deep breath. "I've healed most of his injuries, including a few broken ribs and a collapsed lung. He'll be quite sore for a while. It's a good thing he was in such excellent shape, but that's not what concerns me . . . *Revelá!*"

With a wave of his hand, a runic circle appeared, and the bandages, skin, muscle, and bone faded away, revealing Gideon's clockwork heart, but something was wrong. It didn't move with the same steady beat as it did before. It clicked and whirred with an irregular beat, causing Gideon pain and discomfort as it failed to provide an adequate pumping of blood for his body.

"Perhaps you can explain this modern miracle to me," Lucius continued. "All I can say is that it's not performing as it should be. It's taking all his mana just to make it work as poorly as it is. It's barely keeping him alive."

Jacqueline stared at the clockwork heart and noted its malfunction. It was acting quite differently from when she saw it weeks ago. "Lucius, you must say nothing of this to anyone, nor you Constance," Jacqueline noted, pointing to the two of them. Lucius looked at his nurse, and she nodded her head in agreement as she continued her magic chanting.

"We will be discrete, Jacqueline, but it begs the question as to how to fix this clockwork heart? I have not the knowledge nor the skill to do so."

"Yes, but I know someone who does," Jacqueline replied as she walked over to the nurse's desk and took the quill pen and a piece of parchment to write a short letter. She wrote it with due haste, knowing that time was of the essence. When she finished, she blew on the ink to dry it as quickly as possible before folding it and sealing the letter with wax.

"Lucius, I need Constance to take this to the clocksmith Jacob McMaster on Cintras Avenue and bring him back here post haste."

"Milady, I need Constance to keep Gideon sedated. Her skills at this exceed even my own," Lucius argued.

"I'm sure that is the case, Lucius, but that will not be necessary. We need to place Marcus in a life support cocoon. It will be the only way that Jacob will be able to repair his heart."

Jacqueline's request stunned Lucius. It would leave Gideon inside the spell for nearly two hours, perhaps longer. "Jacqueline, this is quite unorthodox. I would prefer to wait until Mr. McMaster is here before subjecting Gideon to the harsh reality of the life support cocoon."

"There is no time to argue, Lucius," she interjected. "Constance can get there and back, quick and discrete. We must do it this way to keep his secret safe and to keep him alive."

Canon Cordell didn't like it but agreed with her assessment. He nodded over to his nurse, signaling her to stop her spell. She did so, quickly rising to her feet and taking Lady Jacqueline's letter. As she exited the room, Jacqueline sat down on the bed next to Gideon. She took him by the hand, holding it gently as he stirred, and awoke from the spell. He twitched and ached as the pain returned to cause him discomfort.

Jacqueline tried to sooth his pain as she explained the situation to him, about the damage to his clockwork heart and placing him in the life support cocoon while they retrieved Jacob McMaster. Gideon lay there and listened, focusing past the pain emanating from his chest. She could tell his biggest concern was for the armory above anything else.

Gideon violently coughed as he tried to catch his breath. He seemed agitated and unsettled. Barely with a whisper he asked for her to bring him his armory.

Jacqueline looked around until she found the Armory of Attlain. She handed it to Gideon, but before she could pull away, he held her hand to the armory with his. "Should I not survive this ordeal," he whispered, "I entrust you with the responsibility to choose my successor. I do so order this as a Magus of Attlain."

A crescendo of energy passed between their hands and the armory. Gideon released it, as even that little bit of magic wore him down. He did what was necessary to protect the Magus' legacy, entrusting it to Lady Jacqueline. "I accept the responsibility," she said as she cradled the armory in her hands and stood up.

"Okay, Canon," he gasped. "Let's do this."

"Clear your mind, Gideon. Shut out all the noise and sensations as best as possible. Focus on a good memory, something that fills you with joy. That will help you get through this. Hopefully, you won't be in it that long."

Gideon nodded his head as he closed his eyes and tried to find a happy thought. He focused on one thing that made him smile and gave him some peace . . . Wren's smiling face. Ever since he had arrived here, it gave him a sense of belonging. She welcomed him and helped him, something only two people did before her: Master Botàn and Lady Jacqueline. It helped clear his mind as he fell into the depths of the life support cocoon.

The waiting was overwhelming. Nearly an hour passed, and Constance had not yet returned with Jacob McMaster. Lady Jacqueline was beginning to get frustrated. *What is taking them so long? She should have been back by now,* Jacqueline pondered. *I spoke with Jacob about Gideon weeks ago. My letter should have been enough to get him to come here immediately . . . Unless?*

With that, she rushed out of the infirmary. When she stepped out the door, she saw something remarkable. The entire class was still hanging around outside in the hallway, waiting for news on Gideon. They were sitting on benches, on the floor, or leaning against the wall. Their faces were grim and sad as the unknown filled them with trepidation. The worst was Bartholomew, who seemed inconsolable.

Jacqueline was surprised at their concern, which honestly made her feel terrible for how she treated them earlier. She was primarily concerned about Bartholomew, seeing how this affected him, and she didn't want him to lose confidence. Jacqueline needed to talk to him now, but she also wanted to make sure that Constance was on her way with Jacob McMaster.

"Guilfoy, would you please go down to the front entrance and look for Nurse Constance?" she asked. "She will be escorting a specialist. Please bring them here immediately."

Guilfoy darted away, not hesitating for an instant. Jacqueline sat down next to Bartholomew. She wanted to put his mind and the other students at ease as best as she could. Bartholomew would not look up at her. He just sat and stared at the floor. Jacqueline put her arm around him as she looked at all the students.

"Listen to me, all of you. I'm sorry for getting angry earlier. Gideon is special to me because he was my closest and dearest friend's apprentice. I consider it my responsibility to finish his training, so something like this accident upset me dearly, but I should not have taken that out on you.

"As for Gideon, most of his injuries have been healed, save for one . . . His heart," she continued, wanting to explain things without giving away Gideon's secret. "You see, when Gideon arrived in Armändis, he was attacked by bandits, stabbed through the heart, and left for dead. Master Botàn did his best to heal Gideon, but it seems he didn't do enough."

The students listened to her story intently, gathering around close to not miss a single word. "The attack left his heart damaged, and his body was using his mana to keep the wound from getting worse. That's why Gideon couldn't control his mana properly. The consecutive duels exhausted him, and his wounds grew worse."

"So, it was my fault that he's hurt," Bartholomew muttered.

"Yes, Bartholomew, but it's not completely your fault. If we didn't find out about his injury now, Gideon could have been off on some adventure. And then, had it caught up with him there, he may have surely died. You saved him by exposing it now."

Before Jacqueline could say another word, she saw Guilfoy escorting

Constance and Jacob McMaster, but it was who was with them that caught her eye. Administrator von Straithmore followed close behind with two other mages. She recognized them as recently graduated third-year students, both with rather dubious reputations. Jacqueline stood up and walked over to Jacob McMaster. The old man was thin and slim with long stark white hair and a beard. He carried a haversack in one hand and a cane in the other. He wore a pair of wire-rimmed glasses, with many lenses spiraling off to each side of them on his head.

"Thank you, Guilfoy, you may rejoin your class," she said. "Jacob, thank you for coming so quickly."

"Yes, well, Lady Jacqueline, your letter did say it was an emergency." His voice wavered as he pulled out a pocket watch to check the time. "Where is the young man?"

Jacqueline motioned for Jacob to head into the infirmary while she stepped up to intercept the administrator. "Administrator, is there something you need?"

"Well, Lady Jacqueline, when I heard about the incident with Gideon, I took the opportunity to track down Mages Finnegan Osterman and Jules Davidoff. If something happened to Marcus Gideon, I thought it would be prudent to have him transfer the armory to one of them to ensure the security of the magical weapons inside."

"I see," Jacqueline remarked as she bit her lip, trying to contain her anger. "Is that why you delayed Constance from bringing my specialist to the infirmary? So, you could get these gentlemen here first? Are you deliberately trying to get Gideon killed?"

Her accusation smacked the administrator right in the face. He was taken aback and shocked by her accusation. "Lady Jacqueline, I assure you I had no intention of causing further harm to Marcus Gideon. My only intention was to protect the items within the Armory of Attlain!"

"That young man has been in a life support cocoon for over an hour now!" she shouted back at him. "Your delay will more than likely cause him to be in that cocoon for another hour. Do you understand what pain and suffering you have caused him through your arrogance and ineptitude?"

The students were shocked to hear that Gideon has been kept alive in that spell for over an hour. The fact that he would have to spend another hour within its confines angered the class. Many of them paid particular attention to remember this indignation toward their classmate.

"And for your information, Administrator von Straithmore, the armory is in safe hands," she seethed. "Gideon made me the caretaker of the armory until he recovers, and if—God forbid—something happens to him, it will be up to me to choose his successor, not you. Now, get those reprobates out of here; and I would advise you to keep your distance from me. Another misstep like this, and I will personally have you fired."

With that, she turned on her heel and went into the infirmary, slamming the door behind her. The administrator fumed, spun himself around, and trotted off in a huff with the two mages following close behind while grumbling about a waste of their time.

Lady Jacqueline entered the ward with a heavy heart but was thankful to see Jacob McMaster already at work. While Canon Cordell cast a reveal spell over Gideon's chest, Jacob used his intricate optics to get a closer view of the damage to his work. He took his time examining it as best as possible through the spell cast over his chest.

After a few more minutes of close inspection of the clockwork heart, Jacob stood upright and straightened his optics. "What in the world happened to this young man? Did someone beat him with a sledgehammer?" Jacob sounded bemused. "There are several damaged gears that need replacing, and it's severely out of alignment. And what is he doing with my mechanical heart, Lady Jacqueline? I designed and built this device for Henri Botàn."

"Jacob, it is too difficult to explain. Right now, I need to know if you can save his life?"

"Well, yes, it's mostly intact," he observed. "I have everything I need, but I will need to access the heart. That means" —the old man swallowed hard as a lump formed in his throat— "cutting him open."

"Canon Cordell has had training as a surgeon, so he will be able to provide you access while Gideon remains in the life support cocoon, but time is of the essence, Jacob. You must work quickly."

Jacob McMaster repaired clocks, pocket watches, and occasional odd machines, but none ever involved human life. "I will endeavor to do my best, milady. After all, it's my reputation that's on the line. This clockwork heart, as you call it, is my masterpiece."

Jacqueline usually despised prideful people, but in this case, she needed it to save Gideon's life. For the next hour and a half, Jacob worked diligently over his creation, changing out gears and fine-tuning the many nuts, bolts, and screws that held the clockwork heart together. He even replaced the thunderstone core in case the duel damaged the original from a lack of mana flow. When all was said and done, he finished the last adjustment and restarted the ailing mechanical heart.

The old clockmaker took a deep breath as he raised his optics. "Canon, if you would please, release Gideon from the cocoon. We need to see if the heart is working properly for him before we close the wound."

Lucius removed the life support cocoon spell while Nurse Constance reapplied the pain-numbing effect to his head through her cleric healing magic.

Gideon took a deep breath as if he was relieved to be free from the pain and sensory overload he experienced in the cocoon. His breathing became more manageable, not as labored as before. His color changed from a pasty white to a flushed pink as blood flowed again to all his extremities. His clockwork heart now beat at a steady pace, working better than it ever had before. Jacob finally breathed a sigh of relief as he carefully put away his tools.

While Lucius finished up healing Gideon's wounds and bandaging him up, Jacqueline escorted Jacob out of the ward. When they departed the infirmary, she saw that her students were still there, waiting for news. She whispered to Jacob as she stepped over toward them. "Gideon made it through the surgery. He's going to be alright." Her words gave the students a lift of hope from the day's events. Even Bartholomew wept openly in Susanna's arms, something he never did before.

"Now, it's late, and you all still have classes to attend tomorrow. I will get Prefect Onslott to cover my classes as I sit with Gideon until he awakens. Now, off to bed with you. Go!" she ordered as she headed back over to Jacob.

"Lady Jacqueline?" Wren shouted. "Can we assist in watching him for you? I mean, you can't do it all alone, and you need your rest too. We could take turns sitting in there with him if that's alright?"

Jacqueline considered her proposal quite seriously. She was glad to see this class finally coming together. "Very well, I'll let you and Mr. Ostentatious come up with a schedule, starting tomorrow afternoon, but you will still need to complete your assignments. I will not allow any of you to get behind in your work, is that clear?"

"Yes, Ma'am!" they all said in unison, thrilled that they would be able to aid in Gideon's recovery. Of all the students, Wren was incredibly relieved at the news. Her feelings for Gideon were growing, and she didn't know what to do with them.

Three weeks passed since Gideon's surgery and his clockwork heart's repair. He laid in the infirmary since then, sleeping soundly as his mind continued to process the sensory overload from the life support cocoon that contained him for nearly three hours. It was more than a human mind could bear, even for one as strong as Gideon.

As he lay there, stirring now and then, mumbling in his sleep, they watched him closely. His classmates took their turns sitting with him while the nurses tended to his every need. They used elixirs that emitted a billowing mist next to his head to lessen his pain and provide necessary nutrients for his slumbering body. This time out, it was Wren's turn to watch over him.

Wren sat next to Gideon, studying from her textbook while sipping tea. It was late in the evening, nearly 10 o'clock, as she kept to her studies. She stopped and looked up every once in a while when she heard Gideon mutter something, hoping for a sign that he was recovering and would wake up. Still, he slept on, tossing and turning from fever dreams brought on by the prolonged effects of the life support cocoon.

Constance heard him stammering and struggling as she came over from her desk to check on him. She felt his forehead, hot to the touch yet no perspiration. "His fever has returned," she said. "Miss, if you would, please go get some cold water and a cloth from the basin."

Wren put her book and teacup down as she leaped to her feet to assist Nurse Constance. She pumped the handle, pouring water into the bowl, before carrying it over to the nurse with a clean cloth. Constance wet it down before applying it to his forehead. As she dabbed it on his head, she looked down at the bowl of medicine next to him. Barely a wisp arose from the empty bowl.

"Miss Wren, if I may impose upon you to continue to dab his forehead while I run to get the herbs required to brew another elixir to help bring down his fever?" the catsei nurse implored.

"Yes, of course," Wren answered as she sat next to Gideon and took over, wiping his forehead with the wet compress.

"If you can, Miss, please wash it along his arms, neck, and chest as well," the nurse ordered. "It'll help bring his temperature down."

Trying not to be embarrassed by the instructions, Wren nodded and wrung out the cloth again before lifting Gideon's arm and running it along his skin. The sensation was enticing to her, but she tried not to think of it that way. Wren continued to run the cloth across his neck and chest, avoiding his bandages before going down his other arm. She felt his muscles, his skin, beneath her fingers. She was mesmerized to the point that she failed to see or hear Trini come into the room.

"What are you doing, Wren?" asked her friend, bringing Wren back to her senses.

"He has a fever." Wren rinsed out the cloth again. "Nurse Constance asked me to cool him down."

"Yeah, I can see that," Trini joked. "He looks pretty hot from here."

"Oh, stop it, will you, Trini, this is serious," Wren pleaded with her friend as she continued to pat him down carefully. "If his fever gets worse, it could prolong his condition or make it worse."

Trini stepped over to the bed and sat across from Wren, on the other side of Gideon. "I know, I know, it's just . . . Rubbing him down, those huge muscles, it makes you wonder," she said as she started to pull back on the sheet.

"Trini, what are you doing?" Wren implored.

"Well, every time I tried to sneak a peek at him, Nurse Constance was watching me like a hawk. I mean, come on, aren't you even a little bit curious?"

Remembering her encounter with Gideon in the bath, Wren smirked, like the cat that ate the canary. "No," she said, the sly grin strewn across her face. Trini gasped, her mouth agape at her admission.

"Demons!" Gideon shouted and sat upright, startling both girls. He grabbed them by their shoulders as he tried to get out of bed. "City of darkness . . . demon spire . . . They're coming! The demons are coming!"

"What the hell is he babbling about?" Trini asked as she struggled against his strength.

"I don't know," Wren replied before she noticed the blood pooling up in his chest bandage. He must have opened his wound with all this struggling. "Gideon, calm down, or you're going to hurt yourself!"

"The iron golem is failing . . ." he muttered . . . "Must stop the demons!"

Wren knew she had to reach him through the madness he was screaming and try to stop him from struggling. "Trini, I need you to restrain him. Hurry! I'll hold him while you cast the spell."

Trini jumped into action. *"Vinu Liganti!"* As she cast the spell, she blew air over Gideon's body. The air rushed out from her mouth and wrapped around his arms, swirling like a vortex as it held him in place. Once he was secure, Wren reached out and took Gideon's face in her hands, forcing him to look directly at her.

"Gideon, please listen to me, follow my voice and come back to me," she appealed. Gideon continued to mumble on about demons, his eyes glazed over. "Marcus, please, you can leave the darkness behind. Come back to me." Her voice was soothing and calm as it broke through the haze that fell over Gideon.

Finally, he looked out and saw Wren. His mind was clear, and he was awake. He shook his head and looked at the two girls in confusion. "Wren? Trini? What . . . Where am I?"

Both young ladies breathed a sigh of relief as Trini dispelled her "binding wind" spell. Wren helped Gideon lie back on the bed. "You're in the infirmary, Marcus. Do you remember what happened to you?"

Gideon racked his brain, trying to think as he pushed past the confusing haze that still fell over him.

"I remember the dueling arena, fighting Bartholomew," he recalled. "A giant stone fist beat me down, and then nothing. How long . . . How long have I been unconscious?"

The girls exchanged glances, nervous about telling him the truth. "Three weeks," Trini said. "They had to perform surgery on your injured heart. You were in the life support cocoon for more than two hours."

Gideon was shocked to hear it. He knew that the longer you were in that spell, the worst it was for your mind. That must be why he was unconscious for so long. Gideon wondered how much they knew. Do they know about my clockwork heart? he pondered until he realized that something else was missing.

"My armory? Where—" he asked, sitting up quickly, before he winced in pain from his reopened wound. Wren quickly helped him to lie back down.

"Lady Jacqueline has it," Wren explained. "You passed it to her to take care of it while you were unconscious. It's a good thing too."

"Yeah, Administrator von Straithmore wanted you to pass it on to one of his flunkies," Trini interjected. "Well, she put a stop to that and put ole' Dieter in his place." Relieved to hear this, Gideon settled back down on the bed.

"Trini, why don't you go and let everyone know that Gideon woke up."

Trini nodded her head, but, before leaving, she leaned down and kissed Gideon on the forehead, surprising both Gideon and Wren. "It's good to have you back, you big hunk," she remarked before she headed out of the ward. Wren couldn't believe her friend's forward nature. Gideon, however, didn't really mind the attention, although he still felt out of sorts. His mind was a jumble as memories from the past few weeks came flooding back to him.

Wren noticed his obvious pain. "Marcus, are you alright?"

"Yeah, just a headache," he mumbled. "Can I have something to drink? My throat is parched."

"Well, all I have is tea."

"That's fine," Gideon replied as he held out his hand. Wren was reluctant to pour him a cup. "Is something wrong?"

"Well, don't tell anyone, but I put a little honey brandy in my tea," she admitted. "I'm hesitant to give it to you, laced with the liquor, in your condition."

Gideon was genuinely surprised that this prim and proper princess had a little secret vice like that. "I don't think a little honey brandy will bother me," he told her. "It's not like I'm drinking a bottle down." His smile gave Wren the assurance she needed as she poured him a cup and helped him take a few sips. It was sweet and delicious to Gideon as he drank it slowly before lying back down. As he looked over at this beautiful young woman, his curiosity got the best of him.

"How much did Lady Jacqueline tell you about the injury to my heart?" he asked.

"She said you were hurt outside Armändis, stabbed in the chest," she explained. "Your master healed you, but not well enough, it seems. The duel with Bartholomew damaged your heart again. Lady Jacqueline brought in a specialist to repair the damage and heal you properly."

Gideon knew the specialist Wren mentioned must have been Jacob McMaster. It seemed that Lady Jacqueline stretched the truth with the other students to keep his clockwork heart a secret, but he needed to see for himself. That meant sharing his secret with Wren, but deep down, he knew he could trust her.

"Wren, I need you to do something for me, please."

"Of course, Marcus, what do you need?"

"I need you to cast a reveal spell over my chest," he said, his request shocking Wren. He realized she probably never looked at human anatomy before, and the idea of looking at his beating heart was a little bit revolting. Gideon could see the look on her face. "It's hard to explain why; it's just better to show you. I'd do it myself, but I'm still weak."

"No, no, I can do it for you," she answered as she held her hands over his chest.

"I need to warn you, it's going to be a little shocking, and I need you to keep it a secret. Can you do that?"

Wren wasn't sure why his heart would be a secret, but she wanted to earn his trust. With a nod of her head, she cast the spell. *"Revelá!"* she coaxed as the runic circle appeared, pulling back the skin, muscle, and bone until it revealed Gideon's clockwork heart. Wren looked shocked but equally mesmerized by the mechanized organ's steady beat. Gideon also observed his heart, relieved that the gears, the precision timing, everything, worked better than it ever did.

"That's incredible," Wren remarked. "But how? I've never seen anything like it."

"Neither did I before my master put it inside me. Don't ask me how it works. I'm just happy that it does," he said as he looked closely at his clockwork heart. "It looks like he reinforced it too. Hopefully, that'll make it harder to break down."

Gideon lay back as Wren dispelled her magic. He looked at Wren, hoping he didn't spook her with his revelation. "Thanks for doing that. I could have waited for Lady Jacqueline, but I wanted to know it was working okay."

"I appreciate the fact that you trust me enough to share your secret with me, Marcus," Wren conceded. "It means a lot to me. Thank you."

"Well, if you can't trust a princess, who can you trust." That revelation surprised Wren, since she never shared that information with him. Then she guessed who probably told him.

"Lady Jacqueline told you, didn't she?"

"As a warning mostly, not to talk loosely about certain things, like our little encounter in the bath," he disclosed. "Does the rest of the class know?"

"They do, but we keep it casual. During my first year, after I got to know everyone better, I decided to tell the class," Wren explained. "And it doesn't bother you? The fact that I'm royalty?"

"Why should it?" Gideon affirmed. "I mean, you don't act like a princess . . . You know, the spoiled little rich girl, pompous, needy, et cetera. You're just . . . you."

"I guess I'll take that as a compliment, I think?" Wren joked as the two shared a laugh. His impression of a princess was a bit skewed. As she poured some more tea for them, Wren wondered about his ranting and raving about demons and a city of darkness.

"Marcus, when you woke up, you were talking about demons. Do you remember?"

Gideon wracked his brain before he sipped some more tea. He remembered the visions he saw that broke him out of his slumber. "Yeah, I think I remembered something from my past . . . A forgotten memory."

"A memory? I don't understand?"

"I have little to no memories of my past life before I arrived in Armändis. It's all a jumble," he explained. "When my master saved me, he had to place me in a life support cocoon too. When I came out of it, I remembered my name and being a sailor from Bösheen. This time, I guess being in the cocoon for so long brought back some more vivid memories."

"Of demons? What exactly do you remember?"

Gideon took a deep breath before forcing himself to remember the horrors he saw. "I remember sailing into a city glowing with light. The harbor entrance was guarded by a massive iron golem, holding a shield and flaming sword. Suddenly, the city went dark, and a demon spire arose in the heart of the cityscape. Demons spilled out from the tower, devouring anyone and everyone. We fought them off until we were able to escape. The golem kept the demons at bay, contained within the city.

"I remember seeing three letters on a sign," he continued. "N-Y-X, Nyx! It said, 'Welcome to Nyx.'"

Wren was flabbergasted. "Marcus, you couldn't have been there," she stammered. "The demons destroyed Nyx thousands of years ago. It's a day known as 'Demonfall' across Attlain."

"Demonfall? You mean this place, Nyx . . . It's real?"

"Well, yes. As children, we're all told the story. Nyx was the shining jewel of Attlain, just to the northeast of us here near our border with Ishtar. Then, an evil wizard cast a spell that summoned a demon spire, a gateway to the netherworld. The demons poured out of the spire and into the city, killing most everyone there. Those who escaped saw their guardian fight to keep the demons contained on the island city.

"Now, no one goes to Nyx," she concluded. "It's too dangerous, even for adventurers. You must be remembering the story. You were probably told by your parents, just like I was. Kids are told about Nyx to scare us from wanting to become an adventurer."

"Yeah, maybe, it just seemed so real, like I was there." Gideon couldn't get past the fact that these memories seemed so natural, as if he was there, but he couldn't have been. "Wren, why are you here?" he asked as he took another sip of tea.

"What do you mean? Why am I at Basilon? I told you to learn to control my power."

"No, I mean, why are you here, watching over me?" Gideon asked. Wren turned red, a little embarrassed to answer.

"Well, we all took turns looking over you. Even Bartholomew spent some time in here. We all wanted to be sure you were going to come out of it, okay."

Gideon looked at her and saw the concern in her eyes, her face flush with emotion. "Well, I'm just glad it was your face I saw when I woke up."

Wren was caught off guard by his flirting, but before she could say anything, the door opened, and Lady Jacqueline walked in with Canon Cordell and Nurse Constance following close behind. Wren got up and moved away so they could examine Gideon.

"Well, Gideon, you gave us all quite a scare," Jacqueline said, concerned, but he could sense the relief in her voice.

"Yeah, well, it scared me too," he replied as he winced in pain from his chest wound.

"Don't move around, Gideon," Lucius said as he stopped him from twitching. "Let me check on your wound. I don't want you ripping it open again. Now please, lie still."

"Wren, would you please wait outside," Jacqueline asked. "The rest of your class is starting to gather out there. I'll come get you when you can all come in."

Wren gave a little curtsey to acknowledge the request as Lucius and Constance began to remove the bandage to heal his reopened wound. As she turned to leave, she heard, "Hey Wren," as Gideon called out, stopping her in her tracks. "Thank you!" Wren smiled and nodded her head before she left. Jacqueline noted the exchange between them.

"Anything you want to tell me?" she asked.

"Are you asking as my friend or as my instructor?" Gideon remarked, sidestepping the question.

"Both!" she shot back.

"Well then, no, except to say that she saved me from that dark void I was in," he commented. "I was lost, in a sea of endless darkness, and then I heard her voice and followed it back to reality. She saved me, Lady Jacqueline . . . She truly did." Gideon lay back and let the healers do their work. In no time, they completely healed his wound. Jacqueline sat on the bed next to him and cast a reveal spell to see his clockwork heart at work. Gideon didn't mention that he had Wren do the same thing for him.

"Everything seems to be in good working order," she said as she carefully examined the mechanized beating and whirring gears of his heart. "Jacob did an excellent job of making the necessary repairs quickly and efficiently."

"Not quick enough," Gideon interjected. "Wren said I was in the life support cocoon for more than two hours."

"Yes, and I'm sorry about that, but it was necessary to keep you alive. Besides, you seem to have come out of it, no worse for wear."

"I would warn you, Gideon, that you may continue to experience some fever dreams," Lucius added. "I would like to keep you here overnight to make sure there are no lasting effects, and then you need to spend another few weeks on bed rest. You need to build your strength back up before you start any strenuous activity."

"He means no Nært Crid until you're fully healed, understand?" Jacqueline ordered.

"Yes, Ma'am, I understand."

She dispelled the reveal magic and placed her hand on top of his. "You're very foolish, you know. You're a lot like Henri, and that's not a compliment. You need to be more careful. You are the last of your kind, Marcus Gideon, and the world needs a Magus like you to preserve the balance.

"Speaking of which, I have something to return to you," she said as she reached into the air with one hand. *"Sacchetta!"* she chanted as a rip in the fabric of reality opened. She stretched her hand into it and pulled out the Armory of Attlain. Jacqueline placed the armory in his hands.

"I return the Armory of Attlain to you, Marcus Gideon. I lay no claim to the armory or the weapons inside."

"I accept the Armory of Attlain and reclaim it as the sole master of the armory and the weapons herein," Gideon replied as a spark of magic passed between them. Before Jacqueline could remove her hand, Gideon took it in his and kissed it gently. "Thank you, milady."

Jacqueline smiled as a tear rolled down her cheek. Gideon knew Master Botàn thought of him as a son. He surmised Jacqueline thought of him the same way, something they both shared. Gideon wiped the tear from her cheek as she composed herself.

"Lucius, I have several students who would like to come in and say hello, if that's alright?"

With a nod of approval from Canon Cordell, Lady Jacqueline rose to her feet and went off the ward. When she returned, she was followed close behind by the entire third-year class. Everyone was all smiles, happy to see that Gideon was awake, except for one. Bartholomew hung back while everyone shook his hand or hugged him, glad to see he was up and about.

"Man, Gideon, you should have seen Lady Jacqueline put the administrator in his place. It was classic," Guilfoy remarked. "He tried to bring in one of his stooges to get the armory off you, but she told him off. It was awesome."

"Yes, I doubt he'll try anything like that again," Fiona added. "He did seem rather flustered by the whole affair."

"Speaking of flustered, you okay now, big guy?" Trini asked. "You were muttering some scary shit—I mean, stuff, when you woke up."

"Yeah, bad dreams, that's all," Gideon said as he looked over at Wren. She smiled and nodded her head quietly. She knew he wanted to keep his recalled memories a secret.

Gideon finally noticed Bartholomew hanging around the back with Susanna and Killian. "You okay, Bart?" he asked, causing all the students to turn and look at their estranged classmate. Since the incident, he had kept to himself as he wallowed in his guilt.

"Yeah, I'm fine, just glad to see that you're okay," he muttered. Susanna tried to comfort him, but Bart brushed her gesture away. Gideon motioned for him to come forward. Slowly, he stepped over next to the bed where Gideon lay. Susanna and Killian hung back right behind him, as if they were expecting the worst.

Gideon looked up at him and noticed how glum and less confident he seemed. He knew that Bartholomew felt responsible for his condition, and maybe he was a little bit, but Gideon didn't want the young man to get antsy in a fight because of it. It would ruin his future as a magic caster and an adventurer.

"You know you owe me a rematch," Gideon said as he held out his hand. "Our last duel was technically a draw, right?" Bartholomew saw that Marcus was trying to make amends, and he was happy to see he didn't hold it against him. He took his hand and shook it heartily as his smile widened, and his heart was relieved.

"Well, it'll have to wait until Lady Angelica lifts my suspension," Bart replied. "I'm not allowed in the dueling arena right now."

"That's okay. I don't think I'll be dueling for some time either." The two shared a laugh as the rest of the class joined in, happy to see that they resolved their differences.

"Alright class, you can visit with Gideon some more later," Lady Jacqueline said with a clap of her hands. "Let Canon Cordell get back to his treatment. Once Gideon is back in his room, you can all help him catch up on his missed work while he continues his recovery. Now, all of you, shoo!"

Everyone said their goodbyes as the students slowly filed out of the infirmary. Gideon exchanged pleasantries with them, but he kept his eyes on Wren. She passed a glance his way, smiled, and flashed a wink before Trini and Fiona pulled her away. He was falling for her, hard, and it didn't matter that she was a princess. To Gideon, she was the girl that saved him from the darkness, and he was forever hers.

12 A BASILON TRADITION AT THE RED DOOR

Gideon's Journal – I don't know what was worse . . . Lying unconscious or forced bed rest. For someone like me, being stuck in bed was dreadful. Every time I tried to get out of bed, just to stretch my legs, either Nurse Constance or one of my classmates forced me back in under threat of telling Lady Jacqueline. Even I knew better than to get on her wrong side. The one time I did get out long enough to stand up, I got so weak-kneed that I collapsed to the floor, in turn, that ripped open my chest wound, which brought about the wrath of Canon Cordell, Lady Jacqueline, and Wren. So, I gave up on trying and took my time to recover—over a month in the infirmary and another month recovering in my room. I spent the majority of our winter break in bed. The good news is that I'm stronger than I was before. My mana flows better, making it easier for me to cast spells. I think this is what Master Botàn sensed in me when he saved me at the crossroads years ago.

In the meantime, I finally met Jacob McMaster. He is a funny little man, but his attention to detail is extraordinary. He examined my clockwork heart for over an hour through the reveal spell. He was meticulous in his examination as if he was looking at every gear's precision timing, every crank, as it caused my heart to beat steadily. Once he was satisfied, he proclaimed it a rousing success. He was so happy with his work, and he reminded me to stop by and see him occasionally, so he can check on it, free of charge. Even Lady Jacqueline was shocked as she knew his reputation.

Catching up on all my missed classwork was relatively easy, thanks to my fellow students. I don't know if it was guilt or concern, but they all went the extra mile to get me caught up. I can't tell you how great it felt to be brought into this class by the entire group finally. My reputation has grown across the whole campus. Other students from other courses stop by, from time to time, introduce themselves to me and ask all sorts of questions. I think this entire incident may have ended the Magus' stigma, at least for this generation. Now, I can focus my mind and body on becoming one with my magic.

Tonight was a rather prestigious yet mysterious night for the third-year students at Basilon. As tradition dictates, when third-year students reached the halfway point of their final year, they made their way to the infamous Red Door Tavern in Le'Arun. The Red Door was an adventurer's tavern, one of the oldest in the city. It was home for many of the "brave and the bold" that ventured out of the city limits, keeping them safe from the monsters that lurked in the countryside, serving the best beer and food imaginable. It's an honor when invited into this sanctuary, but there was an unknown factor at play. No one knows what happens inside the Red Door, and past graduates won't talk about what to expect with the students.

This has been a rite of passage for more than two hundred years for magic casters. Every one of the third-year students must arrive together, in their student robes, at the Red Door at approximately seven o'clock in the evening. There were many rumors about what to expect, causing some students to consider anything and everything additional they might want to wear or bring with them. The entire evening turned the academy into a gossip factory as whispers were heard from one end of the school to the other.

Gideon finished dressing for the evening as he buckled the armory across his shoulder. Unlike the rest of his class, he didn't have a student robe, but he also didn't want to go out unprepared. He wore his padded leather long coat over his vest and hooded tunic, making final adjustments before holstering his Dragoon as he headed out the door.

He was concerned about running into Duarté Dartagni at the Red Door, as was Lady Jacqueline, which probably was why she asked to see him before leaving for the tavern. However, he was running late, concerned that most of the class was waiting for him. Gideon rushed toward the stairs, running into Wren. She was coming up the stairs as he turned to go down, and they almost bowled each other over.

Wren was dressed as she usually did, with one exception. She wore a rather large rimmed witch's hat. It had a large circular brim, buckled trim with a pointed top—quite the unusual fashion choice in Gideon's eyes. "Oh, sorry, Wren," he started to apologize until he noticed her hat. "Wow, that's some hat."

"Yes, well, it was a suggestion of Lady Gwendolyn, the Royal Magician at Celestrium, before I came here," she explained. "She wouldn't tell me why, just that it would be practical for me to wear tonight."

"Yes, well . . . What is it about this whole event? No one seems to know what's going on, and those that do are very hush-hush about it."

"It's a part of the tradition at Basilon," she replied. "They don't talk about what happens at the Red Door, so no one knows what to expect. Anyway, I was coming to get you. We're all gathering at the front gate. We're supposed to go down to the tavern together as a class."

"Yes, well, you'll all have to go on without me," Gideon explained. "Lady Jacqueline asked to see me at the last minute. I was on my way there when I bumped into you, so I've got to run. You go ahead. I'll catch up with you as soon as possible."

With that, Gideon took off down the stairs and headed toward Lady Jacqueline's quarters. Wren was left speechless as she went to meet up with the rest of the class. Gideon raced across the campus, knowing that time was of the essence. Once he reached Lady Jacqueline's quarters, he caught his breath before he knocked on the door.

"Come in," he heard someone say from inside. Gideon opened the door and stepped inside, finding Lady Jacqueline waiting patiently for him.

"Ah, Gideon, good. You haven't left yet for the Red Door."

"No, milady. I was about to head out when Madam Kokishi passed me your note. What's this all about?" he inquired.

Jacqueline took a deep breath. She needed to talk to him without breaking the "school code" about tonight's events at the tavern. "Gideon, you know you do not have to attend tonight's event at the Red Door. It's technically for students who attend Basilon for all three years."

"I understand that, milady, but I can't do that to these young men and women," Gideon explained. "Ever since the dueling accident, I've been working hard to not only gain their trust in me as a Magus but also to earn their respect. I can't do that if I don't show up tonight."

Jacqueline was impressed that Gideon was more concerned with his classmates than himself. "I understand. In that case, I won't ask it again. Now, I know you're expecting to see Sir Duarté there tonight, and he may very well be, but he usually doesn't engage in events like this. He considers it beneath him.

"Being the high-level adventurer that he is, Duarté has a private room up on the second floor, away from the riffraff down below. Just don't go looking for him, please," she implored. "If he comes to you, well, I know you'll handle it diplomatically. Just remember that the people inside that tavern consider him a God. Besides, there'll be enough going on that you'll get lost in the activities, but just try to keep a low-profile tonight."

"Yeah, about that. What the hell is going on at the tavern tonight? I mean, no one will talk about it, and there's nothing written anywhere about it. Even the locals don't know, or won't say, what is going to happen when we get to the Red Door."

"All I can tell you is that it's a Basilon tradition that every young magic caster has gone through for more than one hundred years. It's not something I agree with, nor participate in, but it is part of the culture here in Le'Arun," Jacqueline said. "I think once you experience it, you'll know what to do, but don't overreact."

With those words, Jacqueline opened her door for Gideon to leave. He got the hint, knowing that his classmates probably already left for the tavern. He bowed politely, taking her last words to heart, as he rushed out the door. As Gideon left, out of the corner of his eye, he saw Jacqueline as she closed the door behind him. He imagined that she would sit and wait, into the night, praying for Gideon and the rest of her class would survive the ordeal at the Red Door.

Gideon rushed down from Basilon through Le'Arun, until he reached the Red Door Tavern. The tavern was a large building, taking up nearly an entire city block. There was no sign or sigil, just its namesake: Two large red doors, standing tall at the center of the building. This tavern's popularity was so renowned that others tried to paint their doors red to lure in adventurers new to the city. It got so bad that the Red Door's owners petitioned the city council for an order that no other tavern could paint their door red. In doing so, the Red Door stands alone with its unique doors as a symbol of its status in Le'Arun.

When Gideon reached the entrance, he heard the familiar tavern sounds—rousing song, drunken cheers, and loud banter—but along with that, he heard crashing booms of objects being thrown across the room, followed by the sloshing sound of spilled liquid. The last thing any adventurer would do was spill their drinks. They're too valuable, especially to those who risk their lives for little reward.

When he stepped inside, it was complete chaos, not something he would expect from the best adventurer's tavern in Le'Arun. Like most taverns, the Red Door had a long bar across the back with tables and booths scattered about the floor. Inside the front entrance there was a long staircase to one side that led up to a second level, reserved for top-level adventurers. There were tankards of ale flying across the room as laughter broke out every time one hit, and Gideon could see where they were aiming.

At a large circular table, his classmates sat together in the far corner. They were huddled under their robes, hoods, and large hats as they were drenched in the sweet, sticky liquid regularly tossed their way. People took tankards of ale and threw them at the corner table one at a time. What caught him by surprise was the fact that they were just sitting there, taking it.

The other thing that surprised him was that different magic casters around the room were not participating in this free-for-all. They sat at the tables with their adventurer parties, sipping their drinks quietly, not even looking at the students. They've been through this themselves and didn't relish watching or participating in the initiation.

Gideon made his way over to the corner table with the rest of the class as he pulled up a chair and sat down. "Sorry for being late. What have I missed?" he joked as another tankard clanged off the wall, spilling ale all over him and the rest of the students. "Okay, somebody needs to explain this to me?" he spouted with anger as he reached for his Dragoon.

"No, Gideon, don't retaliate," Wren warned him. "We have to sit here and do nothing."

"Excuse me?"

"They told us the whole story when we got here," Guilfoy explained as more ale spilled on them. "It seems that, years ago, a group of students from Basilon came to the Red Door to celebrate their last term at the academy. The adventurers thought they looked weak and needed some toughening up, so they started throwing beer steins at them."

"Now, it's become an annual tradition for third-year students," Fiona interrupted. "We were told we have to sit here for the next four hours while they thrash us with ale. We are not allowed to move or retaliate against anyone."

Gideon couldn't believe what he was hearing. To think that adventurers were taking pleasure out of hazing these young men and women who were supposed to join their ranks after graduation. Before he could say anything, a rather large, drunken knight stepped up behind him. He wore a combination of chain- and plate-mail armor and carried a large sword on his back.

"Hey, what are you doing with these kids?" he slurred his words as he slapped Gideon on the back. "Only students from Basilon are supposed to be sitting here."

"I am a student," he snapped at the drunk. "These are my classmates, you moron."

"Well then, you're late," he stammered. "You need to catch up to them!" The drunk poured his entire tankard over Gideon's head as he laughed out loud, causing the rest of his party to laugh and cheer. Gideon had had enough of this, and the others saw that look on his face.

"Oh dear, this is not going to end well," Fiona remarked.

"You got that right," Trini added.

Gideon reached out and grabbed the knight by his armor. *"Congelatu!"* he chanted as a wave of frost emitted from his hand. It spread through the metal armor until the metal froze against the knight's skin. His face went white as the frost that covered his body overwhelmed him. Gideon stood up and pushed the frost-bitten fighter back toward his party. "You might want to warm him up, sweetheart. He's going to need it!" Gideon joked toward one of the female members of his party.

Others around the room stood up and started to draw weapons at Gideon. *"Freya!"* he commanded as he reached behind his back. He didn't want to expose himself as a Magus just yet, so he made it look as if he was drawing it from under his cloak. He slammed the icy mace into the floor, sending out a wave of ice along the path of all the liquid on the floor, walls, and tables.

"Sorry, but I've got something to say about this little initiation of yours," Gideon announced to the tavern. "Afterward, you can do what you want, but if I see anyone draw a weapon or cast a spell, I'll put this entire tavern in a block of ice. Is that clear?"

No one had ever seen a weapon like that before, especially in the hands of a magic caster. They all muttered amongst themselves before they sheathed their weapons and sat back down. Gideon picked up Freya and dispelled its icy magic before moving it behind his back and returning it to the armory to maintain his secrecy.

"My name is Marcus Gideon, and yes, I am a third-year student at Basilon," he said. "I know it's hard to believe, but let's just say I got a late start. These young men and women behind me are my classmates; they are my friends. I came here tonight thinking this would be a grand celebration to honor the final leg of their studies as magic casters, and instead, I find a bunch of drunken reprobates dousing them with stale beer . . . No offense, barkeep."

"None taken. I always give out the old stuff for tonight anyway," the bartender shot back, causing everyone to chuckle a bit. Gideon liked the fact that he was at least honest about it.

"So, am I to understand that this entire exercise in futility is to toughen them up before they become adventurers? Is that right?" Gideon asked. Everyone in the tavern chimed in together, agreeing with that assessment. They all used words like "tradition" and "necessary" to explain.

"Okay, then you all must have gone through a similar initiation, too, right?" Gideon surmised. The mumblings around the room told Gideon that none of them did. "You, barbarian," Gideon said as he pointed to a muscular, bare-chested barbarian sitting across the room. "Did your teachers make you push some enormous wheel of pain for no reason to build up your strength?"

"Bah, no," he spouted, using as few words as possible.

"No, okay, how about you, Ranger?" Gideon asked as he turned to another adventurer in the room. "Did they put fake turds on a trail to throw you off your game?"

The Ranger chuckled at the notion. "Not hardly."

"No, well then, what about you, cleric?" Gideon said to a beautiful female priestess. "Did the high priest take you down into a secret room and paddle your bare bottom while making you recite scripture?" Gideon's scenario caused everyone to laugh and embarrassed the cleric. She turned red as she looked away from Gideon as if he discovered some secret.

"Certainly not!" she huffed.

"I see, so out of all the adventurers in this room, the only ones who go through some sort of initiation are magic casters, am I right?" he ascertained. Everyone in the room mumbled and discussed it amongst themselves, but they all came to the same conclusion. He was right. "And you think that's fair? These young men and women have dedicated their lives to learning magic. All they want to do is be like you, adventurers, protecting the people of Attlain, go out on a dungeon crawl, maybe raid some ancient tomb. And the way you welcome them into your ranks is by pelting them with ale?"

The mutterings amongst the adventurers grew louder this time, with words like "weaklings" and "toughen up" being tossed around with "scared" and "stupid" when describing magic casters. Those comments upset many people, especially the other magic casters in the various parties.

"Okay, fair enough . . . You want to talk about tough," Gideon said as he motioned toward his classmates. "Trini, tell them what you did when bandits attacked your caravan."

Trini paused for a moment before speaking. She stood up and turned toward the room. "I was traveling to Le'Arun from Solara by caravan when bandits attacked us in the Iron Wasteland. We were getting slaughtered, but I was able to whistle up a sandstorm that drove them away."

Gideon smiled and winked at Trini, letting her know she did a good job. "She did that when she was fourteen-years-old . . . Fourteen! I'd call that pretty tough," Gideon surmised. "And you want to talk about scary? Meet Guilfoy Guilderhof. Guilfoy, tell them about the first thing you did when you learned shadow magic."

Guilfoy knew what Gideon wanted him to talk about as he stood up and faced the adventurers. "One of the first shadow spells I learned was how to summon a shadow demon," he explained. "My parents never let me have a pet, so I summoned a shadow demon and played with it like he was . . . well, a puppy."

The room broke out laughing, as did the rest of the class, but they also found it very brave and quite unusual. "How many scared kids do you know that have a shadow demon for a pet? Huh?" Gideon exclaimed as he patted Guilfoy on his shoulder. "And stupid, I think I heard some of you say? Fiona Greenleaf can speak and read all thirteen magical languages, plus ten other languages of the realm on top of that."

"Eleven, actually, Gideon," she corrected him. "I learned Entish over the winter break." Everyone was quite impressed with the young Alf.

"And Bartholomew here, our class leader," Gideon added as he motioned toward Bartholomew. "He has memorized more than one hundred spells, with the possibility of another one hundred combinations of those spells at his disposal. You can't fake that kind of knowledge and power." Bartholomew's chest puffed up with pride, and his chin rose at Gideon's praise.

They were all impressed with Gideon's stories about his fellow students, but they were not wholly convinced. "So, if you want to continue to pelt them with beer, go right ahead," he said as he moved between the room and his classmates, "but I will stand here to stop you. These students have a promising future, and I won't let you dampen it with your stupid initiation."

The adventurers were getting irritated by Gideon's delay tactics—shouting various insults and derogatory hand gestures at him—until someone else spoke up.

"Neither will I," said one of the other magic casters, who got up from his table and stood next to Gideon, defiant of the others.

"Nor I," said another as she joined in. Soon, all the magic casters in the tavern stood with Gideon, forming a wall between the adventurers and the students. Their act of defiance left the students in awe, but they were the only ones. The rest of the room just grumbled when they realized that their fun was going to end here tonight.

"Hey!" shouted one fighter from the back of the bar. "Who the hell do you think you are to spoil our fun tonight?"

Gideon took one step forward, flipped his cloak off his shoulder, exposing the armory, and held out his hand. He knew that this wouldn't sit well with Lady Jacqueline, but he needed to do it. Not only would it help protect his friends from this initiation, but maybe—just maybe—it would let Sir Duarté Dartagni know that there was a Magus in Le'Arun, and he wasn't afraid of him.

"Come to me, Shatterstorm, Sword of the Storm Giants!" he shouted. Out of nowhere, as if it dropped from the heavens, a giant sword fell in front of him. It was a massive weapon, more than eight inches wide and five feet in length, with a hilt more than two feet long. The sword glowed bright blue as lightning danced up and down the blade. Gideon grabbed it by the handle and picked it up with ease as he held the massive sword out in front of him. Everyone in the tavern was left speechless at the sight of this great sword. It even caught the attention of those upon the second-floor balcony as they looked down at him in awe.

"I am Marcus Gideon, the Last Magus of Attlain. You got a problem with that?" Gideon stood there, sword in hand, as he looked out across the tavern at all the adventurers. They stared at him, both at the magic sword he possessed and in disbelief that he was a Magus. No one could have mistaken the Armory of Attlain that sat upon his shoulder. Even the other magic casters next to him were impressed.

As if in unison, the assembled adventurers shook their heads and dismissed any challenges directed toward Gideon. He immediately dispelled the sword as it disappeared back into the armory. Gideon reached into his coin purse and pulled out a small bag of gold he had set aside for emergencies. He tossed it toward the bartender, who caught it and carefully examined the contents.

"Bartender, the next round is on me!" Gideon shouted. "And make sure it's the good stuff and not this watered-down piss!" Gideon's actions brought a rousing cheer from everyone. He knew he made a good impression, and from the congratulations and introductions by the other magic casters, it was a step in the right direction. Maybe he wouldn't be as misconstrued or looked at skeptically as a Magus.

Once all the congratulations were over, he sat back down with his class, who lowered their hoods and removed their hats, grateful that Gideon saved them from any further degradation. "Gideon, why on earth would you buy a round of drinks for the very people that were tormenting us?" Susanna asked.

"Tell her why, Guilfoy," Gideon said.

"The easiest way to an adventurer's heart is through the drink," Guilfoy responded. "Their next adventure may be their last, so they enjoy the night as best they can. Buying them a drink showed them that Gideon respected them and what they do."

"Wow, Guilfoy, you can be insightful when you're not drunk," Trini jested, causing everyone to break out in laughter.

"But, won't you get in trouble for using your armory?" Takeshi asked.

"No, I don't think so," Gideon replied. "My agreement with Basilon stated I would not use the armory on school grounds. We are definitely not on school grounds."

As everyone at the table discussed the merits of what Gideon said, he noticed a calico cat up in the rafters. The cat lay there and stared down at Gideon, as if it was watching him. Before he could say or do anything, the waitress brought a tray of drinks to the students. "Here you go, everyone," the catsei woman said as she passed out the booze. Her blonde hair and buxom frame were offset by her rather large ears and a bushy tail, almost like a leopard's. After she passed out the drinks, she grabbed Gideon by the face and planted a deep, wet kiss on his lips.

"Thank you, love," she said when she finally released him. "You don't know how hard it is to clean this place up after this lot throws ale around for four hours. You just saved the girls and me a long night of cleaning." She picked up her tray and went back to the bar, where there were more drinks to pass around. Gideon smiled, happy with his reward until he saw his classmates' faces. The boys were jealous of him, and the girls were angry that he allowed her to take such liberties with him, and he liked it—especially Wren, who just glared at Gideon.

Before Gideon could say anything, he felt a hand on his shoulder. "Do you mind if I join you?" a voice asked. Gideon looked back at the stranger behind him. He didn't recognize him at first, but he knew who he was in an instant.

He stood tall, very sure of himself, with an air of superiority about him. He had neatly trimmed black hair starting to thin in the front, but it still framed a very handsome face. He had a simple goatee, just on his chin with no mustache and teeth as white as pearls. He wore gold orichalcum plate mail armor under a leather coat with a collar trimmed in white fur. His vambraces and greaves were also orichalcum. Around his waist hung a magnificent broad sword with a curved guard that resembled an angel's wings.

The sword was Durandal, Holy Sword of the Archangel, once a part of the Armory of Attlain. The man was Sir Duarté Dartagni, Paladin of Le'Arun, the man who tried to kill Henri Botàn. Gideon remembered Lady Jacqueline's words about being "diplomatic" should Sir Duarté present himself. He also noticed the faces of his classmates. Their eyes grew wide and mouth agape at this legend standing before them.

"No, please do," Gideon said as he motioned for Sir Duarté to sit down. An adventurer at the next table immediately gave up their chair for the paladin as he sat down next to Gideon.

"Well, young man, you made quite an impression here tonight," he started to say as he sat down, careful to move the sword aside to accommodate him. "I haven't seen anything like that in some time. I—" Duarté stopped himself when he looked across the table and saw Wren sitting there. He immediately recognized the First Princess of Attlain, jumped up from his seat, and bowed respectfully.

"Your Highness, I didn't know you were here in Le'Arun. If I had known you were going to be here tonight. . . ." He continued to apologize until Wren stopped him.

"It's alright, Sir Duarté," she interrupted. "I am attending Basilon as a student, not a princess. No one knows I am here, so I would appreciate it if you would just call me Wren and treat me like one of the students, please."

Gideon watched the awkward position Wren put him in as Sir Duarté slowly sat back down. "Of course, Your Highness . . . " He stopped and then corrected himself. "I mean, Wren."

"As I was saying, your actions caught many of us off guard, my young Magus," Duarté said, directing his comments at Gideon. "Your weapons remind me of a man I once adventured with."

Gideon was curious. Duarté was acting as if he didn't know that Botàn was dead. "Is it an act, or doesn't he know?" Gideon wondered.

"You must be referring to my master, Henri Botàn," Gideon exclaimed as Duarté appeared to feign ignorance of what he did to him.

"Ah, I knew it, Henri . . . How is the old rascal?" he asked inquisitively.

"He's dead; I'm sorry to say, almost a year now," Gideon replied. He watched Duarté closely as he tried to gauge his response. Surprisingly, the paladin was genuinely shocked when he heard the news. Duarté was either a good actor or honestly didn't know.

"Oh, well, I'm sorry too. Henri was a good man and an excellent magic caster. I can see some of that in you, Gideon."

"Thank you, Sir Duarté," Gideon said. "I must admit, you are exactly as Master Botàn described to me."

"Oh, and how is that?"

"Well, at the start of each day, he would tell me stories of your adventures together," he explained. "He often referred to you as heroic, strong, and vividly stoic. Then, as the day progressed, he started drinking, and his opinion of you diminished. By sunset, he was so drunk he called you every name in the book, from a dirty rotten liar to a backstabbing son of a bitch."

The table went quiet as everyone looked at Gideon with their mouths agape. The fact that he just insulted the Paladin of Le'Arun was unbelievable, but before anyone could say anything, Duarté broke out in laughter. It was a deep, roaring belly laugh that even got the other students laughing along with him as Gideon sat there and smiled.

"That does sound like Henri!" he exclaimed as he laughed so hard, he had to wipe a tear away from his eye. "So, where did you train with Henri?"

"Armändis," Gideon replied. "It was a good place to train as a Magus, especially with all the creatures in the Imestrüs Forest at our back door."

"Indeed, indeed, so then tell me, why are you at Basilon? Surely, with your experience, you don't need any other academic training?"

"To be honest, I have been learning a lot at Basilon," Gideon interrupted. "Master Botàn focused his training on basic magic and controlling the weapons within the armory. At Basilon, I am learning so much more about being a magic caster."

"Well, I think you're more than ready," Duarté exclaimed. "I would like to offer you a place in my party. Selene, my wife, can continue your magical training while you play an important part in protecting Le'Arun. What do you think, Gideon?"

It was not the first time Gideon heard Selene's name, the woman who sent out the guild contracts. In an instant, he knew it was a trap to bring him into the fold then kill him to get their hands on the armory and weapons therein. When Gideon glanced over at his classmates, their faces showed how impressed they were with his offer for Gideon.

"Thank you, Sir Duarté, I appreciate your generous offer, but I'm afraid I must decline, at this time," Gideon said. "Master Botàn wanted me to finish my training at Basilon, and I must respect his wishes. I'm sure you understand."

Gideon could see that Duarté was disappointed that he didn't jump on his offer but tried to hide his concern. "Well, I can certainly understand that," he replied. "Perhaps we can talk again after you finish your studies."

"Oh, rest assured, Sir Duarté, we will talk again. You can count on that," Gideon said as he courteously held out his hand to him. The paladin took him by the hand and shook it as a good-faith gesture.

"Well, I will let you and your classmates continue your celebration," Duarté said as he got to his feet. "And well done, all of you." He gave a courteous nod to Wren, still the knight even in an awkward situation like this, as he returned to his compatriots upstairs.

After he left, the others all chimed in at the same time, congratulating Gideon on such a prestigious offer. Typically, students don't get offers until the end of the final term, which was extraordinary, especially if it came from the top adventurer in Attlain.

"Marcus, why on earth would you turn him down? That was a tremendous honor," Wren insisted.

"You're going to turn down Sir Duarté Dartagni? Are you kidding me?" Bartholomew interjected.

"That was a chance at a prime spot," Guilfoy exclaimed. "I mean, do you know the kind of money you can make off a gig like that?"

Gideon sat there and drank his ale, listening to them ramble on about meeting Sir Duarté and the offer, but his mind was elsewhere. He hated the fact that he came face-to-face with the man responsible for his master's death, and he just smiled and laughed, acting as polite as could be. He would have to be patient.

"Gideon?" Wren said, bringing him out of his haze. "Are you alright? What's wrong?"

He hesitated to say anything as he knew how much they idolized Dartagni. They wouldn't understand what he was thinking or what he was going through when it came to the Paladin of Le'Arun. Still, they were his friends, and they might listen to him.

"It's nothing really, it's just . . ." he started to say until he stopped to take another drink.

"It's just what?" Trini asked.

Gideon sighed. "You wouldn't believe me if I told you."

"Believe what, Gideon-san?" Takeshi responded.

"That I just met the man that caused the death of my master, and I didn't do a damn thing about it."

The festivities at the Red Door ended early for the students. As much as they wanted to enjoy the rest of the night, it was difficult to do that after the bombshell Gideon dropped on them. He explained things as best as he could—the bounties sent to guilds by Selene Dartagni, the story Botàn told him about the vampire cave incident, and how the other Magus gave up their weapons in fear of their life. Even with all the facts he presented, no one believed, especially Wren. She chased him through the streets of Le'Arun, sometimes walking backwards so she could get in his face.

"You're wrong, Gideon, you're wrong! You've got to be!" Wren insisted as she pursued him across the academy grounds toward the dormitories. "You don't know Sir Duarté as I do. He couldn't be involved in this scheme to hunt down and kill the Magus."

"I'm sorry, Wren, but I'm not wrong. His wife, Selene, was mentioned by the three people involved in my master's death," Gideon explained. "And you don't toss around a name like Dartagni, especially in a far-off place like Armändis.

"And that ridiculous story of how he received Durandal is an outright lie to cover up the fact that Duarté stole the sword from Master Botàn when he deserted him and left him to die in that vampire's cave," he concluded.

"He wouldn't do that!" Wren shouted as she shot ahead of Gideon and cut him off, poking her finger deep in his chest. Her fingers were flickering with flames as her anger grew. Gideon knew that she would have burned a hole in his shirt if he wasn't wearing his armored jacket. "Sir Duarté and Lady Selene Dartagni have sat at the dinner table with my own family. They are not the kind of people who lie and scheme, and I know that."

"Look Wren, I know you have a history with Sir Duarté, which is why I was hesitant to tell you and the others about this," he tried to explain. "He has a reputation that's undeniable and quite frankly untouchable, but I know the truth."

"No, you know your version of the truth, and I will not let you tarnish the good name of Sir Duarté Dartagni!" Wren shouted before she stormed past him. Trini, Fiona, and some of the other girls went off with her toward their dormitory while the rest hung back with Gideon.

"You can't blame her for being angry," Guilfoy said. "It's like you said, Sir Duarté is a legend in Attlain. It's hard for any of us to believe that he's involved in something like this."

"I know, Guilfoy, and I don't blame you if you don't believe me either. It's something that I have to deal with."

"It's not that we don't believe you, Gideon," Bartholomew insisted. "It just doesn't add up, that's all."

Before Gideon could answer him, he heard a voice that he was not expecting to hear. "Marcus Gideon!" Jacqueline shouted. He cringed as he turned to see Lady Jacqueline standing across the way with Nurse Constance next to her. Gideon remembered back to the Red Door when he noticed the little calico cat watching him from the rafters above. Some members of the catsei can shapeshift into cats, mostly clerics who considered it a blessing by the Goddess Bast. Constance must have been spying on him for Lady Jacqueline.

"Well, this isn't going to be pleasant," Gideon remarked. "Any of you want to help me out here?"

Everyone shook their heads and took a step back. They knew better than to step into one of Lady Jacqueline's lectures. Gideon chuckled. "Cowards," he remarked, but in retrospect, he didn't blame them one bit as he walked over to speak with Lady Jacqueline.

"Good evening, milady . . . Nurse Constance. Nice night for a walk, isn't it?"

"Don't get coy with me, Gideon. What the hell were you thinking summoning Shatterstorm in the tavern? Do you have a death wish?" Lady Jacqueline argued.

"Milady, can we continue this discussion in private, please?" Gideon asked. "I know that Nurse Constance has probably filled you in on most of the details from this evening's exploits, so I would like the opportunity to explain myself, if possible."

Jacqueline bit her lip, then pursed them as she contemplated what to do. "Alright, come with me," she said as she turned to leave. "Thank you, Constance, that will be all." The catsei nurse gave a polite curtsey before turning and went the other way. Lady Jacqueline didn't say another word. She just turned and headed toward her quarters, clanging her staff rather loudly on the cobblestones with every step she took. Gideon knew that she was angry and quickly followed her. Once inside, Jacqueline didn't hesitate to let loose on her student.

"So, which part of keeping a low profile, didn't you understand?" she snapped at him. "Exposing yourself as a Magus for all to see, garnering the attention of every adventurer in Le'Arun, including Dartagni."

"That's right, and he fell right into it," Gideon replied. "I'm sure Constance told you that he came over to our table and had a nice little chat with me. He even offered me a place with his party."

The shocked look on her face told Gideon that she might have left that part out. She either didn't tell her or didn't hear their conversation. "And what did you tell him?"

"I said no, of course, but I left enough rope out there for him to hang himself and his accomplices, whether it's here or at the Helios Arcanum."

"I don't follow you, Gideon."

"Sir Duarté didn't know me or anything about me," Gideon explained. "He was even surprised to hear about Master Botàn and that we lived in Armändis. So, right about now, he's reaching out to his informants and co-conspirators to ascertain as to why none of them told him about Master Botàn or me."

Jacqueline listened to his assertion, and, in all fairness, Gideon could see it made perfect sense to her. "That's why you went to the Red Door tonight. You wanted to draw out his informants."

"Yes, milady, I did. It will be easier to determine who the conspirators are after being put under significant pressure by Sir Duarté. You should inform Lady Gwendolyn of that fact so that she can keep an eye out at Helios."

"Yes, well, that may be a dead-end," she interjected. "She contacted me earlier this evening with some news on her investigation. The Arcanum expelled Selene Dartagni after she tried to take forbidden texts out of the library at Helios. No one at Helios would help her, or else the Arcanum would expel them too."

"So, then the leak must have come from here at Basilon. My actions tonight should draw him or her out."

"Be that as it may, I wish you wouldn't have done this without consulting me first," Jacqueline admonished him. "What would you have done if it didn't work? Would you have fought the entire bar?"

"I was pretty sure they wouldn't attack," Gideon surmised. "Most of them were so drunk; I doubt that any of them were even capable of lifting a sword. Speaking of drink, do you have any more of that Jaxouth Whiskey? I could use a drink right now."

She could see he was hurting. Something happened beyond what he was telling her, so maybe a drink would help open him up. Jacqueline went over to her side table, picked up a cut-glass bottle, and poured out two whiskey glasses. She took one herself and handed the other to Gideon. "So, from the look on your classmates' faces, I take it you told them about Sir Duarté," Jacqueline asked.

Gideon took the glass and drank it down in one gulp, hoping it would ease his conscience. "Yeah, I know, I shouldn't have done that. I'll take the blame for that one. I just felt so bad after meeting him. I needed to tell someone."

"To be honest, I thought that was a good idea on your part," Jacqueline explained. "You're going to need allies in any future fight with Duarté and his people. Your classmates are the logical choice."

"Yeah, well, unfortunately, they don't feel that way. It's like you said, Lady Jacqueline, he's a god to the people of Attlain, especially the young people. I'm going to need hard evidence to convince them that he's not this saintly paladin they believe him to be."

"Especially, Wren," Jacqueline noted. Gideon let out a big sigh. He'd known Lady Jacqueline for less than a year, yet she knew him so well.

"Yeah, especially Wren. She doesn't understand."

"Gideon, you have to understand the royal family. Dartagni did an excellent job of rooting himself into them from the very beginning. He made himself an integral part of their lives. To them, Sir Duarté is a part of their family."

"So, what should I do?" he asked as he finished his drink.

Jacqueline didn't say anything at first. She just took the glass from him and set it next to hers on the bar cart. Her hesitation concerned Gideon, making him question things himself.

"For now, don't do anything; continue with your schoolwork and finish your training. Your classmates will come around once the evidence against Sir Duarté is clear. Give it time, Gideon, just give it time."

13 KIDNAPPING A PRINCESS

G*ideon's Journal – Time is something I have plenty of nowadays. Besides Guilfoy and a few others, most of the class aren't speaking to me. I'm avoided at every turn like I've got the plague. They are really into their hero worship of Sir Duarté, and I shit all over it, so, in turn, they're shitting on me.*

Now that we're near the end of our term, the third-year students can go out on the town on weekends. While the others spend their off time in the taverns—singing, drinking, and celebrating—I spend my time in the library, reading. There's nothing else to do. Guilfoy offered to go out with me, but I declined. He needs to be with his peers, making the rounds to the various adventurer taverns. It's how students get scouted for selection at the end of the term. I don't want to take that away from him. We made it out a couple of times when Montag was in town, but I kept to myself beyond that.

The hardest part of this affair has been the wayward looks I get from Wren. She's so angry with me that she can barely bring herself to look at me. Her stares stab me in the heart like daggers. She's torn between her friendship with me and her family's relationship with Sir Duarté. It has turned her bitter, and that's not a good look for her. I tried talking to her a couple of times, but she ignored me completely, so I've just given up on it for now.

It's like Lady Jacqueline said, the time will come when Wren and the others will learn the truth about Duarté, and when that happens, I'll need their help in bringing him down

Wren sat quietly by herself at a table in the Red Door Tavern. She carefully wrote a letter home while sipping on some honey brandy, her favorite drink. The tavern was sparse as most of the adventurers were out of the city, clearing out the monsters in the outer areas. The few that were there were busy drinking and singing around the bar. Guilfoy and Trini were there with them, making headways into the ranks with the other adventurers by joining in with their drink and song. It's a tradition for them to spend the night away raising the tavern roof in music. Wren was not in the mood for such revelry and just wanted to spend the time finishing her letter home.

She tried to be positive and uplifting in her letter, but she was confused and heartbroken, unable to write. She wanted to ask her parents for advice on what Gideon told them, but she didn't know how to ask. Since she was a child, she had known Sir Duarté, and she couldn't imagine him involved in this affair with hunting down Magus and killing his master. Still, there was no reason for Gideon to lie, hence the conflict in her mind. She didn't know what to do. Her concentration was further interrupted when two figures approached her table.

"May we join you, Your Highness?" Sir Duarté asked as he made a slight bow to the princess. Next to him, his wife Selene curtseyed toward Wren. Selene was a beautiful woman with burgundy hair and full lips, colored the same as her hair. She wore a form-fitting black and white dress, cut low in the front down to her belly button. Gold chains stretched across the fabric, keeping her ample breasts inside her dress. She carried a black oak staff with a white crystal embedded in the top as if the tree branch grew around it.

Their presence startled Wren, but she smiled and put on a good face to hide her confusion. "Yes, of course, please do," Wren said, motioning to the table. "It's good to see you again, Lady Selene. It's been, what, four . . . no, five years since I saw you last?"

"Indeed, Your Highness, at your thirteenth birthday party," she said as she took a seat. "I wish you would have let us know you were here in Le'Arun. We would love the opportunity to host you in our home instead of Your Highness staying in the school dormitories."

"Oh no, I don't mind it, really I don't. It has given me a new perspective on life outside Celestrium," Wren said. "Besides, it was my parents' idea for me to maintain a low profile, so please, call me Wren while I'm here."

Just like Duarté, Wren could see Selene was taken aback by the informality. She just nodded her head politely at the princess. "Of course, Wren."

"It's odd to see you, sitting by yourself," Duarté remarked. "Where are all your classmates?"

"Well, a few of them are up there at the bar, but the rest decided they had enough festivities for one night. I was trying to finish writing a letter home to my parents."

"And where is your friend, the Magus, Marcus Gideon?" Selene asked. "I was hoping I would get the chance to meet him and perhaps persuade him to accept Duarté's offer to join our party."

Wren hesitated, not wanting to present Gideon's outrageous accusations to them. "Well, he's had a lot of catching up to do—with his work, I mean—so he is spending his free time studying." The look on their faces told even Wren that they didn't buy her flimsy excuse.

"He said something about me, didn't he? Gideon, I mean, about my relationship with his master, Henri Botàn," he asked Wren.

His directness took her by surprise. Wren stumbled and stuttered, unable to find the words to answer him.

"It's alright, Your Highness. I expected as much, but you must believe me; none of it is true."

Wren was relieved to hear that her fears about them were unfounded until Sir Duarté began to expound on his comments. "You see, what Gideon doesn't know is that Henri Botàn was a liar and a traitor," he continued, catching Wren off guard. "Henri was one of the Magus who led the Magus Rebellion against the crown. He escaped from the wrath of the king and the Helios Arcanum by running away, something he was very good at doing. When I first met him, he lied to me about his status as a Magus, you see. It was only after I found out who he truly was that I realized I had to do something about it."

Wren couldn't believe what he was saying. Not only did it contradict Gideon's story, but it also rejected what Lady Jacqueline told her and what her own research uncovered about Henri Botàn. Gideon may have lied, but not Lady Jacqueline too. It just wasn't possible.

"So, then, what happened in the vampire's cave?" Wren inquired. "Gideon said you left Master Botàn to die in there?"

"Oh no, it was the other way around," Duarté interjected. "You see, I confronted Henri about his true nature as a Magus as we made our way through the vampire's cave. He got angry and scared that I discovered his secret. He ran from the caves just as the vampire lord attacked. Alone and with no one there to help me, the Archangel Michael blessed me with Durandal to defeat that evil foe. After I escaped, Henri was nowhere around. I decided to let him go unless he showed his traitorous head to me again."

Wren had heard this story before. He told it many times, but this was the first time his story was different. Wren looked at him as she noticed a bead of sweat dripping down from his forehead. He was nervous. She could see that. Duarté Dartagni was never nervous. Wren was starting to believe that maybe there was some authenticity to what Gideon said.

"Listen Wren, we would like the opportunity to tell Gideon the truth about his master," Selene added. "Perhaps you could convince him to speak with us so that we can explain things more clearly."

"You want me to bring Gideon here?" Wren inquired.

"Oh no, it would not be proper here," Duarté said. "You could bring him to our home, at Essex Square. That would be a more private setting, in case, well . . . In case things get out of hand."

Wren could see it now. It was all a ploy to get Gideon alone so that they could steal his armory. They were not the people she believed them to be. I have to warn Gideon, she thought. Wren carefully folded up her unfinished letter and placed it inside her robe.

"I will ask Gideon about it the next time I see him," Wren said with a smile as she tried to maintain her composure. "Is Sunday a good time, say seven o'clock?"

"That would be perfect, Your Highness, but I would advise against telling him it's me," Duarté cautioned. "Perhaps you could just invite him as a guest for dinner with the mayor or some other dignitary of Le'Arun, eh?"

"I'm sure I can do that," Wren said as she got up from the table. Duarté and Selene followed suit, as protocol dictated. "Now, if you'll excuse me, I'm going to head back to the school to finish my letter."

"Of course, Your Highness. Please give your family my kindest regards," he replied with a bow as Selene curtseyed. Wren turned to leave. She wanted to get Guilfoy or Trini to go back with her, but they were having too much fun at the bar, so she decided to leave on her own.

"Do cover-up, Wren; it's starting to rain," Selene warned her. Wren gave a polite nod as she pulled up the hood of her robe before leaving the bar. Wren was afraid, deathly afraid for Gideon. She could see what deception they were capable of, which frightened her.

Gideon walked through the halls of Basilon, paging through a book on protection magic. He crammed as much as he could, preparing for the next leg of his journey once he was finished at the magic academy. Gideon had also been hanging around the school as bait. He hoped that whoever Dartagni used as an informant at the school would zero in on him, but Gideon had yet to sense anyone observing him. They're either very good at deception or biding their time.

Dartagni must know that I'm only going to be here a few more months, Gideon scrutinized. What's he waiting for? Gideon's rumination was interrupted when he saw Bartholomew, Susanna, Killian, Fiona, and Takeshi walking toward him. They were soaking wet as if they had just stepped out of a storm, yet when Gideon looked out a nearby window, the night sky was clear and he could see stars twinkling in the canopy above.

"What the hell happened to you? Did you have to swim across the river to get here?" Gideon joked.

"It's not funny, Gideon. It's pouring rain over the city," Bartholomew said as he shook out his robe. "It stopped just as we crossed the bridge."

The fact that it was raining just over the city was odd to him. Most storms would follow along the mountains, not centered in the valley like that. Before he could ask another question, a familiar voice yelled from behind.

"Bartholomew Ostentatious!" yelled Madam Kokishi as she approached the group quickly, with Administrator von Straithmore following close behind. Her breathing was fast and heavy. Gideon knew something was wrong.

"Bartholomew, where is Wren?" Madam Kokishi asked, her voice quivering with urgency.

"We left her at the Red Door with Guilfoy and Trini," Bartholomew answered.

"What's the matter, Madam Kokishi? What's wrong?" Gideon interjected.

"That's none of your concern, Gideon," Dieter snapped back at him. "We are merely trying to ascertain where Wren is at this time. You—"

"We received word from the Obsidian Court of a potential kidnapping attempt against the princess," Madam Kokishi interrupted. The Obsidian Court was the magical intelligence organization within Attlain. These were wizards, thieves, and assassins—answerable directly to the Crown—that kept a watch on potential threats, both internally and externally.

"Madam Kokishi, that is confidential information," the administrator argued. "He doesn't need to know the reason." Before he could say another word, Gideon handed von Straithmore his book and took off down the stairs and out of the dormitory.

"What the hell is he doing?" Dieter asked as the other students quickly followed behind him.

"I believe he's going after her," Madam Kokishi said with a sly grin.

Gideon ran as fast as he could across the grounds of Basilon, stopping just as he stepped through the gate that led outside school grounds. Before he started on the winding road down the mountainside, he looked down at the city, studying the storm that hovered over it very carefully.

"Gideon, what the hell?" Susanna asked. "What's going on?"

"Look at that!" he said, pointing toward the storm. "It's not moving, yet the wind is blowing to the east. That's no ordinary storm. It's a fifth-tier magic spell, Control Weather. Someone's causing it to pour rain right over the heart of Le'Arun."

"But why?" Fiona asked, and then she realized the answer to her question. *"Mwên Rœnmęn Ænpil!"* she spouted in her native tongue. "They want to weaken her flame magic!"

"Exactly, the kidnappers are already there, which is why we have to move, now!" Gideon said as he leaped over the stone rail. Instead of following the winding path down the mountainside to the bridge across to Le'Arun, he took the direct approach. *"Levitar!"* he chanted, causing him to float on runic circles with each leap over the walls, bypassing the roadway completely.

Takeshi and Fiona quickly moved to follow Gideon, but the others hesitated. "Wait a minute," Susanna said. "You don't believe him, do you?"

"Yes, Susanna, I do. Gideon is rushing to save our friend. What will you do?" Fiona said as she leaped over the rail with the others in quick pursuit.

Wren left the Red Door, sloshing through the mud with every step. The rain fell like weights pushing down on her from above. She could barely see where she was going through the fury of the storm. The water poured down from the sky like a curtain of rain, blinding her vision. In just a few steps, the rain-soaked her to the skin.

Suddenly, Wren bumped into someone. "Watch where you're going, sweetheart," he coyly said as she tried to maneuver around him.

"Sorry," Wren apologized, but he continued to block her movements. "Excuse me, please," she said politely, but she noticed he didn't move out of her way. She couldn't see behind the black hooded cloak covering most of his face. Even his leather armor was dark and dingy.

"Slow down, honey; maybe we can escort you to where you're going," he sneered with a mischievous grin. Wren didn't understand what he meant at first when he said "we" until she saw four others move in to surround her. They were all dressed in the same dark cloaks and light armor, each one carrying either a sword or multiple daggers. They all looked like local thugs, not the seasoned adventurers that usually hung around here.

"No thank you. I can find my way home," Wren said as she pushed her way past him.

But the brigand grabbed her by the arm and said, "Oh, I insist, Princess."

In an instant, Wren knew something was off. They knew who she was, which frightened her, but what did they want? She knew that her fire magic was practically useless in this weather, so she had to try something else.

"Forza Lancet!" Wren chanted as she motioned with her hand toward the stranger. A wave of energy pulsed outward from her fingertips and propelled him across the street, slamming him into the nearby building. He dropped to the ground, groaning in pain.

"Oh no, you don't," said another man as he grabbed Wren from behind, putting his hand across her mouth. "No casting for you, my pretty little witch!"

Wren struggled against him, but the man was quite strong, so she tried a different tactic. Not needing to cast a spell to summon flames, Wren breathed fire out of her mouth, shooting a piercing flame through the palm of his hand, like a blow torch through metal. Even the cold rain couldn't stop her from using her flame power like this. The intense flare burned hot and fast and the man screamed in agony as he released her, but before she could escape, two others grabbed her by the arms and put blades to her throat.

"Say another word, and we'll cut your throat," one of them threatened her.

"You okay, Soka?" the other man asked. He continued to scream as he shook out the pain in his hand, holding it out to the chilly rain to try and temper the burn.

"No, I'm not!" he said as he lashed out and punched Wren right across the face with his good hand. She fell to the ground, landing hard as the mud splashed around her. Soka repeatedly kicked her in the stomach and chest, causing Wren to cry out through her busted jaw. "You damn bitch!" he screamed as he continued to inflict punishment on her.

"Knock it off, Soka. We were told to bring her in unharmed," one of the men told him. "If you kill her, we won't get paid."

"Oh, I'm not going to kill her, but I am going to teach her a lesson! Hold her down!" he ordered. They hesitated at first, but Soka leered at them until two of the men knelt next to Wren and held her down. Soka lifted her on her knees and raised her skirt. Fear swelled within Wren as she knew what he would do to her. She couldn't scream for help or cast any spells as the pain from his attacks overwhelmed her so much that she couldn't fight back. Wren didn't know what to do.

She looked over at the door to the Red Door tavern and saw it slowly begin to open. She knew that someone coming out would help her. Suddenly, standing in the doorway was Sir Duarté Dartagni. The Paladin of Le'Arun opened the door halfway when he noticed what was going on in the street. Wren could see him looking straight at her. Their eyes met through the heavy downpour. He stared at her for a moment, but he just stood there and did nothing. Wren watched as he turned back to the room and offered to buy everyone one more drink. The people cheered, the door closed, and with it, any hope Wren had of being saved.

"I don't know about you, Princess, but I'm going to enjoy this!" Soka said. He adjusted his trousers down as he was about to assault her. Then out of nowhere, a blade-chain whipped out and wrapped around his neck. In one swift motion, his head was cut clean off, the spurting blood mixed with the falling rain and mud on the ground as his body collapsed. The whip-blade retracted back to its source as the other assailants turned to see Gideon standing across from them.

He wielded Bonesaw, a magic sword that extended out to attack from a distance. The whip-blade was especially good at killing zombies, hence its nickname "the Broken Sword of Certain Death." The other students soon came up behind Gideon, drawing their magical arms, ready to fight.

"Takeshi, disarm them!" Gideon ordered as he whipped his sword at the two pinning Wren down. The whip-blade snapped toward them, scaring them off the injured princess as they jumped back toward the others. "Fiona, Susanna, take care of Wren!"

They followed his orders without hesitation. Gideon's battle experience made them listen to his commands. While the girls checked on Wren, Takeshi drew back his bow. *"Kasai!"* he shouted as three magic arrows formed on his bow. They burned blue with a ghostly flame, making them immune to the rain. When he fired them, they flew into their weapons, burning them from the inside out, causing the brigands to drop them instantly.

"Bart, Killian, contain them!" Gideon said as he stood ready if any of them tried to run or fight back. The two earth mages slammed their weapons—a shillelagh for Bart and a hammer for Killian—into the ground.

"Terra Capisce!" the two chanted almost simultaneously. The earth moved like a wave across the ocean as the mud and cobblestones swirled toward the three remaining assailants. Once the rolling ground reached them, the terrain opened and swallowed them all the way up to their necks. The weight of the rock and soil kept them immobilized.

Once the fight ended, Gideon dismissed Bonesaw and rushed to check on Wren. "How is she?" Gideon asked as he looked over her beaten body. Fiona continued to chant a healing spell while moving her wand over Wren.

"She's in bad shape, Gideon," Susanna said. "Fiona's healing magic will stabilize her injuries, but we have to get her back to the school now. Without Canon Cordell's healing, she could die."

Before Gideon could say anything else, the storm overhead increased. The wind howled, and the rain started pouring even harder as thunder and lightning suddenly appeared across the clouds. Gideon looked up as the lightning flashed. He saw a shadow on a nearby rooftop, hands extended into the air. He surmised it must be the sorcerer casting the weather spell, but he couldn't get a clear view of his location because of the storm.

"The wizard casting the spell is up there," Gideon said, pointing to the rooftop. Before he could say another word, a lightning bolt arched down from the sky, right at him. *"Aegis Aspida!"* he shouted just in time, summoning his magic shield to protect him and his classmates from the lightning.

"He's trying to stop us from leaving with Wren!" Takeshi shouted over the storm.

"You think?" Bartholomew shouted. "We need to get up there and stop him!"

"Good luck with that," Killian added as another lightning bolt arched down and struck the shield. Gideon calculated all their options, trying to come up with a plan.

"Takeshi, can you fire a dispel magic spell into the clouds? It doesn't have to be powerful enough to permanently dispel the storm. All I need is an opening for a few seconds."

It didn't take him long to consider what Gideon asked of him. "Hai, Gideon-san, I can!"

"Susanna, I need you to take over shielding us!" Gideon ordered her. Susanna shook her head as she covered her ears, scared as the thunder roared and the lightning flashed.

"Gideon, I can't! The lightning will get through, and . . . I just can't!"

"Susanna, listen to me, you can do it, just like I told you! The lightning won't touch you or any of us. I promise you!"

Susanna remembered what Gideon told him about her water shield. She knew she couldn't fear lightning her entire life. Susanna had to stand up to it and protect her friends at the same time. She nodded her head at Gideon as she took a position directly behind him.

"I'll let you cast your spell before I drop my shield, okay?"

Susanna agreed as she pulled out her orb and cast her spell. *"Come forth oh waters of Aquarius, bearer of seas and bringer of life, to protect me with the power of the ocean and prevent my enemies' strife! Acqua di Aquarius!"* she chanted. The orb glowed as the water pulled in the rain from everywhere around her. It spread out until it was the same size as Gideon's shield. *"Purificà!"* she added as a wave of magical energy burst from the orb. The water within the shield glowed until it became crystal clear. Even as more rain added to its mass, the water remained clean and pure.

Gideon dropped his shield and quickly moved around behind Susanna, just as another lightning bolt arched down. When it struck her water shield, the lightning dissipated with ease. Susanna smiled, happy and relieved that it worked. Gideon gave her a grin as Bartholomew came up and put his hands on her shoulders.

"You are amazing, babe!" Bartholomew said, kissing her on the head to show her his appreciation.

"Takeshi, get ready to fire your spell. *Come to me, Will O' the Wisp, Bright Bow of the Forest!*" Gideon barked as he summoned the alf magical bow into his hand. The sight of this ancient weapon startled everyone, but especially Fiona.

"Gideon, you have possession of *Bow de Sholas Síoraí*, and you didn't tell me?" she asked.

"This is not the time, Fiona," Gideon snapped back as he drew back the bow, summoning an arrow of pure starlight. "Susanna, as soon as the storm disperses, drop your shield." Susanna nodded her head at Gideon. "Takeshi, now!"

Just like before, Takeshi drew back his bow. *"Fusshoku Suru!"* he howled as an arrow of ghostly blue flame appeared on his bow. He released the arrow, and it flew skyward into the clouds. It exploded, sending cascading waves of energy through the storm. In an instant, the clouds disappeared, revealing the dark evening sky. Gideon saw the wizard staring up into the empty sky and took his shot.

Susanna dropped her shield, and Gideon followed right behind her, firing his arrow of light at the wizard. The bolt of starlight raced upward and went right through him. The sorcerer couldn't protect himself. He fell over and off the roof, down to the street below. He crashed onto the mud and cobblestones, breaking his neck.

Gideon dismissed his bow; his biggest concern right now was Wren. He knelt next to her, worried about her injuries. "Can we move her?" he asked Fiona.

"Yes, but we must act quickly, Gideon," Fiona added. Gideon saw that their battle started to draw a crowd as the storm's sudden end intrigued people out of the taverns and homes. Gideon saw the door to the Red Door tavern open. Sir Duarté stepped out and saw the students around Wren, including Gideon. The last thing the Magus wanted was a confrontation right now.

"Takeshi, go get the magistrate and bring them here!" he told the Yamatanese student. He nodded his head and took off to the magistrate's office. "Bart, Susanna, you two stay here and keep an eye on them," he added, nodding toward the captured brigands. "When the magistrate gets here, tell them what happened." Before he said another word, he put his hand on Bart's shoulder. "Make sure you tell the magistrate I killed those two men," he whispered. "I don't want you guys taking the blame for my actions, okay."

Bart nodded his understanding.

"Killian, I need you to come with Fiona and me, in case they have any friends out there," Gideon added as he picked up Wren as gently as he could.

"Don't you worry, Gideon, no one will stop us from getting the princess safely back to the school," Killian stated as he slapped his hammer in his hand.

"Gideon," Wren muttered softly through her busted jaw. "I'm sorry. . . ." She passed out from the pain and went limp in his arms. Gideon held her tight as they took off for Basilon. As they left, Duarté stood there on the Red Door's steps with his wife, Selene, surrounded by his party.

"He's vulnerable right now," Selene whispered to her husband. "We can take the armory!"

"No, Selene, we can't," he snapped back. "There are others with him. If anything should happen to the princess in an attack, it might come back on us. No, not tonight . . ." Before he could say another word, Guilfoy and Trini pushed past them and ran over to Bartholomew and Susanna. They saw the two dead bodies and the captive thugs.

"Hey, guys, what the hell happened?" Guilfoy asked breathlessly.

"They tried to kidnap Wren, but they didn't count on us," Bartholomew said.

"Or Gideon!" Susanna added.

Wren slept, but it was not a comfortable sleep. Her mind stirred with darkness and laughter. All she could see was the face of her attacker, grinning as he kicked her, punched her, and continued to assault her. She twisted and writhed in pain, terrified as her nightmare repeated. Over and over again, she was beaten, bloodied and attacked, until her mind couldn't take it anymore.

"No!" she screamed as she sat up. She found herself in bed, in the infirmary at the school. The pain she felt in her dreams was justified as her body ached from her injuries. She was wrapped in compression bandages to protect her and help her body heal. As she sat up, she went right into the arms of Gideon, who tried to calm her down.

"Easy, Wren, don't move around," he said softly. "It's alright. You're safe now. You're in the infirmary at the school. You're safe."

Her eyes welled up with tears and she started to cry uncontrollably. She fell forward into Gideon, clutching onto him tightly as she buried her face in his chest. He wrapped his arms around her and comforted her as best as he could. As she started to calm down, Nurse Constance came back into the infirmary, carrying some clothes and extra bandages, when she saw that Wren was awake.

"Your Highness, you must not move around," she warned as she set her parcels down. "Please, lie back down."

Gideon gently laid her on the bed as she composed herself. Constance took out a handkerchief and wiped away Wren's tears from her eyes. "Gideon, would you please step outside while I check her bandages and dress the princess?"

Gideon turned to leave but Wren reached out and grabbed his hand. "No, please stay," she pleaded. "Can't he stay, Nurse Constance? Please? I would feel safer if he was in here with me."

Gideon wanted to be respectful toward the princess, but Constance needed to understand the fear behind Wren's request. Gideon knew she wanted him nearby to protect her. His presence was a comfort to Wren. "Alright, Your Highness, he can stay. Gideon, please, turn around if you would?"

Gideon nodded and turned his back to them while Constance tended to the princess. Even then, Wren had some questions for him.

"Gideon, how did you know to come looking for me?" she inquired. Gideon explained about the warning from the Obsidian Court and the rainstorm centralized over Le'Arun, followed by the students racing down the mountain to save the princess. He waited for the one question Wren had yet to ask.

"What about the man who attacked me? What happened to him?" Wren asked.

Gideon paused for a moment, not sure how to tell her. "He won't be bothering you, ever again," he assured her, calmly and succinctly. Wren closely listened and quickly realized what Gideon meant. He killed him. Gideon killed him for what the kidnapper did to her. Wren never thought about another man's death before, but she was glad he died.

Constance finished redressing Wren's wounds and helped her with a nightgown before she lay back down. "Alright Gideon, you may turn around," she said as she picked up the old bandages to throw them away. "I'll inform Canon Cordell, and Lady Jacqueline that you're awake, Your Highness," Constance said as she gave a slight curtsey before leaving.

Gideon sat back down on the edge of the bed and looked at Wren.

"This is a little weird. Usually, it's the other way around," he joked, trying to interject some fun in a bad situation. Wren smiled and laughed, just what Gideon wanted to see.

"Ow, don't make me laugh, Gideon. It hurts," she complained.

"Sorry, Wren. I just like it better when you smile."

Wren tried to compose herself before she reached out and took Gideon by the hand. "Gideon, I'm so sorry . . ."

"Sorry? Sorry for what? Wren, you have nothing to apologize for."

"No, I've been mean and dismissive of you these past few weeks, and I'm sorry."

"Wren," Gideon said as he took her hand in both of his. "It was a simple disagreement between friends, nothing more. You don't have to apologize."

"No, Marcus, I do. I do, because . . . You were right. You were right about Sir Duarté."

Gideon was shocked by her admission and rightly confused. "What do you mean?"

She took a deep breath and composed her words before speaking. "Before I left the tavern, Sir Duarté and Lady Selene came up to me," she started to explain. "They told me that your master was one of the Magus traitors, that he lied to them to hide from the purge. His whole story about the vampire cave changed too. He lied right to my face, and then they asked me to bring you to their house, so they could 'talk to you' about Master Botàn and 'tell you the truth' as they saw it. I knew it was a trap, and I was coming to warn you when they attacked me."

Gideon was furious that they would use her to get to him, but he could tell there was something else she wanted to tell him. "What, Wren? What else happened?"

"He was there, Sir Duarté, in the doorway of the Red Door." Tears flowed down her face as Wren started crying again. "He looked right at me, as that man was assaulting me, and he did nothing. He just closed the door and went back inside the tavern."

Gideon steamed until his rage exploded. This so-called paladin stood by and let that monster assault Wren. He leaped to his feet and started to leave, but Wren wouldn't let go of his hand. "Gideon, wait, where are you going?"

"I'm going to kill that son-of-a-bitch," he fumed. "How dare he call himself a paladin while he stood there and watched you suffer at their hands! I'm going to rip his damn heart out! I'm—"

"No, Marcus, please, don't go. He'll kill you. You can't fight him and his entire party. Please! I . . . I don't want to be left alone," Wren pleaded. "Please . . . Stay with me!"

Gideon listened to her pleas. He wanted to get Dartagni, but Gideon knew that this was not the right time to go after him with anger. He needed to be patient. Right now, protecting Wren was, first and foremost, his only priority. He nodded his head as he sat back down on the bed, not wanting to excite or upset her anymore.

"Where is everyone else?" Wren asked to quickly change the subject.

"Takeshi, Bartholomew, and Susanna were waiting on the magistrate to tell them everything that happened," Gideon began. "Fiona and Killian went to inform the teachers and staff about what went down, and Lady Jacqueline was going to speak directly to your mother and father."

"Why didn't you go with them?"

"Well, I had to stay here to protect you in case there were any further attempts," Gideon added with a smile.

"So, you've appointed yourself my knight, my protector?" Wren joked. She looked at Gideon and laughed, but his face was stone-cold serious.

"From the moment I met you, Your Highness," he said with a stern, straight face.

"Oh please, don't call me that. I hate it when my friends use that ridiculous title with me. Don't ever call me anything but Wren, even though it's not my real name. I prefer it."

"So, what is your real name, if I may ask?"

Before Wren could answer, the door to the infirmary opened. He immediately let go of her hand and stood up to ensure no one would get the wrong idea of anything improper. Gideon expected Lady Jacqueline or Canon Cordell, but instead, Administrator von Straithmore entered with someone he didn't recognize. The stranger appeared to be a member of the magistrate's office by his armor and uniform. He looked familiar to Gideon as if related to someone he knew, but Gideon couldn't be sure.

He wore a sturdy scale mail armored chest piece under a royal blue long coat with armored pauldrons, vambraces and greaves. He carried a long sword at his waist and two daggers strapped to his boots. He was not a man to trifle with, especially in a fight. His reddish-brown hair and full beard hid a rather prominent scar across his cheek, probably from one of the many street fights between adventurers the magistrates break up from time to time.

They both stopped just short of Wren and bowed politely. "Your Highness, it warms my heart to see you sitting up and doing much better."

"Thank you, Administrator von Straithmore, and who is this, may I ask?"

The magistrate took one step forward and bowed again to the princess. "Your Highness, I am Cornelius LoFan, Chief Magistrate of Le'Arun," he started to say. Gideon immediately recognized the name. He's related to Tyrion LoFan in Armändis, a son perhaps. Gideon noted how much he looked like a younger version of his father.

"First, I must humbly apologize to Your Highness. The ineptitude of my office resulted in your attack and injury. I can assure you it will never happen again. For the remainder of your stay in Le'Arun, we will be doubling our patrols and routing out the riffraff throughout the city."

"Thank you, Magistrate LoFan, but no apology is necessary. It was something none of us expected."

"Nevertheless, Your Highness, I must offer my most sincere apology, but I am also here on another matter," he continued. "I'm afraid I must place Marcus Gideon under arrest."

The sudden admission shocked Gideon and especially Wren. "What? Whatever for, Magistrate? He killed that man in defense of my life."

"It is not that man's death that is in question, Your Highness," Cornelius continued. "He was a known criminal, and his actions warranted Gideon killing him. I am referring to the wizard casting the spell over the city, causing the rainstorm. He was from Ishtar."

Ishtar was a small country to the northeast of Attlain. It was a wealthy country with a long line of nobility. With so many nobles in one land, Ishtar spread its influence into other countries through bribery, intelligence, and manipulation. Wren knew immediately why the magistrate would arrest Gideon, but the Magus was still in the dark. "I'm sorry, Magistrate, but what does that have to do with it?" he asked. "The wizard was part of the conspiracy to kidnap the First Princess of Attlain."

"It's obvious you don't know as much as you think you do, Gideon," the administrator interrupted smugly, angering Gideon. "There is a formal treaty between Attlain and Ishtar that protects individuals under the Ishtaran nobles' command from arrest or injury. They have, shall we say, a certain diplomatic immunity."

"So, you're telling me that a wizard, under the protection of an Ishtar noble, was attempting to kidnap a Princess of Attlain, and I was supposed to let him go?"

"You were not supposed to kill him as callously as you did," Dieter interjected. "He would have been held in custody and deported from Attlain, per the diplomatic agreement between our countries."

"He was hurling lightning bolts at the other students and me, trying to prevent us from leaving with the princess," Gideon argued. "If I didn't kill him, Wren could have died. I did what I had to do."

"I understand your predicament, and I empathize with you, Gideon, but I must adhere to the law," Cornelius concurred. "Unfortunately, the emblem he wore was unfamiliar to the Obsidian Court. Until we determine which Ishtaran noble this emblem belongs to, I have no choice." He held up a simple pendant. On one side was Ishtar's seal—a broken, burning shield surrounded by an infinite dragon. On the other side was an off-centered cross with a small circle in the upper left-hand corner and a triangle in the lower right-hand corner. The intricate pattern looked like a mishmash to Gideon, but it was a unique identifier for the Ishtar nobles.

"You will be taken into custody and held until the Obsidian Court confirms both the man's identity and the noble he answered too," Cornelius continued. "It will be up to the noble to determine your fate."

"And what if they can't find the noble?" Gideon asked. "What if that thing is a fake?"

"If there is no determination, then you will be free to go."

"But until then, you will be in the custody of the Magistrate," Dieter interrupted. "And because of that, you will need to surrender your armory to the school for safekeeping."

Gideon knew what the administrator meant. The moment he surrendered the armory, it would find its way to Selene Dartagni. Gideon stepped forward and got right in Administrator von Straithmore's face. His expression of anger and disgust startled Dieter.

"This is the third time you've tried to make me surrender my armory to you, Administrator," Gideon gritted his anger through clenched teeth. "I'm going to tell you now what I told you then. Only the king can take my armory away from me."

Dieter just smiled, like a cat who caught a mouse. "Well, I'm afraid, this time, you have no choice in the matter."

"Oh, yes, he does," Lady Jacqueline interjected as she entered the ward with her fellow teachers—Preceptor de Maestre, Prefect Simralin, and Lady Angelica—and their fellow students. The students quickly went over to Wren and Gideon, standing in support of their classmates. Dieter was furious that he was rudely interrupted.

"This is an administrative matter for the academy, Lady Jacqueline, and that clearly falls under my jurisdiction, not yours; and it certainly does not involve any of these students," he scoffed.

"No, Administrator von Straithmore, this is a matter for the Crown," she said calmly and sternly without looking at him. "And since I just spoke to His Majesty, I am here to relay his wishes. So, I suggest you step back and be quiet." Jacqueline finally looked at Dieter with a menacing stare. It frightened him when she invoked the king's name, so he quietly stepped away.

"Wren, your parents were happy to hear that you are doing better and look forward to speaking to you later after you've had a chance to rest," she started. "As for the rest of you, His Majesty wanted me to personally thank you for your diligence in rescuing the First Princess of Attlain. You will all have a personal commendation from the king entered into your records."

The students were delighted to hear they would receive a personal commendation from the king. It was a great honor for them and their families.

"Gideon, although His Majesty appreciates what you did to save his daughter, he also understands the delicacy of the situation regarding Ishtar. The king asks that you be patient while the Obsidian Court investigates the matter thoroughly," she continued. Gideon nodded his head. He knew Lady Jacqueline wouldn't steer him wrong, especially in something like this. Dieter looked elated to hear that Gideon would still be arrested and detained until Jacqueline added something to the conversation.

"However, His Majesty also doesn't want to interfere in you finishing your training at Basilon, so the senior instructors and I proposed a solution. Gideon will be placed under house arrest, restricted to the academy grounds. That way, he can be closely monitored and finish his schooling at the same time."

"What? No, that's impossible!" Dieter protested. "We don't have the security forces necessary to protect the school and watch over one student."

"His Majesty is sending a contingent of the *Cavaliere* as added protection for the princess," Jacqueline interrupted. "They will be sufficient for the task at hand."

Dieter could not argue with her point. The *Cavaliere* were elite knights of the kingdom. While at the school, Gideon would restrain from any activity outside the school and protect the First Princess.

"So, Chief Magistrate LoFan, will that be sufficient for you?" Jacqueline asked. LoFan rubbed his beard as he considered everything she told him.

"It would, milady, but to be perfectly honest, I don't know this man," he said, pointing at Gideon. "I don't know if I can trust him to abide by these conditions."

Gideon knew how to answer his dilemma. He reached into his coat pocket and pulled out the coin Tyrion gave him before he left Armändis. Gideon didn't say a word. He walked up to Cornelius and handed him the coin. The chief magistrate looked at it closely and was shocked as he recognized it immediately.

"Where did you get this?" he asked Gideon.

"In Armändis, from Magistrate Tyrion LoFan . . . Your father, I believe?" Cornelius nodded, and then flipped the coin in his hand.

"The Magus who challenged Maximillian Herrod . . . That was you?"

Gideon confirmed it was. Cornelius stared at the coin in disbelief, lost in the thoughts of his father.

"I asked him, time-and-time again, to get out of that place. He dedicated his life to that job and the people of Armändis. He just wouldn't leave. You saved him from a lifetime of aggravation." He handed the coin back to Gideon.

"Lady Jacqueline, I am satisfied with your proposal," Cornelius added. "As long as Gideon remains on the academy grounds, he can continue his training as a magic caster, and he can keep his armory."

Jacqueline smiled with a sense of relief as the administrator cringed in disgust. "Chief Magistrate, you can't base your decision on a simple coin. He could've gotten that anywhere."

"That coin came from my father, and he would only give it to someone he implicitly trusted," Cornelius yelled at him. "If my father trusts Gideon, then so do I." Tyrion reached out to shake Gideon's hand. He took it with complete confidence. "Thank you, Gideon. I appreciate what you did for him."

With that, Cornelius bowed to the princess and left the infirmary. Gideon saw the look of defeat on the administrator's face. Dieter was so dumbfounded he decided to leave quietly, but Preceptor de Maestre quickly stopped him.

"Administrator von Straithmore, you seem to have a habit of interjecting yourself in situations outside of your cognizance as to the administrator of this academy," he said. "The board has serious doubts about your ability to do your job properly. Therefore, after this term, we will no longer require your services."

"What? But Preceptor de Maestre, I don't think this is the right time for such a rash decision," Dieter argued.

"Believe me, Administrator, this wasn't a rash decision," he interrupted. "However, this latest incident proves that you are not capable of doing your job objectively. The board has made its decision. I suggest you start looking for another position elsewhere."

Gideon held back his glee as Dieter tried to think of a rebuttal, but he just couldn't find the words. He spun on his heels and stormed out of the infirmary. The students tried to contain their laughter as they waited for him to leave, but before they could do anything, Canon Cordell interrupted them all.

"Now that that's over, I need all of you to leave the infirmary," he ordered. "The princess needs her rest, so my healing can take effect. You can all come back tomorrow to see her. Now go."

Everyone said their goodbyes to Wren as they slowly filed out of the ward. Gideon waited until the very end to say goodbye. Wren looked up at him, happy that it all worked out but sad that he had to leave.

"Can't you stay, please?" Wren pleaded.

"Not tonight, Princess, doctor's orders," Gideon replied. "I'll come by and see you tomorrow, okay? I'll bring you some tea, just the way you like it."

Wren knew what he meant, and she smiled. That's all Gideon wanted to see. He liked it when she was happy, not sad. He glanced around the room and saw everyone was talking and looking away, not paying attention to them. Gideon took Wren by the hand and kissed it gently, a polite gesture in most cultures but quite scandalous when performed on the First Princess of Attlain.

"Until tomorrow," he said before he turned to leave. Wren's heart was aflutter, beating faster as her face went flush red. Nurse Constance came over to administer some medicine when she noticed her composition.

"Oh, Your Highness, are you feeling alright?" she asked as she placed her hand on Wren's forehead.

"Oh yes, Constance. I'm fine. In fact, I've never felt better."

12 A ROMANCE AND AN AMBUSH

Gideon's Journal – House arrest was no different than the past month I spent at Basilon. As promised, I stayed on the academy grounds and worked diligently on my studies. This time, though, it was a little more tolerable. My friends were with me again. After everything that happened to Wren, word spread fast within our class about Dartagni and what he didn't do to protect Wren. They finally believed me about the evil in him. It's nice to have my friends by my side again.

What's even better was that Wren was okay. She bounced back relatively quickly from her injuries. Canon Cordell did a helluva job healing her, even better than the job he did on me. Her spirit has never been more energized. It's nice to have her back, being able to spend time with her. I must enjoy these moments now because, in a few months, she'll be back in that untouchable ivory tower, out of reach for someone like me.

I have these feelings for Wren, and I don't know what to do with them. Am I her knight, her protector? Absolutely. I would put my life on the line in an instant if it meant protecting her. I would die for her. That said, I would love for it to be more than that, but I know it's not possible. She is, after all, a princess. So, for now, I'm just going to enjoy the time I have with her. It'll be a memory that will stay with me for a thousand lifetimes.

The time toward graduation flew for the third-year students. The faculty pressed them with intense studies, end-of-the-year exams, and practical tests. All the while, the students were carefully scouted by representatives from various guilds, city magistrate officials, top adventurer parties, even the military. While most third-year students stressed out with everything going on all at once, Gideon enjoyed every moment. He thrived on the situation's intensity, although he hated all the attention. Being a Magus made him a prime target for recruitment, so it was a standing room only whenever testing in the arena involved him. Gideon felt terrible for his classmates. He thought he was taking time away from them, but that's not how they saw it. They thought his presence brought more attention to them, so they were happy that he was with them.

When it was all over, the students gathered together at the Alchemist's Brew tavern for a graduation celebration. It was a small, hole-in-the-wall tavern near the school run by a former instructor. It wasn't anything extravagant like the Red Door, but they didn't want to go near that place after Wren's incident. Besides, it was a lot cozier and comfortable, and this was a dual celebration. They were celebrating their graduation from Basilon, but they also celebrated Gideon's release from house arrest. After more than a month of confinement to the school grounds, the chief magistrate informed the school that the Obsidian Court could not find any evidence of the mysterious Ishtaran noble. Gideon was free and clear from any diplomatic constraints.

The class gathered around a large oval table in a private room at the tavern. It was piled high with a variety of bread, meat, fruits, and sweets for everyone to eat, along with plenty of ale and wine. Gideon went out and bought several casks of Montag's wine, both to pay off his debt to Guilfoy and to contribute to the celebration. Everyone was enjoying the feast, laughing, and joking around. They were trying to be as cheery as possible since, for some of them, this would be the last time they would see each other for quite a while.

A few of them kept looking at the door as they patiently waited for Lady Jacqueline. She was putting together their job offers from various organizations. Once she arrived, they would know where they were going and what they would do for the rest of their lives. It was the first step in their careers as magic casters.

Gideon sat and sipped his wine as he looked across the table. When he arrived at Basilon, he was an outsider, a stranger coming into their class. Now, Gideon was one of them and couldn't be happier. He had friends, people he considered family, to rely on in the future. The only people Gideon ever thought of that way were Master Botàn, Bok, and even Lady Jacqueline to an extent. But now, he could add a whole new set of names to that list.

Wren sat next to him, smiling and laughing along with everyone else. It was a bittersweet time for her. It was the end of her time at Basilon. She would be returning to the palace and her duties as First Princess of Attlain. She enjoyed the time she lived a relatively normal life at the school. Wren hid her sadness behind her bright smile, especially from Gideon. Every time she looked at him, she knew it would soon be her last. The strange thing was, Gideon felt the same way as she did. Whenever he glanced her way, he took in every detail of her hair, face, smile, and body. He needed to memorize her entirety because he was afraid that he would never see her again.

The barmaids continued to refresh the drinks and bring out more food as the night progressed, and everyone tried to guess where the other was going. "Come on, some of you have to have an idea of where you're going?" Guilfoy asked.

"Some of us do, Guilderhof," Killian interjected. "I have family responsibilities to attend to."

"What do you mean, Killian?" Gideon inquired.

"In the mines of Dyp Halidar, we earth mages take turns protecting the miners from cave-ins and the assorted creatures that live in the depths of the earth," he explained. "As my brother before me, I will go into the mine and take his place so he may go out into the world while my younger sister comes to Basilon next year to begin her instruction. When she finishes, she will return to Dyp Halidar, and I will begin my time as an adventurer."

"The same is true for me," Fiona interrupted. "I will be returning to Appaluna to take my place as a mystic and healer amongst my people. It is to repay the debt I owe them for sending me to Basilon."

"Wow, so there are some things that dwarves and alfs do have in common!" Gideon joked, giving everyone a good laugh.

"Now, don't you be starting any rumors, Magus!" Killian shot back in jest.

"What about you, Wren? Is it back to the life of gilded halls and parties with nobles for you?" Guilfoy asked.

"Unfortunately, yes," she sighed sadly. "My time as a simple student is over for me. I have duties as the First Princess of Attlain that I must return to, but what about you, Gideon? You must have dozens of offers on the table."

"Dozens, I heard that every guild and party in Attlain offered you a place with them," Trini added.

"Well, that may as well be, but they'll all have to wait," Gideon stated, which confused everyone at the table. "I told Lady Jacqueline to inform the interested parties that I won't be available for three to six months."

"What, why not? Where are you going?" Wren asked.

"To Plodoro," Gideon answered. Everyone was shocked at his answer as the room fell silent. Plodoro was the northern-most territory in Attlain. It was the only human settlement, located in the heart of Giant country, at the very end of the Skjem-Tur Mountains. It was isolated and very dangerous for people to travel to and from Plodoro.

"Plodoro? Why the hell would you go to that forgotten place?" Bartholomew asked.

"Master Botàn was from Plodoro. His family—the Botàn Clan—still lives there," Gideon explained. "The head of the clan is also the Matriarch of Plodoro. Her name is Nissa Louisa Botàn, his grandmother. She is called the 'Great Mother' of the clan."

"Great Mother? That's an odd title for a leader," Susanna concluded.

"Well, from what Master Botàn told me, the women of the clan run pretty much everything, while the men are its defenders. It's a system that has been part of the clan since its inception," he surmised. "I don't quite understand it. There's not a lot written about Plodoro since not too many people go there."

"So why would you partake in such a treacherous journey?" Wren pleaded.

"It is the last thing Master Botàn asked me to do. He had not spoken to anyone in the clan for more than twenty years, so they don't know what happened to him, why he stayed away, or that he's dead. I have a letter for the Great Mother and a weapon in the armory that I have to return."

"A weapon?" Takeshi queried.

"It's an ax. Bane, the Great Ax of Annihilation. It's a family heirloom, passed on from the oldest son of the Botàn clan to the next. With his death, it's passed on to the next heir within the clan."

"But it'll take more than three months to travel to Plodoro and back," Bartholomew added. "I've heard of caravans sometimes taking more than a year for a round trip journey. The roads are narrow and treacherous with giants, mountain goblins, trolls, and more."

"Yes, well, I'm not walking there. I'll be flying."

That news got everyone's attention. Even with a basic flying spell, a magic caster can't stay airborne long before their mana depletes.

"I have a friend who's loaning me a griffon for the trip. I should be able to fly up to Plodoro and back in less than three months, give or take."

That was great news to Wren, and it even gave her an idea. "In that case, you should make it back before the end of summer. It would be wonderful for you to come to Celestrium for the Helios Arcanum Magical Arts Competition and Festival."

Gideon looked at her curiously and chuckled. "Magical Arts, what? What is that?"

"It's an annual festival and competition in Celestrium where the top magic casters from across Attlain come to compete in various events, like dueling and magical accuracy," Guilfoy explained. "With your skills, you'd be a cinch to win it all, Gideon."

Everyone at the table agreed with Guilfoy's assertion, voicing their praises on the Magus. His classmates humbled Gideon, honored that they thought so highly of his skills.

"And the winner of the festival gets to make a special request of the king," Wren added. "As long as it's within reason, the king cannot refuse the request."

"Well, that makes it even more tempting," Gideon concurred. "Alright then . . . After Plodoro, I will make my way to Celestrium to compete in the festival."

Everyone started to cheer as they raised their glasses for another toast when

Lady Jacqueline walked in. They were so busy celebrating that they failed to notice her.

"My, my, it appears that there are excessive amounts of celebrating," she commented loudly, getting everyone's attention. "It's a good thing you don't have class tomorrow, or I'd have to put a stop to this."

"Lady Jacqueline, please join us!" Wren offered.

"Thank you, Your Highness, but I'm afraid I must decline. I am only here to deliver these," she said, holding up a set of envelopes.

"Oh, it's about time!" Guilfoy remarked. "What took you so long?"

Jacqueline frowned at Guilfoy's informality with her, only one day after graduating. Trini reminded him of his rudeness with a punch in the arm. Guilfoy sat back down quietly as he finished his drink.

"I apologize for running late, Guilderhof, but I had to ensure the former administrator left the academy grounds before I came here."

"Oh, I wish I had been there to see that," Gideon added, getting a laugh out of the entire class.

"Yes, well, in any case, I have your offers!" She walked around the table and passed out the envelopes to each student, skipping over those few who already acknowledged they had duties elsewhere. The students patiently waited until everyone had theirs in hand. Once they did, everyone ripped through the wax seals and read their offers.

"Well, come on, don't keep us in suspense!" Gideon said.

"Armändis," Bartholomew said first. "I'm heading to Armändis, to the Black Wolf Guild."

"We're heading to Armändis!" Susanna added. Gideon was surprised to hear that they were going there. "We decided that it would be a great place to learn how to be proper adventurers."

"If I want any chance of getting as good as you, it's the best place for me to start," Bartholomew concluded. Gideon was happy to see that they were taking these first steps in their careers. "So, do you have any advice for us?"

"Yeah, stay away from the girls at Marion's Tavern . . . They'll get you in trouble," he told Bart, but before he could answer, Susanna grabbed him by the arm and answered for him.

"Oh, you don't have to worry about that," she said, giving her lover an evil glare.

"Also, the guildmaster is a crotchety old soul, but he's a good man, a seasoned adventurer. You'd be smart to listen to him." Gideon reached into his coat pocket, pulled out the coin Tyrion gave him, and continued, "And if you ever find yourself in trouble, show this to the city magistrate." He tossed Bartholomew the coin. "It'll help you get out of trouble."

"What about you, Trini?" Wren asked her friend.

"I'm heading to the Scarlet Rabbit Guild in Chattaloon, just outside

Celestrium!"

"And near my home in Appaluna," Fiona interjected. "We'll be able to see each other from time to time." The three friends were ecstatic to hear that when Trini saw a shocked look on Guilfoy's face as he looked at his offer sheet.

"What's the matter, Guilfoy? Not what you wanted?" Trini asked.

"No, actually, it is," he gushed. "I've been assigned to the Obsidian Court in Celestrium . . . I'm going home."

Everyone was shocked to hear that he was offered a place on the Obsidian Court. It usually took a magic caster time to garner a reputation to be assigned to the royal intelligence service. It was a rare honor.

"Congratulations, Guilfoy, you've earned it!" Gideon said as he raised his cup to toast his friend. Guilfoy was so overwhelmed, all he could do was just nod his head as he folded his paper and tucked it away. He was finally going home after four long years in Le'Arun.

"What about Takeshi?" Wren asked the last of her close friends.

"I have been offered a place in the Black Scorpion Alliance in Solara," he acknowledged. "Trini-san got me an introduction with the guildmaster."

"He's my Uncle Reza," Trini explained. "Take' wanted to be able to continue to experience life outside Yamatai, so I told him about the alliance. Solara is near the Great Western Sea, so he'll be able to visit home more often than if he was somewhere else."

"But aren't you homesick, Takeshi? Don't you want to go home?" Fiona inquired.

"*Hai*, Fiona-san, I am, but to get stronger as a *Majutsu-shi*, I need to grow outside my homeland. There is a proverb my grandfather told me before I left. 'The bamboo that bends is stronger than the oak that resists.'"

"I don't get it?" Guilfoy remarked.

"He means you have to be flexible to grow against the adversities of life," Lady Jacqueline interjected, and her former students understood the meaning, nodding their heads and muttering amongst themselves. "And that, ladies and gentlemen, is my final lesson for you. I bid you all good night." She approached Gideon then and asked if she could have a word with him.

Gideon got up and walked outside the room with Lady Jacqueline while the rest continued to talk about their new assignments. Once outside in the main tavern, Jacqueline stopped to speak with her charge. She reached into her pocket and pulled out Gideon's holy book, handing it over to him. "Lucius wanted to make sure I returned this to you before you left tomorrow. He appreciates you allowing him to look through it."

"Was he able to decipher anything from it?" Gideon asked as he took it from her hands.

"He said it's an ancient holy book, written in the language of the Saints," she explained. "Unfortunately, it is so saturated that most of its pages are illegible. You did say you were a sailor, so perhaps that could be a clue to the reason why it's in such poor condition. Nevertheless, he found a few words or phrases but nothing worth mentioning. He was able to transcribe one complete passage for you. He wrote it down for you."

She pointed to a piece of paper sticking out of one section of the book. Gideon opened it and looked at the inscription. "Chapter 3, Verse 8, 'I know your deeds. See, I have placed before you an open door, which no one can shut. For you have only a little strength, yet you have kept My word and have not denied My name.'" Even as he read it aloud, it seemed so familiar, and yet, he didn't know from where.

"Does that hold any special meaning for you?" Jacqueline asked.

"I honestly can't say," Gideon surmised as he closed the book and put it away. "I'll try to meditate on it during my journey to Plodoro."

"Ah, speaking of which, I also wanted to tell you that I heard back from Bok. He'll meet you at the rendezvous point at noon tomorrow as requested, with all the supplies you need for the trip."

"Good, I was afraid he was going to back out of our arrangement. I know how much he loves those griffons."

"The thought did cross his mind. For a journey to Plodoro, he's more concerned for his griffon's safety than yours," Lady Jacqueline added. "Still, he said he owed it to Henri and you as well."

"Any word on Duarté and Selene?" Gideon asked. Jacqueline was reluctant to tell him anything, but she knew she had no choice in the matter.

"It seems they are leaving Le'Arun," Jacqueline informed him. "They have packed up their belongings and are supposedly heading to a seaside home near Bösheen. I think that after the attempted kidnapping of the princess, they have given up trying to get the armory from you."

"Don't bet on it," Gideon remarked. "I don't trust those two for a moment. They don't seem like the type to cut and run."

"I agree, but there's not much else we can do right now," she replied as she reached out and touched Gideon on the chest. "You will come by to see me before you leave tomorrow, yes?"

"Yes, of course, milady . . . I promise."

Jacqueline smiled, but he could see the sadness on her face. She leaned in and kissed him on the cheek before she turned to leave. "Lady Jacqueline!" he shouted to stop her. Jacqueline turned back to Gideon. "Thank you for everything you did for me. I wouldn't be here without your help. I am forever in your debt, milady," he concluded as he bowed politely to her.

"No, Marcus, you owe me nothing," she replied. "You have made it possible for me to repay a debt I owed my dear Henri. We are, as they say, even, but I am happy to say that I have someone new that I now consider a dear friend."

Gideon politely bowed in respect, watching as she turned and left the tavern. He was glad that he came to Le'Arun, Basilon, and met Lady Jacqueline Celestra. Gideon realized how lucky he was to have people like Lady Jacqueline, Bok, and Master Botàn at his side. When he stepped back into the private room, he realized something more as the celebration continued. Now, Gideon had a room full of people with him. He would fight for them, protect them, as they would do for him. That was something he knew deep in his clockwork heart.

It was almost two o'clock in the morning when the party finally broke up, and the former students meandered their way back to the dormitories for the last time. Within the week, most of them would be packing up and leaving Basilon for the last time. They stumbled and stuttered with each step until the boys and girls split off to their sides of the dormitories. Gideon helped Guilfoy, who drank a little more than he should have.

"Come on, Gideon, you hardly had anything to drink," Guilfoy stammered. "We've got time for one more!"

"No, you've had enough, and I have to start a long journey," Gideon replied. "I'm taking you to your room, and then I'm taking a bath!"

"A bath? Why on earth would you do that?" Guilfoy cried out.

"Because it'll probably be a month until I have a chance for another one, so come on, drunken idiot!"

"Here, Gideon, let me," Trini said, taking Guilfoy's arm across her shoulders to prop him up. "You go on ahead. I'll put the little man to bed."

"Trini, you can't go into the boy's dormitories. It's against the rules!" Wren warned her.

"What are they going to do? Kick me out of school?" she joked as she followed the boys down the hall, holding up Guilfoy. Gideon loved that about Trini. She was bold and consistently "in your face" about things, always walking that fine line when it came to rules. He turned to say good night to Wren, but she was already walking ahead with the other girls back toward their side of the dormitory. Gideon hoped he would get to see her before leaving tomorrow as he opened his door and went inside his room to change for his bath.

Wren looked back as she watched Gideon go into his room. She didn't want to say good night in the hallway, not like that, especially with everyone around. She knew what she wanted to do.

While everyone made it back to their rooms to finally sleep off the long night of eating, drinking, and celebrating, Gideon soaked in the bath. He enveloped himself in hot water, just letting it soothe his entire body as he stretched out across the wall near the back. Gideon didn't relish the idea of flying through the Skjem-Tur Mountains, living in his clothes with practically no chance of a hot bath like this for more than a month. So, for now, he would enjoy this to his heart's content.

As he closed his eyes and let his mind drift away, he heard the door to the bath open. He didn't know who else was planning on coming here this late, but he just ignored whoever it was. The next sound he heard was a "click" as the bathroom door was locked. That sound alerted him to potential danger. *Did Duarté send an assassin?* he wondered. He kept his eyes closed and stretched out his arms as if he was getting more comfortable, but he was reaching for his armory. It was resting under a towel near his hand. He knew he needed a weapon, so he slowly moved his fingers under the edge of the towel. He just barely touched the armory before he went into action.

"Lionheart," he whispered as the broad sword appeared in his hand. He leaped to his feet, ready to strike at his opponent, when he stopped in his tracks. He was expecting an assassin or the like, but instead, he saw Wren standing there in her robe. She wasn't startled or scared. She just stared at Gideon.

He quickly dismissed his sword and wondered what she was doing here. It reminded him of when they first met, but this was different. "Wren? What are you doing here?" he asked. Without saying a word, she stepped toward the bath, and slowly pulled the robe off her shoulders, letting it fall to the floor.

Gideon stared at her in awe. He remembered when he saw her like this before . . . every curve, every inch of her naked body, and the beauty he beheld before his eyes. Her porcelain skin, her lovely face, full lips, and flowing red hair that fell effortlessly across her firm breasts, all the way down to her curvy hips and long legs. He didn't know whether to turn away or just stare at the angel that stood before him.

She walked down the steps into the water, moving right up to him. "Wren, what are you . . ." he started to say until she wrapped her arms around his head and kissed him deeply. He couldn't resist her delicious lips as he pulled her close and kissed her back, holding her tightly in his arms. They stood there in their embrace, not wanting to let the other one go. Their bodies melded into one and tongues danced around their mouths.

Even though she had locked the door, Gideon became concerned someone might walk in on them. He quickly moved her behind and underneath the fountain at the bath's center.

The fountain resembled a circle of seahorses rising out of the water. From their mouths and the base, the water flowed into the bath, creating a curtain of water underneath it. Behind that curtain, benches were resting at the water level. It allowed students to relax under the flowing water and give them a little privacy.

Gideon sat Wren on the bench while he stood in the bath. "Wren, are you sure about this?" he asked.

Wren smiled. "I've never been so sure of anything in all my life," she cooed. "I love you, Marcus . . . I love you more than anything in this world."

He was shocked and taken aback when she told him that. Wren looked confused by his stark reaction. "What's wrong?"

"Nothing . . . it's just . . . You're the first person ever to tell me that they loved me. I've never heard anyone say it to me before now." His confession made Wren happy as she laughed and kissed him again. When she stopped, Gideon held her face in his hands.

"I love you too, Wren," he confessed to her. "I've loved you from the first moment I met you."

They both smiled, then kissed and embraced each other again. Gideon laid Wren down on the bench as he climbed on top of her. The two made love in that bath as the water rushed around them. Their loving embrace fueled their passion. Gideon was gentle with Wren, being her first time, but he also wanted to please her. He kissed and caressed every inch of her body, loving her with all the passion in his being. She could feel the heat of his body as his strength poured into her, and completely consumed her.

After their first time together in the bath, the two lovers decided it was best to have a little more privacy. Gideon snuck her out of the bath, careful that no one was in the corridor at that time. They cloaked themselves as they snuck their way back to his room and locked the door. Inside, they returned to their lovemaking for another hour until they finally collapsed into each other's arms.

They lay in the bed, listening to their every breath. Wren laid her head across his chest. Even there, she could hear the whirring and clicking of his clockwork heart. Its melodic beat soothed her as she rested from their intense lovemaking.

"You're quiet, Gideon, too quiet," she said, finally breaking the silence.

"Sorry, I was just thinking."

"Oh, about what?" she asked as she rolled over and lay on top of him, resting her chin on her hands so she could look up at him.

Gideon took a deep breath before he answered. "I was wondering . . . What's the punishment for sleeping with a princess? I mean, are we talking years in the dungeon or possible execution?"

Wren laughed, but Gideon was deadly serious. "Does it matter?" she inquired. "Are you regretting being with me tonight?"

"Regrets? No, no regrets . . . Well, maybe just one," he answered, giving Wren a pause for concern.

"Really? And what would that be?" she asked as she sat up, wrapping his bedsheet around her naked body. Gideon could see she was perturbed and sat up himself, wrapping his arms around her and pulling her close to him.

"I regret that we waited until now," he said softly to her. "I wish we didn't wait until the day before I was leaving for our first time together."

Wren smiled, putting Gideon at ease over his concerns. "Well, we couldn't do this while we were still students," she said as she kissed him. "Besides, I didn't want to give the administrator any excuses to expel you from the school."

"Ah, so you planned it this way?" Gideon smirked. Wren didn't argue with that sentiment. "Still, I am concerned . . . about you, especially with your family. I don't know how I will speak to the king about this."

"Well, for now, let's not worry about that," she said as she kissed him again. "We should just enjoy the time we have together. Let's worry about the future later."

"That's the problem," he lamented as he gently caressed her hair and face. "My future is with you, being with you, protecting you, from now until eternity ends, and the angels take me home."

Wren was so happy to hear him say that, then she sighed as if the joy she was feeling just went away. "Unfortunately, you'll be busy adventuring across Attlain while I'll be stuck in Celestrium, performing my official duties as the First Princess of Attlain."

Gideon could see she wanted something more than royal parties and court politics. "Then why don't you come with me?" he asked. "You once told me your father was an adventurer when he was a young prince. Why don't you do the same?"

"It's different for a prince than a princess. I've asked my father repeatedly if I could become an adventurer after I graduated, even if it's for just a few years, so that I could experience things outside the palace. He said no, every time. 'It's too dangerous for the Princess of Attlain to be dirtying her hands, fighting off orcs and goblins,'" she said, imitating his voice and mannerisms. "You don't realize how much it took just to convince him to let me come to Basilon. Even after the kidnapping attempt, he wanted me to come home immediately. It took Lady Jacqueline and Lady Gwendolyn both to convince him to let me finish the term."

"And where does your mother stand on all of this?"

"My mother?" Wren grimaced as she shook her head. "My mother does whatever my father tells her. She has no power in court, and if she speaks her mind, and it's not in line with my father's decision, she backs down immediately."

"That doesn't sound much like a queen," Gideon remarked. "I've read stories about your grandmother, Queen Lyssa, keeping the nobility in line when it came to disagreements with the Crown."

"That's why my father is the way he is," Wren replied. "He saw the way my grandmother disagreed with my grandfather, King Colwyn. He never understood why my grandfather put up with it, so he told my mother what he expected of her as queen when he became king. She had no choice but to acquiesce."

"That's not much of a relationship."

"No, it's not, but they are my parents, and my king and my queen. I must obey their wishes," Wren assured him.

"Well, you said the winner of the magic festival gets to request something from the king. I guess I'll have to make it my official request—to have you join my party as an adventurer."

"What do you mean, your party?" Wren asked, confused. "I thought you were waiting on answering offers until after you got back from Plodoro."

"Yeah, I lied," he admitted. "I didn't want to let the cat out of the bag, as it were. I don't want anyone else running my life, so I'm going to start my own party—No, my own guild—based in Celestrium."

Wren was so ecstatic that she jumped forward, wrapped her arms around his head, and knocked him backwards on the bed. She kissed him repeatedly, so happy that he was going to be there with her.

"I can't believe it! Why didn't you tell me?"

"Well, it was going to be a surprise when I got back from Plodoro, but after tonight, why wait?"

Wren was ecstatic. Gideon planned all this to be close to her. "Well then, I guess I owe you a reward for that," she remarked as she kissed him again.

"I think you more than rewarded me enough tonight," he said coyly.

"Yes, well, the night is still young," Wren said as she jumped up out of bed, picked up her robe, and wrapped it around her.

"Where are you going?" Gideon asked.

"The ladies' bathroom is in the girls' dorm," she said. "I can't use the men's bathroom on this side."

"Does that mean you're coming back?"

Wren walked over and gave him a deep, loving kiss. "Yes, I'll be right back, and don't worry, no one will see me . . . *Invisibili!*" She waved her hand from her head down. Gideon watched as she slowly faded from sight. Once she was invisible, the door opened and closed, signaling she had gone.

Gideon lay back and closed his eyes. He was utterly exhausted, but he wasn't about to let it stop him from enjoying every moment with Wren. He knew he had a long journey ahead of him, but there would be plenty of time to sleep. His time with her was here and now.

He started to drift off to sleep, but he knew she would wake him up when she got back; a few winks wouldn't hurt. Then he heard the door creak after just a few minutes. *I guess it didn't take her long to go to the bathroom,* he surmised as he opened his eyes, but instead of Wren's captivating smile, he saw the angry visage of the former administrator staring at him.

"*Magne Segellu!*" he chanted as he pointed his staff at Gideon. A wave of magical energy covered his body, but it centered on his chest. Before Gideon could say anything, his chest tightened and seized. He was having a heart attack as his clockwork heart slowed considerably. It was as if the spell locked the gears in place. He was in so much pain that he couldn't move or cast a spell. Even his armory was out of reach.

Dieter grinned a wicked smile as he stepped up to the bed and hovered over the helpless Magus. "I think you'll find that your mechanical heart is not working as well as it should," he said gleefully. Gideon was surprised that he knew about his clockwork heart, even more so that he knew how to affect it.

"H-h-ow," he stuttered, with barely enough strength to speak.

"How? Well, that was easy once I was able to track down Jacob McMaster," Dieter continued to gloat. "Lady Jacqueline tried to hide who he was from me, but once I found him, it was relatively simple to get him to talk about your unique condition, although he won't be able to help you anymore. I doubt anyone will be able to find his body for quite some time."

His words made Gideon angry as he fought through the pain. Jacob saved his life, and the former administrator killed him to get information. It was another senseless death associated with Gideon's life.

"This spell is called 'magnetic seal,' used to fuse armor to immobilize your enemy, but I knew it would work on the mechanical gears to stop your clockwork heart. Now then, Magus, where is your armory?" he asked.

Gideon knew that was the only reason he would be here. Revenge was not something von Straithmore would do if there were no profit in it for him. He was after the Armory of Attlain. Gideon gritted through as he tried to focus on any possible way to break free from his spell. Dieter watched him struggle.

"Come now, Gideon, you're going to make me late in meeting Sir Duarté and Lady Selene," he remarked. "I have until dawn to bring the armory to them in Centralia Square. Do yourself a favor and give it to me. I promise to make your death quick and painless unless, of course, you'd rather I torture your lady friend when she returns."

Fear now filled Gideon. Von Straithmore confessed to multiple murders, but worse than that, he knew about Wren. Or did he? *He saw me come in here with a woman, but he couldn't know that it was Wren. He wouldn't threaten her life,* he thought.

"If I were still the administrator here, I would have easily gotten rid of you had I known you were inviting women into your dormitory room," Dieter continued. "Who is it? Some local tavern whore or perhaps another student?"

Gideon wouldn't tell him, but he needed to hear more about Duarté and Selene, so he tried to change the subject. "You helped . . . helped them . . . kill the Magus?" he stammered.

Dieter smiled a wicked, deceitful grin. "Well, of course, I did," he confessed. "After the Helios Arcanum kicked Selene out, the Dartagnis needed information on the Magus. I took this pitiful job just to get access to that information, and for that, they paid me well.

"It was an easy thing to do, right under all the instructor's noses, especially that bitch Jacqueline. I gave them the names of more than fifty Magus. She went through half of them just to perfect her spell. Imagine, she was able to retrieve more than fifty magical weapons before I ran out of names of Magus. Then, they forgot all about me. They started branching out to the guilds, inquiring about armories, to get their leads. But for me . . . I had to stay at this dead-end job just to make ends meet. And then you arrived.

"I never even heard of your Master Botàn until you showed up. All his records were seemingly erased, probably Lady Jacqueline's doing. Still, your arrival gave me a chance to work my way back to their good graces, but they didn't believe me. Duarté screamed at me. He said Botàn was dead and that you were lying. He didn't believe me until your little exhibition at the Red Door Tavern, but then he got angry at me again. He accused me of trying to keep the armory for myself because I couldn't bring it to him."

Gideon noticed how the former administrator grew angrier and desperate with each passing moment as he told his story. He saw how scared he was of Dartagni, but not enough that he still wanted to be associated with him. He wanted the recognition of being with the Paladin of Le'Arun, the chance to be a part of Dartagni's group.

"What . . . about Wren?" Gideon stuttered. "You let her . . . get attacked."

"Well, I wouldn't say I let her get attacked," Dieter exclaimed, jokingly.

"Then what would you say?" Wren asked, surprising Dieter as he spun around and saw her standing in the doorway. She held her robe closed with one hand while holding her other hand out toward him. Her open hand was bristling with fire as it flickered on and around her fingertips. "Move away from Gideon, now!"

Dieter was dumbfounded when he realized that he saw the princess entering the room with Gideon. He didn't know what to do as he stepped away from the bed. Wren moved closer to Gideon, standing between him and Dieter.

"Your Highness, please, I assure you I had nothing to do with the attack on you!" he babbled.

"No, of course, you didn't, but I have a pretty good idea of what you did do," Wren explained. "When you found out about the kidnapping attempt from the Obsidian Court, you sat on the information while you informed Sir Duarté. You both knew this would be an excellent opportunity to draw Gideon out into the open. That's why he did nothing to stop them from assaulting me when I saw him standing in the doorway of the tavern. Is that about right, Dieter von Straithmore?"

He swallowed hard, not knowing how to answer her. His fear grew as she elicited everything precisely as it happened. "Your Highness, I . . . I . . ."

"Do you know what the punishment is for conspiracy against a member of the Royal Family?" Dieter shook his head no. "No? Well, I do . . . *Infernus!*"

Her spell was the ultimate culmination of fire magic. It summoned a column of flame that engulfed Dieter, scorching the room's walls and ceiling. He screamed as the fire consumed him until there was nothing left but burnt bones and his broken staff. Once Wren took care of him, she turned to help her love.

"Marcus? Marcus, my love, what did he do to you?" she pleaded as tears rolled down her face.

Gideon tried to speak as his heartbeat slowed down even more. "Magnetized . . . my heart . . ."

"Magnetized? You mean the *Magne Segellu* spell?"

He tried nodding as best as he could.

"I can dispel it!" she said as she reached out to cast another spell over him, but he grabbed her hands.

"Won't work . . ." he muttered. "The gears are already magnetized. They need to be demagnetized."

Wren thought for a minute as she tried to uncover a solution to the problem. "In Prefect Autorio's alchemy class, to demagnetize an object, you should apply heat." She straddled his lap and placed her hands on his bare chest. "This is going to hurt, Marcus. Please . . . bear with me!"

Gideon nodded his head. "I trust you, Wren . . .," he said as his heart stopped completely, and he passed out.

Quickly she chanted, *"Calore Crescenu!"* Her hands glowed red, burning into his chest. She continued her spell as his flesh began to sear. This has to work, she worried. Please, God, let this work!

Gideon cried out as his heart started beating again, steady and robust. He was alive, and the pain from his chest proved it. "Oh, thank God!" Wren shouted for joy as she wrapped her arms around him before realizing she burned her handprints into his chest.

"Ow, careful, careful!" he screamed at the tenderness of his burns.

"Oh God, I'm so sorry, Marcus!"

"It's okay, Wren," he assured. "You did what you had to do to restart my heart. Besides, the pain tells me I'm still alive." She kissed him as he wiped the tears from her eyes.

"What's going on here?" came a voice from across the room. They turned and saw Trini and Guilfoy standing at the door, both in an undressed state. Trini's bushy hair was quite disheveled, and she was wearing just her robe, which she held closed with one hand. Guilfoy was fumbling with his glasses while he held up his pants with one hand. Once he got them on, he noticed the former administrator's charred remains.

"Holy shit . . . Is that von Straithmore?" he exclaimed. Gideon knew that if they were here, more would soon follow. He had to protect Wren.

"Trini get Wren back to her room," Gideon ordered.

"But Marcus?" she protested, but he kissed her to shut her up.

"Wren, they can't find you here like this. Go get dressed, then come back," he said. She agreed and kissed him back before heading out with Trini.

"Guilfoy, get dressed, then get Lady Jacqueline and Canon Cordell up here. I'll explain to them what happened."

"Really? Can you explain it to me first?" he joked. Gideon glared at him in anger, which clued Guilfoy to get out of there. "Right, later. . . ."

Out in the hallway, Trini and Wren ran toward their room. "So, are you going to tell me what you two were up to?" Trini asked again, grinning slyly as she spoke.

"As soon as you tell me what you were doing with Guilfoy?" Wren answered with a question of her own as Trini laughed.

"Gideon, I'm sorry to say this, but I'm not going to miss you when you're gone," Canon Cordell said as he finished healing the burns on Gideon's chest before applying a soothing salve and bandaging him up. "I have healed you more in six months than I've done for any single student in an entire term."

"Ha, Well, I don't blame you, Canon. I wouldn't miss me either!" Gideon laughed as his healing was closely observed by Lady Jacqueline and Preceptor de Maestre, along with Wren, Trini, and Guilfoy—all dressed more appropriately. Members of the staff had already cleaned up the former administrator's remains. At the same time, Gideon and Wren told the story of his compliancy in the death of the Magus, the attempted kidnapping of the princess, and Sir Duarté and Lady Selene's involvement in the entire affair.

"I can't believe it," Preceptor de Maestre exclaimed. "All this happened right under our noses. We were blind, blind idiots."

"We can look for blame and make the necessary changes to our policies another time, Xavier," Jacqueline said. "We need to make sure the Dartagnis don't get away."

"Yes, you're right. I'll contact the chief magistrate immediately," he said as he turned to leave.

"No, Preceptor, don't!" Gideon argued. "You can't contact the magistrate, at least not yet."

Everyone was shocked to hear Gideon's request, especially Wren.

"Marcus?"

"Why not, Gideon?" Xavier asked.

"If the magistrate shows up at the square at dawn, they'll run, and we'll never see them again," Gideon surmised as he sat up gingerly. "We need to draw them out and capture them ourselves. I have to be the one to meet them."

"Gideon, you are in no condition to do that," Lady Jacqueline said.

"The Canon healed my burns. All I need is a mana boost, and I'll be ready to go."

"Gideon, as logical as your argument sounds, we don't have the manpower to attempt something like that," Xavier replied.

"Trini, Guilfoy, go rouse the others and see if anyone can help," Gideon said. The two started to leave until Jacqueline stopped them in their tracks.

"Certainly not! You cannot ask students to go against seasoned adventurers!" she shouted, raising her hand to them.

"They're not students anymore, Lady Jacqueline," Gideon argued. "They graduated, remember? Plus, beyond the people in this room, they're the only ones I trust to fight by my side. Besides, I'm not asking them to fight an all-out brawl, just to contain any of his party that he might bring along. Plus, we can ask the *Cavaliere* for backup."

Jacqueline and Xavier considered their options, but they couldn't argue with Gideon's logic. "Alright, Gideon, we'll do it your way," Preceptor de Maestre accepted. "Jacqueline, why don't you see to Gideon while I speak to the Captain of the *Cavaliere*. You two, round up whoever is willing to help. We'll meet at the gate in half an hour."

With that, Xavier left the room with Trini and Guilfoy. Canon Cordell got up from Gideon's bed to allow Lady Jacqueline to perform the necessary spell. "Well, since there's a chance there will be some further injuries, I will get the infirmary ready to receive casualties, just in case," Lucius said as he left the room as well. Wren was about to leave when Jacqueline stopped her.

"Your Highness, would you please stay a moment," she asked as she sat down behind Gideon on the bed. Wren closed the door and stepped back into the room. She twiddled her thumbs, anxious about the upcoming fight. Jacqueline placed her hands on Gideon's back before casting her spell. *"Trasmissioni Magicu!"* she said, as the mana flowed from her into Gideon. The magical energy circulated through him as he breathed comfortably, bringing him back to full strength. She let the mana start to flow for about a minute before she finally spoke up.

"Just what the hell were you thinking?" she asked, her voice steady and quite stern.

"It was necessary, Lady Jacqueline, to get Duarté to—" Before Gideon could say another word, Jacqueline smacked him on the back of the head.

"I'm not talking about Duarté. I'm talking about sleeping with the princess, you imbecile," she interrupted, catching both Wren and Gideon off guard with her surprise accusation. "And don't try to lie about it! This room smells heady with sex, and she glows like a bride on her wedding night. I know exactly what you two were doing."

"Well, in my defense, she came to me," Gideon joked.

"Marcus!" Wren shouted, earning him another smack on the head from

Jacqueline.

"That's no excuse!" Jacqueline accused. "Do you have any idea of the political implications of what you have done? You've thrown a wrench into the monarchy going full steam down the tracks, heading toward a curve. What the hell were you thinking?"

Gideon looked over at Wren and knew what to say. "To be honest, milady, I wasn't thinking," he answered. "I love her, and she loves me, and that's all that matters."

Wren looked at him and smiled. He reached out his hand to her, and Wren took it, moving over to stand next to him as Lady Jacqueline got up from the bed as soon as she finished her spell. "What will you do, Lady Jacqueline?" Wren asked. They watched and waited as Jacqueline considered her options.

"At this time, Your Highness, nothing, but I must tell my sister about it when we arrive in Celestrium. She needs to know to protect you should anything come out about the affair. Who else knows? Trini and Guilfoy?" They both nodded their heads. "I will speak to them later, but for now, you two need to put this romance of yours on simmer. Is that clear?"

The two looked at each other before agreeing to her request. "Is there anything else you need to tell me?"

"Yes," Gideon said, looking at both Jacqueline and Wren, "and I need you both to understand. It's something I have to do."

15 THE PALADIN OF LE'ARUN

*G*ideon's Journal – *It was not easy getting a lecture from Lady Jacqueline. It was a bit scary, actually, like being scolded by my mother (if I could remember my mother). Still, she did understand some of the complexities of my relationship with Wren. I think it reminds her of the love she once shared with Master Botàn. Love like that shouldn't fall to the wayside. I think she understands that . . . I hope she understands that.*

Trini and Guilfoy were able to rouse most of the class to help. They were more than eager to jump into the fray, especially when we told them about the administrator and his connection to Duarté. Once they realized how they conspired to use Wren to draw me out, it made their blood boil. It's nice to have friends like that on your side.

After nearly being killed by von Straithmore and discovering just how deep Duarté's involvement was, I am even more determined to take my revenge. The two of them destroyed the Magus in less than twenty years, hunting them down, experimenting on them, and retrieving dozens of magical weapons. Do they still have them, or did they sell them off to the highest bidder? And who paid for all this? These are the questions that the Dartagnis must answer. They'll answer them, or they'll die.

Centralia Square was the heart of Le'Arun. It was more than three hundred yards in diameter. The town hall was at the head of the square, flanked by the two guilds that patrolled the outlying areas around the city—the Silver Phoenix Guild and the Azure Hawk Guild. The rest of the square was home to some of the best mercantile storefronts in Le'Arun. At this time of day, local merchants would bring their carts into the courtyard to fight for a prime spot to set up for the day. Once the square was packed, no more merchants were allowed.

At the center of the square was a massive fountain. It depicted the founder of Le'Arun, Alister Rooney Greyhawk, battling the colossal Steel Dragon, driving the monster out of the valley so he could build this great city. Gideon sat on the wall surrounding the fountain. He waited patiently as the sun rose above the mountain, bringing the first light into the city.

He knew that they wouldn't do anything drastic with all these people around, but even still, Duarté and Selene Dartagni were not one to cut and run. They wanted his armory, and these people were just collateral to them; but Gideon would rely on his allies, his friends, to make sure the people stayed safe.

"Well now, this is a surprise," Duarté said as he walked into the square with Lady Selene by his side. Gideon didn't bother to look at them as they approached the fountain. "You see, my dear, I told you Dieter couldn't complete the task."

"You were right as always, darling, but Gideon, I confess that I did not expect you to be so bold."

Gideon said nothing as he stood up to face them. He did as Master Botàn taught him: calmed himself in the face of his enemy, to quell his rage before the battle. "Next time, do your own dirty work, Dartagni," he shot back. "First Wren, then von Straithmore . . . You have a habit of using others instead of coming at me on your own. You are the coward Master Botàn described to me."

Being called a coward by Gideon and Botàn irked Duarté, but he let it pass, for now. "Come now, Gideon, you can't believe everything that traitor told you. He—"

"Cut the crap, Dartagni!" Gideon interrupted. "The administrator told me everything. How he gave you the names of the Magus, how you killed them, used their armories so Selene could perfect her spell, stole the magical weapons. And I know what you did the night those thugs assaulted Wren. It's over, Duarté, and soon everyone in Attlain will know that the Paladin of Le'Arun is a fake and a coward."

"And who are they going to believe? You? The apprentice of a Magus traitor, or me, a knight of Attlain?"

"They'll believe me!" Wren said as she walked into the square from behind Gideon. She had waited patiently in the shadows, just as Gideon told her to, in order to surprise the couple. Duarté and Selene were caught off guard by the presence of Her Royal Highness.

"Your Highness, I—"

"Don't you dare lie to me, Duarté Dartagni! I heard everything Dieter von Straithmore said to Gideon about the Magus. I know how the two of you let the kidnappers assault me so you could draw him out into the open. I saw you standing in the doorway of the Red Door. You let that bastard nearly rape me and kill me!"

The two stood there, completely dumbfounded. They did not expect the princess to become involved in this. "You came to my home, broke bread with my family, and this is how you repay that trust?" she screamed at them.

Duarté could see everything falling apart, so he had to act fast. He put his fingers in his mouth and whistled loudly. Soon, several men and women—adventurers loyal to Duarté—appeared in the square and surrounded them.

"I'm sorry you had to get involved in this, Your Highness, but I can't let your presence here get in the way," he explained. "I want that armory, Gideon, and if you value her life, you'll surrender it to me now." His voice was severe and strained as he glared coldly at them, but all Gideon could do was laugh, and he could see that it irritated Duarté to no end. "What's so funny?" he asked.

"You really can be a complete idiot, you know that? Did you think I would bring Wren here all by myself?"

Duarté realized what he meant, but as he reached for his sword, a magical arrow came out of nowhere and struck the hilt, preventing him from drawing it. Takeshi stood on a nearby rooftop, ready to hit again if necessary. In an instant, Gideon's friends appeared around them and pointed their various wands, staffs, and other craftworks at the adventurers to hold them back while the *Cavaliere* cleared the civilians out of the square.

"Good morning, Selene. It's been quite a while!" Lady Jacqueline said, sneaking behind Selene, laying her staff across the sorceress's throat.

Duarté tried to defend his wife, but soon, he found Preceptor de Maestre's wand in his face. "Do not move, Sir Duarté! This charade of yours is over!"

"You have no power over me!" he argued. "I am the Paladin of Le'Arun!"

"A paladin does not allow murderers to assault a princess for his wicked gains," Xavier replied. "You gave that title up the moment you took the lives of those Magus."

"And what right do they have to be the only ones to wield magic weapons," Duarté exclaimed. "They hoard them in their armories while others have to fight and claw their way through dungeons just to find one. It is an imbalance that I sought to rectify. Plus, by allowing them to keep their weapons, the Crown was all but asking for another rebellion. I had to stop it."

"That's not your decision to make!" Wren shouted. "If you had concerns, you should have spoken to my father about them, not taken it upon yourself to act."

"Your father is a weak and pitiful monarch," Duarté snapped. "Dangers are walking all around his kingdom, and he ignores them completely. He is a blind fool who will bring Attlain down without him even realizing it."

Wren was hurt deep by his accusations, but Preceptor de Maestre had heard enough. "Then you can explain that to the king when you see him. It's over!"

"Not quite, Preceptor," Gideon interrupted. "I have unfinished business with Duarté."

"Gideon?" Xavier queried curiously. Gideon said nothing to him. He looked straight at Duarté as he stepped toward him.

"Sir Duarté Dartagni, by the Code of the Magus, and for your actions against the Kingdom of Attlain and my fellow Magus, I challenge you to a duel for the holy sword Durandal!"

Gideon's challenge took Xavier by surprise. "Gideon, there is a time and a place for that, and this is not that time," he argued.

"I'm sorry, Preceptor, but it must be now. Who knows what will happen to the sword after he is in custody? He stole it from my master. It is my right to challenge him for it!"

"Jacqueline, please, you must talk some sense into him!" Xavier pleaded, but the look on her face said otherwise.

"I'm sorry, Xavier, but he's right," she concurred. "Gideon has the right to challenge him for Durandal. He must have the opportunity."

Xavier realized that they outmaneuvered him. He had no choice but to relent. Keeping his wand leveled at Duarté, Xavier backed away from him and moved toward Gideon and Wren. "I hope you know what you're doing," he told Gideon.

"So, do I," Gideon confessed. "Please, protect the princess." He moved out into the middle of the square to give them room as the others backed away to the other side of the fountain to watch the duel. Duarté smiled at the chance of killing this Magus as he drew his sword. Durandal shined brightly in the morning sunlight. The dual, sharp edges of the blade were ready for a fight.

"You've just made the biggest mistake of your life, Magus," Duarté gloated. "Go ahead, pull whatever weapon you want out of there. I know them all very well. There's nothing in that armory that can beat Durandal or me!"

"Oh, I beg to differ," Gideon remarked. *"Come to me, Blood Onyx, Crystalline Sword of the Vampire Lord!"* He stood there as a runic circle opened, and a hilt emerged. He reached up and grabbed the hilt, pulling out the sword. It was a broad sword with a forked tip. The blade was a black crystal with runes that glowed red along the fuller. The guard and hilt were made of bone with a skull for the pommel.

Gideon surprised Duarté when he summoned the sword. He saw fear in the eyes of the Paladin of Le'Arun. "That's impossible! You shouldn't have that sword!"

"Really? Maybe if you hung around when Master Botàn fought the vampire in the caves of Golquieth, you would have seen it firsthand, but don't worry, you'll get to know its power!" He charged at Duarté swinging, but a seasoned adventurer like Duarté was ready for him. He matched his moves, blow for blow. Gideon kept him defensive as his attacks increased, but Duarté didn't falter. He pressed back. As Gideon brought his sword down, Duarté shifted his weight and swept him off his feet.

Gideon fell backward and hit the ground hard. Duarté raised his sword to run him through, but Gideon quickly reacted as he placed his free hand on the cobblestones. *"Congelatu!"* he chanted as a wave of frost emitted from his hand and covered the ground in ice. It caught Duarté off guard as he slipped and fell himself. The two of them slowly got to their feet.

"That's cheating, Magus!" Duarté exclaimed.

"Oh, come on, Duarté, I just spent the last six months honing my magic skills. Do you think I want to look bad in front of my instructors?"

Once he got up, Gideon snapped his fingers and dispelled the ice, allowing Duarté to get his proper footing. The two of them began to circle each other, looking for an opening. "One thing I have to know," Gideon asked. "Who paid you to hunt down the Magus? Even an adventurer like you doesn't have the money to pay out five thousand gold coins for an armory. Who's your benefactor?"

Duarté chuckled at his request. "You'll have to beat me to find that out."

"Well then, that makes it easy for me." Gideon shot back as he attacked. He thrust his sword, using the forked front to capture Durandal. Duarté pushed back against him, but Gideon was younger and stronger. He held him back, but not before one of the forked tips put a small cut on his cheek. With that small incision, the runes on the sword glowed brightly. Gideon knew he accomplished his goal and stepped back.

Duarté ran his hand across his cheek but found no blood. "A simple scratch? Is that the best you got?"

"Not at all," Gideon replied. "But it will suffice!" He lowered his sword as if he gave Duarté an opening to attack. The paladin did not hesitate and lunged at him, but suddenly, he stopped in his tracks. He was wheezing as if he couldn't breathe. He dropped to one knee, using his sword to prop himself up, as he looked up at Gideon and saw terror. Gideon's eyes were glowing red, as brightly as the runes on his sword. That look terrified Duarté.

"You never asked how that vampire lord killed its victims, did you?" Gideon asked. "According to Master Botàn, none of them had bite marks anywhere on their bodies, only a superficial scratch. Once he defeated Alucard, he understood the power of this sword.

"You see, it only takes a simple cut to activate the curse. I can stand here and drain you of every drop of blood in your body, killing you, without even lifting my sword again."

Duarté kneeled there and struggled as he got weaker and weaker. His body became thin, almost desiccated, as the sword slowly drained the life from him. Selene watched in horror as her husband was dying before her eyes. "Please, Gideon, stop it! He concedes! He concedes!" she shouted. Gideon closed his eyes, pausing the magic, allowing Duarté to catch his breath. When he opened his eye, they were back to normal.

"Now, Duarté Dartagni, tell me. Who paid you to kill the Magus? Who did you give all those weapons to?"

Duarté huffed as he tried to regain his strength, but it drained so much out of him that he couldn't recover quickly enough. "Answer me, Duarté, or I swear I will take every last drop of blood from your body," Gideon conferred. The paladin bit his lip, not wanting to give in to this boy, but the cries of his wife convinced him otherwise.

"Ishtar!" he muttered. "It was Ishtar!"

Everyone stood there, their mouths agape in disbelief. "Dear God, how could you?" Xavier asked.

"What have you done?" Wren added.

"Keep talking, Duarté. I want you to tell me everything," Gideon said as his eyes glowed red again, warning Duarté to speak up or else his suffering would continue.

"After they kicked Selene out of the Helios Arcanum, we were contacted by a representative of an Ishtaran noble. Don't ask me who because I don't know his name. They wanted to help Selene continue her research, and in exchange, they wanted the first choice at the weapons we pulled out of any armories. They paid us quite well, so in turn, we were able to pay those we needed to help us, like Dieter."

"How many?" Gideon asked as he tried to hold back his anger. "How many weapons did you turn over to Ishtar?"

Duarté swallowed hard, not wanting to answer him, but he was afraid of him. "Twenty-eight," he stammered. "Once we pulled the weapons out, he picked the ones they wanted, mostly cursed weapons. The rest, we either sold or kept for ourselves."

"What weapons did you give them? Name them!" Gideon shouted again as his anger began to boil over.

"The Cestus of the Minotaur, Zzzazz the Lightning Whip, Balroth the Demon Flail of Hellfire, Calypso the Cursed Sword of the Maelstrom, Boreas the Twilight Shield of Eternal Night, and more."

Everyone was stunned into silence. "You know what those weapons can do? Why on earth would you give them to our ancient enemy?" Jacqueline asked.

"The Ishtarans will give those weapons to their spies and assassins embedded in Attlain, spreading death and deceit from Celestrium to Solara," Xavier added.

Before he could answer, Duarté started gasping for air again. Gideon stared at him as he continued to drain his body through the cursed sword. "You killed more than fifty Magus, including my master, so you could line your pockets with gold while arming our enemy against us. You don't deserve to live."

Duarté dropped Durandal as he collapsed on the ground. Selene struggled to rush to her husband's aid, but Jacqueline held her back. "Gideon, you must stop this!" Xavier pleaded. "We need to turn them over to the Obsidian Court to find the identity of their benefactor. We can't do that if you kill him!"

Their words were meaningless to Gideon. His rage overwhelmed him at the loss of his master, his fellow Magus, the attacks on Wren, everything. He would have killed Duarté if not for Wren rushing up, standing between him and the paladin.

"Marcus, please, stop!" she cried out as she touched his face. "Don't become like him!" Her voice broke through the rage as he finally stopped. Gideon took a deep breath as he calmed himself down. He took Wren's hand into his and found his peace through her.

"Thank you, Wren," he said. They looked into each other's eyes, a simple glance that said more than words about the love they shared. Finally, Gideon turned his attention back to Duarté. Kneeling next to him, he said, "I'm not going to kill you, Duarté, but you'll wish I had. And, just in case you get any funny ideas for revenge, let me tell you a little story. This curse will remain on you as long as I don't use this sword on anyone else, and trust me, I don't need to do that. That cut will never bleed, never heal. It'll stay there as a reminder that I hold your life in my hands.

"Come at me, or my friends and I will turn you into a corpse. Do you understand?" Gideon asked. All Duarté could do was nod his head as he had little to no strength to resist him. Gideon dismissed Blood Onyx back into the armory before reaching down to Durandal. He walked away from the fallen paladin, turning his back on him as two of the *Cavaliere* took him, Selene, and the rest of the adventurers away.

Once they were gone, Gideon looked at Durandal and smiled before leaning his forehead against the holy sword. "I did it, Master Botàn. I got Durandal back! You can rest easy now!" Gideon began to choke and gag before he could say another word as he dropped to his knees and began vomiting blood all over the ground. Wren held onto him as he continued to throw up until his stomach was empty.

"Gideon, what the hell, man? Are you alright?" Guilfoy asked his friend in concern.

"Yeah, I'll be fine."

"No, you're not. You've lost a lot of blood. Are you injured?" Wren said as she tried to comfort him, her voice riddled with worry.

"It's not his blood. It's Dartagni's," Jacqueline explained. "Blood Onyx feeds the wielder the blood of the victim. Since Gideon's not a vampire, the blood does nothing really for him except make him sick."

"I'll be fine. Besides, I need to do this first . . ." Gideon struggled to his feet and held Durandal before him. "Durandal, Holy Sword of the Archangel

Michael, I claim you as your master for the Armory of Attlain. As a Magus, I swear to wield you with the honor you deserve. Accept me as your master! Become one with the Armory . . . Again!"

The sword glowed with a heavenly light as it accepted Gideon as its master. A runic circle opened and the sword slowly faded into it until a new rune appeared on the pauldron. It was angel wings surrounded by a halo. Durandal was back in its place in the Armory of Attlain.

Once that was complete, Gideon felt sick and lightheaded. Gorging on the blood had made his condition worse. He stumbled and almost fell over again. Guilfoy and Wren grabbed his arms and helped steady him. Jacqueline checked on him.

"Gideon, I think you need some rest before you start on your journey to Plodoro," she said. "I'll let Bok know about the delay. Is that alright with you, Xavier? I think we can let him stay one more day in the dormitories."

"Yes, but no more," Xavier said. "I agree with Canon Cordell, Gideon. I will not miss you when you're gone. I ask that you don't return to Basilon anytime soon."

Gideon chuckled, but he knew, deep down, that he was quite serious. "I apologize for the problems I caused all of you, Preceptor de Maestre. I will do my best to avoid causing you or the school any further issues."

"Wren, can you and the others please escort Gideon back to his room?" Jacqueline asked. "Preceptor de Maestre and I need to brief the Obsidian Court on everything we learned this morning."

"We'll take care of him, milady," Wren replied. Gideon wanted to smile, but he was too damn exhausted. When they returned to the school, Gideon went right to bed to sleep, and, against Lady Jacqueline's wishes, Wren stayed there with him. She slept right next to him. She had one more day with Gideon, and she intended to spend every moment with him.

She placed every known magical lock, counter, and warning spells around his room to ensure they wouldn't be disturbed or discovered. They slept all day and made love all night. It was even more magical than their first time together. Wren wouldn't have it any other way. She was with the man she loved, and that's all that mattered. Gideon felt the same way. He loved Wren with every fiber of his being and wanted nothing more than to be by her side.

They talked about everything and anything. Gideon wanted to know more about Wren, her family, her life growing up. He listened to everything she had to say. Wren was just as interested in him. She listened to his stories about his life in Armändis, the people he knew. She even tried to find out about any other women he'd been with, but Gideon steered clear of that conversation. He knew better than to talk about old lovers with his current one. Besides, none of them could compare to Wren.

The next day, as dawn broke over Le'Arun, the two of them headed out of town in a carriage. Once they reached a safe distance, Gideon had them pull over to the side of the road. He got out of the carriage, saddlebags flung over his shoulder, and helped Wren down. Gideon carried the sword Lady Jacqueline gave him slung across his back. He looked like he was ready for the long journey ahead. "Please wait here to take the lady back to Le'Arun," he instructed the driver as he handed him a few silver coins.

Gideon and Wren walked a little way down the road. Wren held onto his arm, afraid to let go of him. "So, I'll see you in Celestrium in about three months?" Wren inquired.

"Yes, give or take a week or two. I don't know if I'll run into any difficulties up there, so hopefully, I'll be able to keep my promise."

"God, I don't know what I'm going to do without you for three to four months?"

"Maybe you can come up with a way to tell your parents about us because I have no clue as to how to do that," Gideon joked, but Wren knew he was right. They needed to figure out how to tell the king and queen about their love; otherwise, it might not end well for them, especially for Gideon. "I mean, how do you ask the king for permission to marry his daughter."

Gideon's proposal caught Wren off guard. "What? Marry?"

"Of course, I want to marry you," he said. "I thought I made that clear when I said I wanted to spend the rest of my life with you."

"Well, usually, the man gets down on one knee to propose to the woman first," Wren snapped back at him.

Gideon could see he upset her, but he wrapped his arms around her and pulled her close to him, even as she tried to turn her face away. "And I will do it properly once I get permission from your father," he assured her. He grabbed her chin and made her look at him. "I want to do it right, okay?"

Wren smiled and kissed him lovingly, assured by his words. "I know, I know, it's just—" Before she could say another word, the loud screech of a griffon came from the sky above.

"Ah, it looks like he's right on time." Gideon said.

They looked up to see two griffons descending downward. Bok rode one, while the other was loaded down with supplies. Wren was amazed as she never saw a griffon up close like this before. Their outstretched wings fluttered in the air as they set down gently on the ground.

Wren ignored the massive goblin dismounting the beast as she walked up to examine the griffons more closely. Gideon went over to meet his friend. "Sorry about the delay, Bok, but it was necessary."

"Necessary? What the hell could be necessary to keep me waiting another day?" Bok yelled back. All Gideon did was to point to the new rune on his armory. The one belonging to Durandal. Bok saw and realized what he did.

"You did it? Ha! I knew you could beat that sorry bastard! So, what happened? How did you . . ." he paused for a second when he saw Wren moving toward the griffon. "Hey, keep back there, girl! You don't want to get your hand bitten off!"

Bok stomped over toward Wren, but he directed his anger at Gideon. "What the hell are you doing, bringing a *jillflirt* out here? Is this why you were late in showing up? Damn human, thinking with your crotch again, why I outta rip it off and beat you with it!"

"Bok!" Gideon yelled to get his attention. "May I introduce you to Wren, the First Princess of Attlain!"

Bok suddenly stopped in his tracks when he did a double-take, looking at Wren, then Gideon. "Princess?" he asked as Gideon nodded his head at him. Bok grumbled before the goblin cleared his throat and bowed politely. "My apologies, Your Royal Highness . . ." he politely stated, remembering something he read in one of Botàn's books. "I don't meet too many princesses."

"Oh, that's alright," Wren said, accepting his apology. "I don't meet too many goblins, either."

Her remark caused Bok to break out in laughter. "Oh, I like her," he said to Gideon. "Just, please be careful, milady. They tend to bite anything you put around their mouths."

"I will. Thank you for the warning. She's beautiful."

"It's a he, Your Grace," Bok corrected her. "His name is Zarusasha. That's his sister, Sarusasha," he said, pointing at the other griffon.

Wren looked carefully at the two griffons. "How can you tell the difference?" she asked.

Bok looked at her, confused by her question. "Well, it's just . . . he's got balls." Gideon burst out laughing, but Wren turned red with embarrassment. He pulled Bok away before the goblin said anything else stupid.

"Listen, I need another favor from you. Do you still have connections with those goblin mercenaries in Ishtar?"

"Yeah, I do. Why do you ask?"

Gideon handed him a piece of paper with a sketch of the unknown Ishtaran noble's emblem. Bok looked at it with curiosity.

"I need to know the name of the Ishtaran noble who belongs to this emblem," he said as he reached into his magic coin purse and pulled out a small bag of gems, handing it to Bok. "This should compensate them for their work. You can get a message to me in Celestrium if they find anything."

Bok nodded his head as he folded up the paper and put it and the bag in his belt pouch. "No problem. Now, you remember what I said about flying Zarusasha in those mountains?"

"Yes, put down every couple of hours to let him rest. If the winds get too fierce, take him higher if possible. If not, land and wait for it to die down. What do I owe you for the supplies?"

"Eh, don't worry about it. I'll grab a gem out of the bag before passing it along. Call it a finder's fee," he laughed. "So, you and the princess, huh? I guess I'll need to tell Lyllia and the girls you won't be able to keep your promise."

Wren overheard Bok's comments, and it caught her curiosity. "And who are Lyllia and the girls?"

Gideon swallowed hard. He knew it would be challenging to explain three insatiable naiads to her. "I'll explain later. And yes, you will," he said, pointing his finger at Bok. "Now, can you give me a moment to say goodbye?"

Chuckling, Bok patted Gideon on the back, then headed over to Sarusasha. Gideon took Wren by the hand and pulled her close. "So, who's Lyllia?" she asked, her voice ripe with jealousy.

"Soon to be a very sad naiad, along with her two sisters," Gideon reassured her. "Maybe I'll send Guilfoy down to Ponshu Forest to visit them. He might be able to cheer them up."

"I think Trini might have something to say about that," Wren corrected him. Gideon knew he would have to explain things further to her, but for now, he pulled her close and kissed her deeply. He wanted to remember the taste of her lips until he could kiss her again.

"I don't know what I'm going to do for three months without seeing your face or kissing your lips."

"Well, maybe this will help," Wren said as she pulled out a pendant from her pocket. It was a curved, red glass bead on a leather cord. The glass bead glowed from a small flame that flickered deep inside. Wren reached up and hung it around Gideon's neck. "It's called a *'Magatama.'* Takeshi helped me make it. It's a symbol of good fortune and protection from evil in his country. I wanted to give it to you to keep you safe on your journey to Plodoro."

"It feels warm to the touch," Gideon remarked as he held it in his hand.

"That's because I infused it with my fire magic," she told him. "Whenever you hold it, the warmth will remind you that I'm with you."

Gideon was overwhelmed by her love for him. He never felt the kind of love she gave to him, freely, from her heart. He kissed her again and held her close one last time as a tear rolled down his cheek. "Thank you, Wren. I love you."

"I love you too, Marcus," Wren said as she cried a little herself. "Just be careful and come back to me." She finally had to let Gideon go as he laid his saddlebags on Zarusasha and climbed up on the griffon. He blew her one more kiss before he spurred the griffon into the air. As they rose higher, the griffon screeched a goodbye to his sister and master. They watched until the two were well out of sight.

Bok and Wren looked at each other before the goblin bowed his head politely to the princess. She nodded her head as she turned to walk back to the carriage. "Your Highness!" he shouted, stopping her before she could take another step. "He's a good man, only the second one I've ever considered a friend. Please, take care of him. He's a bit reckless, impetuous, and needs a good kick in the ass . . . I mean, backside, from time to time."

Wren was surprised to hear a goblin talk this way about a human. She didn't know much about their relationship, but she could tell he did care for Gideon. "I will, Master Bok, and thank you for your concern. It's nice to know that Gideon has a friend like you."

No human ever called Bok "master" before. It was surprising and a genuine compliment from someone like a Princess of Attlain. He bowed his head again and waited for her to get back into the carriage before he readied himself to leave. Sarusasha cried out, already missing her brother.

"I know, girl, I know. I miss him too, but they'll be back soon. Don't you worry none. Gideon will keep him safe."

EPILOGUE
ULBRECHT DOMO

To the northeast of Attlain laid the land of noble birth: Ishtar. At a quarter of the size of Attlain, the Ishtar Empire had vast wealth bore on the people's backs. A stoic class system ruled those who lived there, as the nobles prospered from their subjects' work. They kept the lower class in line as slaves, serfs, or indentured servants. From lumber and stone culled from above the ground to coal, precious gems, and minerals mined underneath, Ishtar had all the wealth they needed but no room to expand its empire.

Ishtar needed the mountains and forest to cultivate their wealth, so they lived along the coastline, building massive cities toward the sky and out over the sea. These cities shined from pristine marble, gold, and precious gems used ornately to display their opulence. Over the centuries, they engaged in near-constant war with Attlain to grow their country. And yet, every time they tried, they failed and built farther out into the sea instead of inland.

Building on the water meant that they could bury their secrets in the deep waters off the coast. It put fear into the people, knowing that whenever they walked or rode across the bridges spanning between island city-states, they tread across the graves of those who opposed the nobles. It was the way of life in Ishtar, and everyone accepted it for generations.

The nobility of Ishtar all bore fruit from one lineage: The Charlemont. For more than one thousand years, the Charlemont family ruled Ishtar, creating dozens of other nobles through marriage across the Empire. This many nobles meant a constant clash over the line of succession. Assassinations, mysterious disappearances, and kidnappings were as commonplace as marriage negotiations and discussions of royal patronage, all in an attempt to move closer to the throne.

THE LAST MAGUS: A CLOCKWORK HEART

The current ruler of Ishtar was Empress Katarina Helena Eudoxia Charlemont, known as Katarina the Graceful. The Empress was not only the head of the country, but she was also the head of the family. She divvied out titles to her family to control them. While she gave most lesser titles like baron, duke, or count to distant relatives, only her direct line earned prince or princess titles. They were the ones within the line of succession vying to be the next Empress or Emperor of Ishtar.

A lonely figure sat on a balcony, overlooking the Great Northern Sea, sipping a delicate wine. His blond hair fluttered lightly in the breeze as he stayed back in the shadow. He hated the sunlight, preferring the darkness of the night.

He enjoyed the view; it was his favorite in all of Ishtar. The sea reminded him of power . . . the power he craved and desired every day. It was an insatiable lust, one might say, within his core. *Without it, who would I be?* he wondered.

"Excuse me, Your Highness," came a voice bringing the young noble out of his daydream. "Please forgive the interruption, but I have news from Le'Arun."

He slowly and deliberately sipped the wine, which kept his associate bowing and waiting patiently for permission to stand and speak. It was this the kind of power that the Ishtaran loved. "Go on," he finally said.

"I'm afraid the *Cavaliere* arrested the Dartagnis, Your Highness. The Helios Arcanum confiscated all of the magical weapons in their possession, and—" he spouted off until the noble raised his hand to silence his servant.

"And the princess?" he asked.

"She has returned to Celestrium. I'm afraid she is out of our reach now," he said, bowing his head and closing his eyes, awaiting some punishment or reprisal. The prince took another sip of wine before snapping his fingers, summoning a small boy with a wine pitcher to refill his glass.

"And what of the Magus? Have you identified who he is and where he came from?"

"No, Your Highness, he is as much of a mystery as the weapons in his armory. His master, Henri Botàn, is equally mysterious. Dartagni thought him dead, so we never researched him nor his armory. In fact, there are no records of him anywhere. And now, his apprentice has disappeared. Our spies last saw him flying toward the Skjem-Tur Mountains."

The young noble sat there, drinking his wine while pondering everything he learned. "Have we heard back from Celestrium on my request?"

"The Obsidian Court is doing a standard check, but it appears that they will approve it. You should be able to attend the festival as planned."

The young noble slyly smiled as he took another sip. "Excellent, Uncle

Vincenzo . . . Before we go to Celestrium, send Olaf down to deal with Duarté. I don't want him spilling anymore of my secrets. Do I make myself clear?"

"Yes, *Ulbrecht Domo*," he said with a bow before slowly backing away. With that, he left the prince alone to enjoy his wine as he continued to plot his ultimate plan.

Ishtar and Attlain will be mine, he thought. *I will not let this Magus get the best of me. His armory, his weapons will be mine!*

— THE END —

THE STORY OF MARCUS GIDEON CONTINUES IN

THE LAST MAGUS

DRAGONFIRE & STEEL

ABOUT THE AUTHOR

Mark Piggott, a native of Phillipsburg, N.J., enlisted in the U.S. Navy in 1983, beginning a 23-year career. He served on three aircraft carriers and various duty stations as a Navy Journalist before attaining the rank of Chief Petty Officer. He retired from active duty in 2006 and continues to work as a writer-editor in Washington, D.C. He and his wife, Georgiene, live in Alexandria, Virginia. They have three children. His first novel, *Forever Avalon*, was published in 2009, followed by *The Dark Tides* in 2014 and *The Outlander War* in 2020.